THE HANUKKAH HOAX

A HOLIDAY ROMANTIC COMEDY

AIMEE ROBINSON

AMR PUBLISHING LLC

The Hanukkah Hoax

Copyright © 2025 by Aimee Robinson

Cover by Angela Haddon Book Cover Design

Edited by Sara Burgess at Telltail Editing

This book is a work of fiction. Names, characters, places, and incidents are the product of the author's imagination or are used fictitiously. Any resemblance to actual events, locales, or persons, living or dead, is coincidental.

ISBN: 9781960934116 (trade paperback)

CHAPTER 1

As far as weapons went, few were more formidable than Marisa Silver's customer-service smile. Unfortunately, even that had its limits, especially when the guest in front of her opted to employ chemical warfare.

Holy shit. The *smell*.

Did this guy just—

Right on cue, the fumes hit her while the corporate dude boxing off her only means of escape slid a third cranberry and brie cheese puff onto his already overflowing dish. The silver-plated serving tray she was holding tipped slightly off kilter before she caught it, narrowly saving her from pitching her ass into the nearby candle display filled with very tall and very *real* flames.

Marisa teetered back slightly as the bodies around her shifted out of focus. Dark tuxedos and bright taffeta morphed into candy-colored ripples beneath the wellspring of tears that offered whatever meager protection it could to shield her hadn't-been-20/20-since-2020 vision.

Act cool, Marisa. You've had to work through far worse than flatulent banquet guests. Remember the supposed emotional support

1

Pomeranian that peed all over the smoked salmon roses at the Levin Bris?

She cleared her throat, fighting to keep her lip from curling as the sweaty office monkey in too-tight formal wear swiped a clubbed finger through the congealing pool of crimson-tinted grease on his plate. Only one cheese puff remained. The meager vestiges of puffed pastry crumbs dappling his patchy beard were the sole remnants of their fallen brethren.

"Sir, I have some balsamic-marinated mushrooms I'll be bringing out shortly. They're quite delicious, if you'd like to save some room."

Take the fiber, buddy. Eat the goddamn fiber.

The gentleman—in the absolute loosest interpretation of the word—dangled the final cheese puff refugee above his gullet, then dropped it in like a dragon swallowing its prey whole. A single throat bob was all he wrote on the subject before he downed the rest of his champagne, plunked the glass on her very much *not* empty tray, and waved her off, dismissing both her and her offer of better bowel health.

Well, she had to give him some credit. What the guy lacked in manners and molar usage, he made up for in methane production. On some level, it was probably good to give the cows a break as the sole perpetrators of the planet's ozone depletion. But did *she* have to be the one gifted with that kernel of wisdom?

With her luck, of. fucking. course.

Instead of circulating the room as she was supposed to, Marisa took the opportunity to take a wellness break, her self-appointed employee benefit that had yet to be officially sanctioned during a six-hour shift. She ducked behind the canvas privacy partition separating the waitstaff's entrance from the kitchen into the ballroom. Because God forbid the employees and guests of Mercer, Hoffman, Anders, and Godfrey, Esq., ever learn that the food being served at their annual Christmas party came from an actual kitchen. Just when in the hell did food service become something that needed to be screened off, anyway?

Marisa unloaded her ridiculously opulent tray, tugged at her shirt's scratchy polyester collar, and tried again to scan the crowd for her target.

If there was one thing she knew to be true, it was that no one —the Big Guy included—labored harder during the holiday season than an interior designer working the corporate Christmas party circuit.

Marisa's fingers curled around the edge of the screen, which had also been decorated to within an inch of its life. Flocked verdant boughs of evergreens hung in lush bunches over the top of the otherwise cream-colored ballroom-standard partition. Classic white twinkle lights sweetly speckled each cluster of stone pine and balsam fir branches in a subtle elegance that sparkled just enough to impress upon the occasion but not enough to consume one's gaze.

There was far more available to do *that* job.

At the center of the room was the grand pooh-bah of Christmas preponderance: a Norway spruce that Marisa had on good authority was sourced by a former head gardener of Rockefeller Center, who just so happened to be a major real estate investor for the venue. Extracted from the cozy and picturesque Berkshires of Massachusetts and carted down to New Jersey like a trussed-up Thanksgiving turkey, the evergreen beauty sat resplendent in tastefully crafted string lights varying in shades of warm and cool daylight. Wrist-wide ivory ribbon hugged the needles' branches like a silk veil, while wintery pastel orbs crusted with subtly shimmering glitter poked through the barren pockets. Crowning the top of the tree in true regal fashion was a gilded five-pointed star, thick and bulbous in the middle, with long tapered edges that stretched out like a lover's hand toward different themed catering tables around the room, each abundant in festive culinary offerings.

With the space's unusual arched ceilings that made way for the chandelier currently dripping its opulence all over the mingling partygoers, Marisa couldn't help but think of Walt Disney World. The tree, its own form of Cinderella Castle, and each needle point of that golden star urged guests down one spoke or another, promising them all the fanciful joys of the holiday season decked out in different arrays of splendor.

The whole display was a dizzying veneer designed to keep the good cheer flowing while simultaneously patting the titans of the legal industry—and their notable support staff—on the back for another profitable year.

Profitable.

Had there been a word that had consumed Marisa's thoughts more over the past few years than the very one pulling her lips into an unavoidable pout every time she deigned to utter it, much less wish for it?

"This stollen could moonlight as the bathroom aftermath of what two-thirds of these guests are going to be dealing with twenty-four hours from now. Holy shit, this thing is dense. Good thing I've already hit my dental insurance's deductible for the year. You think they'll let me off early if I crack a crown on company time?" Eden, Marisa's best friend and bartender extraordinaire, unpinned her name tag, plopped it into her pants pocket, and got to work wedging her blood-red acrylic pinky nail into the space next to her canine tooth. "Yours is way better, by the way, and before you ask"—she held up her free hand—"yes, I'm on break. Anthony's covering for me."

"Good. Because if Mrs. Di Paolo catches you with your hair falling out of your bun one more time, especially around these people, she's likely to toss you out with the recycling. Here, gimme."

If being best friends with Eden since they were ten had

taught Marisa anything, it was the value of working fast. Before a thought bubble of objection could even be conceived on Eden's part, Marisa had already yanked the hair tie off Eden's head, caught up handfuls of the long micro braids, and twisted her wrists with a speed only someone who'd worked in candy making as long as she had could pull off. Soon, every last obsidian strand was wrestled back into place.

"There. Tight and right." Marisa smiled with no small amount of satisfaction at her handiwork. "And the stuff they serve here isn't really stollen. It's pretty much just fruit cake dusted with an embarrassingly small amount of powdered sugar so no one has to worry about getting their gowns messed up. The real stollen is called Dresdner Stollen, and you can't make it outside of Dresdner, Germany. The EU gave it protected geographical status, and with good reason. So, everything outside of that region is nothing more than a glorified door knocker dressed up to look like something edible." Then Marisa hung more of her body around the edge of the partition and floated her gaze around the room, looking for a particular anchor that was far heavier than dried-fruit-laden bread. "But thank you," she acknowledged with a wink. "Mine is pretty damn good."

"I do love a woman who knows her worth." Eden smiled, then folded her arms across her chest, her laser gaze aiding in Marisa's search. "So, you find her yet?"

A wave of aggravation heated Marisa's cheeks. "No. But she's got to be here. I heard the chairwoman was a neighbor of one of the partners throwing this shindig. Nothing New Jersey's upper crust loves more than making sure the people in their immediate vicinity know how shiny they are."

"You got that right. And this place certainly is shiny."

And just like that, Marisa was reminded of why she'd accepted this catering gig in the first place. Normally, she'd spend the better part of her December packing orders for her online candy business, tweaking her social media ads, papering the local bagel places with flyers about her custom offerings, and agonizing over the best ways to wrap, secure, and ship her delicate confections so they'd survive the veritable Bataan Death March that was holiday shipping. All while also squeezing in the annual deft avoidance of her mother's phone calls before ultimately succumbing to the well-honed and lethally weaponized Jewish guilt by visiting her family for obligatory latkes, candle lighting, and yearly laments. And doughnuts, even if they were the jelly-filled kind.

Oh, and at some point during that same lunar cycle, her phone's reliably unhelpful AI assistant thought it kind to remind Marisa that her birthday was also coming up. A birthday that usually coincided with the time of the month when parcel carriers stopped guaranteeing delivery by Christmas, leaving Marisa to cry into a vat of royal icing. On that day, Eden would miraculously swoop in, pry Marisa away from her stove and candy thermometer, chuck the apron into the laundry, and take her out for sushi.

This year, however, was a whole other ball of wax. This year, the red she'd been seeing on her ledgers had nothing to do with the all-natural food dye she mixed into her candy canes.

This year, she was turning thirty, and the tenuous grace period of family approval had a few more weeks, max, before the displeased conversations from those around her, spearheaded by her Aunt Gail, wouldn't just be whispered secrets out of the corners of their mouths, but outward discussions of life phase progressions.

Or regressions, as they were.

She's been at this candy thing for a decade now. If it was meant to happen, it would have.

It's fine to have hobbies, but it's not fine to keep sinking your good years into something that's not returning the favor.

Her failure to launch is the ongoing topic in my pickleball group.

Honestly, she went to school for library studies. Sorry, media studies and information sciences. The point is, she's got an entire graduate degree and a whole bunch of expensive letters after her name, and instead of using those letters, she's still futzing around with chocolate and cashew clusters. I heard she even started selling maple-candied bacon.

At some point, one needs to call a spade a spade. Look at me, for example. I always wanted to be a ballet dancer, but when I realized I had one left foot too many and a good six inches of height too few, I learned to pivot.

Passion doesn't pay the bills.

Every snide comment she'd caught from one family member or another set her teeth on edge. The reminders of her failings were so palpable, Marisa was tempted to reach up, grab a frosted garland, and garrote the next person who thought to comment on circumstances they knew nothing about.

"C'mon . . . c'mon . . . where the hell are you? I know you're here," Marisa gritted out.

"I bet she's wearing red," Eden remarked, scanning the crowd. "Like, ruby-slippers red."

"Nah, I'm going with white. Something with sequins. Remember, this is as much of a marketing opportunity for her as it is for me. Monica Freeland is chairwoman of West Meadow's Crystal Christmas Ball. If she's anything worth her salt, she'd saunter out here looking like a snowy frosted cupcake. The event is on Christmas Eve, and if she wants butts in seats, she'd use her own as free advertising. It's what I would do."

"Didn't you *actually* do that when you rented a table at the high school's homecoming celebration and dressed up as a brownie?"

"Ugh, don't remind me. Thought it would be a good way to appeal to the teenagers' parents, who might have wanted something other than stale pumpkin spice muffins to eat while they froze their asses off on the bleachers. But all it did was tempt a bunch of pubescent boys to try and kick me in the walnuts."

Marisa needed her best friend's sharp snort as much as she needed yet another reminder of the lengths she'd gone to in order to—

"Holy shit, you were right. There she is."

"What? Where?" Marisa cranked her neck in the direction of Eden's gaze and was more than happy to let her breath float away on the soft hopes held by the woman gliding into the room on pearlescent kitten heels.

Monica Freeland hadn't worn white so much as she'd been decorated with it. An elegant shawl cozied around her bare bronze shoulders in a thick expanse of snowy—dear God, please be faux—fur, which left just enough real estate for the gown's bodice to garner any guests' attention away from their sparkling wine or spouses. Shimmering sequins twirled along the fabric like snow adrift in a storm. Chins needn't stop dropping there, as the A-line skirt swishing about the woman's ankles was the veritable prized cupcake of tulle and twinkles, with bits of polished pearl studding the fabric and drawing every eye in the room, including the man on her arm, to the splendor that a glittery winter wonderland could offer, whether womanly or whimsical.

Eden let out a low whistle. "Damn. Color me impressed."

And *that* right there was the very woman who could paint the next decade of Marisa's life in vibrant and glorious debt-free Technicolor instead of the drab beige shaded by financial insecurity and familial shame that had thus far marred her twenties.

If the tiny New Jersey town of West Meadow had been capable of true royalty, it'd have minted coins featuring Monica Freeland's well-coiffed profile. Equal parts socialite, philanthropist, town council president, planning board principal, school board member, and, most important for Marisa's sake, recreation committee chairwoman, Monica's influence wasn't only legendary but vital. A single recommendation from her had been known to launch small businesses into seven-figure revenue brackets.

Three years ago, all the woman had to do was take a prolonged sip of a vendor's hot chocolate concoction at the Crystal Christmas Ball. Some photog with a zoom lens got a close-up on Monica's mauve-lacquered lips pressed in rapturous satisfaction after drinking it. Since then, that drink company had opened up a *second* factory, with plans to stock products in ten grocery store chains all over the country.

Monica's was the sort of old-money, life-changing influence that had somehow managed to transcend Internet virality, a feat all the more incredible considering the matriarch only ever used her powers for good.

When she spoke, people didn't just listen. They opened up their wallets and begged for her to be the steward of their hard-earned money.

If Marisa could get on Monica's radar, she'd never have to endure another pleading glance from her family or their weaponized affection. She'd never have to explain how toiling over confections wasn't just a hobby but her *actual* business.

With one golden touch from Monica "Midas" Freeland, Marisa could finally ditch her catering gig and live the life meant for her.

All she had to do was get on The List.

"There she is," Marisa breathed, gripping Eden's arm. "The Queen of Counsel herself."

"What's the plan?" Eden whispered. "What are you going to do?"

"Talk to her, obviously."

"Obviously. Because that's totally normal for waitstaff." Eden squared her shoulders and hooked her hands over the lapels of her bartender's vest. 'Uh, hi, Ms. Freeland. Could I interest you in some coconut shrimp while I take your empty champagne flute and tell you all about how my cranberry Christmas toffee is better than any you've tried because it won't pull out your fillings?'"

"Your vote of confidence is truly inspiring."

"I'm not here to inspire. I'm here to help."

"So far, you're doing neither. Oh my God, look!"

Across the room, standing next to an ice sculpture of a snowflake, Monica rested a finely manicured hand on her date's forearm and whispered in his ear. He smiled fondly, kissed her cheek, and headed toward the bar, where Anthony was currently a dozen guests deep in backup drink orders.

"Shit. I better head over there. Anthony's dying, and the party's just started."

Marisa grabbed Eden's shoulder. "Wait. How long do you think it'll take before Monica's date gets his drink order filled?"

Eden squinted at the lineup of guests waiting at the bar. "None of those people look like they want simple pours. If I had to guess, there will be a lot of unreasonably specific requests and a slew of mixed drinks. You've got ten minutes tops, possibly less once I get over there and help Anthony."

"That's all I need. I've already timed it out."

"Timed what out?"

"My pitch. I've managed to get it down to only four minutes, though it's better if I have five. A whole ten minutes? Ha! Oh, I've *so* got this. By the time Monica's date comes back with her drink, I'll be shaking hands with the future of my dreams."

If Marisa had to slide into her thirties on the coattails of the same shame that had followed her around the ass-end of her twenties, she was going to stab herself in the eye with one of her gourmet candy canes.

CHAPTER 2

Marisa hadn't made it two steps outside the partition before she was spotted by the catering manager, Angela, who had been speaking to another member of the waitstaff.

Angela swung a finger in her direction. "There. Marisa's free. Give them to her."

"Sure thing, boss lady."

The sound of Marisa's name punching through her single-minded focus on Monica was almost as grating as hearing *boss lady* spoken alongside it.

Seriously? Did every position of power held by a woman need to be gender-qualified?

A tray was thrust under her nose. "Here you go. Angela wants you to take these over to that group of guests hovering by the charcuterie display."

"I'm a little busy at the moment. Excuse me." Marisa had begun to push Joey—Johnny?—out of the way, but her strong-arm was blocked by the man's regrettably immovable girth.

"You're too busy for work? Isn't that what you're here for?"

"I'm on break," she gritted out.

"Not according to the schedule, you're not. I'm overdue my fifteen minutes, and Angela just approved it, so here."

Owing to the client's insistence that all the serving trays be silver plated, along with the precariously balanced crystal stemware and greasy food fare perched on top of it, Marisa had two choices: drop it all and make a run for Monica before Angela fired her and had her removed from the premises, or waste precious minutes serving guests before Monica's date came back.

Four minutes, girl. All you need is four minutes.

"Fine. I'll take them over."

The server—Jerry? Giovanni?—scraped his forearm beneath his nose, sniffed deeply, and tunneled his hands beneath the starched polyester covering his beer gut to rest where she presumed a belt lived. "Of course you will. And when you're done, head on back to the kitchen. I've got a few more trays ready to go out that I haven't gotten to yet."

She'd never worked with this guy before and desperately needed to never do so again.

"How is that my problem?" she hissed. "Why are you so backed up?"

"Like I said, just because I was overdue my official break didn't mean I wasn't entitled to some personal compensatory downtime of my choosing. I showed up half an hour early to this gig, and as long as Angela sees me when I need to be seen, it's all good."

"It's all— Did you just say it's *all good*? Seriously? After giving *me* shit for taking a break?"

"I'm always serious. And it's always better to give shit than to take it. First rule of gig work." Jerome—Geoffrey? Geoffry! That was it!—snorted again, this time against the back of his hand, and strode back toward Angela, who was staring intently at Marisa.

Oh, she needed to get the hell out of here. Her soul and soles couldn't take it anymore.

Marisa white-knuckled the silver tray and speed walked toward the charcuterie table, all the while keeping an eye on Monica, who still stood blessedly alone, admiring the ice sculpture. If she were fast, she could offload the goods and answer the obligatory bathroom location questions in about twenty seconds. Given the thickness of the crowd and the pockets of guest clusters, add on another thirty seconds to make it across the ballroom, which would leave her with exactly—

A towering form shifted in front of her only direct path to the display table. With lightning-fast reflexes born from years of working with molten sugar, Marisa somehow managed to rock back on her heels and shelter the stemware behind the cage of her forearm. The drinks jostled slightly, but the drops that had spilled onto the tray were barely noticeable. Likewise, the food had been spared.

Too bad her senses hadn't.

In a ballroom where the finery often wore the guests, the same couldn't be said for the man before her. Dressed in a deep huckleberry suit filled out by a toned thickness not often found outside MetLife Stadium, he stood a good head taller than anyone around him. Unlike those in attendance, however, the courteous expression on his face was mixed with a tinge of boredom that only those expert in observing the misery of corporate event attendees could decipher.

Nothing about this man belonged here. Not the closely cropped dark hair that ended in a widow's peak above his wide brow, nor the charming dimples protruding above a thin beard that hadn't quite managed to shake hands with the mustache haloing it.

Those weren't ordinary dimples. Those were dimples born only of forced politeness and sardonic grinning. She should know because she had a near-matching set, except hers loved to show themselves after the fourth cup of wine during her parents' seder. That was when her dad liked to play it a little too fast and loose with the pours while always making a decidedly unfunny joke about how Jews have sensitive tummies.

All this, of course, right before her Aunt Gail liked to remind everyone that Marisa's *little candies* weren't sugar free.

Marisa slowed her steps in time to the stranger's uneasy shuffle from foot to foot. God, he didn't want to be there any more than she did. Around him, a cadre of suits were laughing and clinking similar glasses of amber liquid while the stranger merely bobbed his wide shoulders on a single tense chuckle and let his boredom-glazed eyes drift over the shellacked heads of businessmen.

Until they landed on her and took in the not-so-subtle fact that she'd been staring at him. Like, a lot.

Marisa sucked in a breath and backed up a step.

"Ow! Watch it!"

The shrill cry was so loud, Marisa's first instinct was to hover a hand over her tray to make sure the crystal stemware hadn't shattered from the high-pitched resonance.

Her second instinct, upon seeing the blooming stain of honey-mint sauce that was meant to coat the lamb skewers she carried but, instead, coated a guest's yellow chiffon dress, was to grovel. Profusely.

"I am *so* sorry. Oh my goodness. Here," Marisa said, placing the tray on a nearby table already overrun with dishes, "let me help." She grabbed a discarded cloth napkin that looked mostly free of stains, dunked it in what she hoped was club soda, dropped to her knees, and began to blot at the smear on the woman's skirt.

"Uh! You're only making it worse."

"If I can just get enough of the carbonation on the stain, most of the green should lift, and it'll blend better. Almost there."

"I don't want it to *blend*. I want it to be gone!"

Marisa's hand stalled out mid-swipe and hovered over the quickly-fading-but-not-fading-enough blemish as her mind landed on the tone and tenor of that word.

Blend.

She'd heard it before. Kind of hard not to when the ad's slogan and its owner had bombarded her social media feed every time she went to research recipe videos.

Blending brilliant care with botanical flair! Scan this QR code for your free estimate on our in-home plant nursery service. But don't wait too long. Holiday season bookings are filling up fast.

Marisa shot to her feet, stain forgotten, and was met with a glare that could wilt the most carefully maintained topiary.

"Plant Nanny," Marisa breathed.

The woman shook out her red hair and lifted the stained corner of her skirt in one hand like a ballroom princess gearing up for a waltz. On anyone else, it would have given *trying too hard*, but on her, it trilled *distressed damsel open for takers*. "Just go, all right? I'm sure there's something you can do to make up for your clumsiness. A complimentary glass of wine with an exceptional vintage, perhaps? Be sure to have someone else bring it over, though."

Marisa had never been simultaneously dismissed *and* employed, but with the woman's back turned to her and the blatant cloud of disgust and expectation fuming around them, there was nothing left for her to do but shake her head as two thoughts held Marisa still.

I just spilled a drink on the Plant Nanny.

I just spilled a drink on the Plant Nanny and missed the opportunity to also stab her with a lamb skewer.

The party guests shifted and pulsed around her, choking out the available air until all that remained was enough to narrow Marisa's focus on the last time she'd seen the Plant Nanny's offerings.

Which had little to do with plants and everything to do with running Marisa's business out of town.

The icy dousing had come in the form of a text from Eden. A single social media post featuring a picture of new customer appreciation gift baskets the Plant Nanny would leave in client homes.

None of that would have been a problem if the baskets also didn't include gourmet plant-based candies and plant-themed treats that had West Meadow residents clamoring for more. Last Marisa heard, the Plant Nanny had been thinking about launching a branch of her business dedicated to the candies and chocolates alone.

And the woman was here. Nearly elbow-rubbing distance from Monica.

If Marisa were looking for a faster way for her small business to die a miserable death before it had a chance to truly live, she'd be hard-pressed to find one.

It wasn't a long shot to surmise there might only be room on The List for one candy maker in town, at best. At worst, well . . . she wasn't ready to think about that just yet.

Marisa caught Eden's eye over at the bar. Her friend was holding up a cocktail shaker and jutting out her chin toward Monica's date, who Eden had just begun to serve. Slowly.

Crap.

Eden had galactic speed when it came to mixing drinks. If she was intentionally putting the brakes on the process just to stall, time was running out.

"Excuse me," Marisa said as she shouldered her way through guests, not even stopping to cringe when her heel squished down on something far more congealed than anything the kitchen was serving. When she finally made it to the rear of the ice sculpture, she took all of five seconds to swipe a few loose strands out of her face and run her tongue along the front of her teeth.

"Here goes everything," she murmured, then stepped out of the frosty snowflake's protection and sidled up to Monica frickin' Freeland. "Ms. Freeland, hello."

The resplendent woman turned and offered her a demure smile before taking in her catering uniform. The confusion was already beginning to crinkle the centers of her brows, but she hid it well. "Hello."

"I'd like to introduce myself."

"You are a member of the serving staff?"

"Well, yes, but in addition to that, I'm also the proprietress of Sweetest Heart's Desire, a confectionery business in town. Marisa Silver. Nice to meet you." She extended her hand and hoped to God it wasn't as sweaty as she feared.

"A candy maker." Monica smiled and accepted her greeting. "Lovely. Are any of your offerings at this event?"

"Not this event, no, but I heard that Brindlewise Bakery and Bon Bons moved their operations to New York City over the summer."

"Yes, quite a loss for West Meadow, though I am thrilled for the company's success."

"I'm sure they're just as thrilled for the significant part you had in helping them achieve it."

Monica's lips twisted in subtle amusement. It was the kind of acknowledgment that both hid and revealed the facts of the matter.

The woman knows her power, and so does Brindlewise. Ten bucks says they probably send her monthly care packages to show their appreciation, but she turns around and donates them to local fundraising efforts.

Oh, she's good.

Marisa cleared her throat and leaned into her pitch. It was now or never. "Ms. Freeland, I'd like to present you with a tasting opportunity of Sweetest Heart's Desire's signature gourmet collection at the upcoming Crystal Christmas Ball. We're really known for blending the traditional appeal of the classics with current inspirations. We specialize in hand-pulled peppermint taffy, bourbon butterscotch, and a delicious macadamia-infused cocoa—"

"Oh, Ms. Freeland, there you are! Such an absolute pleasure to meet you." If Monica's bell-like voice was a blooming orchid, the Plant Nanny's trill was a weed choking out all essential flora. Marisa barely had time to steady herself before she was pushed to the side in a flutter of yellow chiffon, and an open hand was thrust beneath her nose toward Monica. "Phoebe Boyle. I'm the owner of Brilliant Botanical Nursery Services, *the* in-home nursery care providers for all your plant baby needs. You may have seen some of my videos. Many of my wonderful customers have taken to calling me the Plant Nanny."

Monica politely took Phoebe's hand and shook it. "Hello. Forgive me, I'm not familiar with the phrase. Plant Nanny, was it?"

No one's familiar with the phrase, because it didn't exist until the Internet decided it should. Not when anyone can get a self-watering planter for six bucks and free two-day shipping. Marisa huffed away an errant bang and glared at Phoebe.

"I cannot say enough good things about last year's Crystal Christmas Ball, and I'm positively itching to see how it'll turn out this year. Is it still couples-only?"

"I'm so glad to hear it's a beloved event. And yes, it is a ballroom affair that allows West Meadow couples to set aside the frantic holiday needs of their children and families and enjoy the romantic spirit of the season away from the chaos. A bit of Christmas magic and luxury without the need to bring a hostess gift, I like to say," Monica replied, obviously pleased with her marketing pitch. But then her smile faltered slightly. "That is, if the anticipated turnout can meet expectations."

Marisa took a step forward, standing shoulder to shoulder with Phoebe. "Is the Ball having difficulty finding attendees?"

Monica's elegantly manicured hand swiped away Marisa's concern. "Oh, no. I'm sure it will all be wonderful. These things do tend to come through in the end. I was just remarking on the recreation department's community events poll that went out to residents earlier this year. Apparently, the Christmas Ball was one of the items that had decreased in interest from the prior year. It's all a helpful reminder to never let your marketing guard down, even when you think the vendor lists are set. What is that old movie phrase? ABC? Always be closing?" She lifted a shoulder. "The event will be spectacular, I'm sure, if slightly smaller than forecasted."

"Perhaps I can help with that," Phoebe chimed in. "My business has been seeing record growth this past year, so much so that I've been working on a new plant-exclusive line of candies and treats. If I could share with you a few of my confections for your esteemed consideration, I'm certain I could spread the good word about your event to my *extensive* social media following."

Marisa's back teeth met. "Aren't most of your followers in New York? How many of them would be actual West Meadow residents? And this is a *West Meadow* event featuring local vendors, am I right, Ms. Freeland?"

Seeming to notice that Marisa had not exited the conversation, Phoebe speared her with a look and batted false lashes so long they may as well have been extensions of her middle fingers. She took in Marisa's catering uniform and wrinkled her nose. "I'll take a chardonnay, please. And a few of those stuffed mushroom caps I saw floating around earlier."

"Oh, actually, Marisa is another local candy maker. Like yourself! Marisa Silver of Sweetest Heart's Desire." Monica clapped her hands, delighted at the opportunity to make an introduction based on only thirty seconds of information, no doubt.

A skill likely honed while Marisa and the rest of the plebs were still learning to tie shoelaces.

Then Monica's frost-shadowed eyes brightened as a man joined her with drinks in tow. "And this is my companion, Arthur Doley. Thank you, my dear, for getting me champagne. At my age, standing next to an ice sculpture is the only way I'm able to cool down at these things." She leaned forward and placed a hand to the side of her mouth. "Not to put too fine a point on it, but menopause can be a brutal bitch sometimes."

Panic birthed a leaden stone in Marisa's stomach. How the heck did he get back already?

"Monica, the Athertons wish to say hello," Arthur announced, taking her arm and moving to pull her away from the conversation.

Marisa leapt in front of the departing pair. "Wait, before you leave, I also wanted to offer any help I can in garnering support for the Christmas Ball. I'm happy to include marketing materials with all of my business orders that go out from now until Christmas Eve, when the event takes place. They would all be *local* orders, of course, which I know is important to the integrity of the occasion for all those couples in attendance. I tell ya, when you're in a relationship during the holidays, and the bulk of your time is spent taking care of others' needs, it's just so nice to have time for the two of you. You know, around other couples in the *community* who get what you're going through."

Marisa paused, making sure the jab landed with Phoebe right where she meant it to. Judging by the way the woman's skirt was locked in a death grip at her sides, as if the poor fabric hadn't suffered enough already, Marisa had definitely stuck the landing. "And at the Ball, I'll be able to present you with an offering of what you can expect from me and Sweetest Heart's Desire for the upcoming year, in case you know of any West Meadow referral opportunities or—"

"Are you in a couple, then? You live in town?" Monica asked, wide eyes blinking with sincere curiosity.

And that was the moment desperation decided to make an absolute fool of Marisa.

It shouldn't have mattered. It really shouldn't have mattered. But when Monica's expectant gaze was trained on her and was bright enough to spotlight every chink in Marisa's battered armor that her family loved to exploit, as well as some they hadn't found yet, there was only one option left.

"Yes!" she lied. "Yes, I am, and I do. I have a couple—*am* part of a couple. Boyfriend! Not part of a boyfriend. A whole boyfriend! I have a boyfriend. Yes, that I do. Mm-hmm. And he *loves* Christmas. We both do! Favorite time of year. Just can't get enough of it. Yup." Try as she might, she couldn't call back the word vomit. It just kept on spewing out faster than the free booze pouring down most of the guests' gullets.

At her side, Phoebe had gone eerily quiet, the kind of quiet predators with nothing but time on their hands adopted when they had their prey locked in their sights.

Marisa had backed herself into a corner, and somehow, Phoebe freaking knew it.

"A Christmas-obsessed candy-making team does sound like you certainly know your market. You could probably do a nice bit of holiday business with a tag team like that. Does he work with you?" Monica put a staying hand on her date's shoulder, silently urging him for one more moment.

"Uh, he's, well, he doesn't work with me exactly, but . . . you could say he's never too far away."

Phoebe folded her arms across her chest and narrowed her brutal stare. "Is he here?"

Marisa had no idea where to look or what to say. Three sets of eyes, along with the future of her business, beseeched an explanation from her that had no hope of popping up. She toyed with the tips of her fingernails, hoping for inspiration to strike her so she might direct the conversation elsewhere. She'd take anything at that point. The dripping water from the ice sculpture. The crowd mingling around her. The masculine shadow approaching and growing beneath her feet that she hoped to God wasn't Geoffrey coming to give her more hell.

With no conceivable way out, Marisa was about to claim defeat and confess to the misunderstanding, when Monica and her date shifted their attention above Marisa's head and to whoever the shadow belonged to.

Marisa nearly choked on her tongue when the shadow replied, "Yes."

CHAPTER 3

Leave it to Alec to make a right mess of things when he hadn't even been in the States a week. Bloody hell. If his brother, Cal, had been at this stupid party, no doubt he'd be taking the piss out of him for terrifying the poor server with his ugly mug and ruining her evening.

Did he have to *stare* at her like that? Really?

Alec took a sip of his sparkling water and crunched on a piece of ice that hitched a ride with the bubbles. He regretted it instantly when one of his right molars caught the edge of the cube. The dull pain that radiated through his still-sore jaw was yet another reminder of what he'd hoped this foolish event would have taken his mind off.

Instead, the task was accomplished by, of all things, a lovely woman with curious eyes and the most adorable mouth hanging open so wide, his mate Fin could have kicked a ball clean through.

She looked about as desperate to be anywhere else as he was, balancing a tray of drinking glasses taller than her, with her dark hair trying to break free of its ties. It was a comical showing that was also the most earnest and interesting thing he'd seen all night.

And then he caught the moment she registered the rest of his face: the bulge at the top of his nose from being broken too many times, the small scar that, while not too visible from a distance, still made itself known by disrupting his beard growth. On the rugby pitch, his look was all usual and customary. At a corporate banquet?

No wonder she'd turned from him so quickly. After the hits he'd taken recently, most women did. But unlike most women, they didn't usually do an about-face right into his ex-girlfriend, dousing her with condiments.

Dammit all to hell.

What in the ever-loving fuck was Phoebe doing here?

He'd come to this event as a guest of Cal's venture capitalist buddy who'd used the law firm's corporate legal services a time or two. And as Alec could no longer afford to pass up any investment opportunities, he figured he'd tag along while he was in New Jersey. Hell, at least he'd get a few bites of food out of it.

He did *not* expect to run into his ex. Or, to be more specific, to startle a serving woman bad enough so that *she* would run into his ex instead.

No one deserved that level of punishment, and judging by the panicked expression on the woman's face when she stopped wiping Phoebe's gown and fled in the opposite direction, she'd experienced far too much of his ex's hellfire than the job was worth.

Och, he needed to fix this. Phoebe was a handful on a good day, but it was his crass staring that had sent the kind server directly into the jaws of the lioness to begin with.

Alec dragged a hand over his trimmed beard and cursed into his cupped palm. "Gentleman," he said, nodding to the crowd of men whose names he never caught and whose businesses he'd long forgotten, "if you'll excuse me."

Guilt made his stride heavy as he pressed through the crowd toward where the server was talking to a different woman.

Turned out, his guilt was more than a valid concern. The server's hands were swirling around her with a fervor approaching the speed of her nervous speech, which would be less frazzled had he not creeped her out a mere thirty seconds ago. Alec slowed his pace and hung back behind a nearby drink display just so he could make sense of the furor that the slight server was stirring up.

He whistled low and shook his head. And Americans thought Scots were difficult to understand? This wee woman spoke with her hands in such a heated rhythm, it was a miracle her words managed to keep up with her gestured story at all. Alec didn't know whether it was passion, persistence, or timing that kept her going. Miraculously, she held the chairwoman, if he caught the wisps of their introductions right, if not riveted at least in play. Whatever it was, it held him to the spot as well.

More bits and pieces of the conversation floated his way. Interest in a Christmas Ball. Candy making. Business opportunities. It all seemed like standard fare for standard chit-chat at a standard corporate holiday event, though somehow delivered with a magician's flair for visual effects.

He chuckled softly. She certainly was a sight, this one, and if he were being honest, he didn't quite mind being her captive so much. It sure as hell beat the stock market banter from earlier.

Until Phoebe slid into the frame.

Every muscle in Alec's shoulders tensed as if he were preparing for a tackle. His jaw clenched, and his legs widened to absorb the blow.

Except the hit slammed into parts of him that had nothing to do with tightened muscles and readied stance, and everything to do with the banded arms braced across her chest and the stony cast of her features as she joined the server's conversation.

His stomach sank.

"Fucking hell."

He'd been on the receiving end of that pose more times than he'd like to remember, the final time being when Phoebe had all but flung him back to England to *finish giving his body's best years nurturing a sport that would never nurture him back.* Damn if his sore muscles could ever crawl out of bed without recalling those words.

Never mind that he practically grew up on the pitch and didn't know a time when he didn't have a rugby ball in hand. Never mind that he'd promised to live with her in the States in the off-season and visit as often as he could during the series. Never mind that, on the Sevens circuit, he'd made mates for life and was hoping Phoebe would join in his life as well.

The rejection, he'd managed to endure somehow, but the disapproval and disgust?

Well, a year later, he was still gnawing on those old bones, wasn't he? Add in his most recent injury and mandatory medical leave and Phoebe would have all the fuel she'd need to drench him in a rain shower of *I told you so* and use the runoff from his shame to water her fucking plants.

Alec killed his drink and crushed the ridiculous stirrer in his fist as the server he'd been spying on began to falter under the weight of Phoebe's expectant stillness and quiet disdain. It ripped more wounds open because he knew exactly how hard it was to maintain one's composure and not stammer beneath that kind of scrutiny.

All while it was clear that the young woman was trying her hardest to make a good impression with the chairwoman.

"God*dammit*, Phoebe," he ground out, startling an elderly woman whose forkful of pasta missed her mouth and launched the food onto her husband's tie. "Sorry."

Alec handed some napkins to the couple, offloaded his empty glass to the nearest waitstaff, and tunneled through the crowd, intent on at least apologizing to the serving woman he'd startled and fixing his blunder, if not swiping her out of Phoebe's clutches altogether. However, when he got close enough for his shadow to announce his arrival, something had shifted. Phrases like *I have a boyfriend* and *he just* loves *Christmas* spun through the air, followed quickly by the chairwoman's assertion that such a team would do a nice bit of holiday business.

Phoebe hadn't noticed him, which was one of two reasons why she'd yet to pounce on him and drag him to the dumpster.

The second, and far more puzzling reason, was that the regal chairwoman on the arm of the white-haired chap who'd just joined her suddenly shifted her attention to Alec while Phoebe was still watching her prey dangle from a hook.

Which meant that, by the time Phoebe had finally whipped her barbed reply at the server asking where the woman's boyfriend was, fully intent on humiliating the charming girl, a curious solution presented itself. One that felt oddly . . . fun.

Alec smiled, took hold of the idea, and tackled that sucker to the ground.

"Is he here?" Phoebe asked, making a show of scanning the room for someone.

Then he stepped forward. "Yes."

He'd meant to speak the word with a fair bit of venom, knowing it would grate on Phoebe's nerves about as much as hearing her voice did to him, but as was the confounded way of the evening, that went awry when the server gasped and locked her spine as still as a goalpost.

Och, hell. He'd meant to rescue her and fix his fuck-up, hadn't he? Not traumatize her further.

But before the doubt had a chance to creep in, Alec was startled by a boisterous cheer from the man escorting the chairwoman.

"Holy smokes, I don't believe it. You're Alec Elms!" The S in his last name was accompanied by an alarming amount of nose whistle as the man stepped forward and, with two hands, encircled Alec's fist and began pumping his arm like the bloke was tapping a freaking well. "Star forward for Great Britain Sevens. I've never seen a flanker tackle the pitch better than this fellow, let me tell you. Poised to win the championship this year, too. What you fellows are doing out there is pure magic. Arthur Doley of Doley Enterprise Solutions."

"Appreciate it. Thank you. I don't often find such avid rugby fans in the States, especially on the East Coast."

"Oh, I know, and it's a damn shame. Well, you'll be happy to hear I've been working to change that. Just sent in my sizable annual contribution to USA Sevens HQ, along with a few minor suggestions on some outreach endeavors I'm willing to help them with that I believe could really do a lot to positively impact the game's position in the mainstream sports media here."

Alec nodded painfully while trying to discreetly wipe his sweatier palm on any bit of linen in reach. He settled for the tip of his tie that he'd managed to conceal beneath his suit coat.

If he had to hear one more wealthy benefactor spout off about their desire to *save rugby*, he was going to tackle the ice sculpture and try to get pinned beneath it.

"I'm close friends with several guys over at key broadcasting partners in New York," Arthur added in the seemingly ignorant way people from old money often rambled. "Old buddies from college. Actually," he said, sliding close enough for the boozy fumes to carry on his breath, "I know I don't look like it so much anymore, but I *did* play a bit of rugby at my alma mater." When Alec didn't immediately respond, Arthur clarified, "Center. And I filled in for scrum-half when I needed to."

A soft throat clear was the Pavlov's bell Arthur required to abandon the rugby talk, apparently.

"Oh, let me introduce you to Monica Freeland, the chairwoman of West Meadow's Crystal Christmas Ball."

Damn, the man was well-trained. It'd be impressive if it wasn't also a tad terrifying. If that slight woman could get a man like Arthur off the runaway train his mind had taken him down with no more than a simple nonverbal gesture, what the hell could she do with actual words?

"A pleasure," Alec said, though when he went to shake her hand, he hesitated. She'd offered the back of her hand, not her palm. Fucking hell. Just what kind of royalty did this woman think she was?

Alec accepted her hand and, at an utter loss for what to do next, bowed over it before stepping way the heck back lest he get caught in whatever magic web the woman spun that had already nabbed Arthur.

"You are Ms. Silver's boyfriend?" The expectant brightness that lit Monica's face had all the anticipation of a fire sparkler at a Hogmanay festival . . . Right before the bloody thing exploded prematurely, taking precious fingers with it.

Alec risked a glance at the Ms. Silver in question, who had yet to speak a single word, and blanched. *Oh, Lord. What have I done?*

When he had spied her across the dimly lit ballroom earlier, he'd had no notion of the finer tells her features were capable of.

Or how charming they were.

Petrified furrows between her dark brows drew her wide eyes into focus. Her gaze darted from him to Monica and back in a cartoonish gesture made even more adorable by the deep blush staining her cheeks. She was clearly looking for an anchor or an explanation, but her frame's stiffness belied the fear of reaching out for one just yet.

If this woman could make *terrified* look pleasing, what did *joy* look like on such a pleasant face?

For a moment, Alec latched on to her fear as well. Had he made a mistake? Had he misread the room and selfishly declared himself a savior no one had asked for?

Then there was the not-so-delicate matter of Phoebe, who had been staring daggers into the side of his face since he'd opened his mouth. It was only a matter of time before she lashed out and claimed the board for her own game.

God, did he hate mind tricks. Give him something to hit and he was golden. This crap, with all the mental warfare and cunning underpinnings? That had always been Phoebe's arena, and it was bloody brutal.

Alec chewed the inside of his mouth and waited for . . . for what? For the catering server to accept him, a creepy stranger, as an accomplice? For Phoebe to ruin whatever might be left of the young woman's reputation? To stand in front of an influential couple and run the highlight reel of Alec's rugby career down to the final frames, where he'd taken the worst tackle of his life and may not have his contract renewed at the end of the season?

His possible *final* season?

What the hell are you doing, Alec? Come the fuck on, man. You made your stand. Let it go. Let her *go. You and Phoebe are over.*

And he would have let it go, if not for the brush of Ms. Silver's starchy uniform against his suit coat as she took a step closer to him.

"Yup," she said. "This is, uh, Alec. My boyfriend." She'd said the word *boyfriend* with an exhausting accusation that was part incredulity and part relief.

None of which Phoebe cared for or bought, judging by the unnatural arch of that damn left eyebrow she'd always leveled at him when she was about to call him on his bullshit.

"And I love Christmas, as she said," Alec added, moving

closer to Ms. Silver—crap, what the hell was her first name?— and farther away from Phoebe, who he'd not yet dared look in the eye.

"Hold on," Arthur said, putting his palms out and bringing them to his head as if in the throes of prophecy. "What if Alec came to the Christmas Ball as a special guest and was willing to sign a few autographs? It would be a huge draw for the event, having a local sports celebrity in attendance. You know how Jersey's always getting New York's leftovers when it comes to holiday festivals. Well, now we would have our own headliner! We could promote it in our marketing, and I can see if any of my sports buddies in the city would be interested in sponsoring, given the rugby angle."

Alec couldn't be sure, having not died and checked out the Pearly Gates himself, but Monica's excited gasp may have been the closest sound to a full-on angel chorus. "That is such a marvelous idea, love! Oh, there is just so much I can work with there."

She curled her long fingers into a dainty fist beneath her chin and eyed Alec like a bird whose hide was worth more than his plumage. He didn't know whether to be flattered or frightened, but given the way this woman seemed to work men to her advantage, it seemed wise to harbor a bit of both.

Then a wall of yellow consumed his periphery as Phoebe literally and figuratively moved into position. "Not that I don't applaud your ingenuity, Mr. Doley, or your many talents at turning the mundane into marvels, Ms. Freeland," Phoebe finally said, though it was clear her words were directed at anyone but the two. "But I worry that, despite a few enthusiastic pockets of interest, rugby might not hold the draw of other professional sports. Especially in Jersey, I'd argue that very few even know how to play the game, let alone what a team looks like and who to cheer for."

"Oh, don't worry about that," Monica trilled, her voice like that of an alluring siren. "It is my profound experience that people will get excited about what I convince them to. Besides, celebrities are only as big as their following, and I am an expert at curating such followings. Don't worry, Mr. Elms. By the time I'm done with the preparations, you'll be the first and last name on everyone's lips when they leave the Crystal Christmas Ball." Then she took a careful sip of her champagne, and Alec could have sworn to every god his Pictish ancestors had once prayed to that this woman could convince volcanoes to erupt at her command with no more than a smile.

Truly frightening, that.

"You know, another idea just came to me," Monica added before indulging in more champagne. "There are few things people love more than a good celebrity to idolize, except for the one thing that always gets people through the door and drop-ping cash."

"What-what's that?" The squeak at Alec's elbow was a bit closer than its owner had been before, a comforting sign that his accomplice was warming to the role, a partnership he was coming to require more and more, given the stakes.

"Competition." Monica smiled. "I think it would be wonderful to have both of your businesses provide confections to serve at the Ball. Whoever can draw the largest crowds will receive equally large sales numbers, I imagine. Plus, the winner will have my professional and *personal* regards." The champagne hit her lips again and punctuated the implications of her state-ment as the luxurious wine slid, bubbles and all, in a dramatic glide down her throat. Then Arthur took the empty flute from her, and she smiled.

"I don't know if you know this, ladies, but I do have some-what of a reputation in West Meadow. My philanthropic endeavors over the years, along with holding several seats on various local boards and councils, have allowed me to curate a rather exclusive list of vendors I have come to recommend highly. And if the townspeople of West Meadow happen to declare their new favorite candy purveyor at the Crystal Christmas Ball in front of unprecedented crowds, well, how could I *not* add a business that has garnered such local favor to my list?"

"Ms. Freeland, that *does* sound like a wonderful idea," Phoebe said, her lips tightening at the corners, "but wouldn't it be a tad unseemly if one of the competitors is supposedly dating the star attraction? I get the premise of the event for the guests is couples-only, but surely it would deliver an unfair advantage to have that messiness spill over into business in this regard."

Alec narrowed his eyes and moved a shoulder—his good shoulder, the one he'd use in countless rucks to protect the ball and maintain momentum—in front of Ms. Silver. The movement was far more instinct than reason, a behavior that had always served him well in the face of any opponent, whether they wore a mouthguard or lipstick. Regardless, she didn't need to see Phoebe's claws aimed at her. Lord knew she'd dealt with enough of them earlier.

All because he'd fancied a pretty face in a crowd.

Arthur downed his drink and handed it off to passing wait-staff. "My dear, we really should get over to the Athertons. If I don't let David brag about his new property in Boca, I'll have to hear it in the sauna at the club when he knows I only have so much capacity for hot air. I'd rather be agreeable for as long as my martini holds out," he said and laughed at his own joke.

"Of course," Monica said, enfolding her hand within the crook of her date's arm. "Ms. Boyle, how large of a following do your social media accounts have again?"

"Well, to start, I have three and a half million on—"

"Then I can't imagine why you'd worry about anyone having an advantage over you, especially with all those followers on just one platform, after all." Monica squared her shoulders and patted Arthur's bicep, settling and dismissing the matter like a judge's gavel adjourning court.

Except Alec had no freaking clue just what he'd sentenced them all to.

CHAPTER 4

It had taken all of three seconds for Marisa's soul to settle back into her body. It was the only plausible explanation for her lack of involvement in a discussion that, one, very much concerned *her* love life, and two, determined the fate of *her* business. She of Many Words, as Eden liked to call her. And she'd had none to fling! Still didn't, truth be told, given the shock of it all. But oh, they'd come, and as soon as they did, Marisa would be laying down some goddamn ground rules, not the least of which would be—

"Why are you here, Alec? Really?" Phoebe asked, her tone taking on the bored yet agitated note of a woman not used to repeating herself.

The man Marisa had yet to look too closely at simply folded his arms across his wide chest and lifted a shoulder. "I heard they had good raspberry and brie bites."

"Not *here*. In Jersey," Phoebe seethed, but even that was too strong a sentiment for how her words maneuvered around the coiled tension.

"Visiting Cal."

Phoebe twisted her lips and arched one slim brow. "During

the season? You've never visited him before between tournaments. Unless there's another reason you're not on the circuit." She narrowed her eyes at him and raked that razor glare over his finely tailored suit, as if on the hunt for answers Alec wasn't willing to give.

He was having none of it.

"Oh, get over yourself, Phoebe," he said, waving his hand to break her stare before pegging her with a warning glare of his own. "You wanted no part in my life, so why start now?"

Over by the bar, Eden was waving at Marisa, brandishing her cocktail shaker like an aircraft marshal's wand and jutting her chin toward the kitchen door where Angela was scanning the crowd. For Marisa.

Shit.

"You know, I feel terrible about what happened to your dress earlier," Marisa said, planting her fists on her hips and shaking her head in mock dismay, pretending to scrutinize the garment. "Clearly, the club soda was a little light on the bubbles. I'll tell you what." She clapped, hoping to move this show right along. "Why don't I go back to the kitchen and get you a proper drink, this time fully carbonated. And hey," she said, putting her hand to the side of her mouth as though she *wasn't* drowning under boatloads of embarrassment, "maybe I can even bring you that glass of wine you asked about earlier."

It seemed like a fair way to sidestep the consequences, until the meager light shifted and Marisa discovered why Alec had to brace himself behind his thick forearms before squaring off with his ex.

Phoebe Boyle, a.k.a. The Plant Nanny, was the most chillingly beautiful creature Marisa had ever had the misfortune to mire. She hadn't had the opportunity to pay much attention earlier, what with Monica Freeland on the brain, but it was all there in excruciating clarity, as was the unfortunate truth of

Marisa's circumstances and who she'd inadvertently started a war with.

Marisa, my dear. You've messed up. Big time.

Long and vibrant copper curls, studded through with sparkling hair clips, cascaded over bare, slim shoulders that caught the eye of every man and several women. She had the kind of hair that Marisa's muddy curls, which were often too wiry to coil and too frizzy to lie flat, couldn't achieve in their wildest dreams. And that severe side part that always showed off too much of Marisa's patchy temples? It was pure side-swept brilliance on Phoebe. Add in the glittery shimmer dust around the woman's captivating green eyes, which she'd also applied to her ample cleavage and, yeah, well . . . Marisa got the picture, all right?

She'd just pissed off perfection.

Yay. Go team.

Phoebe gestured at Marisa while ignoring her offering. "I'm going to need you to explain this, Alec. I know you're not dating her."

Marisa had been steeped in so much deception that evening that the truth *should have* been a delightful breath of fresh air. She'd never been good at lying and hadn't been since she'd stolen that twenty-five-cent pack of Juicy Fruit gum when she was seven and never stopped to think that maybe chewing the gum in front of her parents, when they hadn't purchased any for her, wasn't the brightest idea. Her mother drove her all the way back to the grocery store to return it, all the while letting her know that her thievery was costing an additional twenty-five cents in gas.

But the truth of her present circumstances hadn't made her feel lighter at all. Instead, everything made her exceedingly uncomfortable. The too-tight, slip-resistant shoes, the hair tie choking her curls, Angela and her classic you're-fired scowl scanning the room for her.

Explaining her deception to two glamorous people while her polyester cuffs chafed her wrists, and what the hell was that yellow stain on her boob? *Really?*

Marisa didn't need the play-by-play of just how unlikely her lie was, and the fact that her brand-new partner in crime was taking his sweet time answering Phoebe?

No way could she bear to have this woman know the truth. The few remaining scraps of her dignity wouldn't allow it.

She needed to get out of there. Fast.

Alec pinched the bridge of his nose. "Phoebe, you're not—"

"Enjoying enough of the party. Go enjoy. Chat soon. Bye!" Marisa yanked Alec away from the conversation, having exactly zero time for any of his thoughts. And hadn't *he* been the one who'd gotten her into this mess?

She needed to have words with the man. Big hairy words. Words that were as thick as his shoulders and had more punch to them than every single one of his rolling Rs.

But first, seclusion.

Running out of options and time, Marisa snaked them through the back of the ballroom and out one of the side entrances that emptied into a few hallways. She picked the first one she saw, dragged him well past the bathrooms, and didn't stop moving until she'd forced them both into a stairwell.

Which he'd let her do, obviously, as there were no real-world scenarios where someone of his size would involuntarily let someone of her size pull him along.

And that just pissed her off even more.

Marisa's clipped "Explain" landed in time with the door slamming, and she had to hold her hands behind her back to avoid fist-bumping the Universe in thanks for the emphasis.

At least someone's on my side.

Alec threw his hands up. "I never meant for any of this to happen. You should know that."

"Then how *did* it happen?"

"Look, can we start over?"

"Why did you say yes? How did you even know what you were saying yes to? You've never met me before, and I sure as hell would have remembered meeting you." Crap. She hadn't meant to say that, but hadn't she, though? Oh, she was making such a hash of this and likely losing her job in the process.

"I'm Alec, by the way. Alec Elms. Figured I'd introduce myself properly at this point."

The hand he held out to her was one of the gentler shocks to her system and made her realize she was standing in a stairwell with a stranger.

A stranger who was attempting to broker peace through what seemed to be a genuine smile and introduction, despite the insanity they'd just fled from.

Aw, hell.

"Marisa Silver." She took his hand and gave the single conciliatory shake she gave to all business acquaintances, but when he returned the gesture with a slight warm squeeze before taking his hand back, she couldn't help but breathe out some of her anxiety.

"It's nice to meet you, Marisa."

"Likewise, I guess," she mumbled.

Then, with his arms clasped behind his back, he hinged forward at the waist. "Will you let me explain now?"

Oh, jeez, how could she not? The rumbling burr he spoke with rebounded gently off the stairwell's concrete walls, calming her overexcited nerves with an oddly comforting echo.

She nodded. "You have five minutes."

"Five minutes?" He arched a single brow in query, but the corner of his lips joined in the conspiracy, lifting as well. The bastard was grinning. Adorably.

"Fine. I'll accept seven."

"You drive a hard bargain." He righted himself and unclasped his hands, as if he would need their aid to answer her. "All right. I joined your conversation because I came to find you."

"Why?"

"To apologize."

"What could you possibly have to apologize to me for?"

He itched at the back of his neck, taming his more rugged features with a splash of boyish bravado. "I feared I may have distracted you a wee bit. When I happened to notice you earlier, I mean. Across the room. Right before you . . ." The swirling gesture with his hands filled in the gaps as to what he was so kind enough not to say out loud: Marisa stalling out and backing into Phoebe, staining her dress and causing a scene she hadn't needed.

"Oh."

"Yeah. I felt terrible, and then seeing that it was my ex-girl-friend you had the unpleasantness to run into, well . . . given the circumstances, I knew she wasn't about to treat you kindly."

Marisa snorted and waved her hand in dismissal. "I've dealt with worse."

"But you also deserve better." The syllabic R on the last word lingered between them, punctuating his stance on the matter. Then he gestured toward the door. "I heard what you were talking about before I joined you, and then I saw Phoebe waiting to pounce on every stuttered word you managed to get out. I could tell you were trying to impress Monica, but if there's one thing that can be said for Phoebe, it's that she can smell blood in the water a mile away."

"Why would you ever date someone like that?"

Alec stiffened and frowned, finding something on the floor terribly interesting. "We've all made mistakes. But the point is that I'm here hoping to correct the one I made earlier this evening. When I knew Phoebe was about to go in for the kill, that she'd trained her sights on you after you ruined her dress, and it was all because of me, I couldn't let that happen. So, when

Monica made the assumption about who I was, I didn't exactly correct her."

"You lied to her."

"Isn't that what you did first?"

"Hey, buddy, if you're going to act all smug, then just go start a YouTube channel like everyone else who needs the validation. My career's on the line here."

"Exactly. So is mine," he said with leashed frustration, the only evidence of cracks in his cool-as-a-cucumber facade up until then.

"What do you mean?"

Alec paced in a small loop on the fractured concrete landing for a minute before leaning against the wall across from her. "I mean that I'm not exactly on holiday, despite my presence at tonight's party. I got injured in my last rugby tournament. It was the middle of November. I took a bad hit during a match, so I'm off the roster for a while. With my contract up in May once the regular season wraps, and given my age, my agent has concerns about whether I should continue to play and whether my team, or any other team, will even want me to. I'm in New Jersey staying at my brother Cal's place to think through some things."

"What happened to you? In the game?"

He shook his head. "It's not important."

Marisa wanted to keep prying, but a shadow passed by the small windowpane in the stairwell door, reminding her that time was not her friend at the moment. She was about to say as much when Alec spoke again.

"What is important, though, is Monica's friend Arthur recognizing and regarding me enough to involve me in the Christmas Ball. It's something that would definitely get my agent's attention, show him that, despite me turning thirty-five in February, I've still got a lot left to give to the game and can draw a fair crowd, which means money for him. And if I can help you in the process by carting you around on my arm for a wee bit as a date so you can still achieve Monica's favor for your business, I can't see the harm in it, really. A bit of awkwardness, maybe, but no harm. The key to us both getting what we want is for Monica to believe we're a couple." Then he lifted his head from the wall and smiled. "Pretty sure that was only six minutes, by the way."

Marisa didn't bother pulling her phone out to check. All she could do was laugh at the man before her and the deal they were about to strike.

"Well, Mr. Elms," she said, straightening her spine and giving him her hand again while praying the yellow stain on her boob didn't ruin her air of authority. And to the man's charmingly sweet credit, he kept his eyes on hers and not her blemished boob as they shook hands before he opened the door and gestured for her to go before him. "For the next several weeks, it looks like we'll be dating."

CHAPTER 5

As far as investment opportunities went, the party was a nominal success. While Alec didn't come away with anything worth throwing money at, he did leave a bit more attached than when he'd arrived.

All things considered, there were worse things that could have happened than landing himself a girlfriend for the holiday season, and a bonny one at that.

Alec closed the door to his brother's apartment and emptied his pockets into the bin on the foyer table. "Hugh! Where are you, you good-for-nothing bastard? Get your arse over here before I—"

Alec's phone on the table began to dance toward the edge, shimmying dangerously close to tumbling onto the floor. In the sink, a couple of spoons and dishes from earlier rattled awake against the metal basin. Amusement pushed Alec's spirits higher as he crouched into a squat, straining a few of the precious trouser seams that hadn't signed up to hold in that much tensed muscle.

From within the shadows of the hallway, four paws as big as saucers hurtled across the hardwood. The black face mask and twinkling mahogany eyes barely came into focus before two hundred and thirty pounds of purebred mastiff tackled Alec to the floor. The tongue bath came next, a favorite pastime of the massive mongrel, but with Hugh's paws firmly set on Alec's shoulders pinning him in place, there wasn't much he could do but throw his arms around the beast's bulk and close his eyes.

"All right! All right! I'm home now. You can stop your fretting. Oh, bloody hell! Your damn tongue touched my teeth!"

Caring not a whit, Hugh continued to deliver his favor all over any available patch of skin in sight and a fair bit of Alec's ruined silk shirt collar. It was only when Alec got his fingers good and buried into the wrinkles surrounding Hugh's ears that the dog eased off him, obediently melting into the head massage that always greeted him whenever Alec was in town.

"That's right. You've got your scratches. All's right with the world." Then Alec leaned closer and whispered, "I know you like my massages better than Cal's. It's okay. We'll just keep that between us."

Hugh barked his agreement and immediately went onto his back, exposing his brawny frame, smooth belly, and the most impressive set of balls Alec had ever seen—no small feat considering the locker room tours Alec had done—and stared up at him with expectant yet patient eyes.

"Fine. A few more rubdowns and then I'll call your dad. Do you want to speak to Cal? Do ya? Do ya?"

The dog's vacant stare and lack of enthusiasm about anything other than a belly rub were unsurprising.

Once Alec had gotten Hugh to resume his usual seat on the dog's personal couch, he'd changed into a T-shirt and sweats and fired up Cal's name on his phone. The video call connected two rings later, and Alec immediately wished it hadn't. Far too much of his brother's pale Scottish skin filled the screen before Cal managed to prop the phone up and stand back from it. The retreating view was far worse, however. Where Alec hoped to see jeans or literally any other pair of trousers appropriate for a man, he instead was met with white tights hugging his brother's meaty legs before cinching him snugly at the waist. To add to the grisly effect, Cal still wore his character's wig: a white powdery number that was pulled back in a neat queue.

"Och, come on, now, Callum. You look like one of those white sausages I had the last time I was in Bavaria. You could have just called me back after you were finished changing."

"And miss the look on your face when you first got an eyeful of my belly lint after wearing a tweed waistcoat for two and a half hours? Never, my man. It was priceless." That familiar gap between Cal's two front teeth made an appearance as he grinned even wider, taking no small amount of pleasure in Alec's discomfort.

Par for the frickin' course, that.

"All right, enough. I figured you'd wrapped for the night already."

"Oh, I did. Just chatting a bit with the crew before I made it back to my dressing room." Cal rooted around at his scalp and pulled out a pin or two before yanking off his wig and placing it off-screen. The bald cap went next, and Cal promptly got to work roughing up his shaggy blond hair. "I tell ya, Jacob Marley is one of my favorite characters to play, but his costume's not made for burly Scotsmen. I popped two buttons today, and Carolyn in the wardrobe department was none too happy pinning things together fifteen minutes before the show started."

"Did she leave a few of her pins in you to express her displeasure?"

"I won't have full circulation back until I get these bloody tights off, so I'll let you know then," he said, laughing. "I wouldn't put it past her, though. This is her twenty-third season costuming *A Christmas Carol* for this tour, so no one wants to get on her bad side and risk any curses, you feel me?"

"Makes perfect sense, especially considering all those ghosts you already have to deal with."

"Exactly. Thanks for staying at my place and taking care of Hugh during the tour, by the way. Show's due to wrap December twenty-third, so I'll be home for Christmas Eve."

"Hugh misses you. Terribly. I don't know how we'll get along without you." Alec positioned the phone so he could get as much of Hugh in the shot as possible, who had already fallen deep into sleep and was hard at work creating a pool-sized drool puddle on the hardwood floor.

"Traitor. Oaf doesn't know what's good for him."

"Clearly."

Cal dabbed some makeup remover onto a cotton pad and started wiping his face. "So, how's Jersey treating you so far? Is it the refuge you hoped it would be?"

Alec took a seat on the couch opposite Hugh—the *smaller* bloody couch—and considered his words carefully, debating how much he should tell Cal. Despite the two years Alec and Phoebe were together, his brother had never warmed to her. Cal had told him so. Often.

"I ran into Phoebe. Or more accurately, I was caught staring at a woman who, in turn, ran into Phoebe. Literally."

Cal paused in his makeup removal, leaving the ghostly pallor and haunting shadows of Marley's eyes to bore into Alec through the phone, reminding him of all his fuck-ups of Christmas past. "I don't know what I should be asking about more. Your ex or the woman who stunned you stupid."

"That woman, believe it or not, is now my fake girlfriend."

"What the bloody hell does that mean? *Fake* girlfriend? Does that come with all the perks of the regular kind?"

"Don't be an arse. Her name's Marisa, and we're meeting up in a few days to discuss things. Nice girl. Ran into a bit of trouble because of me."

"That's not surprising."

"What is?"

"That you're causing nice girls all sorts of trouble."

Alec sighed and launched into the whole messy story, standing and pacing at points when the absurdities became too much to share sitting down. By the time he finished, Cal had changed fully out of his costume and was looking at him with a grim sort of wariness.

Alec knew that look. Hated that look. Wanted to punch the ever-loving shit out of that look.

It was their mother's look. The look of quiet consternation and worry over the hurdles ahead.

"Have you spoken to Dr. Campbell yet?" Cal asked.

The change of topic wasn't entirely unexpected, but Alec had hoped he'd have at least a few more minutes of shooting the shit with his brother before Cal dragged the infuriating sensible storm cloud into the room.

Alec nodded, suddenly wishing he hadn't just mentioned the fuss made about his rugby fame drawing a crowd. But this was Cal. Not his agent or teammates. If there was one person he could talk to about this stuff, it was the man who'd offered him the reprieve of his home to sort through it all.

"I talked to her a few days ago. I've still got some pain in my neck and jaw, but the headaches aren't as bad. Sleeping's a bit tricky, and I do have a bit of double vision at times, but she gave me some prescriptions that should help. Otherwise, I'm to keep at it with my home exercises and call her if anything changes or gets worse."

"Good. That's good, Alec. Really good."

"I—" Alec broke off and shook his head, not wanting to think about what had chased him to the States in the first place but finding it impossible. "I— Look, I'm fine. Everything will be all right."

"I know it will. Eventually. We just don't know what *all right* looks like quite yet, you hear me?"

"Yeah, I hear you," Alec said, resigned to being stuck in the mire of his present circumstances. "I just wish I knew what was coming for me. In the future, I mean. I'm not ready to stop playing. Not yet. Rugby is—" His life? His career? His purpose? After he'd given so much of himself to the game, was there even a possibility of life without it? On some level, he knew he couldn't play forever—that was why he was looking at investment opportunities in New Jersey—but that had always been a tomorrow problem.

And now that tomorrow was at his doorstep, what the hell was he supposed to do with today?

"Go on a date," Cal said, shifting his duffel bag over his shoulder, readying to leave. "With your *girlfriend*. The one you can't stop staring at, if I remember correctly. Sounds like you both could use a bit of company, anyway."

Alec hadn't realized he'd spoken his worries aloud, but it was the lighthearted jest in Callum's tone that softened the grim harshness on the horizon and turned his attention toward far more festive offerings.

It was the holiday season, after all. December held loads more than a weekend rugby tournament he was exempt from playing in anyway.

It held *a date*. Many, if fake relationships followed similar paths as real ones.

"Maybe you're right," Alec mused, trying the cheerful offering on for size while remembering how Marisa's warm hand had felt in his. Surprisingly, he didn't hate the fit of either.

"Of course I'm right. I'm the oldest."

"That literally means nothing."

"Sure it does. You wouldn't understand, because you're not the oldest," Cal whispered out of the side of his mouth, his gap-toothed grin on full display.

"Good night, Scrooge," Alec said.

"It's Marl—"

Alec ended the call before Cal could get the last word in and looked over at Hugh. The dog was nestled in his couch divot, snoring away without a care in the world. No worries about his future. No cares about anything other than the cushions beneath him.

For once, a present-minded focus didn't sound half bad. If it was good enough for an occasionally ornery mastiff, it could be good enough for Alec as well.

The only worry he couldn't shake, however, was whether he'd be any good at this whole fake boyfriend thing. His career wasn't the only one on the line. Marisa's candy making business relied on their deception just as much as his.

He couldn't change what he'd agreed to tonight, but if there was one thing he knew how to do, it was to strategize as a unit. He hadn't been chosen as captain of first Scotland Sevens and then Great Britain's Sevens teams for the past several years for nothing.

It was no different than a match, really, with the Crystal Christmas Ball serving as the pitch he and Marisa would play on, while Phoebe and her plant army stared them down from the other side.

The only thing that remained to be seen was the sort of tactics Marisa was poised to employ.

Because he could think of several that would knock Phoebe down a peg or two.

But first, he needed to meet with Marisa. The thought of it made his chest lighter, and he couldn't help but smile thinking about the tiny woman who'd dragged him by his bulk and chucked him into a stairwell to let him have it.

There was a whole lot of fight packed into that curvy frame, and he couldn't wait to learn what it would be like to fight alongside her.

CHAPTER 6

Few things made Marisa happier than hearing the targeted *beep* of her restaurant supply store's membership card being scanned upon entry. Some safe places designated themselves as such with signs, inclusive graphics, and open-armed social media campaigns. Others, like Dining Depot, were innately safe, especially during the holiday season, for one particular reason.

Only those in the catering and restaurant industries could garner a membership, thus keeping out the general public who would happily judge a woman for buying an eighty-piece bucket of blueberry candy canes.

Which Marisa, with Eden in tow, needed post-frickin'-haste.

"All right," Eden said, doing her best to keep pace while balancing an egregiously large tub of red and green kettle corn on her hip. "So, you have a boyfriend now."

"Fake boyfriend," Marisa huffed out, quickening her steps.

"I don't know. He looked pretty real to me. Nothing fake about the way those muscles filled out that suit. I could see the contouring and definition all the way from the bar, even with the shitty lighting."

"Still a fake boyfriend. Now, where the hell are they? They had the peppermint ones out front, but not the blueberry. Ugh. I hate when they rearrange the seasonal displays. Can't they just keep everything in the same place?"

Marisa's worried thoughts had successfully managed to chase her to the next aisle before Eden, with all that super-human barkeeper's upper arm strength, hooked Marisa's elbow and yanked her to a halt. Cornered in front of the twenty-pound buckets of fondant, Marisa had no choice but to get good and right with the woman leveling a tub of kettle corn under Marisa's chin like a fencer's épeé.

Eden shifted her shoulder to block the candy canes that Marisa was still straining to see. "No, no, no. You don't get to change the subject. For the first time in—"

"Don't say forever."

"—*forever* you have a boyfriend, a booming opportunity to score a spot on Monica's coveted List at *the* holiday event of the season, and we haven't even gotten into the birthday festivities yet!"

Marisa cringed and tried her best to shrink away from the wall of atrocities that was corn syrup, sugar, and water, but it was no use. They both knew she couldn't continue to ignore the scary pile of life-changing events climbing onto her back.

Or the occasionally scarier enthusiasm of her best friend hopped up on Red 40 and Green No. 3.

There was a damn good reason Marisa insisted on using natural food dyes in her candy, and she was looking at it.

"I'm not avoiding anything." Mostly. "I'm having dinner with Alec tonight at Sal and Enzo's. We'll figure out what this whole charade should look like, and we'll go from there." Despite her best efforts to infuse the lowest amount of chill into the remark, even Marisa couldn't keep back a wince. Nerves tended to have that effect. So did spending the past day and a half since the cocktail party reliving every single horrifying rumpled shirt-stained detail of what she must have looked like striking a dating/business bargain with a sports star.

One whose gracious smile she couldn't stop thinking about, a smile she'd be seeing a lot more of very soon.

But she could hardly focus on that when she'd run herself ragged brainstorming what she could serve at the Crystal Christmas Ball and how to entice untold numbers of people to come visit her booth.

Beyond upping her meager ad spend and making more social media posts that the algorithms would suppress into oblivion anyway, she was at a complete loss for how to achieve the latter.

Somewhere during the past several frantic hours of planning, analysis, ledger reviews, customer orders, customer *complaints*, and the two social media posts she'd uploaded that had taken her *four frickin' hours* to design, she'd accepted her fate and spiraled into a depressed heap on her living room floor.

Millions. Phoebe had *millions* of followers, on multiple platforms, likely fueled by a goddamn team of tech-savvy people working around the clock to pump out content about the Christmas Ball.

Knowing Phoebe, she'd probably already ordered merch and was actively sending out influencer care packages about her vendor offerings.

While Marisa had lukewarm coffee, a caffeine headache from said coffee, a combined total of forty-six social media views—screw you, algorithm—and Joe the bagel guy saying he'd make sure her flyers would be put front and center at his shop, right between the twenty-year-old lollipop dispenser and the coffee-can-turned-donation-bin for the local animal shelter.

In other words, Marisa had bupkis.

Her only recourse against spiraling out completely was indulging in the one thing her festive-season-loving heart could always rely on this time of year: artificially flavored and coincidentally Hanukkah-colored blueberry candy canes.

A treat she only ever felt comfortable procuring at Diner Depot beneath its cavernous roof of judgment-free resplendence. Plus, they sold hot dogs.

"And as far as birthdays go, why don't we just keep it low-key this year, huh? You know, pretend like thirty is just another blip on the radar. Perhaps over the Bermuda Triangle. During a freak electrical storm. It wouldn't happen to be a leap year, would it? Doesn't weird stuff always happen on leap years? Stuff we should pretend never actually happened?"

Eden dove her hand into the popcorn bucket but still didn't move an inch. "You mean like people getting to celebrate their actual birthdays for the first time in four years?"

"Sure, that! Weird stuff. So, maybe this isn't the year to lean in so heavily on my birthday. I mean, I get to celebrate mine every year. How selfish is that?" Marisa tried to laugh, but the effect was ruined by a nearby spilled bag of cornstarch that had decided to atomize in her lungs, causing her to choke out the word *selfish* with an inappropriate amount of raspy inflection.

The sole benefit of her near-death experience? Eden finally backed off when Marisa almost coughed into her friend's kettle corn.

"It might be, except that we're talking about two different calendar years, let alone calendar months." Eden narrowed her eyes. "Why are you being weird?"

"Why are *you* being weird?"

"What are you not telling me?"

"Nothing. Can we get my candy canes now?"

"Fine," Eden relented. "You know, you're the only Jewish person I'm friends with who has this as their Hanukkah tradition."

"First of all, I'm your only Jewish friend *period*. And when you can't stand black and white cookies or jelly doughnuts and still want to share in the magic of the holiday season with everyone else, your options are limited."

Eden wrinkled her nose. "But they're blueberry. You don't even *like* blueberry."

"Irrelevant. They're blue and festive and exactly what I need right now if I'm going to make it through the next few weeks."

And that was the crux of the dirty little secret her family had never been able to understand.

When it came to carving out a place for herself, Marisa had long ago landed on the fact that she *was* the blueberry candy cane. An anomaly, a fraud. An unglamorous holiday season misfit that didn't quite measure up to expectations. A fruity treat when everything else was peppermint. The right shape but the wrong color, though still always coming back year after year so Jews like her who were embroiled in all the Christmas wonder could claim them as their own and give them the homes they deserved.

She was the Jewish girl who, after years of floundering and buying degrees she couldn't bring herself to try on fully, had finally found her calling in the sugar-coated fascination swirling around Christmas and other celebratory confections. Her graduate studies couldn't contribute anything to the joy that came with rolling out buttermints or making little marzipan gift-hugging teddy bears.

Which made her a big fat Frosty-the-Snowman-loving fraud.

Of course, it didn't help matters that her love of candy making also coincided with a deeper and far more treacherous crime.

Despite her upbringing, as an adult, Marisa had become *secular.*

The word had been an unspoken stain on her adult life that had unleashed torrents from a wellspring of guilt, which truly had no bottom. She didn't keep kosher, always had to look up when the holidays were, and couldn't remember any of the reasons for celebrating the holidays beyond *Someone tried to kill us. We survived. Let's eat.*

That wasn't to say she didn't have a love for her heritage, but explaining to her family that she always resonated more with the vibes than the plot was like a serial killer trying to convince Santa that a weeklong stretch with no brutal murders had to count for something, right?

Regardless, that never stopped her from buying every bit of Hanukkah merchandise the Internet had the gall to sell or getting swept up in the Festival of Lights, regardless of whether they were from a menorah or a twinkling strand wrapped around a Christmas tree. And blue-and-white Santa hats? She owned three of them, all with varying amounts of glitter.

Even though she had found her quiet happiness and port in the storm, it didn't make her life any less exhausting.

Jewish guilt, man. That shit was a killer.

Marisa had just made it to the bulk candy aisle when the sounds of "The Imperial March" echoed off the concrete floor. Her heart rate lifted out of her chest in time to every *dun dun dun* that projected in all its older-model-smartphone tinny glory from her right butt cheek.

She and Eden shared a look of grim determination before they launched into a synchronized routine as practiced as their senior year of high school's winning lip sync number.

Marisa's ear buds were in her hands a second later, with Eden and Marisa each taking one. As soon as they had them in their ears, Eden gave the thumbs-up. Marisa, huddled between the supportive constraints of her best friend and the stacks of sugar that represented all her adult dreams, accepted the call.

"Hey, Ma. How's it going?"

"I ordered the cake! Marisa Rose Silver, I ordered the cake! Oh, you're going to love it this year. I got Bernie at the kosher bakery to make—get this—a *cupcake* cake. They're all going to be pull-apart chocolate and vanilla cupcakes arranged in the shape of a menorah connected by frosting. I thought about having things shaped like the number *thirty* instead, but I figured a menorah shape could serve more people. And you know your father will put away at least three cupcakes on his own before any of the guests arrive. I'll have to watch him like a hawk. I can't have Sheila and Harry showing up to the celebration with the shamash already eaten."

"Love you, too, Ma. Hey, how about we back up a few chapters, though? What cake?"

"Your *birthday* cake! Seriously, Marisa, didn't you hear a word I said?"

Oh, she heard them. All of them. Which was why Marisa needed things repeated. Slowly. Preferably with enough time in between sentences for a spit take and a bathroom break, because there was absolutely no way her mother could be referring to—

"My birthday cake? Why would I want a menorah for my birthday cake?"

"*Cupcake* cake," her mother corrected.

"Fine. We'll go with that one if it helps the comprehension."

"Your birthday is December seventeenth."

"Yes . . ."

"And do you know when Hanukkah is?"

The air in Marisa's lungs grew thinner, having decided to vacate the space for better circulation in the heating vent overhead. Her pulse pounded a rabbit-kick rhythm against her chest, which only got ten times worse when Eden's eyes widened and her friend made a slashing motion across her neck while also pointing down at the phone.

"Uh, Ma. Can you hang on a sec? I'm getting another call."

Marisa punched the mute button as Eden brought up the calendar on her phone. Marisa looked over her best friend's shoulder and grabbed on for dear life. "No no no. This can't be what I think it's going to be."

"How the hell do you not know when Hanukkah is?" Eden asked, her voice taking on an unsettling shrill of panic that mirrored Marisa's.

"Because it's a moving target and I look it up like everyone else! It's not like there's a committee that sends out monthly emails with coupons or something. Though, not going to lie, that would be kind of killer."

Before the argument could devolve into something even the fondant would judge her for, Marisa stared at the little calendar date, along with its incredibly unhelpful list of daily items it was calling attention to.

Eden squinted. "Yup. December seventeenth is the first night of Hanukkah."

"Which means the last night of Hanukkah is"—Marisa counted eight days off on her fingers because, despite her almost being thirty, math was still her mortal enemy—"Christmas Eve."

The night of the Crystal Christmas Ball.

"Shit," Marisa breathed out.

"Double shit," Eden agreed. "What are you going to do?"

Numb from the news and incapable of any rational decision-making, Marisa shook her head in disbelief. "Tell her, I guess?"

"About the Ball? Really?"

"I don't know." But as the seconds ticked by with Marisa's mother on hold, she knew ignoring the problem would only make it worse. Besides, she hadn't exactly narrowed in on a specific problem yet. There were just so many to choose from, weren't there?

Telling her mother about her failing business, how she had a last-ditch shot to get on The List before she'd have to face some rather unsavory life truths. Oh, and what shade of red the Plant

Nanny turned when she got hosed with hors d'oeuvres before deciding to reap her retaliation in the form of destroying her competitors.

Then there was the ever-present fact that she'd accidentally acquired a fake boyfriend.

She was spoiled for choice. Truly.

"Maybe the party won't be that bad?" Marisa said, despite her voice's upward inflection dragging the needle into the red on her bullshit meter.

Eden pocketed her phone and simply folded her arms. "If you believe that, why is your mother still on mute?"

Marisa narrowed her eyes and mouthed, "I hate you," before picking up again. "Sorry about that, Ma. It was just my mechanic reminding me I'm due for an oil change." On a car her mother damn well knew Marisa hadn't even taken in for a tune-up in three years. Solid.

"Oh, Marisa," her mother said, letting just enough of her disapproval slip through to keep things interesting. "You were looking up when Hanukkah starts, weren't you?"

Dammit.

"No! No, I was just . . ."

"Well, it should be easy for you to remember this year, shouldn't it? Your Aunt Gail and I have decided to throw our annual Hanukkah party on your birthday! Kill two birds with one stone. And who doesn't love an opportunity for double the festivities?"

"Ma, I'm going to be thirty. I'm kind of past the point of birthday parties, don't you think?"

"Are you also past the point of spending some holiday time with your family so we all might indulge in a little greasy food and birthday cupcakes together? The latkes alone will have thousands of calories in them. Honestly, Marisa, it would be downright irresponsible not to share them all."

"I'm not sure I want to have a part in that kind of familial indigestion."

"Oh, please. Your father will have plenty of antacids on hand. He knows the drill at this point." The runaway train that was her mother's enthusiasm would have kept right on running if not for the slight pause that caught Marisa off guard.

Her mother never paused. Like, ever. Even when others were speaking.

A chilly sense of dread crawled up Marisa's spine.

"Besides," her mother added matter-of-factly, "your Aunt Gail was just telling me about a neighbor who moved into her complex, and she thinks he might be a nice person to introduce you to."

Oh, no. Absolutely not. No freaking way.

"Ma, please tell me this person is a woman who has moved through life at the same pace Aunt Gail has moved through life."

More silence and then, "Now, what do you mean by that?"

"You know exactly what I mean," Marisa gritted out. "Is Aunt Gail's new neighbor another one of her retired pickleball cronies?" *Please, please let her be a blue-haired retiree who usually snowbirds in Florida but happens to be in Jersey visiting her grandkids for the holidays.*

"Now, I don't think Jules would appreciate being called a *crony—*"

At the mention of the name Jules, a coil of tension in Marisa's stomach began to unravel. "You know what? It's fine. I'm sure Jules is a lovely—"

"But I wouldn't at all be surprised if he does play pickleball. Or maybe one of those more rugged sports. You know, like bowling! The young man does have quite the athletic build, I will say. I can't speak for his legs, but those arms definitely look like they've had experience throwing a bowling ball or two down a lane. Oooh, I bet he can even use one of those sixteen-pounders!

Your father tried to use one of those once when the cruise ship we were on had a bowling alley. Poor dear broke two fingernails *and* got himself a hernia. Then there was that time when he thought he was good enough to join an actual league. . ."

Marisa wanted nothing more than to drop her phone into the nearest garbage can, grab her candy canes, and crawl into a hole. She didn't need the marked look of sympathy on Eden's face to know that her family had staged the entire birthday/Hanukkah party affair for one specific reason.

She was turning thirty, and if her loved ones couldn't convince her to find a career that actually paid *her* for a change, they could at least try to work on seeing her settled in a relationship more promising than the one she had with the pizzeria she lived above.

The phone in Marisa's hand might as well have been a boulder for all the weight it carried, which only seemed to increase every time her mother mentioned *he's only thirty-two* and *doesn't have family in the area, so he's looking forward to meeting new people.*

Eden mouthed, "Sorry," and held out what remained of her kettle corn in solidarity, but Marisa couldn't even bring herself to smile at the unnaturally bright kernels. Colors that had always made her so happy in their vibrancy and cheer during the holidays now felt like foolish anchors tying her to a life that could only exist in her fantastical bubble.

A bubble that wasn't real. A bubble that saw her fighting for a candy business that she still believed in, even though her family didn't.

A bubble . . . where she had a fake boyfriend.

Marisa straightened and nearly dropped the phone as the idea hit her. "Actually, you know what, Ma?" Marisa said, cutting off her mother's spiel about how doughnuts never quite tasted right ever since trans fats had been banned. "I'm looking forward to the party. Can't wait to see everyone, truly."

"Oh, really? That's wonderful! Your aunt will be thrilled. Just thrilled."

"I'm sure she will be. It'll also be a great time for me to introduce her, and you and Dad as well, to my new boyfriend. See you then. Love you!"

Without giving her mother an opportunity to respond, Marisa hung up, plucked the earbud out of Eden's ear, and neatly folded the little things into their case while she calmly stepped away from the blast zone to find her candy canes.

This was her dream, dammit. Her life that she was more than prepared to go to war for. And if that meant she'd have to call in the reserves to hit the front lines, then that was exactly what she would do.

CHAPTER 7

When Alec initially received the text from Marisa asking him to meet to discuss their first *mission,* he'd been at a loss for what to expect. Or what he should bring, for that matter. It wasn't a date, per se, because they weren't actually dating. He pegged it as more of a strategy session, if he had to guess based on her phrasing.

Or a bloody war briefing, given her copious use of sword and dagger emojis.

He pulled out his phone again as he took in the restaurant's glowing sign of swirling letters above him.

> Marisa: Meet me at Sal and Enzo's at 6 p.m. Assignment tactics are on the agenda. We've got a mission.

The building he stood in front of was nothing more than a pizzeria with a laminated menu taped to the front window that boasted more kinds of toppings than had any right to be put on pizza. But hey, over the course of years visiting Cal in the off-season, he'd come to learn a thing or two about New Jerseyans and their pizza preferences. Or, more specifically, he'd learned

62

to keep his gob shut lest he wanted to walk around wearing his dinner instead of eating it.

Alec pushed through the door with a bit lighter of a step than he anticipated and strode toward one of the tables in the corner. It wasn't hard to find Marisa, with her dark head hunkered down over her tablet and a prominent wrinkle carving its worry into the space between her brows. Outside of the cocktail party's disorienting lighting and instead beneath spotlit fluorescent beams, Marisa appeared far gentler. Oh, there was a fair amount of craze still to be had, what with her hair snaking down past her elbows, with a few mindless waves that seemingly reached for the Parmesan cheese shakers, but it was nonetheless calmer. Peaceful, even, given all she'd been through at his expense.

"General," he announced, taking the seat in front of her. "What are our orders?"

Marisa looked up, surprise lighting her features. "Oh, you're here!"

"I said I would be. I'm a man of my word."

As soon as he said it, she opened up a note on her screen and began scribbling. "Man of your word. Check."

"Am I here to check off boxes? I didn't know there'd be a quiz."

"It's not a quiz for you. More so for me. If we're going to be making this charade appear believable, I think it'd be helpful for us to know certain things about each other."

"Like the fact that I show up on time when I'm asked to?"

"Exactly! You'd be surprised at how many people think tardiness is just a personality trait and have no care for how it impacts others."

"I take it you're not one to be late."

She scoffed, wrinkling her nose. "Are you kidding me? If I'm not early, I'm late."

Alec made a show of reaching into his back pocket, pulled

out an invisible notebook and pen, and pretended to scribble something down. Then he made an elaborate swooshing checkmark in the air. "Hates tardiness. Check."

That won him a smile, and for some reason, it gladdened him. He got the sense she didn't smile often, which was a damn shame because she was quite bonny when she did, even if his words caused her eyes to dart to far corners as if searching for cover from unseen attacks.

Now *that* he didn't like one bit.

He pulled out his imaginary notebook and pen again, making sure to capture her gaze away from invisible worries. "Uneasy with levity. Check. Assignment: immersion therapy."

"Immersion therapy? What's that supposed to mean?"

"It means, as your official boyfriend of record, I'll be tasking myself with making sure cheer sits a bit more naturally with you."

"I'll have you know, I can be delightfully cheerful. Hello? I literally sell sugar for a living. If you know of a more dopamine-inducing product, I'm all ears."

For the second time since he'd met her, Alec had his hands raised in defense. "I didn't say you didn't know your industry. Just remarking that you might enjoy a bit more levity in your life. What's that old saying? The cobbler's children go barefoot? As you said, if us dating is going to have any ring of truth to it, I can't have you walking around on my arm acting like the last time you enjoyed yourself was when you were still fantasizing about men in the Stone Age getting mauled by saber-toothed tigers so the women could enjoy their caves in peace."

He'd meant it as a kind bit of joviality. Something to earn him another smile or at least give him something to work toward, but when Marisa's eyes took on a flinty edge to them and her features slipped back into that mask she'd worn when he'd spotted her through the window of the restaurant, he knew he'd misstepped.

"Hey," he rushed out, grabbing her retreating hand before she had a chance to shove it under the table. "I'm an arse. Forget what I just said. All I meant was that, if we're to look the part of being happy, it's far easier to make it genuine."

Alec had scores of other excuses at the ready and had prepared to dig deep into the reserve of apologies he'd always needed to use with Phoebe, but when the argument didn't come, he was left with a shaky hollowness he wasn't quite sure how to manage.

That and Marisa hadn't taken back her hand.

It was the lightest touch. Barely a clasping of fingers. It could hardly even be called hand-holding, but it was nice. His calloused fingers looked bulbous and craggy caging her smaller ones, but the contrast didn't bother him. It seemed to be the visual representation of what he'd done his whole career. Protecting the ball, blocking the tackle.

Keeping everything, and almost every*one*, out to secure what truly mattered.

He was about to trace his thumb along the top of her hand when she finally, slowly, took her hand back.

"I can do happy," Marisa said with what he was thrilled to see looked to be a genuine smile. "And you're right. This opportunity is a once-in-a-lifetime shot, and I need to believe it'll work."

The tenuous hope in her tone was as much of a rallying cry as he figured she could muster, given the loud hollering of pizzaiolos flinging dough and ringing up takeout orders.

If this was her preferred strategy room, one where she felt comfortable enough to show him even the smallest amount of joy, then the least he could do was share in her belief that they could pull it off.

"This opportunity is significant for me as well," he agreed, nodding. "Speaking of opportunities, what's the plan? You said you had our first mission."

The brightness in her eyes took on a shadowy cast, and Alec immediately picked up on the same shifting discomfort he'd last seen Marisa fight through when she was talking to Monica at the cocktail party.

She was nervous. Did that mean he should be nervous, too?

"There's an event my parents are throwing on December seventeenth. It's sort of another holiday party. Well, no, that's not true. More of a combined party."

"A combined party?"

"Sure. Yes."

"What are the occasions that are being combined? Christmas is one, I'm assuming."

"Not exactly." Marisa chewed her lip before throwing her hands down on the table. "Oh, this is ridiculous."

Before he could ask what was so ridiculous, she walked over to the drink refrigerator, squatted down, rummaged around toward the back of the bottom shelf, then came away with a frosty dark brown can. She cracked open the tab and took a few respectably healthy swigs, then returned to the table, a renewed sense of purpose casting the color high in her cheeks.

Alec scratched at the scar on his face that had long ago ruined his beard line. "Now, admittedly, I'm not as well-versed in pizzeria etiquette as my brother, Cal, who's lived here for years, but I'm fairly certain you can't just take a soda out of the restaurant's fridge and—"

"Enzo! Can you bring over four slices of the white cheese and broccoli?" Marisa shouted to the portly pizzaiolo, who was setting his peel on top of the oven. Then she gasped and leaned closer to Alec. "You're not dairy free, are you? I should have asked first. Oh crap, you eat gluten, right? If not, I think Sal usually keeps some of those cauliflower crust things around."

"I can eat whatever I'd like, but do you always—"

Enzo's booming voice volleyed over the counter. "Sure thing, babe. You got enough crushed red pepper flakes over there? I haven't checked those tables since the lunch rush."

"Got plenty!"

Alec watched the exchange in fascination. For a conversation that sounded like yelling, each phrase was coated with an almost loving appreciation. "I think it would be fair to suspect that you two know each other."

The flush from Marisa's soda swig remained and, bolstered by her interaction with Enzo, had also infused her complexion with more exuberance than he'd yet to see on her. It was utterly adorable.

"Guilty," Marisa admitted. "I actually live in the apartment above the pizza place. Enzo and his brother Sal are always feeding me, and they let me keep my *in case of emergency* sodas in the fridge as long as I tuck them in the back on the bottom shelf so no customers accidentally grab one by mistake."

Alec chuckled, then pulled the can in question closer for inspection, swiping his thumb across the condensation so he could read the letters more clearly. "What's an *in case of emergency* soda?"

"Dr. Brown's cream soda. Occasionally, I go for the black cherry. It's more for fortification than anything else. In my line of work, I try to limit my sugar intake outside of recipe testing and production. But when I'm struggling to stay grounded, I find the Good Doctor always helps."

Intrigued, Alec lifted the can to his lips and took a few good pulls. "Sweet. Pleasant. Heavy on the vanilla. Overall, enjoyable. Not bad." When he brought the can away from his mouth, he was met with a shocked expression akin to what Cal would give him when he'd forgotten to zip his trousers after using the loo.

Marisa's eyes darted from the soda to his mouth and back again.

Alec's misstep quickly sank in, nearly choking him. *Fuckin' hell. I just shared her drink.*

The act had been as natural as blinking, a common occurrence when he visited his brother.

But he wasn't with his brother, and the woman whose soda he'd just tasted wasn't his actual girlfriend.

"Shit. I'm sorry about that. Force of habit when I'm in the States. I don't tend to spend much time with people outside Cal. Not since . . ."

There was something inherently wrong about letting Phoebe invade the space between them, a space that had become a war room infused with basil, oregano, and the pleasant yeasty aroma of hand-tossed dough.

All kissed by a lingering sweetness where Marisa's mouth had been that he couldn't quite put a name to.

And he'd gone and soured it all already. Wonderful.

"Let me get you another." Alec rose to go to the fridge, but Marisa stopped him.

"There's no need. Like you said, if we want this to be believable, we need to start acting the part, right? Couples share drinks all the time."

"Right. Sure."

Alec had never been more grateful to have a middle-aged man's belly almost push him into a wall of windows. "Here you are, babe, for you and your friend. Now, eat these first," Enzo said, pointing to the slices he'd placed in front of them. "The undercarriage isn't going to stay that solid for long." Then he plopped down a plate of garlic knots and marinara that Marisa hadn't asked for but beamed at seeing regardless. "The knots gotta get eaten, too. They've been sittin' a bit."

Marisa stood and kissed Enzo's cheek. "What would I do without you?"

"Probably eat more of that fast food shit."

Marisa grabbed the Parmesan, then clarified, "Enzo believes the only true types of fast food are pizza or Chinese. Everything else deserves the *shit* designation."

Alec smiled. "Well, he's not wrong."

"See?" Enzo said, tossing a greasy thumb at Alec. "I'm not the only one who knows what's what. By the way, your mother stopped by and told me about the party."

Marisa halted a marinara-coated garlic knot inches from her lips. "She did?"

"Hand delivered us invitations and everything. Don't worry. My brother and I won't embarrass you by showing up. I got teenagers. I know the drill. But I didn't know your birthday fell on Hanukkah this year. Let me know if your mother wants to borrow some more cannoli tubes again. Last year, she wanted to fry her own and try those out instead of the doughnuts, but she backed out for some reason."

"That was probably because of my Aunt Gail. She always likes to be involved in the holidays," Marisa said, twisting her lips in distaste.

"Ah. All kosher then?"

"Yup."

"Cool. Let me know if you need anything."

Marisa held up her garlic knot in mock salute. "Will do."

Turned out, Alec needn't have worried about his earlier cock-up. All that awkwardness itching beneath his skin had been steamrolled by the even larger embarrassment of his incorrect holiday assumptions.

"It's a Hanukkah party we're to go to," he said, wishing he could have kept the surprise out of his voice. "And your birthday. That's the combined party you were talking about."

"Again, guilty," she said, wiping her fingers on a napkin, doing all that fidgeting fluff he was used to seeing her do whenever she was uncomfortable.

Bloody hell. That was the last thing he wanted her to feel, especially around him. It'd never crossed his mind that she might be Jewish and celebrate a different occasion altogether.

"It's my thirtieth," she added into the shameful space of his overly loud thoughts. "Yes, it falls on Hanukkah this year, and my family is using it as an excuse to express their disapproval over both my career choice and lack of significant other this far into adulthood by setting me up with my aunt's neighbor. It's going to be absolutely awful"—Marisa took back her soda and fiddled with the can—"except for the fact that I told my mother I had a boyfriend and was going to bring him to the party." Then she pinned Alec with a battle-hardened gaze that would have been better served in a combat zone instead of a pizzeria. "*This* is our first mission. And while we're there, we'll take tons of photos, post them to social media, and start getting people excited for who and what we'll be offering at the Crystal Christmas Ball."

That warbling echo of hope rang through her again, and damn if Alec didn't want to capture that sound and keep it safe from being stomped into silence.

Even if he was the lumbering oaf who'd nearly crushed it to begin with.

The only problem was that he knew as much about Hanukkah as the average American knew about rugby. It couldn't be that hard to learn the basics, though, especially if he were to put on a show of dating Marisa.

Besides, one thing he *did* know a fair bit about was being charming and adaptable. For better or worse, those skills had done him a great kindness over the years, and he saw no reason not to employ them on Marisa's behalf.

"I think it all sounds like a solid plan. I confess, though, you may have to catch me up to speed on a few of the traditions."

Marisa swiped her hand in avid dismissal. "Oh, no worries there. With any luck, we'll be able to duck out of there after candle lighting. The main tradition with my family, unfortunately, usually involves me avoiding everyone as much as possible."

"Even when you're the birthday girl?" Alec tried to let some of his enthusiasm shine through in his grin, hoping to at least somewhat smooth out the crease between her brows that had been a near constant guest during dinner. When the worry remained and she stayed silent even after he stole one of her garlic knots without her swatting him away—which, though he only knew her a short time, somehow seemed like a very Marisa thing to do—he attempted a different approach. They were, after all, in a battle strategy session, were they not?

Alec took a nibbled pizza crust dangling from Marisa's hand, set it on her plate, and linked his larger fingers between hers. That earned him a soft inhale and a delightful spark of surprise flashing through her brown eyes. "If it's a possessive boyfriend you'll be needing, someone to scare away the scrutiny of doting family members and the attention of other men, that's a role I can fill wholeheartedly. I know a thing or two about intimidation tactics. That and I've yet to meet a mature woman I haven't managed to win over. Don't know what it is, but females of a certain age tend to love me."

A ghost of a smile pulled the corner of Marisa's lips a hair higher. It was just enough for Alec to both consider it a win and find encouragement to do better. He'd have her fully smiling by the time the party hit, he was certain.

"It's the brogue/bicep combo," Marisa said, hiding the slight amusement he'd managed to coax out of her with another bite of pizza crust, though she still kept her other hand entwined with his, he was happy to see. "I'm sure the blue-hairs love that stuff. Remember, Sean Connery was their James Bond for most of their hormone-fueled years."

Alec slapped his hand on the table. "Then it's James Bond I'll be, except without any of the smoking, womanizing, or persnickety drink preparation requests. There. It's all settled."

Marisa shook her head. "You're crazy."

"No, I'm your boyfriend. At least for the time being."

As they enjoyed the rest of their pizza and garlic knots, Alec couldn't help but shake his head in amusement at what he'd agreed to.

Or how a greater part of him was actually looking forward to starting their dating rumor.

CHAPTER 8

While it wasn't strictly necessary for Marisa to accept Alec's offer of walking her home, a gaffe he'd charmingly stammered over once she reminded him where she lived, her body still buzzed with the excitement of not wanting to leave Alec just yet. Add in that he'd just witnessed her take down an entire kid's birthday party's worth of pizza, thanks to Enzo refilling their table two more times, and still hadn't made an excuse to leave her for the evening?

Yeah, she had zero problem letting him escort her home, even if the walk was only around the alley that led to the back of the pizzeria, where the separate entrance to her apartment was.

Maybe it was the way her mind still hummed with all the details of their pizza-fueled charade or the image of her mother meeting Alec for the first time, but suddenly, the thought of squaring off with her Aunt Gail's blue-blooded male birthday offering—freaking ew—didn't seem so scary. Not like it had been in the past, at any rate.

Yay for progress.

There was one thing, however, that she couldn't quite seem

to get out of her mind. The little niggling feeling had sprouted at the beginning of their James Bond joke session and hadn't wanted to shake itself loose, even as they laughed over who was the best Bond—Daniel Craig, obviously—and why shaken martinis were for people who liked the *idea* of martinis but not the drinks themselves.

As they rounded the corner from the alley to the street where her front door was, Alec dropped back a bit before shifting his position to her right, the side closest to the street. She wouldn't have even known he'd done it except for the whisper of his presence that slid behind her. Though it wasn't too late in the evening, December's darkness had already taken root around four thirty in the afternoon, so the headlights whizzing past and blinding her as she and Alec turned the corner were the surprise her nerves didn't need.

Marisa squinted against the bright onslaught of the usual nighttime traffic in front of her apartment and put her palm out to shield the glare, but before she could even get her hand up high enough, the shadow of Alec's shoulder blocked out the beams as he tucked his frame around her. With his hand on the small of her back and the lights of the milling traffic abating, he turned them both toward the juniper-colored door she'd stopped in front of, the only door of its kind on the block, which sat exposed among an outline of brick.

"Thanks," she said, though for what she wasn't entirely sure. Walking her the twenty feet to her front door? Keeping her pupils from getting fried?

Agreeing to stand in as her boyfriend so she could exploit his fame for her gain?

Or was it the happy little chill that curled up her spine when he touched her just then? That *had* felt pretty nice.

"Seems like quite the busy street," he said.

"It can be. Though most of the stores close around dinner-time, so it's usually not terrible this time of night. I'm grateful there are no bars or late-night restaurants here." Marisa fumbled around in her bag for her keys and was mildly miffed when she located them so quickly.

She wished she could avoid saying what was on her mind for a little bit longer.

"Alec? Um, can I ask you something?"

"Of course. Whatever you'd like."

Marisa let out a weighty breath and gripped her keys more tightly. Why did he have to be just so goddamn agreeable? Jeez, he was like one of those large, wiry-coated blue-gray Scottish deerhounds, all pleasant and eager with their big amber eyes always looking up as if asking what they could do to either help or make you happy.

Except there was nothing *wiry* about Alec, a point she'd been made increasingly aware of earlier when he excused himself to use the restroom and came back with his Henley pushed up to his elbows and his corded forearms on full display.

It made his ever-looming presence at her back just then, and all his charming thoughtfulness, even more worrisome.

Marisa relished the distraction of her house key biting into her palm before she closed her eyes and turned to face him. "Why did you date her?"

When she'd finally worked out the words and he didn't respond to them right away, she opened her eyes. Sure enough, the question that had been agitating her brain matter ever since they'd met had been flung, not at his stubborn chin but squarely between his pecs, which was all she could see of him until she looked up. Once she did, however, she instantly regretted it.

Alec's jaw had sharpened into harsh angles that even the shadows found ways to skirt around. A steely somberness shook out the warmth in his eyes from earlier, and he shoved his hands—including the one that had just brushed her lower back—into his coat pockets.

"I think this needs to be talked about, given who and what

we're involved in," Marisa said. "I don't need particulars or anything, but I'm about to introduce you to my family. And even though my mother's idea of social media still involves pulling out the slide projector during Passover, she's not above Internet stalking. If there's something that might . . . hurt me, even if you and I know what's going on between us isn't real, I'd still just rather be prepared for all of that, you know?"

"Marisa," he said, though his features remained twisted into that disconcerted sadness. Funny. She'd never really imagined what shame would look like on such a proud Scotsman, but there it was, and it wasn't pretty.

Which meant she really, *really* didn't want to know and most definitely shouldn't have asked.

"Never mind. It's okay. I don't have a right to know that stuff. I mean, I've known you for all of ten minutes. So, forget I ever said anything. We'll figure it all out as it comes, I guess."

"No," he rushed out, pulling his hand free from his pocket and reaching toward her, but he stopped halfway there. "It's not that. It's just a bit—"

Shrouded in shadows, three hulking figures slid out of the alley and headed toward them, drawing Alec's attention. In the paltry glow of the pedestrian crosswalk light, all Marisa could make out were the towering heights and incredibly broad torsos that cut a menacing path through the darkness. They moved in an eerie synchronicity, with one man—a bald, thickly bearded fellow—assuming the lead while the other two fell in step behind him. Then they all stopped. The man in question swept his gaze along the sidewalk through the shadows, until it landed firmly on Marisa, who still had her keys in hand and her purse wide open.

The large man grunted, and all three headed toward her with singular stalking purpose.

Before Marisa could say anything, Alec grabbed her and

threw her behind him. "Run. Get to the nearest open store. Anything with lights. Call the police. Now!"

She stumbled back slightly, nearly tripping over a crack in the sidewalk. When her head popped up, she kept trying to look over his shoulder, but he shifted just as quickly, keeping her out of sight of the approaching men. "Alec, wait!"

"Just run, woman!"

"I think she's fine right where she is," the man in the front said, chuckling heavily. "Besides, I have something for her."

Then the head of the menacing trio advanced into the mild light of a nearby streetlamp.

There, tucked within the wide pocket of the man's winter coat, was the indistinguishable outline of a—

"He's got a gun!" Alec cried before throwing her backward onto the sidewalk and lunging at the man.

CHAPTER 9

Alec had numbed himself beneath his fair share of ice packs in his day, but the clunky resealable snack bag Marisa handed him was a first.

An assortment of loose change, newly chilled from their temporary bout in the freezer, slid between the tracks of his fingers until they'd found a home on top of his swelling knuckles.

Had she really just given him bloody pocket pennies after he—

"I still can't believe you threw a punch. A punch! An actual, literal flying of fist into face. Why would you do that?" Marisa opened and closed cabinets with more ferocity than the injury that had landed him in the States. But it wasn't until she'd slammed the cabinet shut above the stove that he truly felt it, not only in his clenched fingers but the back of his jaw as well.

Damn, the woman was angry, and if this was what an irate Marisa looked like, he'd do well to gird far more than just his fists.

Alec adjusted the—was he really meant to call this an ice pack?—bag and gentled his tone as best he could. "Because three threatening men cornered you outside your door in the dark," he remarked wryly. "Forgive me if I didn't wish to see your pretty head clobbered against the side of a building and all your money stolen."

Marisa paused her frantic rummaging to regard him through sharp brown eyes that were rounder than the coins cooling his knuckles. Her gaze grew more introspective, as though just realizing how her circumstances would have looked to someone with more sinister interests.

Or to someone determined to protect her from those more sinister interests.

Alec took the opportunity to smooth away what fear he could. "I can see the anxiety ping-ponging behind your eyes. Regret doesn't get paid by the hour, so best not give it so much airtime. We're all fine. Besides, I must know"—he reached into the ice pack stand-in and pulled out a silver coin with a gold center—"what the hell kind of currency is this anyway?"

That thousand-yard stare of hers had just come back into focus, earning him a small smile of thanks—another bonny keepsake he'd managed to earn. She started up again with the drawer perusal. "A subway token. And it's not regret that's twisting me up. It's reflection. Ugh. Absolutely nothing about tonight is going as I thought it would." Then Marisa poked her head out of the kitchen and yelled, "Hey, Sid, did you find that antibiotic ointment yet?"

Sid, or Sid the Sparrow as Alec had come to learn, was a sturdy man with a shaved head, an impressive beard, and a preponderance of neck tattoos. He was one of three similarly costumed individuals who were not, as Alec had incorrectly assumed, street thugs intent on hurting Marisa. Instead, they were some of her closest friends.

Friends who had a familiarity with her apartment that had yet to allow Alec's muscles to relax.

Sid and the other two men, who were equally meaty and

tattooed, squeezed out of the small bathroom in cartoonish unison. One of them—the lad with the long queue of white hair down his back but not much on top to speak of—held a tube high in victory between his clubbed fingers. "Got it right here!"

"Thanks." Marisa grabbed it, rising to kiss the grizzled man on his pockmarked cheek, and returned to Alec's place on her couch, where she began dabbing bits of the ointment across his cracked knuckles. "Such a sweetie. You know, Captain's got two older sisters, and it shows. When he told me stories about what those women managed to convince the correctional officers to let them bring to Cap during visitation, everything about him made so much more sense."

Captain grunted, then folded his arms across his massive chest. "Why do you think I got out so early? It sure as shit wasn't for good behavior, I can tell you that much. It was because Emily and Maya made the guards jumpy. I bet those guys figured the less they'd have to deal with my sisters, the better."

Alec took over the ointment application from Marisa but nearly dropped the tube at this little newsflash. "You were in prison?"

Marisa sighed. "They all were. That's how we met. A fact I would have been happy to tell you had you let me get around your freakishly large shoulders downstairs before you went all Street Fighter on them." Then her words cut off, and a familiar chagrin from his earlier point rejoined the conversation. "Not that I wouldn't have been grateful," she added. "You know, if they really had been bad people who'd wanted to hurt me."

Her apology, or whatever she considered it to be, never landed, though, as all the air rushed out of Alec's lungs, abandoning him to choke through its absence. "You-you were in prison with them?"

Marisa's features scrunched in confusion a moment before the fog cleared, and she rounded on him with unnatural shock.

"What? No! I mean that we met through a prison reentry program."

Alec blinked. "Oh, of course. Because that makes much more sense." Then he waited—really freaking patiently, all things considered—for her to elaborate on what the hell any of those words meant.

Once she *finally* registered his worried confusion, her mouth formed a delightfully adorable, not entirely helpful O as she offered an explanation to calm his discomposure. "When I was a freshman in college, there was an activities fair of sorts where different groups on campus and organizations in the area recruited members. One local company was offering an industry skills tour for candy making. It sounded fun at the time and met on the weekends, which was one of the few places that did, so it fit into my schedule. Turned out, the class was also associated with a prisoner rehabilitation program aimed at helping former inmates transition into food service jobs once they reenter society. That's where I met these loves of my life," she said, turning to the three men who had begun emptying their pockets onto her kitchen counter.

"The big bald guy is Sid the Sparrow. Captain Slate's the one with the ponytail, though we just call him Captain, and the mohawk-loving brute who's currently unwrapping his third blueberry candy cane is Manic Boy. And don't let their history fool you. They've come an insanely long way. Actually, together, they now own the largest snack chain in North Jersey called Incarcer-eats, which not only works to employ former pris-oners and offer them a leg up in a society that demands their reformation but actively still refuses to employ them, but they also make the best damn prepackaged churros you've ever put in your mouth."

The one called Manic popped the candy cane free from his blue-tinged lips and smiled an alarming number of gold teeth at Alec. "What can we say? With Marisa, it was love at first Busch

Light. We've all been taking care of her ever since." Then he leaned forward and stage whispered, "And the churros were my idea. Took a hell of a lot of R and D, but we got there. Still our best seller. Oh, and I'm sorry I bit your hand. What can I say? Old habits die hard, and when you rushed me back there, my golden chompers sort of went on autopilot. You got in a good hit, though." Manic pulled down the collar of his graphic T-shirt to show the barely pink patch of skin that Alec had thrown all his bloody power into after the man's *teeth* broke through Alec's skin.

Alec's head hinged back and forth among the inhabitants of Marisa's small apartment. "Are you lot taking the piss out of me?"

Captain ran his hand over his chin. "Not sure what any of that means, but we always wipe the seat down after we use Marisa's bathroom." Then he punched his thumb into his chest. "Older sisters, remember?"

"Older sisters," Alec said through a throat gone way too freaking dry. "Right."

"No, we're not teasing you," Marisa added from over in the kitchen, where she was holding up all sorts of pumps and tubes the men had brought her, which only added to the bizarre picture Alec's brain was frantically trying to piece together. "Oh my gosh! You guys got me a sugar pulling hook! Wow, it's all here. New cylindrical chocolate molds, a sugar-blowing pump . . ." Marisa kept digging around at everything the men had placed on the counter, pure elation lighting her features. "Phoebe will never know what hit her. There's no way she'll put out anything at the Ball even half as good as I can, not with these puppies."

Manic chomped on another bite of candy cane and raised his hand like an eager and remarkably well-behaved kinder-gartener sitting cross-legged on a classroom carpet. "Can *I* hit her?"

Marisa twisted her lips in what Alec hoped was mock

contemplation. Then a defeated sigh fled her lips. "I'm going to say no."

"Boo," he said, his voice full of dejection, and lowered his oafish hand.

When she returned her attention to the silicone molds and lifted them higher for closer examination, Alec saw the curve they took, especially when rolled for transport, and how they looked suspiciously like the barrel of a gun.

A gun he had *sworn* Sid the Sparrow had been carrying when he'd approached Marisa outside.

"I . . . Wow," Alec said, shocked by just how much vocal fry shame and fear could wreak on one's words. "I am so, *so* sorry, lads. I thought you all were carrying a gun."

Curious glances passed between the three men, which made Alec certain he'd just been put on some sort of list that he didn't want to be on.

Then Sid lifted a brow. "And you still attacked us." A statement. Not a question.

With his faux ice pack abandoned, Alec stood, his voice dropping into a register he only ever used when some big, hairy center on an opposing team saw fit to get mouthy before a match. "You're bloody right, I did."

He hadn't meant for his words to be threatening or to scare Marisa into dropping her equipment on the floor.

But he had *meant* them, even if he wasn't sure why.

Sid stepped forward, with Captain and Manic standing on either side of him. Together, they looked like a wall of monstrous muscle that hadn't just been carved from a mountain but had terrified entire rock structures into creating mountain ranges around *them*.

In the kitchen, Marisa still stood quiet, her nimble fingers that had cared for his a moment ago now twisting into knots of uncertainty.

Despite it all, Alec wouldn't budge. If there was one thing

that could be said about him, even with his aging body and even more aged career, Alec Elms didn't fucking back down from a fight.

Especially not when it came to a woman he'd sworn to help.

Then Sid leaned his tall frame over Alec, his bald head eclipsing the living room lights and casting them both in an eerie shadow. "Good. We'll let her keep you, then."

The handshake that came next was so strong, it nearly crushed Alec's swollen knuckles. But his muscles had managed to strengthen themselves just in time, especially as the back slaps and shoulder squeezes came into play.

From within the cheerful circle of newfound pseudo-acceptance from Marisa's friends, Alec had yet to check on his own friendship with her, however.

Was that what they had? A friendship? Or was it more of a partnership? One that had originally been steeped in surface-level deception but had now come to grow with far deeper implications? After what he'd done this evening and who he'd met and had likewise somehow ingratiated himself into their company, though he still had no fucking clue how?

Calling what Alec shared with Marisa a mere friendship, though, felt equal parts right and wrong and made his chest itch.

As if owing to his tumultuous thoughts, when his gaze sought Marisa out and she threw him another one of those quiet smiles, he hesitated. The reward wasn't quite as sweet as before. No, this time, it was strained.

Because before, he'd not met firsthand the people in her life who loved her enough to defend her heart—with perhaps less-than-legal tactics—if he were to crush it.

And crush it he would. Because none of what they were doing was real, was never supposed to *be* real. After the holidays, he'd have to go back to England, where he'd hopefully be cleared to resume play and prove to his agent and team that he wasn't just owed a new contract but worthy of it.

For the first time, he saw the true dilemma of their charade. The hesitancy in her smile. The lack of certainty in her eyes.

Without examining things, they'd entered into something there was no going back from. Not easily, at least. Not without a bit of pain on her part. Pain he would acutely, selfishly, cause when he'd return home so he could get on with the life he'd worked so hard to build.

But the stakes had been made clear and were punctuated by three blokes with criminal records who now had an abundance of money, resources, and immense brotherly affection for the woman Alec had just claimed to care for, in a way.

If he broke Marisa's heart, even falsely, he'd have far bigger problems to worry about than a stupid contract renewal.

Problems that came in the form of a mess he'd be leaving Marisa behind to deal with on her own.

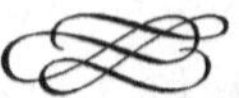

If guilt was the emotional throughline that tied the majority of Marisa's family interactions together, then shame was the glitter all over the package that never left any surface clean.

Marisa sat in Alec's car outside her parents' house and looked for any excuse not to go inside. At first, the heating vents had to get her Goldilocks treatment of finding *just* the right angle, then she'd pulled down the visor and checked her makeup, wondering whether a third coat of lipstick would be too much—it wouldn't have been, but she restrained herself anyway. By the time she'd started burrowing through her bag for a possible piece of gum she hadn't carried on her in at least the past two years, she'd reached the end of her rope, and Alec finally had to call an audible—or whatever the rugby equivalent would have been.

"We don't have to go if you don't want to. It's your birthday, after all."

"Of course I have to go. I said I would."

"So? Just because I'm a man of my word doesn't mean you

have to be a woman of yours or that the words can't change if you're uncomfortable."

Marisa banged her head against the back of the seat, then rolled toward him, cursing the good-natured smile encouraging her to take the out he offered, which helped not a whit. In what world could she disappoint a man who looked that good *and* had braved toll roads to get her there?

Not having a clue how fancy to dress as the guest of honor for an event that was more to honor the woman paying for the affair rather than the star attendee, Marisa couldn't offer that much help to Alec when it came to appropriate party attire. For her, she'd pulled on her standard-issue black sleeveless cocktail dress that she always doctored with cardigans of various colors. Tonight, the cotton-poly blend covering her shoulders was a royal blue—a nod to the occasion, she supposed. Topped off with simple stud earrings, her one pair of heels that *didn't* destroy her instep after thirty minutes, and just enough makeup to look like she'd tried but not too hard. It was about as glamorous as she got these days.

Which was a goddamn shame because Alec Elms and *glamorous* obviously had a very different relationship.

Forget the one wedding/funeral/Bar Mitzvah suit that always made appearances by most of the guys she'd dated. Alec had foregone a suit altogether in favor of a silk burgundy button-down shirt that hugged more than it hid, expertly tailored gray slacks, and a charming smile that hadn't left his lips ever since he'd picked her up and chariotted her across two full Garden State Parkway exits, *plus* an interchange.

Again, she wondered whether all Scottish men were so annoyingly cheerful and friendly or if she'd been blessed with the most good-natured one in the bunch.

Certainly the most good-natured one in Jersey, at any rate.

"I swear, you really are like one of those Scottish deerhounds," she huffed under her breath.

Alec quirked his head to the side in a very doglike fashion and smiled. "What?"

"What?"

"Did you just say something about—"

"Never mind. I guess there's no point in waiting in the car any longer. If I'm going to face the firehose of criticism, best get it over with sooner so at least I'll have time to dry off later." She could already hear how it was going to go. The questions about her *little candy business*, whether she'd looked at any of those new housing developments offering rent-to-own options, and what her plans were now that she'd turned thirty, essentially serving all the standard *when are you finally going to start adulting* fare.

As if there were a drastic difference in her schedule between the final Tuesday of her twenties and the first Wednesday of her thirties, other than that Wednesday was laundry day.

Which she was notably missing so she could party it up with latkes, hopefully decent liquor, and a cupcake if she was lucky.

Marisa hitched her handbag strap higher and reached for the door handle, but Alec stopped her.

"Wait. I've got something for you before we go in." Alec rose and twisted his torso around so he could reach the back.

That left Marisa at eye height with a wall of muscle that seemed to be doing its level best to make itself known through the thin veil of silk concealing it. The proximity to all that strength pulled up fiery goose bumps along the back of her neck, especially as he adjusted himself and the fabric stretched even tauter, letting her see every lower ripple of his stomach as they tightened before he settled back into his seat with a rectangular box in his hands.

"Happy birthday, Marisa," he said cheerfully as he handed her over a silvery package wrapped in a dark blue ribbon.

"You didn't have to get me a present."

He shrugged as much as the car's tight confines would allow

his large shoulders. "This may be my first Hanukkah party, but it's sure as hell not my first birthday party. I know better than to greet the birthday girl's mother without having given her daughter a birthday present. I'm not that insane. I've got a mum, too, you know."

Smiling, Marisa held the gift up to her ear and shook it slightly. "It's clanking, sort of. Is it metal?" Then a wash of horror overtook her as her suspicion landed on another item. "Oh, God, it's not jewelry, is it? Because we never agreed on anything like that. It goes way beyond the bounds of what we—"

Alec narrowed his eyes and put his hand over hers, bringing the gift safely back down to her lap. "Just open your present, woman."

"All right, all right. No need to get all growly about it."

"I'm not bloody growly."

"He said with a growl."

"Will you open your damn gift already?"

"Fine. Yes. Thank you. But you do snarl sometimes. Just saying." Marisa pointedly ignored the eye roll Alec tossed her way while she slid a finger beneath the wrapping paper and ribbon.

He'd gotten her a present? An actual *present*?

But no amount of anticipation could have prepared her for what she found inside.

Her breath sawed in and out of her chest, and her eyes got to work ruining her carefully applied mascara with the single-minded efficiency of Christmas elves.

Within the carefully molded plastic packaging sat three shiny and rather unassuming metal cookie cutters. They were made of the same stainless steel as any other cookie cutter might be, with their dangerously flimsy framework and in-no-way-dishwasher-friendly coating. Wholly ordinary, except for their shapes.

A menorah, a dreidel, and a Star of David.

While Marisa sat there, shocked into stillness, Alec carefully cleared the brush of wrapping detritus from her lap. "I don't know what your plans are for the treats you'll be making for the Christmas Ball, but I can honestly say—and most red-blooded men would agree with me on this, I wager—that I didn't much care for the way you were going all gooey-eyed over that sugar hook thing your friends gave you. I didn't know whether you wanted to kiss it, kill with it, or castrate the next poor bastard who looked at you wrong. Instead, I figured these might suit you just fine. And to be clear, I'm not saying you need to use them for the Ball or anything. There are only three cutters, and I imagine you've got grander plans for your big reveal than what these wee things can help you achieve, but they were amusing and reminded me of you." Then he covered her hand, the one *not* stroking soft pets through the plastic along the menorah's shamash, and squeezed his comfort into her. "You have a beautiful heart, Marisa, and you want to make people smile with your work. That's something worth defending and something any family should be proud of."

Marisa held the small symbols of her life—for that was exactly what they were, a grossly mismatched mix of who she was and what she loved—closer to her chest, doing her best to release her throat from the tightness her unbidden emotions were inflicting upon it.

In the end, the only remaining avenue was a single nod of thanks.

"You're welcome." Alec pulsed her hand again. The gentle pressure in his touch was warm and weighty, anchoring her to the tiny moment where she was locked safely in his car, holding to her heart the baking equivalent of her blueberry candy canes, and could just exist, without explanation, in the magic of the moment.

Of the season.

Of his kindness.

Of his presence.

She still hadn't said anything, but the effort was massively hindered by the man sitting next to her, balling up the wrapping paper and ribbon in one hand and silently supporting her with the other. In the cocoon of their little car cave, she could finally see him in a way she hadn't before. There was something about the windows around them, the darkness shadowing the car that allowed for them to look out at the world, but not for the world to look in, that made her feel as if she were truly sharing a special secret with Alec, one that went far beyond the lie they'd agreed to front for both their sakes.

And he knew it, too, she suspected, or at least knew *something* he wasn't prepared to share with her just yet.

Which was fine. She was too busy acknowledging the true beauty of the man before her. Dark eyes, which had usually been hidden by garish lighting either from a cocktail party, Enzo and Sal's fluorescent bulbs, or had been tempered with worry and shock following his run-in with Sid and the boys, now charted a map of her features. And damn, it was just ten kinds of not fair for a man to have lashes that luxurious, but even more so when they caused her to wonder what they might feel like brushing against the tops of her cheeks if she moved just a little closer.

A flurry of insistent butterflies had pulled the choke on her long-cold physical attraction motor, and there was no cutting it off now. Her imagination scooped up her thoughts and ran them far away from her sane and civil mindset, leaving only admiration, wonder, and curiosity about the man sitting before her.

On instinct, Marisa pulled on his hand, perhaps for strength or support, she didn't know, but it brought him the tiniest bit closer, a move he didn't seem to resist. The top button of his silk shirt was undone, revealing the bare beginnings of smooth hairs that dusted light shadows over his skin before the collar stole them away from her.

God, he was handsome, in that rugged way only found in men who tackled life head-on. Marisa knew he played rugby. Though her knowledge of the sport was minimal, she was at least aware that it came with its own intensity and physicality. It was evident in not only the strength filling out his skin but also the way he treated her.

Like a teammate. Like a woman.

Like someone . . . worth defending.

The weight of Alec's words made Marisa's fingers go slack in his hand, but instead of pulling away and leaving her to yet another hyper-emotional moment, he moved closer and turned her palm upward in his.

Then their fingers joined, interlocking together in a neat little cage of security, his hardness bolstering her softness, protecting it, defending it.

Any other time, she would have said it was all too much, that they were no more than business associates and should stick to the plan. However, what the hell kind of plan was there for a fake relationship with a rugby player who was about to light the Hanukkah candles with her family and fend off her aunt's bizarre boy of a birthday present, all while she tried not getting grease stains on his silk shirt?

It was the Jewish mother of all bad scenarios.

So, why the hell was her heart one hot minute away from saying, *eh, fuck it?*

She leaned forward, close enough to scent both his cologne and Alec's earthiness beneath it, and knew that she much preferred the latter. His lips parted slightly as he nuzzled the side of her nose with his, testing the limits of what she'd started.

"Marisa," he said, and the rolling R in his accented version of her name did interesting things to her insides. Man, she could listen to that all day and twice on one of the umpteenth Jewish holidays she'd long ago forgotten. It was just so exciting, so attractive, so—

He reared his head back and dropped her hand. "Are you crying?"

The record in her mind ripped a teeth-clenching scratch through her fantasy.

Was she? Well, the moment *had* been beautiful, and he'd given her those wonderful, perfect cookie cutters, and for the first time, she had a teammate to face down the holiday with.

So maybe . . . yes?

She lifted her hand to swipe at her cheek, but Alec's fingers were already there.

"Och, don't be doing that, getting all weepy on me. I wouldn't want your mother to think I'm the type of lad to make her daughter cry or anything." He leaned forward and swept a curled finger beneath her eye, catching the one tear that had managed to break free of her emotional dam, rescuing her from having to explain to her nose-in-the-air aunt why she'd worn a cardigan with wet spots all over it to her—not Marisa's, but *her* —party.

With a face all fresh and clean, she simply shook her head and smiled away the memory. Then she set the cookie cutters beneath her seat and grabbed her purse. "No tears tonight. I promise. C'mon. It's time we entered the belly of the beast."

As they walked toward the front door to meet their fate, Marisa figured it wasn't entirely inappropriate, given the occasion, to hope for a frickin' miracle.

CHAPTER 11

lec wasn't sure what to expect, but the twinkling grandeur that dripped over the main staircase's balustrade as he escorted Marisa into her parents' house wasn't it. Granted, he'd been to zero Hanukkah parties in his day, but when Marisa had told him it was technically a combined Hanukkah/birthday party, he'd envisioned more . . . banners, maybe? A few of those paper numbers that spelled out *Happy Hanukkah* or *Happy Birthday* or some such thing that were always dipping far too low that he feared one good sneeze would cause him to headbutt the garlands and take everything out clothesline style, making a right arse of himself.

Something more DIY, he figured.

Boy, was he wrong. About so many goddamn things, apparently.

A few moments ago, Alec's mouth had been separated from Marisa's by millimeters, with his desires being held together by even less of a distance. Bloody fucking hell. And he'd almost done it, too. In his stupid brother's borrowed car, parked beneath a stupidly too-dim streetlight, in trousers far too tight to be useful at hiding anything, he'd nearly kissed her. A woman who was more akin to a business partner than a romantic one, despite the odd nature of their arrangement.

Och, sure, he figured there'd be a bit of hand-holding and cordial affection that would eventually be required. A peck on the cheek and a few hugs for photos and whatnot. Social media sweet, he'd heard it called.

But there had been nothing sweet about where his thoughts went when he'd seen the mistiness in her eyes as she took in the gift he gave her. Like she had just learned the difference between being taken care of and being cared for.

It fucking shredded him, especially since, though he couldn't commit to doing the caring once their time together ended, he also didn't much like the idea of leaving it to someone else to take over.

Someone who was foisted on her by her family. Someone who didn't make a private game out of earning her smiles.

The lone tear that had tracked down her cheek had been a life preserver saving him from a decision his body was still angry at him for getting bloody wrong.

But he wasn't there for his needs. Certainly not the kind that made him want to jump across the front seat in all his brutish glory and determine whether Marisa tasted as sweet as she always smelled.

No, tonight, he was there for her, acting the part they had agreed he'd play.

Though he'd yet to meet her family, judging by the decorations in the foyer alone, when he *did* meet them, he'd do well to look for a ring to kiss or a firstborn child to offer.

Holy shit, he'd never seen so many lights in his life.

"This is brilliant," he breathed out, hanging up his coat and taking in far more twinkling lights than any Christmas tree, real *or* fake, could hope to safely wear.

"You get used to it. Here." Marisa opened a drawer within one of the tables near the entryway and, after digging around a bit, pulled out two pairs of tinted glasses. "They're to help with light sensitivity and irritability. Dad always keeps a bunch on hand this time of year, as Aunt Gail doesn't know what the word *understated* means." She plucked one from the pile—a horned-rimmed pair with rose-tinted lenses—and tucked it into the pocket of her cardigan.

Alec just stood there, unsure whether accepting a pair would imply he thought the décor too harsh or whether *not* accepting a pair would be akin to refusing the host's hospitality.

As if she sensed his unease, Marisa's eyes softened, and God fucking bless the woman, she helped him through his moment of analysis paralysis. "I'm going with the blue-tinted frameless ones for you, and why don't I just hang onto them for the time being?"

"Uh, thank you. Is this . . ."—Alec gestured at the rows of long tapered white candles bracketing the stairs, the blue-and-white icicle lights cascading at the opening of every entrance-way, and the glittered gold paper lanterns shaped like dreidels hanging from the ceiling before pointing back to the glasses—"normal for Hanukkah parties?"

"Oh, God no! This is purely a Silver family thing. Even though it's my parents' house, it's my Aunt Gail's party, and the woman is nothing if not severely over-the-top and disgustingly wealthy. She married young to a rich businessman who'd gotten in on the ground floor of a few very profitable investment opportunities. And to my Aunt Gail's misfortune, or fortune, I guess, her husband died young and left her a shit ton of money. And though she remarried my uncle, my dad's stepbrother, technically, she still insists on maintaining the prestige she enjoyed while her first husband was alive. It's why she won't accept no when she throws her money at the rest of the family and offers to pay off student loans, fund vacations, and replace roofs and furnaces and whatnot." Marisa dug her hand into a crystal bowl full of gold and silver chocolate coins on top of the entryway table and began peeling one. "Unfortunately, she can't host the size of crowds she wants to in her condo, so she throws her parties here and foots the bill instead. Pisses the neighbors right the hell off, I can tell you that."

"Why?"

She handed him a chocolate coin before popping another one into her mouth. "Because all the street-side parking is taken up by her guests, so there's nowhere else for people to park to gawk at the Christmas decorations the neighbors worked so hard to display. The McCauleys three doors down sync their lights to music and have a sign on their lawn to tune into a certain radio station so you can hear the music in your car in time to the light show, but it doesn't do them any good if people can't find a place to park to enjoy it."

"Isn't it a public street? Can't anyone park anywhere they'd like?"

Marisa winked at him and scooped her arm through his. "Exactly. It's a whole lot of not my problem and one of many reasons I was more than happy to leave my hometown."

When they entered the kitchen, a silver-haired woman, barely taller than the counters she was somehow lording over, cut off her conversation with a small group of people, untied her apron—another glittery number, except this one had powdered sugar all over it and said *Fryer-in-Chief, so I'll take no grief!*—and gave Marisa a huge hug.

"Happy birthday, my dear!"

"Thanks, Ma." Despite the squishy hug that passed between the two women, Marisa's shoulders still had a stiff set to them.

"Now," her mother said with a tone that had quickly slipped into social director mode, "I told all the guests who brought birthday presents to put those over on the kitchen table, while any Hanukkah presents can go on top of the piano. And look, I made it nice and easy for you." Her mother scurried over to a blue-and-yellow grocery store shopping tote with a big, blaring menorah on the front and jangled it next to her head. "There are mainly cards inside, but I couldn't resist the gift bag. Don't you love it? You can take it home with you, too."

"Ma, it's not a gift bag. It's a shopping tote."

"Which I'm using to *gift* you things. You see? It's all a matter of semantics. And you know how hard it is to find Hanukkah items out in the wild like this during the holiday season. I couldn't *not* buy it. Besides, I figured you weren't really in a position to turn it down. Weren't you telling me recently how all your grocery bags were so tattered?"

Next to him, Marisa's hand clenched into a fist so tense he suspected it could smash the marble counters—or his jaw, if he wasn't careful.

"Yup. Thanks," she clipped out.

"My pleasure." Then her mother's eyes lit with an impossibly livelier interest as she noticed Alec. "And who is this?"

Alec stepped forward and extended his hand, hefting an ocean's worth of charm into his smile. "Alec Elms. A pleasure to meet you, ma'am. Your daughter's told me so much about you."

"Beatrice Silver. How lovely to meet you." Her mother shook his hand with far more force and enthusiasm than he thought capable, but he was also smart enough to know not to question it. "Did Marisa get you some glasses?"

"I believe she did, yes."

"Wonderful! Most guests don't need them the first night, as there aren't as many candles to light, but we do love our opulence when it comes to the Festival of Lights." Then she flashed him a smile that showed a bit too many teeth for his liking. "The McCauleys aren't the only ones who get to be *extra*." The last word was said with air quotes that made Marisa wince.

"Ma thinks everyone should be able to drain down the power grid from time to time. She's an equal opportunity electricity hog."

"I am not! I just think that there are plenty of watts to go around, and just because we don't have illuminated lawn ornaments or Christmas twinkle lights lining our eaves and railings for two months shouldn't mean we can't throw off our own sparks during this time of year as well."

"Well said, ma'am." Alec nodded, figuring it better to be agreeable, even though he didn't understand the argument.

"Oh, please. Call me Bea." She dismissed the formality as if she were shooing off a bug from her macaroni salad. "The only one who calls me *ma'am* is the cashier at the grocery store, likely because I'm the sole person who still uses an actual human being to ring up my groceries and he needs to practice talking to somebody. I'll admit, the moniker does sting a bit, but at least it's better than *bruh*. By the way, Marisa, what does that even mean? Is he saying *bra*, like a brassiere?"

Marisa's mother looked at her huge shelf of cleavage that her apron was struggling to stretch around, as if the offending answer could be found within the cavernous crease between her breasts.

Alec's throat chose that moment to wedge a frog in his vocal cords. He was saved, thankfully, when a tall bald man with bits of what looked like icing dappling his mustache joined them and swept Marisa into a hug. "Hi, honey bun. Happy birthday."

"Hi, Dad. Thanks. This is Alec, by the way."

"Alec, nice to meet you. Hank."

"Likewise, sir. And Happy Hanukkah."

"Oh, damn." Marisa's dad swiped a thumb across his mustache to remove the offending evidence of festivities enjoyed too early. "May have gotten into the cupcake cake a bit too early." Then he shielded his mouth and whispered to Marisa, "Don't tell your mother."

Marisa gave him a lopsided smile as she looked over his shoulder. "Too late."

"Double damn." The man had the good humor to look appropriately chagrined as he turned to his wife. "Honey, now that Marisa's here, why don't we sing 'Happy birthday' first, then light the candles?"

The corner of Alec's mouth quirked up in appreciative fondness. He sure as hell knew that move. Cal had practically perfected the bloody thing with their parents when he and his brother were teenagers.

Nice diversion tactic. Well played, sir. Well played.

Bea's eyes narrowed into all-knowing slits, the kind of expression that said, *I know what you did, but what I'm going to do to you later will be so much worse.*

Alec instinctively dropped his fists over his crotch on the elder man's behalf.

"Fine. Hank, call everyone else into the living room, please."

While he and Marisa brought up the rear of the processional leaving the kitchen, Alec took the opportunity to steal a quiet word. "Everything all right so far?"

She nodded tightly but still accepted the offer of his folded arm, curling her delicate hands around his bicep. "Sure. Not looking forward to enduring a happy birthday montage usually reserved for little kid parties, but I can deal."

"Easy now," he chided. "Some of my favorite people are former little kids. It may not have occurred to you, but I, myself, was once a little kid. Fucking loved birthday parties. Always stole Cal's portion of cake when he wasn't looking. Left him the icing, though. Too sweet." He wrinkled his nose in distaste.

Marisa's harsh chuckle forced the tension from her shoulders, lightening not only her grip on his arm but the grim cast that had prevented her smile from surfacing all evening. It was out now with all its former splendor, and he mentally added one more check mark to his win column.

"You're too much." She shook her head.

"Nah. I'm just right, I wager, kind of like the way you were fiddling with my heating vents in the car earlier to position them how you liked. I may need a bit of guidance and direction from you, but I always get to where I need to go."

Marisa drew them to a stop once they entered the living room, where a crowd of people had begun to gather around a grand piano. "Just remember you said that," she whispered, then tightened her hold on him and sidled up to her parents.

For the second time that night, Alec's expectations, a bit muddled though they were, evacuated from the scene posthaste. In their place stood a grand display of what could only be described as a true Festival of Lights.

By that, he meant every single light. All at once. Including things he hadn't thought should light up in the first place. Did those couch cushions really have light-up letters that said *Relax! It's Hanukkah. Have another doughnut?*

A grand chandelier hung from the center of the room just above the piano. On top of the resplendent instrument stood a large silver menorah with glass cups filled with oil and candle wicks, in addition to various gifts.

The feature presentation, most notably, but definitely not the only one.

All around the room's perimeter were several other menorahs, some holding candles, some electric, but all with different shapes and flows. They were arranged in an elegant, tapered processional that would surely chase away any shadow that had the gall to try and lurk around.

Those were already lit, however, along with all the decorative votives dancing beneath the hanging glittery lanterns that cast light throughout the rooms like disco balls, bouncing off silver candleholders and guests' crystal wineglasses. The only menorah that wasn't lit was the main one on the piano, which made sense. There had to be at least a dozen menorahs scattered throughout the space. If Marisa's family had to light each one all at the same time, they'd never get to the food before it got cold.

And speaking of food, rich and savory aromas perked up Alec's stomach and yanked his attention toward the source, which was no easy feat given the visual spectacle. Lined up around the adjacent dining room were buffet-style serving dishes and platters, all adorned with neat little note cards declaring their offerings and heaped high with a whole lot of golden, brown, and delicious. Alec had to suck back the puddle of saliva that had formed in his mouth as he squinted, damn near desperate to read each little tented card from where he stood.

There were crisp potato pancakes in russet, sweet potato, and mixed veggie varieties, glistening folds of smoked salmon adorned with red onions and capers, bagels for days, cream cheese and applesauce tubs the size of kiddie pools, sugar-dusted doughnuts, and those were just the things he recognized as symbols of the holiday. All this to say nothing of the cheesy stuffed shells, fried mac and cheese balls served in shot glasses with toothpicks, and a lone platter of what he figured were the obligatory roasted vegetables offered up to the gods of fiber and good colon health. Likewise, the cupcake cake arranged in the shape of a menorah, with a few notable cupcakes missing, sat off to the side, its cheerful *Happy birthday, Marisa!* capping off the buffet like a prize at the end of the finish line.

Between the living room and dining room, there wasn't a surface or ceiling that hadn't reached its limit in terms of festive abundance.

It was absolutely cornea-singeing.

But it was also bloody lovely.

It was a different kind of festive than he'd ever experienced, and strangely enough, it reminded him of a phrase he'd been taught by a former Italian teammate he'd played with for a handful of seasons. Abbondanza. Or the Italian concept of too-muchness, as Alec understood it. The idea of a pleasant fullness that magnified one's joy *because* of its excess, not despite it. Alec bit back a laugh and covered his mouth with his fist, pleasantly surprised at just how much he enjoyed this fake date.

Because it was excessive, every bit of it. But it was also joy. Excessive, unapologetic, and insanely gaudy joy.

He leaned close to Marisa's ear, intending to tell her as much, when an elegant woman who seemed to be around Marisa's parents' age separated from a group surrounding the large menorah at the piano and came to greet them. "Marisa, happy birthday, my love."

"Hi, Aunt Gail. Thanks. Nice spread you got this year."

"Oh, thank you. The party planner worked miracles with the decorations," she said with air kisses on each side of Marisa's cheeks. "The caterer, not so much. I had a bit of trouble with the order, but in the end, they came around. It all worked out."

Bea started passing out skullcaps—yarmulkes, he'd learned—to those who wanted one, then coughed into her wineglass. "Because you threatened to contact the Better Business Bureau over false advertising when you ordered off the printed catering menu you still had in your kitchen drawer, instead of the updated one on their website."

"Oh, Beatrice," Gail said, rolling her eyes, "It really shouldn't have made a difference."

"It's not that we're not all grateful for the spread, *dear*, but the caterer is allowed to change the menu. It's not their fault you don't know how the Internet works, nor should it be my burden to talk the poor employee off the ledge when *you* asked me to call to see whether they could add cinnamon raisin and walnut cream cheese to the order *thirty minutes before it was supposed to be delivered.* You know that's not on the menu anymore. Hasn't been for five years. It takes time to soak all those raisins. You can't just add them to the cream cheese all hard and shriveled." Then she took a deep breath and exhaled through pursed lips, attempting to adopt a calm-down technique Alec had seen far too many women do. He always wondered whether it really worked.

Hank leaned forward, lifted the mostly drained wineglass out of Bea's hand, and whispered next to her, "Remember, kindness," but Marisa's mother just shrugged him off in favor of tossing another chocolate coin into her mouth.

Alec made a mental note that the calm-down technique might have a far higher chance of success if chocolate were involved.

Unfortunately, it did little to calm down Marisa's aunt.

Gail's eyes turned into icy slits, and strangely, Alec relaxed a bit more, comforted to know that Marisa's family holidays could be just as noxious as his own. Some things were universal, he supposed.

Marisa fiddled with her fingernail. "Can we just light the candles, or sing 'Happy Birthday,' or do whatever it is we need to in order to get to the food? I promised Alec a good meal, not dinner and a show."

It was under the weighted and, thanks to Marisa's comment, spotlit stare of her entire family and loved ones that the two of them realized their huge mistake.

A big bloody albatross of their fake dating lie.

They'd yet to come up with a story of how they met.

Her Aunt Gail, who had been about to strike a match to light the first candle, instead put the matches down. "Who's your guest, Marisa?"

"Uh, um. Alec."

"Alec Elms," he offered, awkwardly waving his hand, as if that would be explanation enough. It most definitely wasn't.

"He's my, uh, my . . ."

"Boyfriend," he said, smiling, plunking down that word like a man betting it all on red because he had an in with the dealer.

But to his abject horror, his smile, *the* smile, didn't so much as even soften the shock on her family's features.

The matches hit the floor, their task long forgotten, as Marisa and Alec just stood there, bracing themselves against the chorus of questions fired their way.

CHAPTER 12

It was a damn good thing there was a mine's worth of sterling silver between Marisa and the rest of her family. Anything less and there wouldn't have been enough counterweight to keep the table from flipping as her family slammed their eager palms down.

"Yes!" her mother trilled. "*Finally.* Please, let's do proper introductions. You know, Marisa, I was really trying to wait as patiently as possible for you to acquaint us on your own, but there's only so much patience a woman of my age has left. Damn near used it all up raising you, as your father can attest to."

At the mention of his name, her dad walked back the dreidel-shaped sugar cookie he'd attempted to pluck from the dessert tray and pushed his glasses higher on the bridge of his nose. "That's right," he affirmed, clearly having no idea what he was agreeing to but habitually proclaiming it, nonetheless.

The gelt that Marisa had pounded earlier threatened to revolt. She looked to Alec, desperately hoping mind reading wasn't actually a made-up thing and just hadn't been widely studied yet.

Yeah, his tense stare returned a big fat *nope* on that front. She could practically see the question mark thought bubble ballooning above his head. Wonderful.

"Well, we actually met at a party in New York."

"Yes," Alec chimed in, trying to follow her lead. "A party for . . ."

"Rugby players! Alec plays rugby. For Great Britain! Which has Scottish players, too, because he's, uh, Scottish!" As soon as the words left her mouth, Marisa cringed and wanted so desperately to call them back. Or alternately, find a table to crawl beneath, preferably one with half a ton of silver weighing it down.

Which has Scottish players, too? Because he's Scottish? Fucking really? Is he also a masculine man who prefers things made out of wooden wood, as opposed to metallic metal?

"Hmm . . ." her dad mused, smearing his chin with powdered sugar as he put on his proverbial thinking cap. "Can't say I know much about the sport, but I sure know a Scottish accent when I hear one."

"Right," Alec said, forcing out the fakest chuckle that had ever been chuckled.

Meanwhile, her mother had somehow unearthed another bottle of wine, uncorked it, and was letting the liquid breathe . . . on its way down her throat. "What were you doing at the rugby party?" she asked Marisa. "Were you on the catering staff?"

"Um." Marisa's wherewithal was falling as fast as her spirits were sinking as they continued to get pummeled by the lies surrounding her truths. Her insides twisted with indecision. How could she tell her mother, in front of all these people, that even at a fake party where she would have met her fake rugby star of a boyfriend, she'd still just been a fucking cater waiter?

"Actually," Alec broke in, surprising her, "Marisa was selling her gourmet confections. Sweetest Heart's Desire had a booth at the media event. There was this beautiful dark-haired lass handing out loads of sweet tea-infused caramels, and I'm a sucker for anything my dentist hates, so I couldn't resist. And that's where it all started."

A wellspring of emotion lodged itself in Marisa's throat, but it was immediately forced out by the smile she couldn't contain. In the short time she'd been around Alec, she'd never known him to use the word *lass*. As far as she'd heard him tell it, where he was from in Scotland, the only men who still called young women lasses were working on great-grandfather status and solidly collecting their state pensions.

Regardless, it worked like a freaking charm and added a thrilled sparkle to the eyes of every woman in the room.

Except for her Aunt Gail.

"How long have you two been dating?" her aunt asked, folding her arms across her chest. "It can't be that long, or I'd have heard about it."

"It only just happened—"

"About a few months or so—"

Shit on a fucking shingle.

Marisa turned to Alec, her panicked gaze colliding with his as quickly as their words had. "Uh, I mean," Marisa hedged, widening her eyes and hoping Alec got the freaking hint that he needed to come up with something good pretty damn quick.

"What Marisa means is," he said, drawing out his words, "that it *feels* like it only just happened. It's all pretty new still."

"Do you know what else is new?" Marisa hurried out. "My birthday and Hanukkah! First night turning the big 3-0 and first night we all get to experience shared regret over the amount of fried food we all stuffed our faces with."

Her dad leaned toward her mother, silently stole a sip of the woman's newly refilled wine—which already had been drained by two-thirds—and lifted the glass in solidarity. "It's game time, honey bun. I'm so ready for this."

After she and Alec fielded a few more of what Marisa deemed as requirement questions—How much time is Alec on the road? Is the long distance between the two of you challenging? Can I get free tickets to a match sometime?—the festivities commenced, for better or worse.

Marisa snaked her arm around Alec's bicep and held on for dear life as she whispered, "Safety glasses on," a Bill Nye reference she was thrilled he understood when he chuckled softly. She gritted her teeth through "Happy Birthday" and then chanted along softly when the blessings were said to light the candles.

"I'll say, Alec, I do have to commend you," her dad said after swiping off his light sensitivity glasses and stowing them into what Marisa always thought of as the Dad Pocket on the front of his button-down shirt, "you're braver than I was the first few times we went all out for Hanukkah. My poor corneas couldn't take this much light, even with it being celebrated in the evening." He gave Alec a friendly pat on the back, then threw his hands up. "Just don't send me any optometrist bills. I haven't quite met my deductible for the end of the year, so I'm still on the hook for our healthcare costs."

Marisa's mom moved the tray of cookies farther out of her dad's reach. "Then you should have taken your Lipitor before you got into the sweets. C'mon. Help me get the paper plates out so we can start serving, or do you want to keep stealing bites and pretending I don't see?"

"You mean I have a choice?" he asked, though Marisa wasn't entirely sure whether it was a genuine question or her dad mocking his lot in life. She decided she didn't want to know.

With the ceremonies out of the way and the guests having finally been released from their assigned spots and given free rein to mingle toward the food, Marisa was left to take in all the high-production value of the spectacle around her.

"You know, this would be a good time to take some pictures and post them. Most of Aunt Gail's friends have already started carving out their feeding troughs, so who knows when we'll get the star centerpiece of the party all to ourselves."

"I'll do it," Alec offered, pulling out his phone.

"You better. You've got those orangutan arms."

He gasped in mock affront. "Are you calling me a beast, woman?"

She smiled. "No. I'm calling you a very intelligent man who handled my sometimes-unbalanced family perfectly, who also has an arm span ideal for making sure all my curly hair gets in the picture without any of it getting lit on fire."

"Och, hush. Come here already and get in the picture, will you? And I'll have you know," he said as Marisa staged them both in front of the large menorah's festive display, "I happen to like your hair."

She was just practicing her *say cheese!* smile when his comment caught her off guard. "You do?"

Alec's lips curled into a grin, and the image prickled the tips of her ears and nose as she remembered just how close those lips had been to hers. Then he moved to her side, and instead of putting his hand on her shoulder and pulling her close like she expected, he curved his hand around her waist and cradled her against his side. "Aye."

There was no escaping Alec. He was everywhere at once, both flush against her body and running rampant in her thoughts. His natural scent from earlier, the one that caused her to imagine a bit too comfortably, perhaps, what it would be like to *really* date this man, was now consuming so much more of her. It was all one giant bad decision, a bad decision that would eventually end once he went back to England and she no longer needed his influence to help her business. Right now, that bad decision was just *waaay* too sticky for her liking. Or maybe because of her liking? Hell if she knew. The only thing she *did* know with any amount of clarity was that she liked it. Way too much.

Kowtowing to the sway of the moment and knowing on some level that the pictures of them as a couple needed to hold more believability, Marisa sank into Alec's embrace and let her hands go where they wanted. It wasn't until her right arm banded around his back and her left hand settled on the flat of his chest did he finally whisper, "That's better," then tightened his grip on her hip and started snapping photos.

And it *was* better. With each fresh strategic cuddly pose staged around the festive décor throughout the room, any apprehension that had compressed her muscles had fled the scene in favor of a situation that carried her heart and hopes to new heights.

"There," Alec said, leaning over to show her the photos he took. "Not half bad."

"Not half bad," Marisa echoed, admiring the genuine joy that shone off her in each new picture. Her smile, her skin, even her freaking hair all looked like they were showing up not only to play but to win.

"You look happy," he added, putting words to the sentiment she'd struggled to name.

And she *did* look happy. It had just been so long since she knew what happy looked like on her features that she couldn't recognize it. Perhaps it was because, standing next to Alec, eating meals with him, getting to know about his life and his career, having him meet her farkakte family and former-felon friends, were the things that had more of a hand in her happiness than they should have.

It was another reason her nerves had been firing on all cylinders. As if she didn't have enough to worry about, now she had to worry about—*gulp*—catching feelings as well?

After Alec posted the photos across all his social media plat-forms—to followings way, way larger than Marisa had—he pocketed his phone and rubbed the back of his neck. "It would be a good time to tell them, you know."

He gestured toward where her mother was rearranging the tower of bagels so they were more foundationally supported while her father kept scooping up all the good plump capers onto his cream-cheese-mounded plate.

"You can't be serious. One, I just introduced you as my boyfriend to my parents. Two, my dad *just told you* how he hadn't met his health insurance deductible for the year yet, so do you really want me to go give him a heart—"

"About the Ball, you daft woman," he said, snatching up her hands as they flew about her face to aid her in conversation. "You should tell them about your offer from Monica."

Marisa snorted, taking her hands back so she could rightly set them on her hips. "You mean how I managed to get into a candy competition with your ex-girlfriend, who's very likely to put me out of business."

"Stop it. That's not what I mean, and you know it." The word *know* was doing a lot of work in that statement, primarily unearthing a shame she'd hoped to cover up with a cupcake cake. No dice.

"Do you speak fluent hard-ass or something?"

"No. But I have been known to comment on the truths around me, and it's plain as day that you're bloody proud of the opportunity you've gone after for your business. From what you've told me, the Crystal Christmas Ball is an event not to be missed, and of all the vendors who've been dying to get their chance, *you* were the one to walk up to Monica, stained shirt and all, and put yourself out there. It's amazing and an incred-ible honor, regardless of the outcome with Phoebe. You're a headliner, Marisa, and I think it'll do you some good to start sinking into that feeling and letting it take you where you want your business to go. There's no one better qualified than you to sell to a Christmas crowd. No one else has the amount of fight you do. Take it from someone who knows a thing or two about winning tourneys. Fucking hell, you could make your own version of those delicious chocolate coin things and likely print your own money. What are they called again, by the way? Guilt?"

Marisa barked out a laugh. "Gelt."

"Right. Gelt. As I figure, it's money either way, and I've seen your family. Odd as they may be, they'd love to support you. Just give them a chance. Why are you already regretting your loss when you've never even given yourself the chance to envision the win?"

"God, you are so annoying," she said, hoping the statement would cover up her nerves after he'd gone and rudely sheared off their protective layer. But the truth was often annoying until it grew up. Then it was just a big fat reality Marisa had to learn to either dodge or deal with.

Problem was, after so many years, she only had so much fight in her, and what was left was running on emergency reserves.

And emergencies made a person do crazy things.

"I'll have you know," Marisa said, poking a fingernail between Alec's pecs and enjoying the wide-eyed surprise on his face. "I have been selling Christmas cheer for a goddamn decade. No one knows how to make better candy canes, peppermint fudge, and caramel clusters than I do, to say nothing of my marzipan and frangipane work." The brighter her pride grew, the stronger the force pushing Alec back into the breakfront behind him. "I've got recipes for ribbon candy that have taken me *years* to perfect. And what does the Plant Nanny have? Chocolate Christmas tree molds? Give me a fucking break."

"A hook!" Alec added, curling his hand around her pokey

finger to stem off any more attacks. "She doesn't have one of those angry hook things your adjacently law-abiding friends brought you."

"Exactly!" Marisa cried, pointing to the ceiling with her other hand and nearly snagging a string of paper lanterns. "She doesn't have a sugar pulling hook! Probably wouldn't even know what to do with it if she saw one."

"Or one of those blow pump gadgets."

"You're right!" Marisa breathed, cradling her forehead under the realization of just how much she had going for her and how much of it she just couldn't see until Alec pointed it out. "My business is more than the sum of its parts. So much more. I just need to get in the game and make some noise about it."

"And speaking of noise, I bet this'll help." Alec pulled out his phone and showed her his screen, specifically all the notifications that had come within a span of only a few minutes. There were more likes, thumbs-ups, smiley emojis, and *Can't wait to go!* comments than any one of her posts had ever received. Page after page of people asking how they could buy tickets to the Crystal Christmas Ball, what other kinds of candies Sweetest Heart's Desire would be offering, and which one of Marisa's treats was Alec's favorite.

Mentally, she'd tried racking up the numbers, but her brain stalled out when the comments bled over to subsequent pages. If even just a fraction of the people who interacted with this post actually bought tickets and showed up at the Ball, Marisa wasn't only going to win a spot on Monica's List, but she'd be in business for who knew how long.

Wave after wave of emotion flooded her system, causing her cheeks to heat and misting her eyes with good tears for a change.

But then another notification popped up on Alec's phone. A single text message from a man's name she didn't recognize.

Alec's face pinched and sank into a worried scowl. "My

agent. Wants me to call him back. Must be in L.A. Give me a moment."

"Sure."

She didn't know why, but when Alec let go of her hand to take the call, she worried he was letting go of something far greater.

CHAPTER 13

Alec excused himself and ducked out onto the back patio, one, to give his retinas a rest, and, two, because he didn't want Marisa's family to hear in case Brennan's mouthiness caused him to inadvertently slip about his story.

Without his coat, his muscles felt the shock of the mid-December air in a way they did not appreciate, and boy, did they let him know. A prickling tension seized up at the base of his neck, shooting straight into his skull and behind his eyes, a stark reminder that he'd been slacking on Dr. Campbell's exercises and his body had earned the right to file complaints.

Bloody perfect. As if speaking to his agent alone wouldn't have given him enough grief.

"Hey, Brennan. Are you out at the Los Angeles Sevens tourney?"

The sour Irishman's gruff guffaw wasn't the reception Alec expected, but he couldn't say it was entirely surprising. After more than ten years working together, he'd learned to make peace with whatever needed to come out of Brennan's mouth, as it usually made them both loads of money.

Until the damn fool had started bringing up Alec's possible retirement.

"I am, and watching some smarmy bastard mangle the shit out of your routes."

"Is Marty not playing flanker?"

"Nah. His dad took ill. It's more serious than he thought. Had to fly home to be with his family."

"Shit. Can Fin step in to help?"

"And who do you think's trying to train up the other two fly-halves while also keeping our conversion numbers up? We barely pulled out a win against Fiji yesterday, and that was because half their best players are dealing with a bout of food poisoning. It sure as hell wasn't because we were stopping them from scoring. Fin's doing more than his contract's paying him for, I can tell you that much. And speaking of contracts . . ."

Through the patio door, the party shrank down to a speck, threatening to implode along with Alec into whatever black hole Brennan was surely about to throw his way.

Alec pinched the bridge of his nose. "If you're going to go on about retirement again—"

"I'm not."

"You're not?" Alec quickly had to pull back the fight that was on the tip of his tongue.

"No." Brennan paused for a few breaths, which would normally have been silent for anyone else, but for him, they were solid grumbling wheezes that likely portended certain doom. "I'm talking about a trade. And before you get on my arse and protest, you owe it to yourself to at least hear me out. I can already tell you've not been taking your meds, 'cause I can practically hear your teeth grinding through the phone."

Alec willed his jaw to unclench. "I'm taking my fucking meds, Brennan. My anger has nothing to do with my concussion, and you bloody well know it. A trade? Really?" Just saying the words left a sour stain on his tongue, to speak nothing of the sting of betrayal they left all over his heart.

"Yes, really. And once you hear what I've got on offer, you'll be thanking me more than cursing me."

"That is highly, *highly* unlikely."

"Well, good, then. I'd rather have you angry than stupid. You always played better when your blood was up anyway, so here's to hoping your emotions will finally let you hear some sense. While you've been recuperating, I've been shopping you around."

"Shopping me around? Jesus Christ, Brennan. I'm not a fucking collegiate rookie hoping to show promise to scouts. I've been team captain for more years than I wasn't. I trained up a good three-quarters of the mates I now play with, and they're some of the best in the league. And now you're coming in here talking about *shopping me around* like I haven't even broken in my mouthguard yet?" Alec wasn't hearing this. His brain, for all it had been through recently, knew better than to give any sort of credence to the drivel that was coming out of his agent's mouth.

"Argentina's interested. They're offering a two-year contract. The bonuses aren't what you're used to, but you don't really have a lot of options, and they're playing halfway decent this season. Even made a few good moves for the Cup. With your help, they're likely to make it further than they have in the past. Not to the finals, no, but enough to be encouraging for the program. It's a young team, and they lack veteran leadership. It'd be a great place for you to pass on what you know, leave that legacy for the game that you've always wanted to."

Vaguely, Alec heard the rest of the pitch package, with numbers far lower than anything he'd been offered since his third or fourth year playing. It wasn't that he didn't like the team. He'd played against the lads many times, and they were all a good group of players who seemed to work hard but suffered beneath the weight of an underfunded sport in a football-dominated country. Without a large cache of wealthy patrons and a damn near perfect marketing department, no amount of training or veteran players could ever turn that team around, and both Brennan and Alec knew it.

That meant this whole trade negotiation was little more than a peace offering. A way, on the surface at least, for Alec to go out on his terms, rather than publicly face the rejection that would come if his contract didn't get renewed and he wasn't picked up by another team before the new season started.

"You're asking too much of me, Bren."

"I'm not asking anything. I'm offering. We don't always get the choices we want. And as your agent, who's watched you get patched up more times than a person ought to at your age, it's my job to give you the facts and negotiate accordingly."

That familiar chill crept up Alec's spine, the one that had nothing to do with the weather and everything to do with his nervous system's response that came whenever he heard Brennan use the word *negotiate*. "What aren't you telling me?"

A hesitant silence hung between them before Bren cleared his throat. "I know you're on the mend, that it's the holidays, and you're visiting your brother. I just didn't want it all to come out this way."

"Come out *what* way? What the hell are you keeping from me?"

"Great Britain's recruiting flankers, all right? Any loose forwards who are a good fit for your position are what management's been ordering the team to go scout for. There are always holes in the roster, but yours is a fucking massive one, and they're not taking chances you won't be able to perform to your fullest in the long term when you rejoin the team next month *if* Dr. Campbell clears you."

Whatever remained of Alec's equilibrium seemed to catch the last chopper out of the battle zone. His right knee buckled slightly, but it was enough to collapse all sixteen stone of him onto a frigid Adirondack chair that took the abrupt intrusion out on his tailbone.

"They're replacing me already? Are you fucking serious?"

"No one's replacing you yet, Alec. You're under contract until May."

"Which is the end of the bloody season!"

"And Great Britain's doing exactly what they're supposed to be doing: keeping an eye out for talent, building where they can, nurturing where they need to, and putting together a team that stands to win the Cup. The same can be said for Argentina or Fiji or South Africa or any other Rugby Sevens team out there. The difference is that Argentina's asking and offering for you, whereas the others aren't. I'll keep doing my part to get you the best of what's out there, but it'll be easier for everyone involved if you take the time you have now to reevaluate what you want, what you *really* want. Invest in whatever opportunities come your way in the States, sure, but I'm asking you to focus on what your playing future looks like. Nothing lasts forever, but you've at least got options on how you want your career to end. Most of the blokes I manage don't even get within pissing distance of such choices, so keep that in mind."

Alec barely managed to grunt out a goodbye before he hung up. It was bad enough his heart threatened to explode out of his chest, which would have been a far neater experience than the soup his brain was turning into, but Argentina? Bren wanted to trade him to fucking *Argentina*? For what? So he could leave a goddamn legacy for younger lads to step off?

He didn't give a ripe fig about legacies. Those were for men with egos so large, they thought a lifetime wasn't enough to contain them, so they insisted on others carrying their accomplishments on their backs.

All Alec wanted was to play a game he'd always loved and had always been good at. He wanted to go out on his terms, to shake hands with Bren after years together and say *job well done*. He wanted to retire when he was ready, not because some bloody bulldozer of a man got the better of him in a tackle and knocked him unconscious for the first time in his life.

He wanted to remember what it was like to bounce back up from a fall. To imagine, just for one more day, how it felt to be infallible.

Inside, the cheerful din of the party thumped its joy through the glass slider, reminding him of everything else that insisted on passing him by that evening. The large menorah already had a fair bit of its oil drained down from their wee cups, while several of the other candles decorating the living room had been burned down to nubs, with a few extinguished entirely. Tragically, regardless of how beautiful the blazes were, they also had no say in their futures. Eventually, every flame burned out, no matter how long the wick.

Next to the menorah, nursing a glass of wine with her elbow resting above her forearm across her chest, stood Marisa, talking to someone. Among all the glittering lights, cloaked in the armor of her blue cardigan, the woman seemed like the brightest light in the room when, given the luminous power pumping out of the place, she had every reason not to be.

Still, he considered her, the way the candlelight flickered in the subtle auburn of her hair or how his hand still remembered the precise slope of her back when he'd held her close to take a photo. It was strange, this partnership they'd somehow forged. Strange, perhaps, because he felt wholly entitled and unentitled to her at the same time, no matter where his admiration of her led him.

Because if he played his very fucking limited cards right, it all had to lead him back to building a name for himself at the Ball and, more direly, doing what he could to impress the hell out of that Arthur bloke. If Alec could draw a crowd that would get that man and his New York media connections interested enough to pique Bren's notice, then his agent would have no choice but to fight for him the way he ought to, the way they'd fought together for years.

Alec pulled out his phone and smiled at the growing likes and shares his pictures of him and Marisa were getting. If he could get that kind of response from just a single post, how much more notice could they garner for the event from a far more structured social media campaign over the next week, especially if Monica's and Arthur's connections were as good as they were purported to be?

"You've got this." Reenergized, he slapped his knees and stood to head inside, but when he gripped the handle of the sliding glass door, Marisa shifted, and Alec got an eyeful of the man talking to her.

A man with his hand on her arm, whispering something into her ear.

The flood of feelings that roared to the surface of his mind caught him off guard like a tackle from behind. Trained to respond to trauma as he was, his body clenched tight, his fingers clutching nothing but air, the muscles in his face shutting down to absorb the shock.

But it wasn't the sort of shock he was used to. This sort of shock had been stirred up by a hive of bees, all its inhabitants compelled to attack on instinct rather than reason.

And reason was missing from the bloody equation. Alec had to remind himself that he had no right to stop a true romantic interest from forming between Marisa and another man if that was what she wanted. He had no right to any of Marisa, just as he had no right to the thumbs-up her dad kept throwing him through the glass or the third plate of artfully arranged potato pancakes her mother had offered him.

They were partners. Nothing more.

Alec swiped a hand down his face and let the cold night air carry away his curses, hoping the breeze would return with something useful, some course of action he could take that didn't involve storming back in there and—

Marisa laughed at whatever the man said, but the lines around her mouth weren't the sort Alec earned each time *he* made her smile.

These were tense, short. Unwanted.

Alec considered the scope of his actions for only half a second before he moved. If he needed to be her boyfriend, then this fool and everyone else needed not to think otherwise, and there was only one way Alec knew to send such a message.

When he saw Alec coming, the man lifted his head and backed away from Marisa.

Good thing, too, because with all of Alec's muscles in lock-step to get to Marisa, there was no one left upstairs in his brain to halt the train and tell him that grabbing her and kissing her in front of her family was a bad idea.

So he didn't stop.

CHAPTER 14

By all objective measures, Marisa was pretty sure there was no right amount of alcohol to make a night go by faster, but she'd always prided herself on her experimental spirit. One glass of wine down, with number two in her hand, and the seeping warmth that unspooled within her veins was doing little to cast out the impending doom blanketing her. With Alec gone, even temporarily, the ruse they'd engineered felt far more fragile.

Add in her genetically spawned anxiety and Marisa was quickly spiraling from unsettled into unhinged.

Just as she was going to throw up her hands—well, her one free hand—and add some latkes to soak up the wine sloshing around nervously in her belly, a handsome man approached her. "Rumor has it you're the famous Internet lady with some really good sugar."

And just like that, unhinged morphed into unbelievable.

Ugh, gross. Worst opening line ever.

"That's the rumor," she said into her wineglass.

"I'm Jules," he added, holding out a hand and flashing a smile that had gone a little too heavy on the whitening strips.

"Marisa." She shook his hand, inwardly groaning at why her aunt's neighbor had chosen that moment to show up. "You're not one of those people who talks about gut health a lot and is oddly obsessed with the microbiome, are you? Nine times out of ten in my business, when someone starts talking to me about sugar before they even tell me their name, that's usually the case."

The man laughed heartily and shook his head. "Nah. Just trying to talk to someone who's not carrying an AARP card and doesn't seem to be perfecting their Pinot Grigio mom strut every time they hit the smoked salmon station. If I'm asked to hold one more handbag, I'm liable to start charging baggage fees."

Against her earlier inclinations, Marisa couldn't help but snort a laugh through her latest sip. But before she'd barely gotten through the sting of red wine singeing her nose, Jules was already holding out a napkin for her.

"Happy birthday, by the way. When your Aunt Gail invited me, I didn't really have the heart to tell her no, especially if I was going to be living next to the woman for the foreseeable future. I mean, she cornered me when I just got back from a run and was in the middle of taking in the garbage cans. I got the sense that if I didn't shut down the conversation real quick and appease her, she'd have me out there inspecting for visitor parking passes or asking my opinion on whether the homeowner's association is paying too much for their snow removal contractor. I know a yenta when I see one. Besides, wouldn't have been the first time I've had to make nice with the new neighbors."

"You volunteered to go to a Hanukkah/birthday party with a bunch of people you'd never met before just so you could get away from your neighbor and back into your house as fast as possible?"

"In my defense, I was in the middle of my *West Wing* rewatch.

After my run that morning, I was planning on eating my oatmeal while President Bartlet comforted the signalman in the hurricane. I had a fair bit on the line there. So, I'd say I didn't so much volunteer to attend the party as was volun-told. Plus, I knew there'd be doughnuts."

"Oh my God, I can't watch that episode. Not unless I want to spend the entire day making sure my eyes don't leak into my caramels."

"Hey, you never know. Maybe selling a new batch of candies called *The Signalman's Salted Caramels* might be a runaway hit."

Marisa shared a careful, yet pleasant laugh with him before the wine unhelpfully let loose what her brain had been guarding. "I'm sorry, and I know this is going to sound the way it's going to sound, but I was sort of under the impression that my aunt wanted to . . ." *Don't make me say it. Please, buddy, don't make me say the words.*

A humorous expression came over his face, one that played perfectly off the half-smile curving his lips. He leaned forward, grabbing her elbow and bringing his mouth to her ear. "I didn't want to make a scene with your aunt or anything, but I'm pretty sure the guy I just started dating at my new gym would take offense."

The peal of laughter that rattled Marisa's lungs was so intense, she had to slam her teeth together to keep her family from thinking something was wrong or, worse, far too interesting to go a minute longer without their inspection.

And that was the last thing she needed.

"Oh, I can't believe this," Marisa said, shaking her head and pounding her fist against her chest to beat back the burn.

"Believe it," Jules added, picking up a decorative dreidel nestled within a puddle of gelt on the table and spinning it for effect. "When she mentioned her niece, I knew exactly why I was being invited, but I didn't want to be rude. And I wagered that anyone who had an aunt like yours probably needed as many distractions as possible to get them out of your business so you can have some peace. I do know what that's like." A sad look of commiseration highlighted his angled features, shocking Marisa even more. On anyone else, she would have found his ability to get such an accurate read on her sourness annoying, but all things considered, she didn't mind the sympathy.

Jules took a sip of his drink. "Then you introduced your boyfriend to everyone earlier and saved me the headache of having to perform." His eyes took on a new life. "But I had no idea you were dating *him*. Took me a few minutes to connect the name with the face, but I knew I'd seen him from somewhere." Then he pulled out his phone and scrolled through a feed of photos until he landed on one and held it up to her.

Whatever air had remained in Marisa's abused lungs from the near spit take a moment ago vanished. In a sea of stadium-goers, Alec's joyful face stared back at her. With a backward hat on, a beer in one hand, and a carefree smile that could disarm even the most strident drill instructors, he was the picture-perfect epitome of a sports fan.

Right down to the beautiful woman draped beneath his other arm. None other than Phoebe Boyle wearing a too-large rugby shirt in Great Britain's colors.

Marisa was immediately slammed with the desire to find the nearest bathroom and lock herself in it. Grief followed that up, riding in hot and angry, but it wasn't the ancient and oppressive kind that, as a proverbial member of the tribe, she was used to. Instead, the frustrated anguish that was doing a bang-up job of stealing her words could better be ascribed to the grief of Charlie Brown.

More of the eternally unfortunate sort.

If there was one thing Marisa excelled at, it was woeful and perpetual sadness, especially the kind that sprang up in the form of reminders she'd rather forget.

Like how Alec and Phoebe used to be romantically linked. And how he'd yet to explain any of it.

Unaware of her quiet despair, or perhaps uninterested in it entirely, Jules took his phone back. "Used to date a guy who was a goalkeeper for the New York City Football Club. I'd go to games when I could, and every now and then, when the Jumbotron operator got wind of a few famous people in the crowd, they'd direct it around in the stands, spotlighting some of the celebrities attending. I'd always snap pictures because, hey, they're celebrities, right? Even though most time, I had no fucking clue who any of them were. I deleted most of them when I had to clear out my phone storage, but this fellow?" His voice was full of a wistful smokiness that Marisa suspected had nothing to do with the rapidly extinguishing candles in the living room.

Because Atlas himself couldn't have held up the weight of Jules's sentiment without shattering a shoulder blade or two. The photo of Alec was a beaming portrait of a man who could be the sentinel of his sport. A shining star that attracted everyone around him into his orbit. There, radiating back at her, was the evidence of just how magnanimous the man was.

And how he was absolutely getting the shit end of the deal in their little arrangement. She was staring at documented proof that he didn't need her, not in the same way she needed him. Not really.

It made the whole charade feel like she was being kept at arm's length from the true manipulation, as if he were some sort of agreeable renegade to a cause he refused to share with her.

When Marisa had tried to wrap herself in her denial all over again, doing her best to project an outward appearance of *Yup, that's my boyfriend and we're definitely super, super into each other,* the sentiment stretched over her like a soggy parka she'd forgotten to dry out the last time she'd worn it, leaving her feeling steamed in all senses of the word.

Jules's eyes softened, but then he took a step back as someone approached from behind her, their shadow climbing up his body.

Suspecting it was her father finagling an Everest-sized mountain of sufganiyot without her mother catching him, Marisa turned, ready to aid and abet in his culinary heists, as she always did.

Instead, what she got was the all-encompassing presence of Alec Elms as he gripped the back of her neck, pulled her close, and kissed her.

So many things began to fire at once, bringing all the micro-components of the situation into awareness. The grain of Alec's short beard rasping against her chin. The way his hands shifted from the back of her neck to the sides of her face, angling her mouth higher while he lowered to meet hers. The thrill rocking her body as it desperately tried to match the energy he surrounded her with.

If this deception was a performance, she could think of a million and one reasons for never bothering with the truth again.

Marisa's ribs desperately tried to expand with the enormity of the emotions flooding her body, but the damn things seemed to have no more room for anything other than breathing in Alec's essence. His wine-kissed lips, that familiar earthiness from earlier, and the subtle sweetness of dark chocolate gelt that paired so wonderfully with all the rest of him crowded out the party until all she cared to focus on was the gift he was giving her.

He was kissing her. They hadn't agreed to it or discussed it beforehand. Weren't there rules they should have put in place so her emotions wouldn't get all sticky like this?

Because when his lips pressed against hers, urging her tongue to join his and dance along to the rhythm he set, it didn't feel like an agreement between platonic business partners.

It felt like more, like he actually *wanted* to kiss her, instead of doing so out of duty or obligation.

When he finally pulled away, he took most of her breath with him but left just enough for her to add so incredibly lamely, "You . . . just had one of the Nutella-stuffed doughnuts, didn't you?"

The satisfied smirk looked just as at home on his face as the arms that now held her to him felt, and it was more than enough of an answer for her confused mind.

But then he went and added his rumbling "Aye" to the mix, and as sure as she felt every bit of his brogue down to the tips of her heels, she knew one thing.

Their relationship may be fake, but there was nothing fake about that kiss.

CHAPTER 15

Normally, Alec was quite fond of snow. Moving around in it tended to do a good job of working his muscles and kneading out the bits of tension his trainer always managed to miss. Winter in New Jersey, however, made him bloody hate the stuff.

Sitting right smack in the center of the Mid-Atlantic Coast, the state wasn't far north enough to know how to reliably manage nor'easter-levels of snow, nor was it south enough to miss out on snow entirely.

There were too many damn people in the state to make maneuvering in winter anything other than a clusterfuck of traffic, dangerously narrowed lanes, and snowbanked sidewalks that everyone thought was everyone else's job to clear.

But after what he'd done with Marisa, Alec didn't think he was in a position to debate roles and responsibilities with anyone.

Alec skirted around a slushy gray snow pile encroaching on the walkway and nearly cursed when an oncoming stroller, whose owner was far less inclined to share the concrete than he was, almost ran over his boot toe.

"What a mangled mess," he said, shoving his hands into his coat pockets, secretly wishing the bagel shop where he'd asked Marisa to meet him had decided to close due to three inches of snow so he wouldn't have to explain the what and whys of his mistake.

No, not a mistake. His actions.

He'd kissed Marisa. Not just kissed her but stormed over to her during her family's holiday celebration and captured her as if she were the last survivor in a gruesome battle theater he'd been charged with protecting. A bit dramatic to think of things in such a way, but he hadn't exactly been working with an abundance of common sense lately, had he?

Desperation made for lousy decision-makers. Though, try as he might, he couldn't bring himself to regret his choice. Oh, he certainly didn't love the open-mouthed stares and barely shielded giggles that had tittered around him as his arms sank into the curve of Marisa's lower back and he savored the moment when she relaxed against him, the anxious tension fleeing them both.

But when he'd seen that man—who he later learned had zero interest in Marisa—get so close to her, touching her elbow and breathing against her ear, and her forcing out a smile Alec didn't bloody well care for, something inside him had snapped.

And because he'd always been a right bastard when provoked and a particularly selfish one when it came to Marisa, he was finding out, Alec had held her against him longer than he needed to.

Longer than he had any right to.

Essentially, his brutish body had taken over once his brain had been benched.

Alec cupped his hands to his mouth and blew heat into them. Even as he fought off the chill of the snowy morning, his fingers still remembered that slight shudder that had run through Marisa when the air left her and she'd finally settled against him. He was fairly certain essential parts of him were now dedicated to that little shiver.

Then everyone started snapping their damn photos, and before Alec could muster the urgency to tear himself away from her, the social media storm he'd hoped to carefully and strategically craft with Marisa's say-so ignited like bloody wildfire, and there was fuck all he could do to call it back.

He didn't know how much of the social media storm she'd seen yet, but if she'd been tagged in at least half of the gossipy posts he'd been, all because of his foolishness . . .

Alec's elbow bumped into a pine garland snaking over the doorjamb to the bagel shop, karmically knocking a chunk of snow onto his T-shirt.

Thankfully, unlike when he'd met Marisa at the pizza place, which was clearly an establishment devoted to her turf and terms, the bagel shop he'd chosen was closer to Cal's apartment, in a different side of town from where Marisa lived.

Plus, he was thirty minutes early, and due to the snow, the place was blessedly quiet. No way in hell was he going to apologize to a woman who'd already been given the upper hand by letting her choose her battlefield and set up camp early. He wasn't *that* thick.

When the wee bell above the door chimed and Marisa finally joined him, the five different scenarios he'd run through his mind of how their conversation might go evaporated. Stuffed beneath the egregiously chunky scarf that seemed like more of a shield to hide behind than a way to ward off the weather, Marisa's lips were tight, her face drawn in frustration. Her eyes, though, were unmistakable in their messaging.

In the new light of her thirties, Marisa Silver was scared. All because he'd bloody kissed her.

Alec stood and gestured to the seat in front of him, where a steaming to-go cup sat far more patiently than he had. "Hey there. I got you coffee. Wasn't entirely sure how you took it, but I figured—"

Marisa's scarf hadn't even unwrapped from her hair fully before she plopped down and took the lid off the cup. With the practiced precision of a woman who'd likely cut her teeth on Jersey diner caffeine and convenience store carafes, she didn't say anything as she took in the black coffee, reached for the little cluster of half-and-half creamers Alec had brought to the table, and dumped in two. She didn't bother stirring it. Instead, she simply swirled the cup around until the liquid obediently lightened to her mental specifications.

Once satisfied, she took a sip, let her eyes fall closed, sighed, and only *then* did she bother taking off her coat. "Coffee will forever and always be my favorite person."

When she opened her eyes and came back to him, her worried gaze returned, and her expression had taken on a bit of a lecturing look that seemed to silently plead for an explanation.

It was the sweetest form of condemnation he'd ever witnessed, and it was bloody effective at making him feel two inches tall.

"I should never have kissed you," he blurted out, hating the lie as soon as it left his lips. If his heated blood was anything to go by, he most definitely *should* have kissed her, thoroughly, eagerly, and with as much expediency as the fire lit beneath his heels granted him. Which had been just shy of a metric fuck ton. But how the hell could he say that when they weren't even dating in the first place?

Marisa halted the cup she brought to her lips, her features morphing from aggrieved to . . . Was that hurt? Or was she just sick of his words already?

Bloody fucking hell, he was making a mess of this.

"No, what I mean is that I shouldn't *never* have kissed you," he added quickly, "but I never meant for you to suffer because of it." Alec took a sip of his black coffee, hoping to find answers in something with more experience being so bitter. He got nothing except a burned tongue and a mug of judgmental sludge.

"I wasn't suffering for it," she replied, looking down into her coffee. "It was—"

"Unexpected and out of line, I know. My agent called me and gave me some shitty news, telling me that, basically, unless things change, come the spring, I'll likely be traded to Argentina as a veteran player tasked to lead their young club, or I can retire. Great Britain's apparently already shopping around to replace my position, and everyone seems to have forgotten that I'm still on the fucking team, even when my doctor says I'm on track to rejoin in January for the next tournament. Brennan's a good guy and all, but he's not hearing me. None of them are. They haven't even given me a damn chance to prove what I'm still capable of, and they're already moving on to the next name on the roster. So, right when I finally hung up on all of that mess, I looked through the patio glass door and saw that blonde bloke moving in on you, trying to make you laugh but mostly seeming to make you cringe, and I wanted to fucking kick myself for abandoning you there when I promised to be by your side."

He was beginning to spiral a bit, but he didn't care. The seal had been broken, and it felt good to get it all out. "I kissed you because if we *were* really dating, I'd want people to know that you're worth keeping, worth claiming, even if I'm not. I'm so sorry, Marisa. I should have asked earlier. I should have gone over some ground rules about how you wanted things handled. And I bloody well shouldn't have put you in a position where half the fucking Internet gets to see me pawing at you in an unstaged intimate moment."

A chilled silence stretched between them, settling around the word *intimate* like an avalanche of poor choices. Alec winced at just how few favors the confession did him, especially the ripple of awareness that crept beneath his skin and started to get his blood up when he saw just how crimson Marisa's cheeks had flushed after he'd said the word.

Oh, for fuck's sake. Was there anything he could say that *wouldn't* land him mired in shit and anxiety? Lamely, he glanced toward the food counter, hoping that one of the line cooks would take pity on him and lob him onto the griddle along with the bacon and eggs.

No such luck. To Alec's eternal misery, all he got back were indifferent shrugs and pointed glances that said *Apologies still don't get you free refills.*

"I was going to say," she added, smiling and seeming to take a particular joy in his distress, "that the kiss was . . . nice."

His balls could have been buried in two feet of snow, and he still wouldn't have moved.

Nice. *Nice?* Had the woman just said his kiss was *nice?*

Alec let Marisa conceal the enchanting smile that followed behind the rim of her coffee cup, because he couldn't fathom a reason why she'd gift him with it after what he'd confessed. "Did you not hear me?"

"Oh, I heard you." She nodded. "But I believe *you* didn't hear *me.*"

"I'm sorry. I don't follow."

"I said the kiss was nice. More than nice, if I'm being honest."

Alec's breath froze behind his ribs. *Please be honest. For all the bagels in Jersey, even those peculiar French toast numbers, please be honest with me.*

"Jules showed me the picture he took of us before he posted it," she confessed. "I said he could."

Well, that was a ripe piece of news. "You did? Why?"

"I was a bit tipsy, and also . . ." To his utter astonishment, Marisa tried to look anywhere but at his face. "He had a picture of you on his phone."

"He did?" Well, that was bloody news to Alec, though

whether it was the nightly news kind or the tabloid kind remained to be seen.

Marisa nodded slowly but still wouldn't meet his eyes. "Jules said he used to date a soccer player for the New York team. He saw you in the stands one time and snapped a photo."

"Why would that bother you? I mean, don't get me wrong, I don't exactly relish the idea of being in some bloke's phone gallery, but it's not an uncommon occurrence, I guess. I play all over the world and can be a bit recognizable in certain circles, so it's bound to happen."

However, his explanation didn't soften whatever had set her on edge. She shifted uneasily in her seat and kept tapping out a rhythm on the table with her thumbs.

Alec placed his elbows on the table and leaned forward. "What aren't you telling me?"

"The picture was of you and Phoebe."

Ice flooded his veins, and the shock of it somehow crisped up the circumstances he found himself in.

"Ah. It must have been from a few years ago, then." Alec raked his memory bank, and sure enough, he'd gone to a few local sporting events with her when he was in the States.

"Why did you break up? Or I guess the bigger curiosity I have is, why the hell did you date her to begin with? You never answered me, and it's still been on my mind."

Outside, the light snow had begun to collect on the edge of the window glass, pooling in a slanted hill that seemed determined to frost over as much of the world beyond and block out any distractions.

Even the weather was conspiring against him, forcing him to reveal the truth lest he be buried beneath the weight of it.

Again, Alec looked for answers in his coffee. Again, he found none. "We were together for some time. Met her in New York at one of the opening night parties for a show Cal had been in. She had a friend who worked for the theater, so she got in as a guest, and I was on break in between rugby seasons and not opposed to a bit of fun back then. *Break* being the keyword in that scenario," he said pointedly. "The way our tours work is that, each month, we play one jam-packed Friday-through-Sunday weekend of rugby in a different city around the world. There are seven legs, you see, all leading up to the Grand Final at the end. It's a lot of travel, and though most people may not think so, it sets a grueling pace of play, pace of life, really. Playing Rugby Sevens at that level is not conducive to settling down, and at the time, I wasn't interested in changing.

"Phoebe, however, was, despite the fun that my lifestyle afforded her. She was convinced that, with me getting on in years, all she had to do was wait out my career, and eventually, the ruthlessness of the game would decide in her favor. When it didn't and I saw just how unhappy my professional happiness was making her, we ended it, though far later than we should have. I suppose I used all the travel as a convenient excuse to be a coward. It's a bit easier to hide your injuries and true worries over video chats."

It had been bad enough to have Brennan's disgruntlement breathing down his neck over Alec's desire to keep playing, but to have someone who supposedly loved him tapping her foot every time he took a tackle and spent longer in the infirmary than he had when he was younger had been the wrong sort of confidence vote.

"She didn't have anything nice to say about the photos online," Marisa added. "A few passive-aggressive emojis seemed to be the extent of her interest in the matter."

"I'm not surprised."

"Does she know how you got injured?" A bit of trepidation laced her curiosity as she tried hunting for answers she likely guessed others already knew.

"I'm willing to bet she does." He sat back in his chair, leaning on the rear legs, and barked out a laugh. "I don't even have a good story to tell you about that one. Probably should just make one up, to be honest."

"I like made-up stories," Marisa said, lifting a shoulder. "Did Santa have a mid-air collision during sleigh testing and land on your shoulder?"

He shook his head, grinning. "No, but the lad who tackled me during the Vancouver match might have weighed about as much as the Big Fella." Then Marisa gave him the space he needed to talk about the fear that had chased him all over the globe. "I misjudged the pitch and my opponent. Took on more of a bloke than I could handle and didn't land properly. A total rookie error. Woke up in a hospital bed with a concussion diagnosis and the worst headache you'd ever imagined, and that was *before* I got an eyeful of Brennan's mangy jowls flapping at me, screaming about how I owe him a new suit for causing him to spill his drink all over his crotch when I didn't get up after taking the hit. Even through the pounding in my skull, I managed to tell him it didn't matter. Any equipment that may have been affected between his legs had been inactive for so long, I doubted window dressings would have made it work again."

Marisa laughed cheerfully, brightening his spirits. "No you didn't."

"I did."

"No wonder he doesn't like you."

"Oh, he likes me fine. He just doesn't understand me. No one does, except Cal and sometimes Hugh."

"Who's Hugh?"

Then the inkling of an idea sifted through his thoughts, one that just might fix his execution problem when it came to this whole fake relationship charade.

"My roommate while I'm in Jersey. Snores like a beast and eats all my good steaks. Hates any food that's green and gets mighty irritated when I turn off the TV, even though he's already fallen asleep to it. Would you like to meet him?"

At that, Marisa's eyes widened. "Meet him?"

"Sure." Then Alec set their coffees aside and clasped her hand, the one that hadn't been holding the cup, and rubbed away the remaining bit of chill with his fingers. "Listen, I know I fucked this up. That kiss wasn't exactly planned."

"But it was effective," she added, gesturing with her chin toward her phone sitting on the table. "Word's spreading. Even Monica liked the photo, which I'm still not sure how I feel about. Either way, it definitely made people sit up and take notice, including a few rugby organization names I didn't recognize liking the photo as well."

"If that's what we can achieve with an accidental spark, imagine what we could do with an intentional fire."

Marisa's brow furrowed. "Huh?"

"The Ball's coming up, and we won't have many more public opportunities to drum up business, so let's make one. This time, you and I will have ground rules set in advance. No kissing without consent. No touching without prior approval. Everything staged and thought out beforehand. Think of it like a director's shot list. What do you say?"

Marisa bit her lip, and for a moment, he was terrified she was going to send him packing, having dealt with far too much of his shit and all the stink that came with it. But then she smiled at him and raised her coffee cup. "I'm in. On one condition."

He faux clinked his paper cup with hers. "What's that?" he asked, taking a sip.

A flash of something he couldn't quite place lit her eyes. "That there be more kissing."

He turned just in time to spit his hot coffee all over the frozen window and watch in shaky fascination as the hot liquid melted away every inch of snow that had been choking out his escape route moments before.

CHAPTER 16

Marisa's tired shipping label printer had just successfully spat out the last postage label of the evening despite its wheezing protestations.

"There. Done," she said as she started gathering what was supposed to go in the order so Eden could pack it up. "Shop's officially closed until after the holidays. Now I can finally focus on the goods for Monica's event. I think I've got the recipes nailed down."

"You freaking better," Eden added from her place on Marisa's living room floor as she grabbed the next bundle of orders and began packing them up. "I'm generally not one to worry for other people, but you're not other people, so congratulations. You have my worry."

"Thank you?"

"You are cutting things really close here. Like, heinously so."

"It's not heinous. It's Hanukkah. This is all totally normal."

Eden snorted and popped another sweet and sour gummy Christmas tree into her mouth. "Could have fooled me." The silence that followed lasted just long enough to tear Marisa away from her laptop screen and mark the track of Eden's eye roll, which landed squarely on the saddest excuse for a Hanukkah celebration collecting dust on Marisa's mantle. "Pretty sure that menorah has more wax build-up than what an ENT sees when they go elbows-deep in an ear canal. It's what, the third night? Isn't that thing supposed to be lit? Like, what the hell, girl? I usually work any holiday that's willing to pay me time and a half, and *I* can even manage to remember pulling out my tiny fake hot pink Christmas tree and setting it on my coffee table."

"I've had a lot on my mind, all right? At least I remembered to take the menorah out of the closet this year."

Eden snorted around a mouthful of gummies. "Pretty sure that thing wanted to stay right where it was. Sterling silver can sense shame, you know."

That was true, and Marisa's weepy menorah was nothing if not judgmental about it. The once-polished hand-me-down was from her grandmother, who loved to hoard shiny shit and made damn sure everyone in the family had an appreciation for her collection as well. When Marisa went to college, the thing had been shipped off with her, along with a gleaming new bank account and a boatload of silent expectations. She'd never asked for it and yet had been tasked with its upkeep, or, in her case, the guilt that came when she didn't clean and polish it regularly. Or light it regularly to boot.

Her eyes fell on the sealed box of candles perched next to it. *Shit. Forgot about those, too.*

As far as her version of Hanukkah usually went, tarnish was just another word for tinsel and a far cry from the opulent splendor her Aunt Gail always insisted on showing off at every opportunity. For Marisa, her lack of proper spirited fanfare, as her mother always called it, was a befitting image for the general dishevelment that had become her life. Oh, she had every *intention* of doing the candle-lighting routine—minus the blessings, because who the hell even remembered those when not mumbling along with the rest of the crowd?—but the Christmastime push her business seemed to always need tended to get in the way.

Along with the stacks of unassembled pastry boxes, industry-sized rolls of cellophane wrap in various festive colors, and a galley kitchen that had about four ovens too few and three cracked tiles too many. And then there were the catering jobs she picked up as often as her bank account needed her to

. . .

Bottom line: if it was winter, Marisa was working, though no one else in her family saw it as such. Even in her mind, she could hear Alec's brogue-laced cursing, criticizing her, albeit as sweetly as the Scot could manage, for not taking the time to celebrate her holiday as she should.

"Fine, I'll light the candles. The menorah doesn't look that bad, though, does it?"

When Eden didn't answer immediately, Marisa blew out the match, trying to make sure her temper didn't spark too hotly and light anything else on fire.

"Not really, no."

Marisa glared at her. "Then why the hell did you pause before you said that?"

Her friend's poor attempt at tactical evasion did no favors for Eden's authority. "Because I'm still trying to figure out what your grand plan is, other than watching K-dramas with me and avoiding the fact that you told a certain Scottish rugby player, who you're not really dating, mind you, that there would be more kissing in his future."

Marisa cringed and was a hairsbreadth away from banging her head against the mantle in frustration before she remembered the actively lit candles that seemed eager to see what she'd look like with less hair.

She *had* mentioned the kissing thing, hadn't she? When she replayed their coffee-date-thing-whatever over in her mind, all she came away with was one glaring set of ground rules between them: kissing. And more of it, please and thank you.

"I can't believe I said that," she muttered, grabbing her laptop and plopping onto the floor next to Eden. "It just sort of fell out of my mouth." Her embarrassment had been a tangible thing, so solid that even Eden couldn't refrain from flashing her a sad look of commiseration.

When Alec had presented her with his plan for a staged outing, the entire situation had run away from her before she'd even had the opportunity to deploy logic. Instead, her other senses had elbowed their way into the picture, not giving a rip just how messy the situation was.

He'd been honest with her, laying out his vulnerability like a grocery store birthday sheet cake about to be cut up and obliterated by a pack of wild five-year-olds, and he'd done it *before* she explained her take on the Kiss. Because she did have a thing or two to say about it, all of which stemmed from the way her skin tingled when he held her flush against his body. Or how everything in the room had shifted from a crisply focused picture to an amorphous blob of heady happiness. Vaguely, she recalled lights and people and murmuring, but mostly, she just remembered a viscous amount of Alec stealing her breath while she resisted the urge to rub herself all over him like a scent-marking cat.

"Oh, please." Eden swiped a dismissive hand in front of her face. "It hardly sounded like you both weren't thinking the same thing."

"That's the problem. We're not supposed to be thinking that."

"And why the hell not?"

"Because this is not real. None of it is. It's all an act. And he'll be heading back to England, if all goes well. It's a sort of business agreement, I guess you could call it."

"Wait. He'll be leaving if all goes *well*? Really? That sounds like the exact opposite of well."

Marisa folded her arms across her chest, uncertain where her indignation was coming from but feeling the need to defend it, nonetheless. "It's just complicated. It's hard to understand."

"Damn right it is, but that's hardly your biggest problem." Eden swept her arm across the living room floor, which was nearly bowing from all the packages that needed to get sent out. "When are Manic and Sid showing up for all this crap?"

Marisa sighed, grateful for the change in subject, though only slightly, because the next object of her mangled life seemed to be in similar shambles. "They said they'd be over around nine. They're letting me use some of their warehouse space tonight to store everything, and then Captain's taking it to the post office in the morning."

"That's awfully nice of them. How much did that cost you?"

"Manic wants some of my homemade Red Hots, Captain asked for a gift card to the movie theaters, of all things, and Sid made me promise to watch the entire original *Baywatch* series with him so he can accurately judge the remakes." Marisa pinched the bridge of her nose. "That's going to be brutal. There are eleven seasons, and because they originally aired on network TV back in the nineties, each season has, like, twenty-two episodes in it. I don't know where I'm going to find that kind of time."

Eden smirked. "Ah. The things we do for love."

"I guess." She sighed and lifted her laptop onto her crossed legs. "As for what I'll be serving at the Ball, here's what I've got for the lineup. I'm going with classic gingerbread but infused with Jamaican ginger. It's way more potent and punchy than the stuff most Americans are used to, and I've found, especially at this time of year, that people are a tad more willing to try something new and interesting if it looks and feels like what they're familiar with."

"Like blow-your-ass-off spicy gingerbread men that'll have people running to the bathroom all night?"

"No. The eggnog will do a fine job of that, I imagine. I'm talking about a traditional gingerbread man, a Christmas staple with the royal icing eyes and everything, but with the bolder flavors of the West Indies. It'll be comfortable but memorable. I got the idea after you and I were in the city for the West Indian Day Parade over Labor Day weekend. You remember the Jamaican bulla cakes we tried?"

A fond recognition crept over Eden's face. "Oh, those were so good."

"Exactly. I think it'll be a hit, and it's something I can easily and quickly make in large quantities with smaller cookie cutters. Besides, thanks to Alec's lovely lip-locking-session-turned-social-media-stunt—"

"Which you ate up. *Literally*." Eden's smile invited an argument Marisa was just not in the mood to have.

Marisa rolled her eyes and returned her attention to her laptop. "Anyway, thanks to, well, *that*, I've got quite a few more eyes on my social media accounts than I used to, so I did a little poll." Then she flipped her screen around to show the latest post to Eden, whose eyes widened at the number of votes for the Jamaican gingerbread to be featured at the Crystal Christmas Ball.

Impressed, Eden said, "Wow. That's—"

"A lot of enthusiastic people who are interested in attending Monica's shindig if I can keep them flowing in treats. I'll be making one treat box filled with an assortment, as that's easier to manage. It'll have the Jamaican gingerbread, a sampling of old-fashioned ribbon candy, and hand-twisted mini chocolate peppermint candy canes. The sugar work I can bang out in advance and can store easily at Manic, Sid, and Captain's warehouse until I have to truck it over to the event. It's a solid treat box offering for sure and one that'll definitely put me on Monica's radar, but it's all hinging on the gingerbread."

A low whistle rumbled through Eden's lips, which was

followed by a slow clap of dramatic proportions. "You're a goddamn evil genius, and I've never been so proud to call you my best friend."

The corner of Marisa's mouth ticked up with pride as she went to the website of the small West Indian grocer about an hour away that always had plenty of the good Jamaican ginger extract in stock. "I'm not an evil genius, just an incredibly stressed-out woman who doesn't like Santa breathing down her neck."

"You're right," Eden agreed, her voice turning silky as she plucked another fistful of gummies from the dish, leaned back, and plopped them, one by one, into her mouth like a Grecian goddess at a bacchanalian festival. The Cheshire Cat grin that surfaced after the swallow was concerning, to say the least. "You'd much rather prefer that a certain other man do the breathing."

Marisa's fingers stumbled across the keys, nearly making a mess of her search bar. Not enough of a mess, however, to prevent her from erecting her Jersey-born-and-bred, always-at-the-ready middle finger. "A gift, madam."

"Aw," Eden said, hugging a throw pillow. "And here I was hoping my true gift would be hearing about a steamy holiday tryst featuring a sex-starved candy maker and a hot Scot in a kilt. Either that or something smothered in chocolate."

Marisa resumed her focused searching, though not without admonishing Eden with a single raised eyebrow. "He doesn't wear a kilt. And the rest of the chocolate I have is reserved for guests of the Ball or the few family members I always give care packages to. I don't have any supplies left to spare."

"Great! Then I'm your cousin now. See? We're family!"

"That's so crazy, because my cousin owes me money."

The raspberries Eden blew at her were a bit much but not entirely out of the realm of what Marisa expected. But once the grocer's webpage finally finished loading, a new annoyance managed to successfully cling to her cranium.

"Out of stock?" she barked.

Eden tossed the pillow aside and scrambled to see what Marisa was looking at. "Damn. That's not good. Is this the only supplier?"

"The only one who'd be willing to work with me on such short notice, yeah. If I had more time, I *might* have been able to go to the city, but not now." No way was New York a viable option. The upcharges for the last-minute order alone would kill her, and New York suppliers were so expensive, to begin with.

"Well, what are the odds his website's up to date? You said he was a small grocer, right?"

"I did," Marisa said, letting her worry stretch out the words.

"Then I'm willing to bet the online inventory hasn't been updated since the Netscape days. Watch, after Christmas Eve, I'm sure the owner's got some college-aged nieces or nephews who'll be home for the holidays and will be tasked with updating things."

The logic was there. Marisa couldn't argue with that, no matter how much she'd like to. "I don't use them often, but now that I think of it, I do usually just call them. I only ever go on their site to check their hours of operation."

"Exactly! Give them a call tomorrow morning. I'm sure they've got exactly what you need. Oh!" Eden grabbed the remote and unmuted the K-drama that had been languishing in silence for the past twenty minutes. "No freaking way. Do you see that? Do you *see* that? Quick. Get your phone out and pull up the timer."

Uncertain of what the hell was going on, with her mind still chewing over the worry of not getting the single-most important ingredient she needed, Marisa blindly did as ordered.

"Aaand *stop*. Okay, how long was that?"

Marisa looked down at her phone. "Um. Twenty-three seconds."

"Now *that* right there, ladies and gentlemen, is some goddamn romance. That was twenty-three seconds of a solid hand linger. Not even a full holding of hands. Just a *linger*. His index finger was the only thing touching her pinky!" Eden said with her hands on her head, her eyes alight with amazement. "I'm telling you, Western media would just about shit their pants if they had to spend that much time on two fingers barely brushing against each other. The Koreans, man, they know a thing or two about yearning. That and fried chicken." Before Marisa could respond, the doorbell rang. Eden paused the episode and popped up off the floor. "I'll get it."

"It's probably the boys picking up the shipments," Marisa said, though the daze that still held her enthralled had nothing to do with helping Eden load orders into Manic and Sid's car.

Slowly, she closed her laptop and tried to make sense of the lingering hands on the TV, but her mind kept tripping over other images. All starring emotionally charged moments where Alec, as if on instinct, had captured her hand, always pressing and prodding his reassurances into her tension points every time her doubt began to creep in.

The Hanukkah party . . .

The car *outside* the Hanukkah party . . .

The pizza parlor . . .

Since their arrangement started, she was hard-pressed to find a time when he *hadn't* been there, holding her hand, urging his strength into her.

Lingering.

And now, with the chaos of Christmas swirling around her in boxes, she couldn't remember what it was like without him.

CHAPTER 17

Alec settled his hands on his hips and evaluated the pop-up tents stationed around West Meadow's dog park. Three tents in total, with an adoption day crowd that was nothing to sneeze at. No, it wasn't the largest gathering, but it was a fair bit better than anything else he could call to mind for a staged outing with Marisa, given the time constraints.

Where there would be kissing.

Might be kissing.

Very hopefully would be touching of some sort. If she needed him to.

If she let him.

"Oh, bloody fucking hell." Alec threw his fingers into his hair, angling for the distraction that usually came when he was looking to tug out his frustrations, but then he recalled he'd opted to keep his hair short the past several months.

Because it impeded his play during the season.

Because it required too much upkeep otherwise.

Because he was *responsible* and had a bloody *job to do*.

The self-criticism had been a touch overloud, apparently,

because at his side, Hugh snorted his thoughts on the matter into the crunchy snow around them, painting the light crust with a drool string that dried on contact.

At least Hugh hadn't pissed all over Alec's boot like the last time the cur felt the need to criticize his plans.

Alec crouched down and gathered up the wily beast's wrinkly face. "Now you listen here. I'll be introducing you to a new friend shortly, and I want you to play nice. Play better than nice. Play the nicest you've ever played. That means minimal slobbering, no jumping, and keep the tricks to fetching a stick and bringing it back. This is what we call a photo op, which means we need to look and behave our best."

Then he leaned close so his nose was almost touching Hugh's snow-covered snoot. "And whatever you do, do *not* run after whatever strange scent you might pick up on. There are a ton of dogs here, as well as families all looking to give one of them a home. It won't do to have you barking and grinding all over a pack of eight-year-olds because one of them has dog treats in their pocket."

The cunning look that flashed in the mastiff's brown eyes wasn't the reassurance Alec had been hankering for, but it was what he'd have to work with. Huffing, Hugh settled into the snow and began nonchalantly crunching away as if Alec had said nothing important.

Infuriating creature. He'd gotten kinder lectures from Brennan after he'd blown a match. To Argentina, of all teams.

"Alec!" Marisa churned up a flurry of chunky snow as she trotted across the field from the parking lot.

His chest tightened, and he couldn't help but smile. Och, she was like a veritable bouncing puppy coming to greet him, all eager limbs and floppy enthusiasm. The crocheted hat she wore sat flat over her ears and cheeks, ending with two pom-pom-studded tassels that swayed in time to her steps. He chuckled to himself.

Could she be any *more* adorable? Not bloody likely.

With her high-necked puffer coat and massively oversized furry hood, there was very little to distinguish her from several of the other double-doodle-dog whatnots prancing about in their Christmas coats and jingle bell collars.

Except her smile.

A fluttery sensation warmed his skin, and his heart nearly sprinted out of his chest at the sight of it. Quickly, he searched his brain for what he'd done that could have earned him such a greeting so he could be sure to repeat the effort, but all that came to mind was her wanting to kiss him again.

And him being way too fucking eager to oblige.

Contrary to his earlier pep talk, he was not responsible.

Hugh stood up, let out an eager bark, and began whacking Alec's calf with his tail.

"Easy, Hugh. You'll get your sniffs in. Just be patient."

"And who would this be?" she asked when she greeted them, all flushed and cheerful, holding out her hand for Hugh to smell.

"Marisa Silver, I'd like to introduce you to Hugh, my brother's frequently unenthused mastiff and, for the time being, my roommate."

Her bonny eyes brightened, and her delightful smile widened. "Oh, so *you're* the one who eats all of Alec's steaks."

"Only the *good* steaks, mind you. The bastard nabbed an entire ribeye clean off the counter before it had even finished resting. The meat wasn't there for thirty seconds before it leapt into this knucklehead's gaping maw, and I had to settle for frozen pizza for dinner."

"Well, I hope you at least heated the pizza up first."

"Haha," he remarked dryly, folding his arms across his chest. "The loss was survivable, but I'll have you know I suffered greatly for it."

At her feet, Hugh was rolling around like a pig in shit, giving her as much of his belly to rub as could fit in front of her. And like a perfectly pleasant woman used to disregarding men in favor of furry animals, she got right to work laying her hands all over him.

Alec was *not* jealous, nor did he yank on Hugh's harness just a wee bit tighter, dragging the beast upright sooner than the dog appreciated so they could get on with what Alec had planned.

"So, what's on the schedule for this morning?" Marisa asked, rising to her feet and dusting off the snow from her coat. "Are we adopting a dog?"

"No," Alec said, leading them over to the rest of the plowed walkways that led toward the tents. "But we *are* here to be seen. This is the annual adoption event where a bunch of the local animal rescues team up to try and find their critters new homes before the holid—" Alec stalled out, remembering that the world *holiday* was not synonymous with Christmas for everyone.

"Christmas, you mean," Marisa finished for him. "It's okay. You can call it the holidays. I won't be offended. Remember, I sell Christmas cheer for a living this time of year. And I also feel that my *boyfriend* should know that about me." She winked at him, and whatever tension that had wrapped itself around his lungs eased each time the corner of her mouth tugged higher.

It was a curious thing to hear the word *boyfriend* and how it had begun to feel so much more than a casting choice. There was still a heft to it, aye, but one his muscles had become accustomed to lifting. It was a good weight, too, one that sat comfortably around him, commending him for finally wearing a skin that seemed to suit so well, as if the life he regularly carried around was a perpetually poor fit.

Hugh took Alec's moment of silence to curl around one of Marisa's legs and rub his swaying jowls all over her boots.

Alec sighed, knowing when another's affection was favored over his. "Here, you want to walk him a bit while we chat?"

"Do I ever?" Marisa eagerly reached for the lead and looped

the handle around her wrist while Alec double-checked Hugh's harness buckles.

"Just hang onto him tight. Mastiffs are huge, powerful animals, but they don't have the energy of, say, a border collie. He likely already expended his maximum allotment of energy for the day just rubbing all over you, but with all these tiny yappers around, there's no saying something won't spook him. And once he pulls—"

"Let me guess. Hang on tight?"

Alec slowed his stride, snatched up her mittened hand, and stared down at her. "No, you hang onto *me*."

In the parking lot, cars began filing in, with doors opening and closing one by one as families, all red-nosed and cheery-cheeked, strode eagerly toward the adoption tents. There were several fenced-off areas where dogs of all shapes and sizes—and decked out in an abundance of flippant finery that had no busi-ness gracing any creature larger than ten pounds—leapt and rolled through the snowy mounds erected by the volunteers for canine enjoyment. Rows of kennels and crates housing all the unamused cats available for adoption were set farther back from the larger crowds but not so far as to be forgotten or left out. The event was small and cozy, with only two food vendors selling wares: one dispensing hot apple cider, hot chocolate, and coffee, and the other handing out warm soft pretzels with tiny tubs of that melted plastic cheese Americans were so fond of.

It was the perfect holiday photo op for what he had planned, set against the backdrop of frosted pine trees and nearby street-lamps adorned with wire snowflakes that would light up as soon as the sun went down.

As expected, Hugh had walked over to the pretzel maven, tugging Marisa and Alec behind him. The two of them engaged in good-natured conversation with people, and Alec bought two pretzels and two coffees, let some of the kids pet Hugh, and made sure everyone's phone was out when he gave donations to the animal rescues while encouraging people to follow Sweetest Heart's Desire online and directing them to the site for Crystal Christmas Ball tickets.

Eventually, his hand had somehow slipped from simply holding Marisa's to banding behind her back and pulling her close. When he finally realized just how personal and cozy he was getting, he remembered they'd yet to discuss those bloody ground rules he'd promised to establish.

As if his conscience were mocking him.

Marisa was just finishing up chatting with a lovely couple who was interested in the Ball when she turned to him, beaming with the glow of what he suspected was a new scheme. "That was the fourteenth couple I've talked to today who expressed interest in seeing us at the Ball. They normally don't even consider going, because it means they'd have to get a babysitter and those are hard to find on Christmas Eve, but they're going to try. They seemed super intrigued with the ribbon candy I plan on throwing in the treat boxes."

"Not the Jamaican gingerbread? I thought that was your fan favorite so far."

Marisa pulled away from him slightly and hugged herself, and whatever comfortable cadence they'd found with each other that morning turned stilted and worrisome. "The grocer I usually work with is completely out of stock of the extract I need. I called him this morning, hoping that perhaps their site just wasn't updated when it said they were out of stock, but nope, it was accurate. Sure, I could try making it with other ginger, but then I worry it wouldn't be distinguished enough. People are paying a pretty penny for tickets. There's no way I can risk anything that would taste even remotely ordinary. I'm going for traditional flavors with flair. I can't do that with the powdered shit, raw ginger isn't suited well for this application, and there isn't enough time to make my own ginger extract. It takes too long to distill properly."

"Did he say when he's expecting another shipment? Or is there another supplier in the area that I could pick up an order from?"

She shook her head. "There's no time. I'll have to think of something else."

"Have any of the other photos of what you'll be serving racked up the interest that the Jamaican gingerbread has?"

"Not even close. But," Marisa said, lifting her chin and squaring her shoulders, doing her best to walk in stride with wherever Hugh was now dragging them to, "I've got some other concepts to try. They're not fleshed out yet, but I'll get there."

Alec heard the trepidation in her voice and the even stronger ring of her determination to fight through it. It was a grit he was very familiar with.

"You're bloody brilliant, you know. Truly." Alec swallowed against the insistent shiver snaking down his spine, the one that urged him to move closer to her like the wholehearted idiot he'd become whenever she smiled at him.

Marisa tugged on Hugh's lead slightly. The mastiff instantly ceased his lumbering and eagerly obeyed, plopping his arse into the snow at her feet in a way he'd never done for Alec. Bloody smitten bastard.

And then another thought flitted through his mind as his chest tightened when she turned to face him. *I'm right there with you, pal.*

"People really seem to like us together," Marisa said, wringing the lead between her hands.

He nodded. "That they do."

"So many people have taken pictures. I haven't checked my phone in a minute, but it keeps vibrating in my pocket. I'm guessing I'm getting all sorts of tags and mentions."

She shifted Hugh's lead to her left hand, leaving her to fidget and pump the right one absentmindedly, as if she were trying to ward off a chill that had set in. Made sense, as she'd largely been keeping her fingers clenched around the strap all this time.

"I have this crazy idea," Marisa said, biting her lip.

"Oh?" He pointed two fingers at her cramping hand and gestured for her to give it to him. Following the most dramatic eye roll he'd ever seen, she finally relented, pulled off her mitten, and gave him her hand.

Bloody Christ, her fingers were freezing and tighter than his joints after a post-match ice bath. He got to work with single-minded focus, immediately rubbing warmth back into them.

"So, about my crazy idea," she said, sighing as she began to move her fingers more freely. "What if you kissed me in front of the large pine tree over by the pretzel cart and made it really convincing that we were together? You know, as per the ground rules."

The ground rules they'd never gotten around to discussing because he was too caught up in whatever sacred magic Marisa always seemed to carry with her.

Roaring heat flooded his body. "I have a crazy idea," he said, lowering his head as he hunted for more of her fragrance with a determination that had begun to border on worship. "What if we didn't call it crazy?"

She lifted her mouth to his, and he bent down, more than eager to claim what she offered, to warm the other parts of her as well, her cheeks, nose, lips—

Hugh's ears perked up, his large body tensing against the lead. Then his broad-skulled head whipped toward the woods right next to the walking path they were on, and Alec caught the flash of orange that had snagged Hugh's attention.

A fox.

Mother*fucker*.

Knowing exactly what was coming, Alec wrapped one arm tightly around Marisa, who was still holding the lead slackly in her left hand. With a speed born of instinct, he yanked her to his chest, barely having time to secure her head beneath his chin before he grabbed the lead from her with his free hand and braced for what was coming.

A massive spray of snow was kicked up against them as Hugh bolted toward the woods, dragging them both to the ground.

CHAPTER 18

Alec gritted his teeth as his back slammed against the cold pavement.

Of course, they'd not had the luxury to fall on the *acres* of padded snow around them. A fiery ache shot up his spine, pinging the precise spot at the back of his head with the echo of his earlier injury.

Thankfully, Marisa had tumbled down with him, landing on his chest with a comfortable weight that eased the pain hammering him from behind. Dark disordered coils of her hair fanned over his eyes, getting in every sort of way, while his brother's beast of a dog nearly pulled Alec's meat from his bones. With one arm still banded tightly around Marisa, he flexed and pulled, his biceps straining with the effort of holding back two hundred and thirty pounds of motivated muscle.

"Hugh, you fucking bastard! Stop your pulling and get your arse back over here *now*!" But the threat lacked the true weight of Alec's ire as every other word was broken up by him spitting out strands of Marisa's hair, and dear lord, was she *giggling* into his chest? Was she for real?

"Holy shit. Holy shit. Holy *shit*!" Marisa shrieked with glee and burrowed closer into his chest, which Hugh had already kicked a fair amount of snow on.

Bloody hell. Didn't the woman have the good sense to sound properly terrified, instead of like a thirteen-year-old going on their first upside-down roller coaster and spewing every curse word they could get away with saying?

"Are you hurt?" Alec ducked his chin down and tried to holler around Hugh's ear-ringing barks, but all that got him was more hair in his face, this time with some snow tossed in for variety.

"No," she mumbled between his pecs, her shoulders bouncing. "Just, you know, horizontal when I wasn't a moment ago."

His stomach tightened with the one amused chuckle he had to spare, likely a result of Marisa's infectiously humorous fierceness and complete lack of good sense. Then he asked in earnest, "Can you stand?"

"Probably."

"Good." Alec dumped her in the snow and quickly rolled to his knees, which brought him face to face with the dog's back end. "I've about had it with you and your snarling, lapping—" Alec went to adjust his grip on the lead, and the slight jostle was the opening the beast needed.

Hugh leapt forward, wrenching the lead out of Alec's hands, and bolted into the woods, funneling a spray of snow behind him and coating the few remaining parts of Alec that had managed to stay dry.

Alec stumbled to his feet and ran after the dog, holding back a curse as a second chunk of snow slid beneath his trousers and down his backside. Once he picked his way through the wooded area, he cornered Hugh, who had his snout down to the ground in front of a small den, with his arse in the air, his tail swaying from side to side as though he were waiting to collect his prize.

Alec snatched up the lead, squatted down, and brought his face right fucking close to the bastard, grabbing fistfuls of whatever scruff he could hold. "Do I need to call your father? Hmm? Or I'll do you one better," he said, adopting his best dad voice. "Do I need to cut back on your treats? Were the two whole pretzels the size of hubcaps that you demolished earlier not enough? Oh, I know. I think I'll fancy switching to a vegan lifestyle for a bit. See how happy you'll be once I replace your rib eyes with those genetically engineered plant-based meat crumble things."

The threat earned him a drool-laced *harumph* that flung sticky strands all over Alec's coat collar.

"That's what I thought. Next time, you'll think better about chasing after a bit of foxy skirt."

"How do you know the fox was female?" Marisa ascended the shallow embankment and leaned her hip against the only patch on a nearby boulder that had managed to stay clear of snow and Hugh's havoc.

Upon seeing Marisa join them, Hugh perked up again, and that tail became a speedy metronome of excitement against Alec's sodden leg.

Exhausted, he groaned as he got upright, rolled his sore shoulder out a time or two, and gestured grandly toward the canine *and* the dog's unavoidable erection, both of which were cheerfully engaged in lusty adoration upon seeing Marisa. "No male like him runs that hard after a creature unless he's sure she's a woman. It's not worth the energy, otherwise."

Marisa leaned down where Hugh was sitting and cocked her head, squinting in the general direction between his legs. Alec smothered a laugh, then waited for it as, sure enough, she jolted upright and immediately looked skyward, a heated flush creeping up her cheeks.

Yup. She definitely saw it.

Any other time, he would have enjoyed stretching out their bit of banter. It had become something he looked forward to with more regularity. Her teasing and him feigning tolerance for it. But there was an uncertainty sparking in her eyes that he didn't like, and he was reminded of where they were and how much time he had left to be the one responsible for her care. Per their arrangement, at least.

"Are you all right?"

She rubbed her shoulders. "I'm fine. A bit shaken up, but I'll survive."

I'll survive. He liked those words about as much as he liked the prospect of playing for Argentina. By all the beer in Scotland, there had to be so much more to the human condition than just fucking survival, right?

"Wait here a moment. Let me tie him up, and I'll check you over."

This time, Hugh obligingly meandered toward the tree Alec selected, which had a nice flat patch of undisturbed snow perfect for a mastiff-sized crater to be carved out in. As expected, the dog got to work immediately scooping out his own sort of den, then circled the space twice before finally settling down for a bit.

It wasn't until all the noises had fallen away that Alec noticed where they were. Hugh had pulled them off one of the park's paved walkways into the woods but not so far that they couldn't still see and hear the people and dogs over at the tents. The sounds were there but muffled, like the quiet hum of tenants in an apartment building behind closed doors as they moved through the hallways. Tree trunks of various sizes cordoned off most of the view across the fields but didn't shield them away from the world entirely. At the edge of their wooded haven, nature had been kind enough to grant them a little snowy cocoon of seclusion.

And if there was one thing Alec knew as a figure in the public eye, it was that privacy rarely stuck around as long as he needed it to.

He returned to the boulder where Marisa had situated herself, but now both of her mittens had been removed. Her hat, on the other hand, still sat sturdily on her head, framing her lovely face. "How on earth did that hat stay on through all that mess?"

She grabbed a fistful of hair that poked out and hung over her shoulder, along with one of the pom-pom tassels, and shook it for effect. "Behold the power of frizz. Able to adhere to woolen fabrics with a single touch. Once the molecular bond is fully activated, no known substance can ever remove its—"

Alec leaned forward, swiped his hand through some snow, and slid his slick palm beneath the wool, freeing the hat neatly from her head.

"Hey!"

"Water dissipates static electricity." He held up the garment for emphasis, then shoved it into the pocket of his coat. "Besides, you're quite bonny without it."

The admission was a happy thing, he found, allowing some of the tightness in his chest to alleviate whenever he was caught off guard by how enticing she was.

Marisa shifted on her feet, seemingly uncertain where to look. "I think that's the adrenaline talking. You're still probably hyped up on all those fight-or-flight hormones. Your judgment's compromised. You can't be trusted." As soon as the words were out, Marisa paled at what they'd seemingly implied and fluttered her hands in front of his face as words of apology slipped from her lips. "I didn't mean that. Shit. I'm so sorry. There's nothing wrong with your brain. You can absolutely be trusted. Otherwise, I wouldn't have asked you to kiss me in front of hundreds of people, or asked you to pretend to be my boyfriend, or wondered whether all those times you put your arm around me was part of the ground rules. You know, we really never did hammer those out. But regardless, they have nothing to do with your injury, and I was a complete asshole for cracking a judgment-based joke at your expense."

"Oh, hush, woman. My mind is fine. I took no offense." He

swept forward in a smooth rush and caught her up against him, holding her beneath his chin and rubbing her back until he could somehow convince her central nervous system that it didn't need to be in survival mode all the damn time. At least not with him.

"Are you sure? Because I am really good at saying stupid shit when . . ."

If he hadn't become so finely attuned to her, he would have missed it, the way her heart kicked up just a bit higher against his, hammering him with a fine flutter he could feel even through their coats.

He held her away from him and lifted a brow. "Are you nervous?"

She twisted her lips, which had turned pouty and pink from the cold. "Maybe."

"Don't be. Besides," he said, grinning, "as you carefully pointed out, we haven't yet defined any ground rules. We've not broken anything because there's nothing in place to break."

"This all just feels so messy at times."

Hmm. Messy. Not sure he liked that word, at least in the context she meant it. "How so?"

"Well, today has been a flurry of ups and downs that would put anyone out of their right mind. The supply of extract I was relying on for my treat boxes isn't available, but then I met Hugh, and thanks to his charm—"

"And mine."

"Of course." She patted his bicep in reassurance. "But thanks to that, we got all this wonderful exposure from the animal rescue event. Then Hugh ran off, and I tripped all over you—"

"I grabbed you so you'd land on me and not the other way round."

"I guess," she mumbled, and he did *not* like the shift in her tone, the one that was filled with indecisiveness and her ever-present worry. "But then you and he were okay, and we both don't exactly seem in a hurry to more solidly structure the framework of whatever the hell we're doing."

"Ah. I understand."

She glanced up at him, her big eyes searching for something he worried he'd let shine through without meaning to. "Really? You do?"

"I do. It's all just . . . nice."

She stilled and stared blankly at him. Then smiled and echoed, "Nice?"

"Yeah, nice. Like after we first kissed. You were the one who said it was nice, if I recall."

"Oh, yeah. I did say that."

"See? You were right from the start. You're not the least bit messy." Then she snorted and buried her forehead against his chest, pulling at his coat lapels for support, or a shield, if he had to guess, but before she could start spewing whatever counter-argument her mind was surely working through, he tacked on, "That's how I know you're human. Muddling through all this is part of what makes the journey so beautiful, even if you can't see quite where you'll end up or how you'll get there just yet."

He hadn't expected to be hit so hard by his statement, but he couldn't very well ignore the truth that he'd just dangled above them like bloody mistletoe.

Marisa's slim arms squeezed him tighter around his middle, pushing warmth into his core and clearing away the haze that had threatened to take over. "When all this is over, would it really be so bad for you to join Argentina if you got to keep on playing and doing what you love?"

Oh, sweet, beautiful woman. How on earth was he supposed to make sure she was keeping her head above the fray when she went and robbed his thoughts from where they'd rather be? On her. Around her. Just *about* her.

"I haven't decided yet. But there's no need to worry. Brennan has it all in hand, and the awareness I'm drumming up is doing exactly what it needs to do," he lied. "It'll all work out in the end."

"That sounds messy."

Messy. The damn word was quickly becoming the bloody tagline of their whole affair.

He poked her side, tickling her a bit and making her squirm. "Quiet, you. We've got more important things to discuss, like those ground rules."

"Ground rules," she repeated as she came down from a laugh that was also thick with an alluring sigh.

And then his own fucking ground rules changed right quick.

She huddled closer against him, and his body thrilled at how perfectly she fit in the cage of his arms. How her scent seemed to meld with the fragrances of the forest, pulling up primal urges and making him wonder just how nice other things would be, things that definitely had no place in the sort of agreement they had.

Alec dipped his head lower, testing the space between them. When she didn't pull away, he brushed her hair to the side, enjoying the wee patch of her neck still visible. She was quite bundled up, as she should be, but that didn't stop him from imagining further.

Tasting her. Kissing her there, right at the tiny hollow behind her ear.

"Marisa," he breathed against her neck. "Regarding ground rules . . ."

"Yes?" The word was more of a sigh than a question.

"Are there any objections to—"

"Oh, shit! I forgot!" She slapped her hand over her forehead and fumbled around in her pocket for her phone.

"What?"

She opened up her calendar and groaned. "My last catering gig is tonight, but I told someone I'd cover their earlier shift, which is right before mine. They'd done a favor for me a few weeks ago, and it totally slipped my mind that I was pulling a double tonight."

He tried to conceal his disappointment. "Oh."

"I won't get home until around eleven. It's the last one I'm taking before Christmas, though. After that, I'm free to work on the treats for the Ball."

He took out her hat and adjusted it on her head, trying to ignore the flutters of frustration knocking around his stomach. "Text me when you get home tonight."

"But it'll be late."

"Just promise me."

She blinked. "All right. I promise. I'll text you the moment I walk in the door."

He nodded, then stole a quick, searing kiss before he winked at her, grabbed Hugh, and led them out of the woods, where they could still pretend to be a proper couple for both their sakes.

And so no one could blame him if he picked up where he left off: regarding her with a bit more affection than was strictly necessary.

For the benefit of the bit.

CHAPTER 19

It was almost midnight by the time Marisa finally plopped her exhausted ass into bed, though not before creeping around her living room like a teenager who was afraid of getting caught out after curfew.

It wasn't that she was afraid of getting caught, per se, but more so shamed.

By her once again neglected menorah.

It was the fourth night of Hanukkah, and there she was, thirty years old, coming home from a double shift and speed walking in the dark past the only relic of her own damn holiday that, despite the inanimateness of the menorah's silver-pedigreed existence, seemed to judge her more than her family. For a microsecond, she thought about making a cup of Earl Grey tea and lighting the candles just to show some belated form of solidarity, that she hadn't forgotten about Hanukkah entirely, that she was, hand to God, still Jewish—though perhaps with a bit more emphasis on the *ish* part. But she just didn't have it in her to fight sleep long enough for the things to burn down on their own.

Maybe she could plug in a night-light in the outlet next to

the mantle? Would that qualify enough to be considered conciliatory?

Likely not.

In the end, bed won out, which sucked on multiple fronts because, up until then, she'd been relying on her supreme exhaustion to keep Alec and the events of the morning from her mind and focus on what she was being paid to do. However, once she was finally alone with her racing thoughts, there was nothing to prevent her from simply plugging her phone into the charger, opening up her texts, and typing out the bare minimum of a message.

Except it was late. Like, so so *so* late. Nearly-the-next-day kind of late. And bothering someone during what she considered emergency hours with a nonurgent thumbs-up emoji was the epitome of rude in her book.

But he was expecting to hear from her.

Her thumbs, locking up with indecision, hovered above the keys, while she took out the sweet memory of Alec's departing kiss and replayed that reel for the umpteenth time.

The smoky, scratchy insistence in his voice when he demanded she text him after she got home.

The way her skin prickled beneath his regard, which had nothing to do with the snow or cold.

The entire lungfuls of breath he'd stolen when he'd snuggly tucked her back into her hat and thieved a kiss, which all happened right before her nerves said *to hell with ground rules* and she almost started shimmying up and down his body like Santa short on time and long on chimneys.

"Fuck a giant Christmas duck. What the hell am I doing?" Marisa fell back onto her pillow, flung her arm over her eyes, and waited. And waited. And waited for the excuses to come, for the reasons why she shouldn't do what she wanted, what he'd freaking asked of her, and just text him.

And they were there, the reasons. There was the whole *he's not your real boyfriend* one, followed by the *he's leaving after the holidays* one, and rounded out by the ever-popular *besides, wherever he winds up, it'll be on a literal other continent, and whatever you might think of Phoebe, you can't fault her for her reasoning on long-distance relationships and wanting to settle down when Alec couldn't.*

Plus, your passport's expired. And you hate flying.

Her body, however, was having none of that. Despite her exhaustion, the damn thing still thrummed with a distracting vibrancy, so much so that she knew she wasn't getting to bed anytime soon.

Marisa sighed and rested her hand over her runaway heart, letting her fingers fall in the valley between her breasts and her mind wander where it would.

But all that did was remind her that she was feeling a whole lot of heated flesh right now and that she was supposed to be talking to Alec.

And she sure as hell wasn't supposed to be thinking about those two things together. But then her thoughts drifted again, along with her fingers, and well, willpower just seemed like the most uninteresting thing to prop up at the moment.

Maybe restraint wasn't what she needed.

Maybe she needed a bit of indulgence, something to take the edge off the past several grueling hours and acknowledge the sweet fantasy of the morning.

A fantasy that was exactly that, but one she wouldn't mind living in a bit longer.

Marisa dragged her fingers down her belly and began to slide them beneath the waistband of her shorts—

Her phone blared through her quiet bedroom, scaring the ever-loving shit out of her and nearly causing claw marks that would be mortifying to explain to any emergency department triage nurse working the night shift.

She jolted out of bed and reached for her phone, which was still plugged into the charger. Any restraint she may have fancied flew out the window as Alec's name appeared on her screen.

"Uh, hi! Hi there. Sorry I didn't—"

"You're home." Alec's words definitely weren't a question, nor were they filled with the smooth confidence she'd always known him to command. He almost sounded . . .

"Were you worried?"

His pause was brief but noticeable, and she imagined him casting his eyes up, as if asking for someone to save him from intuitive women. "I hadn't heard from you. Wanted to make sure you got home okay."

"Because you were worried for me," she needled, smiling.

"Because I asked you to text me when you got home."

"So you wouldn't worry."

The long-suffering sigh he gave was delicious. "So I wouldn't hunt down your felonious friends and see whether they were throwing a party you went to without me. And also," he added, infusing his words with what she suspected was a mollifying smile, "so I wouldn't worry."

The earlier tingle she'd abandoned fluttered to life again, except this time, she hardly knew what to do with it, so she just snuggled down into the comforter and gripped the phone tighter to her ear. "That's got to be the cutest, coziest thing anyone's ever said to me."

He snorted. "Not sure I've heard that before, but I'm in no place to argue with a woman who knows her mind."

"Oh, please. I don't know my mind so much as I am a slave to it. Besides, if I were certain about half the things I should be, I'm pretty sure you and I wouldn't be using deception and a pet adoption event as a battle strategy when it comes to figuring out our lives."

"I wouldn't say that. You seemed pretty sure of yourself this morning, in all the ways. It looked quite bonny on you, that self-confidence. I've noticed it a few times now, the glow you get when you've settled into your own skin. It's a different sort of radiance."

Radiance. Whoa. She had no idea what to make of that or what the late hour was doing to her inhibitions, because she most definitely wasn't the sort of woman who would ever ask—

"Alec, can I ask you a question?"

"Anything. So long as it's not what side of the bed Hugh likes to sleep on, because I'll go to my grave before I admit to being the little spoon with that arsehole."

She laughed, and man, it felt *so* good, in the way things could only feel when one's brain was too exhausted to care about *woulds* and *shoulds* and, instead, just happily floated among the *maybes*, only firing the neurons it needed to, *if* it needed to.

No alternate mode. No safe topics. No eggshells. Just . . . joy.

"I like the way that sounds," Alec added. "Your laugh. I wish I were there to see it."

"See what? Me laughing? It's not as glamorous as you might think. Spoiler alert: I snort more often than I don't. I'm practically a farm animal at times. My mother couldn't take me anywhere when I was a kid."

But despite her attempt at humor, her mouth still had gone dry waiting on his next word, while her brain, ever the A student, sprinkled in all the extra credit tidbits the rest of her body sure as hell never forgot.

Like the exact heat his large hand gave off when he gripped her lower back, or the way his scar scraped ever so slightly against her upper lip when he kissed her, making her nipples harden.

His gruff voice pulled her back to the present. "To see what genuine humor looks like on you, without all the fluff of trying to be funny or laughing so others will like you. It's so bloody tiring, the game we're playing, isn't it?"

Marisa's throat had tightened to the point where she wasn't even sure she could still push out the words she'd wanted to ask.

God, he sounded just as exhausted as she felt, yet he still spoke to her like she'd not only hung the moon but the entire freaking galaxy. So what even were words at this point, when the only comfort her mind could wrap around came in the form of imagining Alec as he was, not as their arrangement presented him to be?

"Alec," she rushed out over a swallow.

"You had a question for me," he said heatedly, as if he knew exactly what she was about to pose. Was expecting it, hoping for it, even.

Then her fingers returned to where she'd left off before he called. "What if we played a different game? One where we didn't have to pretend?" She took a deep, sobering breath, then added, "The one we started in the woods?"

No force on earth could slow Alec's racing heart. It had flown off the runway and was veering toward whatever words Marisa chose to grace his senses with. And he'd fucking take all of them, even though he had earned none of them. Hell, she could curse him out in Gaelic, which he spoke not a word of, and he'd happily set her melodic profanities as his bloody ringtone.

He was in trouble. Big fucking trouble.

But the decision had already been made when he'd claimed her in front of the most influential people in town, and then again in front of his ex-girlfriend, and then again in front of her parents, random social media followers, his fucking brother's dog.

So, what did it matter if he claimed her in this small way as well? For him and him alone? The way his body had been longing to?

And even more terrifying, what if she let him?

Alec shifted in his bed so he was flat on his back, his phone on speaker and lying on his heart. With his limbs free, he managed to kick Hugh out, though it earned him a threatening look of retribution made even more ominous by the dog's angry jowls and preponderance of retaliatory drool.

His new boots out by the front door would probably suffer for his actions, but like he bloody well cared at the moment.

The only care he had in the world was for Marisa.

When he gave her back his full attention, he was met with little jitters of breathy sounds that weren't filled with the confidence he'd heard in her a moment ago but were laced with more of that uncertainty she was always fighting off when they were in public together.

Did she want this? Want *him*? Fuck. Had he read things wrong? She was exhausted, that much he knew, and they were both still hurtling toward this mammoth deadline. Perhaps this wasn't the best idea, even as his cock thumped out its disagreement against his leg.

Ornery wanker.

"I don't want to play any games," Alec said, and it was the truth. Games had winners and losers, and he couldn't bear to see Marisa's face on the other side of whatever it was they were playing at if she thought she'd lost.

"Oh," she said, disappointment thick in her voice.

"Because right now, it's just you and me. And that's what I want. Just you and me. And we don't have to do anything you don't want to do."

Another "Oh." Then a heartbreakingly adorable gasp, followed by a more enlightened "*Oooh.*"

He smiled at what her lips must have looked like, all plump and pink, pushed out into a fetching O that pulled her beautiful brown eyes wider. It was enough that she was with him on the phone, that she hadn't hung up on him after he'd called her at —he checked the time—near to bloody midnight when she'd just worked her arse off all day catering to people who likely didn't appreciate her the way they should. It was enough that she—

"Alec?"

"Mmm?"

"I'm, uh, wearing a tank top."

He'd never been more convinced the woman was out to kill him.

Alec nearly choked on his tongue, with his most recent breath doing its damnedest to ensure he didn't have a next one.

"Aye?" he croaked out while his lower abdominals tensed in time to the T's she'd spoken in *tank top*.

"Aye," she mimicked rather fucking cutely.

Bloody hell. Did the woman not know what state he was in, with his cock about to mutiny over his brain?

"Was that too much?" she asked. "Should I not have said that? I don't know how to do any of this—"

"Where's your hand?"

Fucking Christ. Had he really just gone and blurted out the first thought that came to mind, like a creep with an agenda? He fisted his hand in his hair, *again* wishing he hadn't cut it so short. He was about to apologize, to beg for forgiveness, mercy, blessings, anything she'd give him, when what she said next froze every bone in his body—except one.

"On my breast."

Fuuuck.

Alec coughed. "I'm wearing a T-shirt," he said, like a fool. What was it about this woman that stole whatever was left of his good sense?

"If you were with me, would it bother you if I said I wanted to see you without your shirt on?"

Before the T had landed on the word *shirt*, he'd ripped his off and resettled the phone on his bare chest. "Already gone. And no, it wouldn't bother me at all." Then he paused, his thoughts growing darker through the filter of the phone. "What would bother me would be not knowing how you'd like your breasts touched."

They were doing this. She was really fucking letting him do this, and he was at a complete loss for why he hadn't gotten in his damn car and driven over to her place a good ten minutes ago.

"Slowly," she breathed. "Nothing too aggressive."

"There's no force in the world that would prevent me from taking my time. Tell me, how do they feel?"

"Heavy. The nipples are sensitive."

"Only delicate affection, then. Bloody perfect. I'd want to take my time. Savor every bit you'd want to offer me. Learn what you like."

He slammed his eyes shut, his chest heaving as he imagined worshipping every flawless inch of skin that had been carefully concealed from him thus far.

"I like your kisses," she said airily.

"Then that's what you'll get. As soft or hard as you please. I'd start by tracing the curve of your breasts with my lips."

"Mapping out a breadcrumbs trail?"

He chuckled. "Wouldn't want to lose my way, though I wager it'd be a happy accident to get lost in the valley of your curves."

"Oh my God. You're so—"

"Where would it lead me, such a trail? If I kept going with my kisses?"

Alec was being bold now. Way too bold, and the heat in Cal's apartment must have been set to scorching. The sweat misting his skin was beginning to make him forget he was in bed alone and not with the woman his hands itched to caress.

"You'd go lower."

Please let me go lower. For the love of any holiday with miracles still on offer this late in the game, let me go lower.

Through the phone, he could hear the distinct rustle of sheets, the rearranging—or was that pounding?—of pillows, and he cursed the too short of a time he'd spent in her apartment, when he was regrettably at his least masculine, getting his damn boo-boo iced by Marisa while three of her mountainous male friends, all with criminal records, casually threatened him with implied New Jersey hospitality if any harm came of her at his expense. And having spent enough time in the Garden State with Cal, Alec knew what that hospitality likely entailed.

Him wearing a pair of cement shoes and enjoying a trip down the Hudson River.

But he'd not seen her bedroom, and *that* had been a catastrophic mistake, especially as he took himself in hand and imagined ducking beneath her sheets to taste what only she could offer.

At this point, words fell away from them both and were replaced by throaty breaths and short, eager moans.

"Alec . . . are you feeling . . ."

"I feel you, lass. I feel you all over me. God, Marisa, you're perfect. You're bloody perfect. Come with me." He pumped himself harder, angling his hips toward the ceiling in rushing thrusts, relying on the power of his fantasy to provide any sort of anchor lest he fly off the bed entirely.

She wasn't really his, but his heart remained focused on the duties that would have been his responsibility had she been.

Helping her seek out her pleasure and ensuring she took it from no one else besides him.

It was that single thought that proved to be his undoing. Alec roared his release into the darkness of his bedroom, echoing in time to the lighter cries from Marisa as she found her pleasure alongside him.

And it was through the hazy aftermath of the strongest orgasm of his life that only her sweet voice managed to penetrate.

"It's after midnight."

"Aye," he agreed, though how she could make sense of anything, let alone tell time, was beyond him.

"A new day."

"So it is, and a happy one at that."

"It's going to be a good day." The brightness in her tone warmed him, because he'd likely had something to do with putting it there.

"A perfect one, after you get some sleep."

"Oh, I suppose," Marisa said, though even she couldn't fight back the yawn trying to break free.

"Have coffee with me tomorrow."

"Yes, sir. Whatever you say," she said drowsily.

"Then sleep well."

After Alec cleaned up and checked that Hugh hadn't made leather confetti out of his boots, he hobbled back to bed with the biggest shit-eating grin on his face. But when he went to plug his phone in to charge, he accidentally brushed his thumb over the email icon. He had every intention of closing it right back down, until he saw Brennan's name at the top of the heap, with an all-caps subject line titled ARGENTINA CONTRACT OFFER.

Alec's stomach sank like a stone, then threatened to drag the rest of him down with it as he took in the most lucrative contract terms he'd ever expect to see at his age. It was more money than even Brennan originally thought they could get and scores more than he would ever hope to negotiate out of Great Britain again.

But it was for a coaching position. Not as a player.

Which meant that if he had any hope of staying in the game, the only way to do so would be by leaving it.

Alec leaned forward with his forearms on his knees and cursed.

If this was what Argentina would offer him, he wouldn't just need Arthur's New York sports spotlights and praise. He would need the entire hemisphere's worth of sports reporters to even convince Great Britain to counter effectively.

And if he accepted the offer, everyone, Phoebe included, would know he couldn't go out on top as he'd hoped and boasted about and bloody sacrificed for.

That even titans were still expected to hold up the weight of a world, even if the world was content to spin without them.

Whatever he decided, whether signing with Argentina or holding out for a renewal with Great Britain, either option cast a grim pall over his future.

Because both choices saw him oceans apart from Marisa.

CHAPTER 20

Marisa had never been more grateful for some solid alone time, even if that definition had turned out to be rather relative.

While the cold strip mall bench she was sitting on did absolutely nothing to warm her hind quarters, Hugh's hot breath, on the other hand, was doing a bang-up job of cooking her calf to a nice medium-rare within her jeans.

It was the most sensorially confusing hot seat she'd ever found herself in.

Through the window of the coffee shop Alec had ducked into to call his agent, *again*, a new wave of heat warmed Marisa's body, one that had nothing to do with the meaty mastiff she was currently babysitting—or being babysat by, given the amount of wary canine side-eye he kept sliding her every time she lifted her head to check on a certain Scot.

Alec had squished himself into a tiny booth near the front window, and though his broad forehead seemed to furrow deeply at times, setting all sorts of worries in Marisa's mind, he always managed to toss her a lopsided grin and one of those little two-fingered waves every so often during his conversation.

It did jack shit to calm her pedaling nerves.

Because it was that damnable grin and set of fingers that had kept Marisa up well past the appointed bedtime Eden had informed her naturally came once one hit their thirties.

Marisa puffed out her cheeks and stared at the man responsible for the first decent orgasms—plural—she'd had in months. It made sense, of course, especially when morning-after-phone-sex Alec was still just as brutally charismatic and charming as the model she'd previously become so well-versed with.

Never in her life had she let loose like that. Never had she wanted to, not with any former boyfriends, at least. Though the notion brought a secret smile to her lips and caused her to bite down on her lower one in homage to the prior night's festivities, it also brought to mind another fact that was becoming stickier and more of a mess than undercooked ribbon candy.

He wasn't her boyfriend, but what he'd done last night was undoubtedly a boyfriend thing to do, right down to his whispered words of worship that bestowed every throbbing ache with way more attention than she thought possible through a phone connection.

That man. My *God.*

Over the past several hours, the quiver in Marisa's stomach had perfected its gymnastics routine, expertly volleying between imagining what it would feel like if he had *actually* been against her and he had them both properly naked, and the hollow ache that would torture her if she never got to experience that at all.

Then there was the little matter of how her heart had been feeling, it, too, going through a whiplash routine that had yet to settle on an exit strategy that would see everyone out safely.

Marisa leaned her head back, looking to the sky for answers.

When none came, she offered the only appropriate lament for the situation. "Oy."

But she didn't want to think about feelings or impropriety, especially not when she caught Alec smiling at her again, always flitting a glance her way to check if she was still right where he left her. She supposed that had something to do with Alec swearing that Hugh had given his double-dewclaw promise not to leave her side again so Alec could speak to Brennan. Marisa hadn't been privy to all the particulars, but she got the gist that the dog's manhood may have been threatened.

A cruel tactic but effective, it seemed, as the dog decidedly stayed put.

Around her, the West Meadow strip mall had turned into a beehive of holiday activity. Whatever snow had fallen recently had been cleared, and the walkways had even been dusted of the finer powdery particles that tended to stick around and make the ground unexpectedly slick. Hugh's double coat must have been doing him a world of good against the nippy air, and the cheerful Christmas music drifting from the building's outdoor speakers, along with the tiny, yet crucial cup of whipped cream Alec had brought out for him from the coffee shop earlier, kept the dog properly distracted in between spot-checking her well-being.

Which was good. It allowed Marisa a few minutes to finish her blueberry candy cane and sort out what the hell she was going to do with her gingerbread issue. The ingredients for the other treats—peppermint, cocoa, sugar, a few various fruit flavorings—were all simple enough and easy to come by, but the one thing that people online had clamored for the most, and the sole reason they were even interested in checking out her booth at the Ball, was looking like the one thing she wouldn't be able to deliver.

Perhaps galangal might be an option? Or maybe she could—

Hugh growled as the shadow of a well-coiffed woman

holding a cinnamon roll stretched over his cup of cream, blocking out the remaining good bits at the bottom of the cup.

"Easy, boy. You're fine." Marisa scratched his butt the way he liked it and instantly regretted the action the moment she saw the curtain of red hair tumbling out of a fashionable slouchy beanie in riotous waves.

With not a cotton swab's worth of frizz in sight.

"Hello, Marisa."

"Phoebe. Um, hi!" Not knowing what the appropriate greeting was for one's fake boyfriend's ex-girlfriend, who was also her business competitor and a well-known name in the community to boot, Marisa jumped to her feet, abandoning her candy cane and Hugh's butt, and jutted her formerly itch-scratching hand out in acknowledgment.

Smooth.

Phoebe's well-lacquered lips curled in amusement. Then she extended the tips of her fingers and gripped the ends of Marisa's in a cluster before giving the barest shake possible. "So," she said, breaking off a piece of gooey cinnamon bun and popping it daintily—who the hell ate a cinnamon bun daintily? —into her mouth. "You've been very busy on social media, I see. Looks like you've got some rather popular options for the Ball."

"Yup. Sure do." And that was when Marisa realized two things simultaneously: first, that Phoebe had been paying attention to her competition. Second, and the one that had far more dire implications, Marisa realized in horror, was that she hadn't checked on anything the Plant Nanny had posted regarding the Ball. Like, at all.

Shit shit shit.

Marisa's fingers itched to pull out her phone to see just how monumental the scope of her mistake had been, but she couldn't do that with Phoebe standing there. Instinctively, she glanced at the space in front of the window where Alec had been sitting, but he wasn't there. Instead, his back was turned to her, and he was pacing in small circles with his phone to his ear, gesturing animatedly.

"What are your plans, if you don't mind my asking? Since you know what I'm preparing and all, and it's pretty late in the game to change course or anything." Oh, the lie tasted like whatever Hugh had just decided to start licking off the walkway. "You speak to Monica at all regarding how your recruitment's going?"

"Oh, we're in touch regularly."

"Really?" Marisa liked that not one bit.

"Of course! Well, I had to be to see whether she could create a promo code for some of the guests I was sending her way."

Marisa's thoughts nearly stalled out. "A promo code? How is that fair? I didn't even know that was an option."

"There are always perks to volunteering, so why would the couples-only Crystal Christmas Ball be any different?" Phoebe swiped a dollop of icing with her pinky, and Marisa and Hugh both held their breaths, tracking the dangling drop just as her tongue caught it at the last second. The moan that escaped the woman's lips could have been turned way the hell down. "I know you and Alec have been doing an amazing job at bringing in guests, and quite frankly, you were right. I just wasn't able to convince the New York contingent of my coupled-up fans to schlep all the way out to Jersey and pay for a two-hour Christmas Eve event. You'll definitely be beating me on the revenue there."

There was sincerity, as well as a bit of sadness, in the remark that nearly caught Marisa off guard and caused the tension in her chest to ease ever so slightly.

"But when Monica and I discussed the volunteer option—"

Volunteer. There was that word again. "What volunteer option?"

Phoebe's smile widened. "Well, since Alec is so well-loved, especially by Monica's friend Arthur and his sports connections,

I decided to see whether anyone would be interested in attending as a volunteer. Doing so would give them free access to the Ball, therefore lifting the couples-only restriction that's a requirement of admission, and in return, as volunteers, they'd have the opportunity to meet Alec, and everyone else, in person before the official start of the event, as well as sample any of the wares at no cost."

Marisa's eardrums nearly ruptured at the explosion of bull-shit the woman in front of her just spewed, because surely she didn't just say— "At no cost? But it *all* costs! That's the entire point of this thing. To drum up business and sales."

Those red lips pursed tighter, and Phoebe picked off another bite of thickly iced cinnamon bun to savor. "Of course there's a cost. That's why I suggested the donation stipulation for all volunteers."

"Donation stipulation?" She was not hearing this. Nope. She was not hearing any of this.

"Any volunteer I recruit would be given donation cards containing exclusive details of all the future programs Monica will be running in the New Year. They'll be granted advanced access and opportunities to sign up to attend and donate their support before anyone else, but only if they fill out the cards and turn in their pledges and payments before the Ball is over, like a stroke-of-midnight kind of thing. I thought it was fitting, given the theme."

"And doing that would allow your volunteers to claim their charitable donation as a tax credit before the year is out, and Monica's organization gets a convenient influx of cash before the fiscal year ends," Marisa breathed, piecing it all together behind the haze of the angry red nightmare swimming before her.

"Exactly. See?" Phoebe shrugged. "That's why you'll defi-nitely have me beat in the ticket sales department. Now, as for treats, I've got quite a popular assortment planned."

Marisa wasn't hearing this. She wasn't hearing any of this, not between the blood pounding in her ears and Hugh barking his disapproval at whatever squirrel likely had the gall to encroach on his sweet treat. She searched for Alec, but all she could see were Phoebe's perfectly tailored shoulders, stuffed into one of those premium parkas that would cost Marisa three months' rent plus some good kidney payout.

But Hugh's barking didn't relent, and when he began to tug more insistently on the leash, she saw what had intrigued him, and a new horror struck.

Phoebe brought the final mouthful of icing-smothered cinnamon bun to her lips, but not before a dollop of icing dripped free. Like a fly to shit, Hugh lunged for it, leaping and planting his front paws high on her coat, dead center on her breasts. The look of indignant shock on Phoebe's face was all but wiped clean as Hugh's big tongue whipped out and captured the icing mid-air in one drool-laden lick.

The ripping came next, and it was the most horrendous sound Marisa had ever heard.

One of the metallic buttons on Phoebe's coat caught the edge of the very full and flimsy poop bag loosely tied to the back of Hugh's harness. Marisa stared, frozen. One by one, turds tumbled out like well-trained soldiers and followed the arc of the air before landing expertly, painting Phoebe's fine coat in shades of dog shit.

Phoebe and Marisa screamed at the same time. Hugh barked and jumped with excitement. Somewhere nearby, a gaggle of teenagers wheezed through intermittent laughing fits, all while Bing Crosby provided the *White Christmas* soundtrack to Marisa's own personal hell.

"Oh God, it's in my ring!" Phoebe hollered, flapping her hands over the soiled fabric while inadvertently swiping her fingers through Hugh's morning finest. "Fuck, I think it just got in my cuticle!"

Marisa yanked out the roll of clean poop bags, at a complete loss for what to do except, well, clean up poop. Quickly, she ripped out two bags, shoved her hands in them, clicked her plastic-encased fingertips together like lobster claws—as one does when they're about to get to work—and rushed toward Phoebe.

"I'm *so* sorry! Let me clean up what I can." Marisa ran her hands down the front of Phoebe's coat in large oven-mitt-sized swaths, hoping to clear as much as she could, but instead, she only aided in turning the woman's coat into a monstrous shit-filled finger painting.

"Get off me!" Phoebe whirled away from Marisa just as Alec came running out of the coffee shop, pocketing his phone in the process.

"What the bloody hell is going on?" All it took was for Alec to look at Hugh—who now sat upright, proud as he pleased, and had just let out a lip-fluttering burp—then back to Phoebe for understanding to dawn on his features. "Jesus fucking Christ. Phoebe, are you—"

"Don't say another goddamn word," she seethed, finally undoing the coat buttons so she could rip the thing off and toss it into the nearest garbage can. "I'm noticing a pattern, Alec. You're always more than happy to fall in line with messy fantasies than real life, which explains so fucking much about this ridiculous setup you two have going on." Then she glared at Marisa with enough fire in her eyes to incinerate every marsh-mallow west of the Hudson. "And might I suggest you rethink any industry that has you looking after customer welfare. Or interacting with people entirely, for that matter."

Her words slapped Marisa in a way that no amount of family disapproval ever had. And it stung ten times worse because Alec was there to witness it.

God, what must he think of her?

Marisa's throat tightened as Alec took the leash from her,

and she desperately tried to sink back into her coat and hibernate inside it until spring.

"Phoebe, enough of this," he said, tossing the woman his jacket out of courtesy. "I'm sure it was all an accident. If you've a quarrel with anyone, let it be me you fight. Hugh's *my* brother's dog. Marisa had nothing to do with it. She was only trying to—"

"Help?" Phoebe asked. "Like when she spilled food all over me at the cocktail party? Was that another accident, too?"

Alec's face reddened, and his brows sank low in warning. "You bloody well know it was."

"Do I? I don't know anything, apparently. For example, I can't for the life of me figure out why you'd choose a game, one that damn near tried to kill you at every turn, over me. I was there for you, Alec. I was waiting for you, quietly loving you, ready for you to choose me, and instead, you choose this? *Her?*" Phoebe pointed a finger at Marisa, and God, she hated how Phoebe was wearing Alec's coat when she did it, how his presence was somehow wrapped around the woman in support as she doled out her jealous fury. "And you're *still* playing all these games? When are you going to grow up, for god's sake? You're almost, what, thirty-five now? Isn't it time for you to start taking things seriously?"

It was hard to imagine what dejection would look like on such stony, handsome features, but Marisa got her answer, and it gutted her for so many reasons, not the least of which was because she knew what it felt like to wear that sort of perpetual disappointment.

"I've told you before, and this'll be the final time I say it. You and I didn't fit."

"And you two do? You both are happy to just fall in line with whatever this game is that you're playing?" She punctuated the point by waving her shit-stained hand in their general direction.

"*Yes.*"

The force of the word was like an insistent finger beneath

Marisa's chin, pulling her attention toward him. As he stood there in just a Henley shirt and jeans, otherwise bare to the cold except for whatever insulation his anger provided, he didn't look like a fake boyfriend. Or fake anything, for that matter.

He looked *real*, like someone Marisa wanted in her corner for everything life decided to throw at her, who actually wanted to be there, had been the first to sign up, even.

He looked resplendent and powerful, with his tense muscles firing in defense of her and championing every ridiculous dream she'd ever shared with him.

Then, as Phoebe stormed off and Hugh began licking his paws, Marisa's breath caught and her throat tightened as the final truth of what she saw turned her eyes liquid.

He looked like *hers*.

CHAPTER 21

Alec waited, but by the time Marisa came out of the coffee shop with her hands freshly washed, his mood hadn't improved much, nor had his relationship with Hugh. He'd just finished texting Cal this very thing when the damn dog started whining again at her approach.

"The closer I get to this stupid Ball, the more I think I'm not cut out for any of this," Marisa said, twiddling with her hat's tassels and looking anywhere in the fucking universe except at him.

"*Any* of this?" he said slowly, not liking the way his heart clenched with the same vigor as his fist holding Hugh's lead.

Marisa's hand flew out in exasperation toward the direction Phoebe had fled. "She seems like she's ten steps ahead of me, when I was foolish enough not to keep tabs on her. That was my fault. And now she's got this volunteer payment scheme that's a complete blow out of left field. I feel like I'm back at zero again, especially when I can't even deliver the cookie I promised to everyone."

"You were too busy with your own life to worry about hers,

as you should be. The woman meddles far too much in other people's affairs."

"But it's working for her. This whole competition just to win Monica's favor? This isn't business. It's blood sport. I never intended to go along with all that. All I wanted to do was to craft candy and make people smile."

"Do you regret it, what we agreed to do?" Beneath the words he said were the ones he couldn't bring himself to truly ask. *Do you regret me?*

Marisa twisted her lips and sighed, then looked at him, her expression softening. "No. Not in the least. Let's face it. If I weren't begging Monica, I would have been trying some other scheme to make Sweetest Heart's Desire work. It would have been a cruelly unfair pill to swallow, not being able to quit my catering job after I worked so hard to do so, but I would have kept going and found a way. Resilience is in my DNA, after all. Well, that and high cholesterol."

Alec chuckled, relief sitting high on his heart at her ability to still crack a joke after what he'd witnessed. "So, what you're saying is that Hugh was actually doing a good thing by trying to save you from coming into close proximity with the cinnamon bun. Fending off all those triglycerides in the icing and whatnot."

Her spirited smile returned, warming him against the chilly air. "A true mitzvah."

"It was a sacrifice of *mastiff* proportions, you might even say."

"Oh my God, stop." She pinched the bridge of her nose. "I can't take the groaners."

"I'll stop when you realize that Phoebe's got nothing on you. She may be the Plant Nanny and can diaper a fern while her customers are down the shore or whatever the fuck it is that people with more money than sense pay her to do, but she doesn't know what makes people happy this time of year."

"How can you be sure?"

Then he pulled out his phone. "Because she doesn't sell Christmas. She sells anxiety. Look."

Marisa came near him, and he had to resist leaning into her subtle scent as she read the screen. On the Plant Nanny's home page were scores of services ranging from the *Weekender's Weeping Willow* package to the *Vacationer's Violet Indulgence* à la carte offerings, all words he'd never thought a grown man like himself would ever read in that order.

He was already itching to clear his browser history, but he held his phone steady so Marisa could see more of the ridiculousness Phoebe was offering.

The one common facet pasted all over the Plant Nanny's website was her abundant use of scarcity marketing tactics. There wasn't a single product image or graphic that didn't have the words *Time is running out!* or *Limited quantities available!* plastered across it. Phoebe even had an auto-play video banner at the top panning through calendar pages, each one filled with angry red Xs, presumably crossing out another open service slot a customer narrowly missed out on.

And the same thing went for her Christmas confections, which she'd yet to fully show off in detail, choosing to create an air of mystery around what she'd be revealing at the Ball. That didn't stop her from blanketing *Preorder now, because when they're gone, they're gone!* all over the fucking order buttons.

"She's afraid," Alec said, hoping his words could soothe some of the tension that had tightened Marisa's jaw. "Just plain running scared. That's all any of this is. As long as I've known her, she's always been a driven woman, not always in a healthy way."

Marisa drew closer, bumping her shoulder against his, as if trying to keep *him* warm, when her touch alone turned his body into a fucking furnace. "I see what you mean. The color scheme by itself tells the story pretty succinctly."

Again, she wasn't wrong. Everywhere over the screen, he was assaulted with shades of fluorescent orange, fire-engine red, and lime green—that last one not even fitting the usual calming verdant hues he associated with most flora. Odd choice for a supposed plant enthusiast.

"Holy hell," Marisa said, squinting and waving her fingers in front of her face in mock offense. "It looks like a Teenage Mutant Ninja Turtles convention. All that's missing is the . . ."

She scrolled down farther and abruptly stopped when they were both assaulted by a collage of what Alec could only describe as aggressively toned pansies in shades of McDonald's Grimace purple and that electric blue raspberry color one could only usually find in convenience store slurpy dispensers.

"Ah, there it is," Marisa said, nodding sagely. "For a second, I was worried we weren't going to see any Leo or Donnie representation."

"I was always partial to Splinter myself."

"Hmm. I'm not really getting rat sensei vibes from you."

Alec shrugged. "Well, you haven't seen me attack a frozen pizza yet while Hugh's breathing down my neck. It makes you appreciate the kind of patience that rat had for mealtimes with animals. It was a wonder Splinter got fed at all."

And just like that, her smile returned in full force. Unfortunately, his chest didn't even have time to expand from the joy of seeing it before it deflated.

Because a text from Brennan popped up on the screen, and he wasn't able to swipe it away fast enough before Marisa read it.

"Am I allowed to ask what that's about?"

Alec pocketed his phone and started walking them through the parking lot, letting Hugh freely sniff now that they were away from people. "I've got an offer."

"From Argentina?"

"Aye."

"Is it something worth considering?"

"Honestly? I'd be foolish not to consider it. They want me to coach, though, and they'll pay me well for it. Far better than I can reasonably hope to get out of Great Britain or any other team that would have me as a player."

He briefly filled her in on the details of what he was coming to suspect might very well be his reality once the season was over. After he'd gone through laying out all the terms, he wasn't sure what he expected to see on Marisa's face. Pity, resignation, perhaps some eye contact avoidance, especially given the verbal lashing Phoebe had handed him in front of Marisa. Instead, what he got was a stony look of determination.

It was the same look she wore when she'd instructed him to meet her at Sal and Enzo's, where they initially mapped out their battle plan for how they were going to sort through all of this mess and persevere.

God, had it only been a few weeks ago, if that?

It seemed like he'd been devotedly following his general's orders ever since he'd marked her at the cocktail party and bothered to listen to his curiosity for once.

"Sounds like your heart's not in it, Alec."

He shrugged. "Not sure whether I have the luxury of—"

The backward tug on his arm was the only indication that he had been mindlessly moving down the walkway. Alone. However, the vise grip Marisa held his wrist in was anything but mindless. Nor was the stern, rather drastic slant of her brows, or the shards of accusatory shame dancing in her eyes she seemed about ready to slash him with.

"Sounds like your heart's not in it, *Alec*." The words were slow to come, with each syllable stomping its emphasis into the frigid pavement. But his name landed like a crater and had her voice wobbling with the sheer force of her insistence.

"No," he admitted. "My heart's not in it." There. He'd confessed his fear, and the unfortunate reality that Phoebe had shone a spotlight upon for Marisa to see and judge. "I wish I could be as brave as you, sometimes," he whispered, scratching at his scar so his free hand had something to do other than punch out the nearest car window. "I don't think I can live with the scrutiny of my choices the way you can. It seems like a learned skill that a brute like me could never have much of a knack for."

"You're wrong." Marisa moved closer and kicked her chin up with practiced precision, as if it were the blade by which she held all other threats back. "Choices are options. Sometimes they're favorable, and sometimes they're nothing but dilemmas, but they don't have to be permanent. Sometimes, they just need to be a stopover on the path you're meant to take later on." She slashed her eyes down at Hugh, but Alec didn't miss the sheen that had begun to form there. "I wasn't meant to be a librarian, and I'm sure as shit not meant to be a cater waiter. I'm not meant to be a disappointment or another failing business owner who can't get her life off the ground. I'm not meant to be any of those things, but that doesn't mean I avoid choosing them if I have to, if I know that those choices, incredibly sucktastic as they may be, will eventually lead me toward my goals. And that is the business I stand on." She brought the shimmer back to him, her eyes like warm chocolate with enough bitterness to give the sweetness backbone, and he wondered why he ever bothered thinking he could fake this.

Because there wasn't a chance in hell he could. Not anymore. And maybe he never had.

Alec cradled Marisa's head in his palms and kissed her, wrapping himself in whatever beautiful, drugging essence she possessed. He smiled against her surprise, especially as her lips softened and she wrapped her hands around his neck, molding her body to his, somehow making him feel lighter despite her added weight. Rather than fighting for every extra hour he could have with her, he finally let himself wonder what it would feel like to just . . . be.

It was strange and not entirely comfortable just yet, but he desperately needed more.

Alec moved to deepen the kiss, not giving a ripe fuck how many teenagers had stopped to gawk at them, when Marisa groaned into his mouth and pulled away.

He liked it not one bloody bit.

"Get back here. I haven't decided whether I prefer the blueberry flavor on your tongue more or the peppermint. I have many more choices to make. General's orders and whatnot." He dipped his head down, chasing her mouth, and was rewarded with a half-hearted feint on her part.

"As much as I'd love to continue making good choices with you, I have to get over to the boys' warehouse. These treat boxes aren't going to put themselves together, and Captain reorganized part of the facility's kitchen space so I could use it for the next few days."

"How long will you be there until?"

"Late. But if I can get over there now, it shouldn't be too bad. The ribbon candy will be the trickiest to get right, but once it's all pulled out and shaped, the hard part's over, and things can move more quickly from there."

"Text me once you're home. And I promise not to be an arse about it this time." He meant it as a joke, something to pull her smile out, but an unfamiliar expression flitted over her features, one he'd never seen in person but had dared himself to imagine last night.

Marisa pulled away from him. "No."

Alec's body revolted, responding to the betrayal on an elemental level. He nearly lunged for her, but Hugh chose that moment to get up and stretch, his elongated barreled body blocking Alec's way.

A fine fucking time for that beast to be making bloody choices, too.

"No?" A wellspring of hurt began to scratch beneath the delicate hatch he'd only just begun to latch down.

Had the kiss backfired and instead of drawing her closer to him, it'd only succeeded in giving her more time to mull over Phoebe's antics? Had he fucked this up just like everything else?

He tried to swallow against the torrent of emotions and fear, wracking his brain for how to make her believe that he was more than the venom Phoebe spewed about earlier. "Marisa, I—"

"I don't want you to text me, Alec," she said firmly, freezing him to the spot. "Because I want you to be waiting for me in my apartment when I get home."

CHAPTER 22

The fact that Marisa could even turn her doorknob was a miracle in and of itself. God, her fingers were numb, and her swelling knuckles were even worse, gnarled to the point where dunking them in ice wouldn't help so much as likely freeze them in place.

If it were possible to have one's ass kicked by a molten-sugar-coated candy thermometer and what surely amounted to miles of pulled ribbons, she'd succeeded. And then there was the monster gut punch of having to scrap her gingerbread concept.

Without it, all she had to offer Monica's guests was what amounted to a smattering of hard candy found in every grandmother's foyer candy dish at Christmastime. True, they'd be the best hard candies anyone ever put in their mouths, the kind people would cheerfully snap a tooth on and say *worth it*, but regardless, it had been hours, and she still hadn't come up with a gingerbread replacement, let alone a showstopping one.

For some reason, defeat tasted even more bitter when coated in sugar.

After toeing off her shoes and dropping her bag and keys

somewhere in the vicinity of her kitchen table, she was met with a soft glow coming from her living room.

Alec.

He was there, lying on her couch, waiting for her, just as he said he would be. And he looked appropriately rumpled.

Once he caught sight of her, he smiled, and memories of her earlier gingerbread trauma faded. God, he looked good on her couch. More than good. Extra good.

And Marisa stared down at herself and winced. She looked like she'd been pulled through a sugar paste extruder.

Alec kicked off his sock-clad feet from her couch cushions, paused whatever he had been watching on her TV, and rose to greet her, not even bothering to smooth down his shirt or pull the hem free from where it had gotten snagged on a belt loop. The overhead lights were off and the curtains closed. The only lights left on to offer any sort of illumination were the dimmed ones from the kitchen and—she gasped—the glowing Hanukkah candles in her shabby menorah, which must have just been lit, judging by how little they had burned down.

"Why are my . . .?" She was about to ask why he'd bothered lighting them at all, let alone close to eleven thirty at night, but her words were swallowed up by the Korean couple frozen with lips centimeters from each other on the screen. "Wait. Were you watching my K-drama?"

Alec's cheeks reddened, and Marisa got the distinct impression that, had he been wearing a hat, he would have yanked it off his head and mangled the brim nervously in his hands. "It was on your watchlist, and it looked interesting." Then he cleared his throat. "Um, so, how'd everything go?"

Oh, she'd have to unpack that reaction later. Preferably with Eden present and a few bottles of soju under their belts.

"Good. I made decent headway on all the sugar work. The ribbon candy is all shaped and cut. I just did two flavors. The first is a blackberry cream, and then, to keep it easy, I just repurposed my homemade Red Hots syrup into the second batch but toned down the heat slightly. Eden's stopping by tomorrow to help me bag those up while I work on the mini chocolate peppermint candy canes."

"I can help too if you need it."

Marisa nodded distractedly, her thoughts roadblocked by the lit candles and the glow they cast across Alec's stubbled face. "That would be great." And then she asked, "Uh, why did you light the candles?"

Alec shrugged and walked over to the mantle, where a second box of candles sat next to her sad seen-better-days box that still held at least half the candles from last year that she'd meant to light and hadn't. "It's Hanukkah. Still the fifth night, right?"

"Yeees," she said skeptically. "But it's well past sundown."

"So you missed the sunset." He shrugged. "It's not your fault you forgot. Just because you were busy doesn't mean it didn't happen."

"But it won't count." Right? Hadn't that always been the fear holding her lackluster holiday practices in place? That doing the small bits could manage here and there would be seen as wasted effort, so why bother?

He scratched the back of his neck and seemed to reflect on how she'd forgotten yet again to celebrate her own damn holiday.

Had she been thinking ahead, she could have brought her menorah over to the warehouse. Could have spared all of the ten seconds it would have taken to light the candles so she could at least feel a small connection to her tradition, instead of constantly feeling adrift in a sea of other people's festivities.

"You know, when I used the spare key you gave me and first got here, I didn't like the look of what you had going on."

Marisa bristled but bit back anything she might say that would inadvertently make her shame flare hotter. The thing was already on a roll and didn't need the encouragement.

"I went to three different grocery stores, until I found one that still had some Hanukkah candles left. An older woman helped pick a box out for me. Apparently, these were the last *good* candles, whatever that meant. I wanted to light them when you got home because I remember how bonny you looked staring into the flames at your parents' house on your birthday, during the first night of the holiday. You just seemed happier, with the fire glowing in your eyes and bits of gold dancing in your hair. And your candles looked like they'd had a rough go of it, so I thought I'd help and give your set a refresh, aye? Because if this is what makes you smile, then it all counts."

Marisa joined him and wished she didn't feel so goddamn fragile all of a sudden.

"Sometimes there's a lot of pressure, you know?" She sniffed back the emotional strain, but not before Alec curled his arms around her and pulled her close. "At times, I'd miss a day lighting them because I had a catering gig or I had too many orders to fulfill, and the guilt of missing it would ramp up all over again. That if I couldn't even manage to do the barest fucking minimum of lighting a few candles for what's considered a minor Jewish holiday, then it felt like too much to bother with the rest. What was the point?"

"The point," he said firmly, with all the confidence she didn't feel, "is that it's pretty and festive and a part of you, and it doesn't need to be anything more than that. One of the best things about joy is that it's generally very forgiving. Otherwise, why on earth would those blueberry candy canes be so popular? It's not the taste, that's for damn sure. By the way, do you know you have half a dozen boxes of those things in your cabinets? Are you worried there'll be a shortage and that all the holidays will be canceled next year or something? I hate to break it to you, but they're the sorts of things that come round regularly."

He looked down at her with tempered amusement. Then a harsh laugh squeezed through her lungs and chased away the tremors from the emotional vise grip her throat had been stuck in.

"Hey." He chuckled, pulling her away from him slightly and lifting his fingers from her shoulders to try and aid his argument. "I don't make the rules."

Whatever remained of her exhaustion winked out of her body as she started to see things in a different light. Whatever magic was in those *good* candles was clearly working miracles that, before Alec entered her life, she'd had no access to.

They stood there, socked feet mere intimate inches from touching each other while her heart hammered out the very insistent reminder of *why* she'd given him the key to her apartment. Why she wanted him to be waiting for her and why a full-blown Mardi Gras parade was taking place in her stomach as his powerful chest seemed to reach for her each time he breathed.

Oh, who was she kidding? Fake girlfriend or not, she would happily be caught in whatever spell he wove, especially since the more exhausted she was, the more likely it was that her shame and inhibitions delighted in expressing their competing interests.

Marisa's toes betrayed her, lifting her higher to Alec's mouth, but whatever sweetness she had been expecting him to deliver as he kissed her was quickly thrown aside once he wrapped his arms around her waist and savored what they'd never had the time or opportunity to explore.

All sorts of deliciously spirited grunts rumbled through Alec's chest, each one thrilling Marisa until her toes curled. His fingers dug into her waist with deliciously possessive hooks that had her opening her mouth to him wider, her tongue seeking out more of whatever it was about this man that her heart had latched on to.

Instead, what she got was a mouthful of subtly sweet and unapologetically artificial blueberry.

"You wicked, judgmental thief," she said against his lips. "And after you just spent how many precious sentences berating me over my candy cane choices?"

His sensual lips slid over her jawline until they were bestowing apologetic kisses into the hollow behind her ear. "I had to know what all the fuss was about. Besides, I'm thinking blueberry might be my new favorite candy cane flavor."

"And why would you say that?" Just when she expected him to do something far more wicked with his mouth, he surprised her yet again by doing the wicked thing with his words instead.

"Because you're fond of it, and I'm fond of you."

There had been precious few experiences in Marisa's life where she'd been rendered speechless, and Alec Elms accomplished the task while tasting of chemically crafted fruit, wearing no shoes, and lit by the backdrop of Korean lovers who didn't know they were lovers yet but were on the cusp of finding out. (She'd seen that episode already.)

What she hadn't seen yet was how her own story would play out. There were just so many knobs and gears that she'd been juggling to turn right and left lately, hoping each new combination would be the winning one that would allow her to live the life she wanted without having to shave off any more serial numbers that made up who she was.

Yet there she stood, being smothered by every depiction of what her wants looked and felt like: Alec's heated mouth trailing over her neck, the hardness of his cock pushing against her hip bone, her skin prickling as she pressed her breasts closer against him.

It was enough to make her head spin. And whether it was all real or imagined, she wasn't ready to get off the ride just yet.

Marisa found Alec's hand and pulled him behind her into her bedroom, smiling at how he gaped at her.

Never in all her life had she been so thrilled to put an end to a conversation.

CHAPTER 23

Alec had never given much thought to the finer qualities of bedrooms. Perhaps that was because they'd always been so utilitarian. A place to lay one's head during months-long stretches of travel. A bed was pretty much a bed. Firm? Soft? He'd never bothered to care enough to differentiate.

But oh, he fucking cared now.

Marisa was all softness, and the bloody woman mocked him with it as her generous hips swayed in front of him while she pulled him down the hall. His damn erection grew more eager, gleefully tying itself to the teasing rhythm of her body.

A body he'd soon have against him, sprawled out naked on what he had no doubt was the softest bed he'd ever deigned to sully with his sixteen stone of Scottish bulk. Hell, for the past month or so, he was used to sleeping next to an odorous mastiff fond of kicking him in the balls during doggy dreams and slobbering all over Alec's pancake of a pillow the mutt had claimed as his own.

He'd waited—really fucking patiently, it was important to

note—until the backs of her legs were brushing the bed before he resumed his worship of her mouth, still not believing for one second that he was here and being given the privilege to cherish her properly.

Alec slanted his lips over hers again, cupping her cheeks and tracing his thumbs across the smooth planes of her cheekbones. She sighed against him, delving deeper into the kiss and molding her luscious body to his. For the briefest of moments, his mind threatened to short-circuit, but then a bit of sense settled back over him as he recalled what he'd intended to do next.

"I'm coming back to this mouth of yours. Don't you worry."

"Where are you going?"

God, even her words had turned thick, as if he needed one more reason to happily give her every spare bit of breath in his lungs.

Alec skimmed his lips over the slope of her neck, whispering words of adulation over every smooth surface of bare skin that had painted the backdrop of his fantasies. His fingers flowed easily into the coordination his body had honed for years, working in tandem with his mouth to peel away the layer of her crewneck. Once all her wild hair was freed from the collar, it resettled over her shoulders, framing her breasts like intricate vines draping a marble goddess in a museum.

Every gasp and moan that Marisa breathed into his neck fed his hunger. Good Lord, was there anything about this woman that wasn't bloody perfect?

He got his answer when she deftly grabbed his hands and guided them around her back to her bra clasps as if he'd been plucked from a lottery and was the luckiest son of a bitch on this earth. A few seconds of tricky fingerwork was all it took for the cotton to fall away, taking the entire reservoir of his sanity with it.

Marisa stood before him, everything above her high-waisted leggings unapologetically bare to him, while he stood there, blinking, like the daft fool he was, eyeing the sweet lushness of her displayed with all the confidence he'd clearly, and right fucking stupidly, left behind somewhere else.

She bit her lower lip, and the rosy peaks of her breasts pebbled sharply, splitting his attention in two. Or three.

He took two steps toward her and drifted his fingertips over her nipples. Her gasp of delight all but reached out, grabbed him by the cock, and pulled him over the precipice he'd been trying to avoid for weeks but now couldn't think of a reason to stay away from.

The more he felt of her warm skin, the more he was certain there was no possible future where he could exist as a complete whole of himself without Marisa.

"I think it's your turn," she said, pouting as she let him ease her back onto the bed.

With military precision, he whipped his shirt over his head and bowed his allegiance to her marvelous breasts, mounding and kissing what he'd only dreamed of.

Marisa lazily drifted her fingers down the sides of his neck, then dug tiny divots into the meat of his shoulders with her fingernails when he bestowed a slow, wet kiss on one nipple before bequeathing like-minded praise on the other.

She could carve out entire craters in his back and he'd happily hand her the shovel to do so . . . and tell her to dig deeper. Fuck. He'd buy her a whole host of landscaping tools if she stayed pressed to him like that and kept dragging her hands lower.

When his cock twitched painfully against his thigh, he sat up and paused for a moment. Disappointment briefly flashed across her flushed face, but it was quickly replaced by something he was far more familiar with: a Jersey girl's irritation.

"Why are you stopping? No no no. Don't stop. Please, Alec.

We're not at stopping time yet." She was borderline whining, nudging her toes into his legs and getting all squirmy beneath him, which was helping his cause not a whit.

Jesus Christ, she was trying to kill him, wasn't she?

Alec grabbed up her wrists in one hand over her head and braced his other palm against his heaving chest. "Oh, I have no intention of stopping. I just need a minute." Or five. Maybe ten? Would she fault a man for taking the time to lecture his soldiers lest they rebel against him?

"Is it too much? Too fast?" That worried wrinkle reappeared between her brows again, and a concerned expression swept in right behind it, which had no place anywhere near this moment between them. "This is a violation of the ground rules, isn't it?"

"No," he said firmly, infusing his insistence that what they were doing was right and needed and fucking perfect.

But the wrinkle remained. "Then why did you stop? Was your head bothering you? I never turned off the overhead lights. They're still the old incandescent bulbs. My landlord won't swap them out until he absolutely has to. Are you sensitive to light? Maybe we can—"

"Woman," Alec growled out, dipping his forehead against hers and impressing just enough of his weight, and his cock, upon her to make his point. As soon as she felt it, her beautiful brown eyes grew wide with wonder, and he grinned at her. "There could be a damn fireworks finale going off above my head, and I'd make you scream until the next showing."

He wasn't normally one to assert his prowess, but well, he really could do with a goddamn second to breathe, and if she kept looking at him like that, with her breasts molded against his slick chest and her shapely curves wriggling beneath him, he was about to come up really fucking short of what he knew he could give her. What she deserved.

And anything less than that was unacceptable.

"I want to do this right," he said, kissing away the furrows on her forehead and releasing her hands. "I need to do right by you."

"I'm pretty sure there isn't anything you could do wrong."

He chuckled and moved his mouth across her stomach. "I appreciate the vote of confidence. Truly, I do."

"Then I'm confident in your appreciation," she said smugly.

"Little minx. This can't be over before it starts."

"Agreed."

Alec proved the truth of his words by sliding off her leggings and underwear, but not before silently asking for permission with a heated stare and delicate kiss to her navel.

Marisa's acceptance came in the form of an "Oh my God!" that had her hands covering her face and her head hitting the pillow, clearing the way for Alec to savor every goosebump as he moved his mouth lower.

Her sweet blush and all the emotions that hid behind it were the last things he saw before he dropped a stream of kisses in a trail down her inner thigh, first the left, then the right. The curve of her legs rose to meet his palms, sinking their delicious weight into the expanse of his hands and giving him something to hang onto while he explored what her moans let him. He allowed his tongue to play first, swiping and coaxing little mewls out of her that made her legs shake beside him. Smiling against the playful part of him itching to come out, he shifted his shoulders so her legs rested comfortably on top of him, opening her wider to his attentions.

"Oh my *gawd!*" The muffled cry made him smile against her core.

"Do you want me to stop?"

The yank at his short hairline lacked the punch he suspected she craved, but it effectively delivered her message. "If you even think of stopping what you're doing, I'll satisfy your earlier curiosity and show you exactly how a man can die at the end of a sugar pulling hook."

"It would probably be the sweetest death I could imagine."

"*Alec!*" Marisa swatted his arse with her heel. Hard.

"Only jesting." And he was, partially. The more he tasted her, the more of his strength he wanted to offer her, the more he realized what the days ahead without her would feel like. And even just the slight possibility of never holding her softness to him again—or worse, imagining someone else doing so—was enough to put too frightful an emphasis on the concept of la petite mort.

The thought spurred him faster. He became more eager than ever to claim whatever he could of her, and her pleasure seemed far more desirable than any World Championship.

With a grunting scream from both of them, because, dear God, the woman hadn't let go of his hair, Marisa came apart in his arms.

"You're lovely when you unravel," he murmured against the curve of her hip, the tender space between her ribs, the underside of her breasts. "So fucking lovely."

"Alec."

He wasn't sure of the emotion she put behind his name, but he didn't have a mind to question it. Her sly little fingers had already undone his trousers, found the condom in his back pocket, and gripped his cock with an urgency any red-blooded male knew not to question.

The rest of his trappings fell away and could have burned in a fire for all he cared, save for the condom she'd cleverly sheathed him with.

Because Marisa lay naked before him, bathed in all the beautiful energy-inefficient lighting her thoughtless landlord had gifted him with. Whatever magic was in those bulbs cast a dewy sheen to her eyes and warmed her skin in a way that made Alec want to drag his mouth again over every enticing curve offered, lest he'd neglected a few the first time by mistake.

He placed his palm on the side of her face and kissed her like the universe was at his back, eyeing him for all his faults and flaws and was determined to take her away from him at any moment.

Then their bodies started to move, his strength cradling her softness, providing all the hollows for the wondrous parts of her to explore. He was more than happy to be a map of her wildest imaginings if she let him.

Slight shivers cascaded down his spine. Alec bit down and breathed through his teeth as she reached for his cock and slowly guided him to her slick entrance. He had no recourse but to kiss her again and again, gripping her jaw firmly when her heel urged him forward, sliding him into her welcoming core.

"Jesus fucking Christ, woman," he ground out against her mouth, shifting above her and sliding to the new natural rhythm they both set.

Marisa's lower lip had slackened, but that didn't stop her from gasping for breath and nodding her approval. "Wrong crowd, but I appreciate the sentiment. Oh!"

Alec lifted her leg higher and swiveled his hips, grinding forward with a ferocity that sent Marisa's body quivering. She whipped her head to the side and was met with the wall of his bicep. He would have moved, but then her neat teeth sank into him, pinching the taut skin there and sending his hips pistoning with pleasure.

Whatever he'd thought was unreadable in her expression before crystallized into a snapshot of ecstasy. Her brown hair thrown wild, her brows knitted together, her lower lip slack and swollen from his kisses. It all screamed its own type of release, one that had nothing to do with sex and everything to do with the intimacy they'd forged together.

It would be the expression he'd tattoo on his heart, and when the time came that his heart was close to breaking, he'd use that image as the emotional engine that propelled him toward wherever they were headed next.

Wherever *he* was headed next.

He lowered his head and kissed her through the earth-shattering tremors that claimed them both, never wanting to take his mouth off hers. If he did, a terrified part of him worried he'd never find his way back.

CHAPTER 24

The only reason Marisa even bothered to crack an eye open at the ungodly morning hour was because the running water in her bathroom was most definitely *not* the result of her toilet's sticky valve.

The shower cut off, and Maria snuggled deeper into her sheets, her eyes fully open as she waited for the unimaginable truth of her night to walk over the threshold of her bedroom door.

Her cheeks heated, and she curled her toes farther into the sheets, remembering just what those sheets had served as a backdrop to a handful of hours before.

She'd made love with Alec Elms. In her bed. At least a prime number's worth of times.

How's that for fucking ground rules?

In the light of the new day, the haze of her sex-addled mind reluctantly shuffled away, pulling back the curtain on the shit-storm of her reality, which Alec's clever tongue had done wonders to keep at bay for a time.

Though they'd yet to talk about it explicitly, as their mouths had been engaged in other affairs, Alec was still leaving.

But the way he'd made love to her last night wasn't with the fleeting affection of someone who didn't plan on sticking around.

Quite the opposite, actually.

Marisa's eyes drifted toward the ceiling as she recalled what her body had yet to forget.

"Put your arms around my neck, Marisa. That's it. Don't let go. I've got you."

"I love how your hair wants to trap me against you. Like you're stealing me away, keeping me for yourself. Nothing would make me happier."

"I need to see you come apart on top of me again. Now and every day after."

Admittedly, Marisa didn't have a *lot* of experience in the casual sex department, but those hardly seemed like things a man would say if he planned on leaving soon. Right?

The bathroom door creaked open, and Alec strode into her bedroom, freshly showered, wearing a pair of boxer briefs and an adorably tousled look that showed she wasn't the only one still humming after their late-night escapades.

And that was when she got a good look at him and just how much of a man she had invited into her bed.

Not a man. A professional athlete. A rugby player.

The defined ridges and planes that she'd only known through a careful physical sensory analysis had nothing on what all that strength looked like stacked on top of each other. His wide shoulders, which she had never paid much attention to on a man before, now served as the armored mountain peaks of his body from which great ranges flowed. Alec's torso was a map of exquisite contours and honed rippling muscle, to say nothing of his powerful thighs and perfectly sturdy backside.

It was as if everything about Alec Elms, from his scarred smile to his sinewy strength, was designed to thrill and excite.

It would have been enough to make any woman lose her mind.

Except Marisa didn't have the luxury of lost faculties. Instead, her brain blitzed out and coughed up the craziest idea she'd ever had. Even crazier than what it would be like if it were all real.

Crazier than if he stayed.

She took a fortifying breath. "I have to—"

"If you say, 'draw me,' I'm going to gently remind you that I've seen *Titanic*, and I know what happens after Leo draws Kate like 'one of his French girls.' If you want me to make love to you in the back seat of a vehicle, you don't need to go through all those hoops. I'm easy to please, especially if you're the one I'll be pleasing."

Gulp.

Marisa tried to quell the butterflies in her stomach long enough to keep her train of thought on the damn rails.

She failed spectacularly.

And all Alec could offer for her fish-like gaping was a charming chuckle and sliding all that gorgeous male confidence into bed next to her as if her mind hadn't already started going through their prior activities list in said bed.

He tucked her against his chest and dropped a kiss to the crown of her head. "I'm sorry. I shouldn't have startled you that way, even if you do look cute when you're flustered."

"Oh, you most certainly *should* have startled me that way," she said, wrapping her arm around his rib cage and smiling against the warmth of his bare chest. "But I feel selfish thinking about . . . us. What we just did and all."

"Hmm." Alec didn't offer up any more than that, and Marisa had no idea what to make of it.

"Was that hmm a *we really should have set ground rules hmm* or was it a *'tis the season for being selfish hmm?*"

He squeezed her a bit more tightly, twirling a clump of her

hair around his fingers, and she let her ping-ponging nerves relax into his welcoming weight. "It was a *hmm I wonder what your skin would look like in the Argentine sun and whether Brennan would have my balls if I tried to negotiate more administrative duties into the offer, ones that would keep me working remotely from the States more often hmm.*"

Marisa's head shot up. "What?"

"You got me thinking about choices and how the right one for the moment doesn't always need to be the best one." Alec looked away from her, seeming to lose focus in the hair behind her ear. "You're right. The Argentina coaching contract is likely the right offer for me right now, but not if it takes me away from you for eight months out of the year."

"Wh-what are you saying?"

"I'm saying that I'm not ready to give up rugby yet, but I'm not ready to give you up either. There are assistant coaching positions that, while still having plenty of on-field training time that one does need to be present for, also deal with lots of administrivia—tour management, budgets, player recruitment, stuff like that. Less glamorous, for sure, but just as crucial and, in my mind, all work that can be done remotely at times from, let's say, the tri-state area."

The jerk winked at her, as if he hadn't just told her he would amend a major competitive sports contract with beaucoup bucks on the line so he could essentially work from home. *Her* home.

Well, her home turf, at any rate.

"Now, I don't want to get either of our hopes up. Coaching of any kind would still require a heavy on-pitch presence for the majority of the season, but I'm optimistic that Argentina will be inclined to bend on some terms if it means they'll still get me joining the coaching team. Besides, as an assistant coach, they wouldn't have to pay me as much. All they'd have to concede to is more travel compensation on my part, since I'd be splitting my time between here, Argentina, and wherever the touring circuit takes the team."

Marisa lay on top of him, feeling the beat of his racing heart arcing through her fingers. A reserved sense of hope sat expectantly in his gaze—a gaze that never wavered from her face, even when it clearly cost him to push out the words that would put an end to his playing career, at least for now. It was a temporary choice made with a not-so-temporary feel to it.

But she could tell he was still nervous. The unease was there, written all over his wide brow and thinned lips. Yet his hands were warm and solid against her back, rubbing into her the reassurance he seemed to need more than she did that his decision was the right one.

"You're my choice, Marisa," he said, the force of his words stunning her for all the conviction they held that his earlier ones hadn't. "Not a fake girlfriend or a relationship born out of convenience. You're my *choice*. The right one *and* the best one, and I'm willing to do whatever it takes if you'll have me, if you'll accept that when I'm away from you, it's only because I've not yet worked out all the roads I need to take to stay by your side. But I will. I promise I will."

"You want this? Want me? For real?"

"No. I *need* you. For real. I'm through pretending." Then he brushed his thumb down the curve of her jaw and swiped it over her bottom lip, pulling free the dopey-ass smile she couldn't contain any longer. "Though I can't say I was really pretending much of anything to begin with."

"Oh, Alec. We can make it work. Whatever it takes, we can make it work." She didn't even give him the chance to respond. Her mouth was on his, seeking out his signs of happiness. Not to brag or anything, but she'd kind of gotten pretty good at deciphering them.

"Wasn't there something you wanted to tell me?" he asked in between taking slow sips from her mouth.

"Something I wanted . . . Oh! Yes!" Marisa scrambled off the bed, stealing all the covers with her and leaving a prone Alec and his chilled nipples shocked to the point of delightful worry.

"It's fucking freezing, woman! Get back here!" He lunged for her, but she danced just out of reach.

"No, hear me out!" Marisa finished tucking the sheets around her breasts and ensured everything stayed in place with a little shimmy-shake of her hips so she could call on both hands to aid her in explaining her hairbrained idea. Then she smiled her biggest high school musical opening night smile and swept her hands across the air in front of her in one long, slow pull. "Fudge."

Alec blinked. "You want . . . fudge? Now?"

"No, you gorgeously obtuse man. I'm going to replace the original concept I had for the Jamaican gingerbread with a gingerbread *fudge*."

"Have you found a new supplier? What's changed?"

"Nothing. But I think I've figured out a way to deliver on expectations *and* give people something exciting that I know they'll adore. Something coated in the flavors of the holiday but adorned with something completely irresistible and delicious."

"What's that?"

"You."

***

IT WAS late in the afternoon when Alec finally left Marisa, aided by Eden and the unlawful trio, to her candy making with the promise to return later with dinner for everyone.

He had an errand to run, one that would be rather unpleasant, but if all went well, it might ease some of the pathways ahead of him. And he needed as much smooth sailing as possible.

The jangle of the bar's door was perhaps the only bell sound during that time of year that set his skin to crawling, not for its tinkling tone in particular but for who it announced his presence to.

The crowd was as thick as expected this close to Christmas. A few empty tables here and there, but otherwise the place was filled out nicely, with an assortment of weary heads all wearing the same distilled haze of disappointment bent over glasses filled with liquids of various depths.

Alec knew those looks. They were the disillusioned expressions of people who'd just had the shit kicked out of them by a holiday that hadn't even happened yet.

Poor bastards. I can relate.

Without sparing them another glance or look of commiseration, Alec found his quarry sitting at the bar sipping a dirty martini with—he narrowed his eyes and cursed—*three* olives.

Fuck.

Phoebe only indulged in that many olives when she was in one of her cryptic *these calories don't count* rages.

He took the seat next to her, the one with the coat he'd loaned her the day of the dog shit debacle draped over its back, and declined the offer from the barkeeper to get a drink started. "You didn't have to return it."

"I had no reason to keep it." She smoothly took another sip without so much as glancing at him.

"Well, thanks anyway." Then he caught her profile. "I haven't noticed those before. Your glasses," he said, pointing to the thick black frames that seemed a bit too bulky for her face, but like hell he was about to point that out, especially when she was holding a metal martini skewer not a foot from him. "Have you started needing a prescription?"

"Since when do you notice anything that isn't rugby related?"

Fuck. He knew this was coming. Knew it, prepared for it as best he could, and still bloody hated it.

"I came to make peace. I didn't do right by you. I know that now. I was incredibly selfish and had no business stringing you along. You deserved so much better than I could ever have hoped to offer you. I was damn foolish for treating you the way I did."

Phoebe scoffed, her polished lips lifting on a sneer. "No, Alec. You weren't the fool. I was. I knew I was staying longer than I should have, but I suppose I just didn't care."

"Then let's not make any of it worse now." He pinned her with his stare, giving her no choice but to face him. "I know what you did, and I'm giving you the chance to make it right."

Her stony expression betrayed nothing. "I don't know what you're talking about."

"Don't make me say it. Jesus fucking Christ, Phoebe, you're better than this. *I'm* better than this. I shouldn't even have to be here telling you the difference between right and wrong."

She adjusted her glasses but still didn't acknowledge his words.

He sighed, hoping things would have gone differently, but not surprised they hadn't. "I know you were the one who purchased the lot of the Jamaican extract from that West Indian grocer. I called the place on Marisa's behalf, trying to see whether there was something I could do to get another shipment in for the Jamaican gingerbread treats she was planning on serving at the Crystal Christmas Ball. I spoke to the owner's nephew, who said they'd just sold their last bit of supply to a woman offering to pay double the retail price if it could be delivered the same day. I asked whether he recalled the name, and thank goodness for clueless teenagers, the bloke told me who'd placed the order. It was arranged under the name Phoebe Boyle."

Phoebe rolled her eyes and plucked an olive from the skewer. "We live in a free enterprise market, Alec. A woman is allowed to conduct legal business however she sees fit."

"Look, I get it. It was a mistake for Marisa to post what she was planning on serving online, and you were within your rights to compete, but this has all gone too far. I'm the one you should be attacking and dragging through the mud, not my girlfr—"

Alec knew it was a mistake the moment the word began to fall from his lips, but as much as he tried to pull it back, there was no erasing the hurt that had struck Phoebe's features so harshly.

Fuck. *Fuck.* He dragged a hand over his face.

"She's not your girlfriend," Phoebe stated.

"No, she's not. I mean, she is now, I think, but wasn't before, though even that doesn't sound at all fair." Goddammit, he was making a hash of this, and he hadn't come to drag Marisa's name into his mess. He'd come to get her out of it.

"What is she, Alec? It's a simple question."

"She's . . ." He blanked, not knowing how to categorize things himself, let alone explain them to a woman who had no love for either him or anything in his life anymore. How much clarification did he owe to Phoebe, to the world, or to himself when the only straightforward offering his brain could come up with was the most basic one?

"She's mine. And you'll be leaving her alone. I'll not have another woman suffering for her association with me."

He rose out of his chair, nearly toppling the thing once he yanked his coat free, and stormed toward the door. But before he walked out, bitterness had him slowing his steps as his throat thickened with the pain he'd seen mirrored in Phoebe's eyes. Pain he'd failed to grasp so long ago because he'd been too busy darting from country to country seeking praise and glory from everyone except the people he'd left behind.

The ones who had always been waiting, more than ready and eager to give their praise, if only he'd chosen to be there to receive it.

"Be well, Phoebe. You can hate me for as long as the hurt lasts, for as long as you need to. I hold none of it against you and deserve every bit of it. I truly do. But I also hope, perhaps foolishly, that one day, you can finally move past this. Not for me but for the next person in your life who you think is worthy of your attention. I've robbed you of enough. The last thing I want is to rob you of a happy future as well."

Alec let the jangle of the entry bell show him out, but its somber tinkling wasn't enough to drown out the worries that kept cycling through his mind.

And the cold realization of just how far away Argentina was.

CHAPTER 25

The audible whines of Marisa's stomach weren't the only groans echoing around the commercial kitchen she had commandeered from her friends. Poor Captain had probably fared the worst.

Marisa spread out the last of the cooling mint chocolate candy canes and grimaced as her beloved pal sat at a table, an array of shimmering plastic treat bags stuffed with ribbon candy before him, with withering determination in his eyes as he grappled with his clubbed fingers' greatest enemy: thin scraps of quarter-inch ribbons.

"Do you want me to switch to a thicker ribbon? You don't need to sacrifice your dexterity for candy."

"I said I got it." Captain's tongue curled around the corner of his upper lip, and his eyes narrowed as he tried to pull the last piece of ribbon through the loop to make a bow. Once success had been acquired, he leaned back in his folding chair and finished off his second longneck beer. "I tell ya," he said, bringing the still-frosty bottle to his forehead, "I will never underestimate the skill required to make friendship bracelets ever again. I don't have the finesse for this shit. No wonder

Emily and Maya were always so happy to braid my hair. They knew their handiwork would stick around for a while, because my fat fingers could never summon the patience to undo it."

"But I love you? Does that help?"

"It would help a lot more if you got me another beer and something to eat that won't send my glycemic index spiking."

"Alec's on his way with real food. And I need you to know this." Marisa took both of his stiff hands and massaged the tender joints with her thumbs. "I absolutely love the shit out of all of you for helping me. I'm serious. I couldn't have done any of this on my own."

"Like we'd let you." Sid chuckled as he loaded up another box of finished ribbon candy and set it with the others, while Manic was at the sink, cleaning the last of the sheet pans.

It had taken all day, but with their help, Marisa had finished prepping all the candy canes and ribbon candy. It was impossible to know how many to make in advance, so she'd gone off last year's Ball attendance numbers, which, according to Monica, had been lower than the event organizers usually liked to see for the occasion. So, Marisa tacked on an extra twenty percent of product, which pushed her to her absolute limit in terms of production, given the timeline, and, at Eden's suggestion, printed up some promotional cards for the table that offered customers a discount on sold-out items when purchased from the Sweetest Heart's Desire website.

There was only one thing left to do.

Eden's car keys announced her arrival as she backed into the kitchen door with her arms full of the one machine Marisa's hopes and dreams hinged on. Unfortunately, before Marisa could take it from her best friend, she froze, expecting to be blown backward by the steam that was surely about to erupt out of Eden's ears.

"Oh no. What happened?"

"This is the last fucking time I'm picking up anything from those online auctions you always win out on."

"But this was the one for government surplus products. The reviews were really good. They partner with different municipal and government agencies to auction off equipment municipalities don't need anymore. I thought that since the edible printer was coming from the local community college's auction, it wouldn't be sketchy."

Eden hefted the machine onto the counter and plugged it into the nearest outlet while Marisa unhooked the plastic bag dangling from her friend's wrist. Then Eden wiped her brow and full-on *glowered*. "Your instructions said to meet the seller in lot A."

"Yes, that's what he wrote down."

"There were *four* lot A's."

"What?"

"Oh yes." She stormed over to Captain, yanked the freshly opened beer out of his hand before he'd had a chance to take a sip, and chugged her feelings. After a third of the bottle was gone, she dried her mouth and sighed. "That place was fucking huge, and all the lots were color-coded and *then* sorted by letter. I wasted thirty minutes driving through every goddamn color in the rainbow before I found the right place. It was like some Sesame Street episode from hell."

Marisa casually plucked the beer from Eden's hand and discreetly handed it back to Captain behind her back. Then she rubbed Eden's shoulders and gave them a good pat. "You did well, soldier. I'm proud of you. Big Bird would be proud of you, too."

"All I can say is that I am dying, *dying*, for those auction site motherfuckers to send me a survey. And not one of those *How many stars would you rate your experience?* surveys. I'm talking about a full-fledged text box with unlimited characters."

"I'll be sure to forward you anything they might—"

"Thirty minutes, Marisa! I was driving in circles for *thirty minutes,* hungry out of my mind and wondering whether I'd have to gnaw off the rest of my fingernails just to get some freaking protein in my system."

"Well, thank goodness you didn't, because the nail technician who painted the sparkly snowflakes and winking snowmen on your nails truly outdid herself. I'm so jealous."

Eden sniffed as Marisa's compliment injection started to do its work. "I know, right?" Then she held her nails up, admiring them. "They're just so cute."

"They are. Plus, I love you." Marisa scooped Eden into the hug she knew the woman needed. And she needed, too, if she were being honest.

"Who's hungry?"

Marisa had never been happier to hear that rumbling R tumble off Alec's tongue. The man waltzed into the kitchen, his bulging arms laden with five pizza boxes from Sal and Enzo's, along with an assortment of bags that, based on the smell, contained a spirit-fortifying selection of fried food.

Manic lifted his chin. "What's in the bag?"

Alec plopped the essentials on the counter, along with—bless him—two more six-packs of beer. "I wasn't sure what everyone wanted, so I got—"

"Everything on the appetizer menu?" Eden asked, her voice full of hope.

"Basically."

Soon, the kitchen was filled with the unctuous aromas of garlic knots, mozzarella sticks, hot wings, chicken tenders, onion rings, and enough french fries to fill out a few McDonald's worth of deep fryers.

It was all gloriously greasy and far too perfect for the occasion, given that it was still Hanukkah. To say nothing of the wink Alec fired her way.

This man, I swear.

Then he clapped his hands. "So, once you get yourselves all fed and watered, what's my next assignment, general?" The two-fingered salute he threw her way garnered more than one inquisitive look from those around them, but Marisa was too hyped up on good sex, sugar, and saturated fat to bother explaining.

"Did you bring your rugby uniform?" Marisa said.

"Aye. Though I can't for the life of me figure out what my kit has to do with all of this." He gestured to the grand sugar spectacle around them. "Or how it ties into fudge."

"*Gingerbread* fudge."

"Right," he said, the word suspended in the air, waiting for the explanation she'd been holding just out of his reach for the past few hours.

A good thing, too, because for better or worse, she was so far beyond anyone talking her out of it.

At this point, it was either this or giving up on the Crystal Christmas Ball altogether, and she hadn't suffered through a dozen sugar burns just to admit defeat.

"I can't pull off the flavors I wanted to, but that doesn't mean I can't pull off the flavors people *need* me to. Gingerbread. It's a Christmas classic for a reason. I've decided to make a gingerbread fudge. Super simple, super basic, and can easily be made in large quantities within a day. It's honestly the perfect mass-produced holiday product. But what *won't* be basic about my version is the edible image adorning the top of every piece, capturing the eyes and hearts of anyone who walks past our booth."

Marisa held her breath a moment, then let out the kernel of genius that had hit her earlier that morning when she'd gotten an eyeful of a post-shower Alec looking all dewy and dreamy. "Alec Elms, the number one player for Great Britain Sevens and one of the most famous rugby players in the world, on full display in his uniform, personally wishing everyone a Merry Christmas with each bite."

Alec laughed and shook his head, a hint of, well, she hoped it was eager mischief dancing in his eyes. "You're crazy, woman."

"Crazy brilliant, though!" Eden chimed in. "Think about it. If Phoebe's playing her game where all her bullshit volunteers get free access to you and the festival's wares, essentially taking money out of Marisa's pocket, why not beat her at her own game?"

Sid stroked his beard, gesturing toward Alec. "She's not wrong. If that plant lady is more than happy to exploit you for her own recruitment purposes, wouldn't it be better if it was Marisa's products that left the strongest lasting Alec impression?"

Manic waggled his eyebrows. "Hey, man. The ladies think you're a stud."

"A stud whose face they'll want to eat," said Captain.

"A stud who'll gain lasting and literal face time with every one of Arthur's sports media buddies who have to show up at an event their wives dragged them to when you know those romance-clueless fuckers would rather be working," Eden pointed out, brandishing her fried mozzarella like a pointer stick.

Marisa slipped her hand into Alec's arm and slyly walked her fingers up his taut chest before he caught them against his heart. "What do you say? Are you up for a little Hanukkah photo shoot?"

The room fell as silent as it could given everyone's aggressive nervous chewing while Alec carefully assessed her, keeping his decision locked tight behind those discerning eyes. She hugged his arm closer to her chest, granting him a good-natured squeeze, and though she'd never been able to claim a pair of sweeping lashes, she batted the hell out of what she did have until, finally, a hint of a smile cracked his stony expression.

Alec leaned forward and held her chin so it was impossible for her to look anywhere else but at him. "You're ruthless when you're determined. You're like the goddamn Tony Soprano of Christmas."

"Hmm . . . maybe Willy Wonka would be a better comparison?"

"I couldn't say, honestly. I haven't seen you wear that much purple, but I *have* seen your fondness for Italian food."

Eden swiped a garlic knot. "And she *is* from North Jersey, so . . ."

"All right, fine." Alec released Marisa and picked a duffel bag off the floor she'd been too entranced by gluten to notice earlier. Then he grabbed her around the waist and kissed her. Hard. It was the first time they'd crossed their undefined and completely irrelevant ground rules in front of her friends.

But before Marisa could sink into the taste of him, he pulled away and hiked his bag higher. "Now, where the hell is the bathroom in this place? If I'm to show off for my girlfriend, I'll not do it with a bunch of felons eyeing my arse and her best friend taking bloody notes."

Eden shot her arm out toward the bathroom while Marisa basked in the stupor of Alec calling her his girlfriend for the first time.

LEAVE it to former rabble rousers to turn anything into a gym, especially one as industrial and gritty as what Marisa and Eden had in mind for the backdrop of Alec's mini photo shoot. The corner of the main warehouse space had been quickly cleared of shipping equipment and, in a matter of minutes, been crammed full of strategically placed gym mats, a few free weights, and the only other props they'd been able to muster: the rugby ball Alec had in his trunk—seriously, was that a guy thing?—and a Santa hat.

Eden was futzing with the camera frame on her phone, trying to position the tripod correctly while Captain, Sid, and Manic hooked up some extra lamps.

"Are you sure this is going to work?" Marisa asked, gnawing off her last good nail.

"Of course it'll work." Eden stood back from the setup and held out her hands. "There! It's as good as free labor will get you."

"Hey, Alec fed you, and I'm paying you in promises that, if you die first, I'll delete your e-reader history before your brother gets to your stuff."

"Oh, please. That's not the flex you think it is. Who do you suppose I got half, if not two-thirds, of my book recommendations from?"

Marisa pegged her with a calculating stare. "I was talking about your *younger* brother."

A touch of Eden's confidence flickered, and she snapped her attention back to lining up the shot. "Heartless woman."

"I'm sorry. I'm just nervous. We've got all of fifteen minutes to take an amazing picture, edit it, figure out the correct sizing for the fudge squares, which I've yet to also make, and hope like hell the community college's edible printer and icing sheets hold up to their end of the bargain."

"What did you pay for all this stuff again?"

Marisa tried to work out a knot in her shoulder, but she had trouble finding the spot, as if the damn thing meant to stay just out of reach until she offered up the honesty Eden deserved. "Couple hundred," she muttered.

"And would it be fair to say that the couple hundred wasn't in Mexican pesos?"

Marisa toed at a spot on the floor. "It would be."

"Yikes."

"But it came with the ink, right?" Shit, *did* it come with ink? Marisa hadn't bothered to check and hadn't owned a printer, food-grade or otherwise, since grad school. She just assumed the plastic bag hooked on Eden when she'd walked in held the rest of the stuff needed to make Marisa's dreams come true.

Her insides twisted horribly and had her questioning, for the umpteenth time, what part of any of this was a good idea.

A foreign cluster of taps pulled Marisa away from her spiraling thoughts as Alec's cleats joined the conversation, reminding them all that it was show time. In more ways than one.

Eden looked up from her phone at the exact time Marisa did. "Oh, holy Jesus . . ." her friend said breathily, any of the prior fastidiousness over the camera placement long gone as she abandoned the thing to its lonely tripod.

Marisa nodded stiffly through her own dazed appreciation. "Still the wrong crowd," she murmured mindlessly around a throat gone arid, "but I'm starting to get it now, I think."

She and Eden both tilted their heads to the right as Alec continued his catwalk across the concrete. The corner of his lips lifted with that Scottish charm that told Marisa one of two things: yes, he knew the effect he had on women, and no, he wasn't above using it to make her go insane.

"It's got to be painted on, right?" Eden reasoned out of the corner of her mouth. "Otherwise, how would he get in and out of it?"

"Not sure. But those are definitely four-inch inseams."

"Or less."

"But the shirt," Marisa stammered. "The sleeves. The . . . the . . ." The complete abundance of visible flesh. Well, except for the socks, but even those seemed to know their place when it came to the lines of his calves.

Alec joined them. "Are we ready to do this?"

It occurred to Marisa that she'd made yet another grave

mistake, far worse than any earlier surveillance she'd failed to perform on the Plant Nanny. In all her time with her nose in front of a screen, she'd yet to pull up video of what Alec Elms looked like in his rugby uniform.

Kit, she mentally corrected.

A truly egregious mistake, and, boy, oh boy, was she paying for it now.

He wore familiar colors, navy blue, with slashes of red and white lines running vibrantly across his impressive chest like a New York subway mural. The effect was marvelous and speckled him in a sort of war paint, the threat of which one only saw coming once it was right on top of them.

The short neckline and sleeves were another matter entirely, stopping just shy of his prominent collarbones and biceps. Tucked into the skin-tight fabric as he was, there was nowhere to hide any of his power or potency. All of it was proudly on display, from his ribbed abdominals to his muscular thighs, the latter of which stood just far enough apart to draw Marisa's eyes to another proud display, indeed.

And goddamn that arrogant Scot. When Marisa finally found the courage to meet his eyes, he countered with a mischievous gaze that glowed with a knowing flame that lit her wick of desire. All while Alec stood there, smirk in hand and a scar so lickable that she wouldn't put it past herself to paint him in sugar and launch herself at him.

He even had the chutzpah to flash a smug grin that very much said, *Look your fill now, because I'll be enforcing some ground rules of my own later.*

And now, with that lovely thought pole-dancing through her mind, she had a photo shoot to get through, who knew how many hours of work ahead of her, and barely a shred of dignity left to do it all with.

CHAPTER 26

It had taken the rest of the night and the better part of the following day, but Marisa was finally done with everything. Or *finished*, as her ninth-grade science teacher liked to say, before always emphasizing that only food was *done*. As far as Marisa was concerned, she was both those things, and she wanted nothing more than to throw her fingers into a pair of hydration hand masks and let voice control run her life until the New Year.

Marisa tossed her sugar-splattered apron on a hook and twisted her hair into a messy bun while she surveyed what they'd all managed to accomplish. She'd lost count of how many treat boxes they'd assembled or how many sinfully gorgeous Alecs she'd printed and plastered on gingerbread fudge squares she couldn't wait to surprise people with.

Last Eden informed her, once the sugar dust settled, they'd landed somewhere in the three-digit range. Meanwhile, Manic and the boys had faithfully stuffed and stacked every single one of the ribboned boxes into optimal height and width ratios for easy transport come the morning. That was another thing Marisa had failed to consider, but she was beyond grateful she had friends who had.

Tomorrow, the Crystal Christmas Ball would arrive on the heels of the final night of Hanukkah, as well as Christmas Eve. And just like Santa, whatever was loaded into the sleigh was all she had to work with.

Solid hands settled over her shoulders, bringing with them Alec's comforting strength and, more than that, a steely reassurance that warmed her belly and sent a new set of flutters jittering along her nerves.

"You've done all you can."

"I know. I'm just . . ."

"What?" He turned her in his arms, and every insecurity that still beat a rhythm in her brain felt like a betrayal for all the man had given her, for all he'd endured because of her.

For all he *would* endure.

How the hell was she supposed to stare into those soft, unguarded eyes and tell him that the heated storm behind them was the one thing that had made her feel beautiful and powerful? And that the only thing she'd ever lived up to was other people's disappointments?

Marisa lifted a shoulder. "Nervous. There's going to be a lot of attention flying around, and while I'd love it if it were focused on Sweetest Heart's Desire and what's in the treat boxes, I'd be stupid to think that's likely to be the case. And yes, I know that was the point of all of this"—she gestured to the small space between them—"and we manufactured it for a reason, but that doesn't mean I haven't been here before, to a degree. I guess what I'm trying to say is, this feels different, and well, I'm not interested in losing this time."

God, even her worries sounded like whines, painting her with a new brand of pity that was unbecoming in all shades. She didn't want Alec to feel sorry for her, and she sure as hell didn't want to count herself out before the big show even started, but despite how strong her internal defiance sounded, it was still hard to drown out years of Aunt Gails and Plant Nannies and behind-her-back whispers.

"I'm not of a mind to lose either," Alec said, squeezing his encouragement into her arms. "Never was. But it's important to know one thing."

"What's that?"

"You deserve every bit of praise. And aye, the spotlights may be brighter than usual tomorrow, but that's only because they've yet to capture a star like you."

Marisa's mouth fell open, her brain short-circuiting on the wealth of emotion that threatened to pour out of her in droves.

Goddammit, the man got her. Not just got her but genuinely understood her, down to dissecting the sandy bits that made up the sea sludge of her chaos, knowing there was a precious gem or two hiding beneath.

Waiting for him to find.

"I'm done," she reiterated, insistence paving way to urgency as she marked the way his throat worked on a swallow and every muscle beneath her fingertips went taut.

She needed to kiss this man, not just often, but deeply, and everywhere. She needed to wrap herself in Alec until all the worries in her mind were pushed out by his overwhelming presence.

But overwhelming in the best way, the way that made her heart lighter and gladder and eager to greet what the world threw at her because she knew he'd be throwing punches right alongside her.

"Come home with me, Marisa," he whispered against her cheek, his words filled with thrilling promises.

"What about Cal? Isn't he due home tonight?"

Alec chuckled, then took her hand in his and guided them toward the door. "Enjoyed himself a bit too much at the cast wrap party. He's crashing on a mate's couch tonight, but don't worry, he'll be joining us at the Ball tomorrow."

"He better. I'm looking forward to meeting the man Hugh first let himself go home with."

"Not too eager, I hope, because tonight, I've got plans."

"Oh? What sort of plans?"

Alec opened the car door for her, then held her gaze as she slid into the seat. The muscles in his neck strained against his collar, and the streetlamp's glow forced all her attention on his scarred smile.

Pinpricks of arousal danced along her skin, igniting her body even further as the determination in his expression hit her in full force.

"I'm locking Hugh in the guest room and taking my girl-friend to bed."

As they drove off beneath a vast sky dotted with light snowflakes and darkened not by deadlines but by desire, Marisa bit her lip and knew one truth with thrilling certainty.

When Alec spoke those words, he wasn't faking a damn thing.

THE DRIVE across town was an exercise in suspended animation. Every breath that puffed out of Alec's lungs seemed to enter Marisa's, until there was no safe quarter for her being so close to him. He had become elemental. His scent, his smile, his laugh, the way his knuckles groaned against the steering wheel's leather when his impatience started to get the better of him—they were all signs that had begun to build in the vital helix around her heart, so much so that by the time they'd reached his brother's apartment, her limbs had turned to jelly.

Good thing, too, because when she went to open her door, Alec was already outside, grabbing her hand and freeing her from the stuffy car's cabin, a strained eagerness creasing his features.

Her lungs tightened further around her racing heart as he all but sprinted with her across the parking lot.

So she wasn't the only one trying to hold it together long enough to avoid a public indecency charge.

The only respite he'd allowed her was when she rested her flushed cheek against his broad back as he punched in the keycode for the apartment. Three times. On the fourth try, she had to bury her laugh between his scapulas while Alec's brogue-laced blasphemies pelted the poor locked door.

"Damn fat fingers. I fucking hate this thing. A key. All I need is a bloody key!"

"I happen to like your fat fingers." She giggled, curling around him and punching in the code he was trying to enter. The light instantly turned green, and the metallic lock clicked open in time to Alec's jaw grinding its frustrations.

"You did not just say that to me."

"I did," she said smugly. "What are you going to do— *Uf!*"

Alec captured her face within his strong hands and sealed his lips to hers. Vaguely, she was aware of him backing them into the apartment. A door closed, she was sure of it, the lock snicking into place right after. There was a fair bit of mastiff-flavored barking, some mumbles against her lips that sounded like *fuck off, pest,* the hasty removal of outerwear, and then her feet were off the floor.

Something about being weightless in Alec's arms drove her passion to heights that had previously been well above her salary bracket. The way he lapped and suckled and swiped against her lips was an exercise in reverence, as if each kiss he claimed was a careful prayer and her body was the altar upon which he'd bestow them.

"Alec," she whispered against his mouth, not quite sure what she wanted of him but just knowing that she *wanted.*

"Not done yet," he said against her lips, settling her onto the couch and shifting his attention to the hollow divot at the base of her throat. Lord, his mouth felt wonderful on her skin, every press a mixture of silk and just the right amount of scratch from his short beard, mimicking the delicious strain in her chest.

Seemingly overnight, what started as a strategic deception had blossomed into an essential need. With Alec's lips on her, kissing her, consuming her, he'd somehow managed to push out all the doubt and disillusionment that had marked her as a failure among her family and replaced it with far more joy and passion than anyone had a right to experience.

He marked her as worthy. As precious. As his. As something worth loving.

Maybe? Hopefully? She gulped at the thought.

And because she had no earthly clue what to do with a gift as precious as what Alec was offering, she did the only thing she could: shared as much of her heart with him as he'd accept.

She gentled her hands at the sides of his ribs, using his strength to steady what her limbs could not, but so much of his greedy touch and eager mouth unhinged her to the point of giddiness. When that clever tongue of his found her aching nipple through her shirt, she couldn't help but suck in an excited breath.

"Oh, you are an evil, evil man."

"Hush, woman. I'm busy tending to things." He pulled her shirt higher, dipping his head to pay homage to any patch of skin he seemed to begrudgingly omit from his prior attentions. At the same time, she worked to squirm out of her jeans, doing her damnedest to feel as much of this man against the vital parts of her as possible.

"You are so bossy."

"Team captain," he reminded her as he freed her breasts and his shirt in one admittedly impressive maneuver. "Comes with the territory." The sexy smugness with which he spoke was overloud in her ears, calling every nerve ending to attention.

As if there was any part of her makeup that could ignore what this man was doing to her.

Decidedly not.

But whatever sex-crazed witty rejoinder had been on her lips was tossed aside as Alec shifted on the couch, preparing to undo his fly, while Hugh let out an overloud cry.

With a startled yelp, Marisa threw an arm wide, offsetting her entire equilibrium, as well as Alec's. Together, they tumbled onto the carpeted floor, her foot clotheslining the contents of the glass coffee table.

Alec's hand shot out and cupped Marisa's head to his chest, cushioning what would have been a nasty blow against the table's edge. Once the rest of her had settled safely, wedged between the soft, high pile and Alec's broad body, she exhaled through a nervous laugh.

His only response was a sweet kiss to her forehead and a delightful display of tenderness as he brushed his thumb across her cheekbone. "Don't know why Cal insists on glass furniture, but if it's stars you want to see, I'd rather my body claim the credit."

That annoying heat in Marisa's cheeks returned. "You're too athletic for your own good." *And mine, apparently.*

Alec squeezed her bare hip with his large hand, and a curious concern flitted through his eyes, as if he were trying to uncover a deeper meaning behind her thoughts. "I'm beginning to think that all those years on the pitch, tackling blokes twice my size and running until my lungs ached, was all just conditioning for whatever sort of service you'd need from me. If my strength and agility are what you require, then take it all, Marisa. Give them a purpose. Make them yours." Then he swallowed, and Marisa marveled as the tendons in his throat shifted in preparation. "Make *me* yours."

In all the years she'd been struggling to fulfill other people's purposes, turning herself inside out to feed their expectations, she'd never imagined what the reverse would feel like. To have requirements of her own and a man like Alec want to fill them. And not just *want* to fill them, but would eagerly show up and do the work without asking for a list of justifications in return.

She had no idea what to make of his declaration. Any response she could think to push out seemed wholly inadequate.

What she did know was that his statement was needlessly encouraging because her body was already begging for more of his touch.

"I don't want this to end," she said, lifting her leg higher so more of her filled his palm, making his eyes take on that unfocused haze she loved to see.

"Don't worry," he said, lifting her hand and placing a hungry kiss on her pulse point. "Obsessions never do."

For the second time in as many minutes, another foreign sound broke through her swoony stupor. This one, however, wasn't barking. It was crinkling. And sticking to her elbow.

"What the hell?"

Pasted to her sweat-slicked forearm was a single sheet of paper that really shouldn't have been as sticky as it was. She sniffed the air. "Why do I smell frosting?"

Before Alec could reply, Marisa plucked the intruder from its handhold on her and finally noticed the slew of papers she'd knocked off the coffee table. She gathered them up and couldn't keep the note of surprise out of her voice. "Is this your latest contract? Printed on my icing sheets?"

Alec scratched the back of his neck. "It was the only paper I had handy, and I wanted to review what Brennan sent over this morning. Because blue light and tiny text give me headaches on a good day, yes, I'm one of the few people under forty on the planet who still print things out to read them."

"I'm not sure you have any business being adorably defensive." Marisa sat up, covered her breasts with a nearby throw pillow, and tried not to smile as Alec flipped Hugh off, presumably for good measure, before snatching up a pair of reading glasses that had also managed to go flying.

But Marisa didn't even have time to imagine how sexy he'd look in black-rimmed spectacles because her misty eyes were too busy blurring every other word of the contract. Her voice thickened with strain as she looked at him and asked, "Is this for real?"

"Aye." He nodded, his expression full of sincerity. "Argentina's amenable to my terms. I was going to sign it after the Ball. I'll still be keeping my flat in England for the time being, might even rent it out as an investment, but once the season starts, I'll be able to travel a bit more freely when I'm not . . . actively coaching."

Actively coaching meant living in Argentina, an entire hemisphere and culture away from West Meadow, New Jersey.

"You're really doing this?" Marisa worked to keep the strain out of her voice but had exactly zero luck now that the tears had begun to fall. "But you'll be taking a pay cut. You won't be playing anymore."

Alec took the papers from her shaking hands, dammit, and set them down on the table, then gave Hugh a big, *long* side-eye that had the dog slinking off down the hall. Then he pushed the offending table away and pulled her down on top of him.

Something like determination steeled his features, as if she'd hit on a nerve he'd trained himself to deflect. "I'm not choosing Argentina," he said, his voice gentling. "I'm choosing you."

Whatever emotions Marisa had been managing to keep at bay roared to life, erupting with a passion that fused their mouths. He rose and kissed her deeply, thoroughly, but it was messy, their actions uncoordinated.

The subtext and intent were real, though, and somehow, that sort of seemed like the crux of all of this.

He was unapologetically and deliciously real. Always had been.

Desperation lit a fire within her belly as she helped him rip off his jeans and whatever inhibitions that still stupidly decided to cling to their bodies. She'd have none of it. Nothing but Alec.

"You taste like sugar." He groaned, trying to chase her lips but failing as she pulled away, smiling, then rested herself on his hips, triumphantly holding up the condom she knew to ferret out of his jeans. "Bloody thief, you are."

"A careful thief," she corrected, rolling it on, suggestively squeezing the tip of him for good measure, delighting in how it caused his top teeth to bite down on his lower lip.

Her heart kicked an exuberant rhythm behind her ribs, making her toes tingle.

How, in all the world, could she ever have doubted this man? Especially when he gazed at her with so much more than mere affection in his eyes?

There wasn't just heat there, but a compulsion, an essential obligation, as if Alec would run out of air if he could not get to her fast enough.

She'd never been crucial before, and yet there was no other way to describe the impression he made on her.

Alec growled. "I'll be needing more of your sweet mouth."

Letting herself fall further under his heady spell, Marisa situated her body above his hard length. "I just need more of you."

Alec gripped her at the waist, then gently guided her into position, an act that robbed sawing breaths out of both of them. He filled her, stretching her slowly but perfectly, easing her comfort by kissing whatever bits of skin he could access: a finger, a wrist, the fleshy pad at the base of her thumb.

All erogenous zones, apparently, as she leaned her head back and worked her hips against him.

"Oh, God," she breathed. "You feel so good. You feel—"

"More." As promised, Alec rose up again and claimed her mouth as he moved within her, his pace punishing in its depth but not nearly as punishing as the passion he wrought out of her.

"Alec, my skin's on fire. If you keep that up—"

"Then I'll burn happily alongside you."

"I'm not entirely sure that's something I should encourage."

"I am." Seeming not to care one whit about his imminent demise, he snaked a hand through her hair and secured his possessive grip to the side of her face, once again fusing their mouths as he pushed her higher and higher toward a bliss she hadn't bothered with for far too long.

Whatever had or hadn't been said yet, Marisa was a thousand percent sure that Alec owned her heart. Just straight up stole the damn thing out of her chest and tucked it away, protecting the bleeding thing from judgment and scrutiny behind all that adorable Scottish bulk.

Keeping her safe, as he always had.

She moved faster, her body writhing with more insistence now that she'd wholeheartedly decided to claim all this man had freely given her.

Fake, real, none of it fucking mattered.

Because with one sweeping cry rippling through her body, she collapsed against the man, who captured her pleasure into his kiss as he clutched her close and shuddered through his own release.

Somewhere in the distant corners of her mind, beyond all the tense thoughts of Christmas Balls and Argentina and Plant Nannies, sat one little kernel of delight. Marisa plucked that thing and held it close to her heart as she snuggled in against Alec's warm chest.

I wish I could keep him here forever.

Alec tugged at the sleeves of his suitcoat for the third time while he waited for Cal to park the car. He probably should have driven, but he didn't entirely trust his movements.

Or motivations.

Fomenting fratricide wasn't anything he'd previously given (a lot of) thought to, but when Cal stumbled into the apartment that morning way the fuck earlier than expected, he'd mortified Marisa out of Alec's arms and sent her scrambling to the bathroom. After a brief introduction and a few parting words of *see you both at setup*, she'd kissed Alec hastily, ignored Hugh entirely, and left man and beast alike glaring daggers at Cal.

So, yeah, he had zero qualms about sending his brother to park the car in the back lot and have him meet Alec at the Green.

The bastard could fucking walk and freeze his arse off.

Murderous thoughts aside, the few minutes of alone time did give Alec the opportunity to appreciate the splendor that Monica and the rest of the recreation committee put on. He'd have whistled his admiration if his scar didn't pull at his lip so uncomfortably.

The Crystal Christmas Ball had arrived at West Meadow Green with no shortage of enjoyable fresh snowfall and sparkling stupor. White flickering string lights flowed in intersecting patterns from tree bough to tree bough high above, crafting a breathtaking net of sparkles that illuminated the entire area. Old sentinel trees stood as pillars in the corners and were wrapped with intricate netting, which dressed up the otherwise sleeping giants in their festive finest, outlining all the ancient knots and charm that normally went unnoticed.

Like any other wintertime festival, there was an assortment of strategically placed, *tasteful* light-up candy canes and reindeer, with an ornate sleigh display piled high with illuminated gifts.

The rest of the magic likely happened in the large, heated tent that enveloped every other available inch of the Green, the one being fed by scores of gorgeous couples as they made their way down a lit walkway through shimmering open flaps.

There was no way to tell just how many of those couples Phoebe had lured in with the promise of exclusive access to him as part of her bullshit volunteer scam, so he hadn't been inclined to show up earlier than needed. Besides, Eden, Captain, Manic, and Sid all ensured Marisa had no shortage of adequate setup help, so coming a bit later with Cal in tow had been a welcome strategy.

"There you are," Cal rasped out, trotting over with a hand on his chest. "Fuck, that took for-bloody-ever. Parking's a total shit show. I had to wait in line. Would you believe they're doing valet-only for this thing?"

"If you're seeking sympathy, you'll be waiting in another long line."

Cal threw his arm over his brother's shoulder. "Och. Still mad, are we?"

Alec bit back a growl and shrugged the arsehole off him. "A bit."

"Well, don't worry. I suspect you'll be making it up to her tonight."

Alec could have done without the ludicrous wink or the obnoxious thumbs-up.

Or the heart-thumping eagerness that had him cutting a path through his brother's sarcasm and spearing toward the tent's back entrance, where all the volunteers and organizers bustled in and out.

"C'mon. If you're not going to behave, at least be helpful."

"When am I ever not helpful?" Cal asked, his words hefted high in mocking astonishment.

"When your mouth is open. Now, get in here, and remember, we're representing Marisa. We're supposed to be part of her vendor team."

Grinning, Cal tugged on his lapels and led the way. "Understood. Besides, it's not like I need any encouragement when it comes to acting."

But once they walked into the tent, the glamour around them had blessedly managed to accomplish what Alec had failed at: shutting up Cal.

Crossing the threshold escorted them into a true winter wonderland. Various cocktail tables draped in shimmering white linen dotted the far end of a dance floor, while illuminated ice sculptures accented the perimeter. Alec strained his neck, marveling at how, no matter which way he looked, there was always something to impress his eye and take his breath away. Hanging garlands of frosted evergreens dotted with ice-blue lights draped elegantly around the sizable space, while white-gloved waitstaff moved through the dancing crowd, holding their platters high.

At one end of the room, a band was playing, their lively strings and cheerful bells setting an exuberant pace for the couples who had already assembled on the dance floor. Pockets of champagne, spiked eggnog, hot cider, and various light culinary assortments were accented throughout the room, allowing for excellent crowd flow and maximum enjoyment. As it was a ball and not a formal dining event, the food was light and suggestive, with the event organizers placing an emphasis on movement and dancing rather than sitting and eating.

The design was bloody brilliant, as each guest acted like a drifting snowflake swirling within a couples-only snow globe.

"Is this Monica woman a magician?" Cal asked, equally impressed.

"No. Just a chairwoman."

"A chairwoman magician."

But Alec wasn't in the mood to debate the magical merits of anyone other than one woman in particular.

The woman who had taken up permanent residence in his heart and had made him a miserable bastard to be around when he couldn't have her scent in his lungs.

The lights toward the back of the tent were far dimmer, making the series of glittery shadows and gowns that were congregating around the tables in the area all the more eye-catching.

He ducked beneath a garland, pushing toward the cluster of people, and pointedly ignored any volunteer donation card stack perched on various table ends. He had just about reached the rear of the tent when he stopped short.

Alec's chest squeezed, and every part of him ached as he took in Marisa, standing quietly behind her vendor table, conversing with Eden. A dark green floor-length gown painted her contours in muted opulence. Her shoulders were bare, but the neat lace three-quarter sleeves that pulled the subtle pattern from her bodice gave her a sophisticated elegance that full-blooded queens would be hard-pressed to achieve.

Alec's fingers twitched, and he had to shove them into his

pockets lest they pull him across the room to finger the two locks of mahogany tendrils framing her smile. The rest of her hair had been pinned up in a subtle fashion, and the only jewelry she wore was the twinkling silver headband capping her crown.

It was all Alec could do to steady himself against Cal, who had caught sight of the verifiable goddess handing over a treat box to a young couple. Or several treat boxes, as it were, as they'd walked away with a staggering stack and an excited smile.

Then he saw it. The line to get to her table was forming more of a tail than he'd realized, and his damn pride was not handling her popularity as well as he'd hoped.

"I'm going to go out on a wild limb and guess that's Marisa."

Alec nodded, trying to peel his tongue away from the roof of his mouth. God, she was a vision, a miracle in her own right, regardless of whatever bullshit approval or permission the likes of Monica would have her believe she needed.

"Aye." It was the only word Alec trusted himself to properly articulate. As he could no longer rely on his senses, he thought it best to save whatever words his stammering heart could muster for Marisa's benefit.

"And you're going to go over there right now and tell her she looks bonny."

"Aye."

More tightness in his throat. More tender feelings he wasn't sure what to do with.

Then Cal gave his frozen shoulders a slight push, and Alec stumbled forward like a damn teenager who hadn't come into his larger limbs yet. "An object in motion stays in motion, so best get to it. You're doing no one any favors dawdling over here with your thumb up your arse."

"Aye."

Aye . . . aye . . . aye . . . Was that all he could manage to say? For fuck's sake, he sounded like Jack goddamn Sparrow.

Alec's blood pumped at a sprinter's pace, but he wasn't entirely sure it could claim the lightheadedness he felt.

That likely belonged to the beauty before him, who was beaming one of her enchanting smiles his way while he nearly tripped over a table leg to get to her.

Real fucking smooth, Elms.

"You look amazing," Alec said, leaning over to kiss her cheek, and smiled at the scent he pulled off her. Blueberries. "Enjoying those candy canes again?"

She twisted her lips. "Maybe. They're stress relievers."

"If you say so." And Alec made a mental note to stock up on the suckers before the stores stopped selling them, which would likely be the day after Christmas, given the speed at which capitalism moved on to the next holiday.

After Alec offered up introductions on Cal's behalf and Eden quickly grabbed his brother and started showing him how to process payments on the tablet, he asked the question that had been gnawing at his curiosity—and yeah, a wee bit of his vanity. "So, is it working?"

It meaning the gingerbread fudge.

It meaning the final photo of him that Marisa and Eden had selected to print onto each piece of fudge and package up with the rest of the treats.

He wasn't sure what to make of the look Marisa flashed him, but it was easy enough to follow the pattern of people she indicated with her fingers.

And the squares of what he'd forever come to think of as face-fudge they were shoveling into their mouths with uncomfortable relish.

"Holy shit," he breathed.

Each tawny brick was slathered with an edge-to-edge picture of Alec in full rugby kit, with his arms flexing on his hips and a Santa hat perched on his head. The grumpy face he was sporting had been a joke during the shoot, a way to make everyone laugh and cut some of the tension of their deadlines, but the ladies had run with it, apparently, even to the extent of including a thought bubble poking above his head saying, "Bah, scrum-bug!"

"Has anyone ever told you two that you'd make excellent crime bosses? You can't be serious with all this." But even he couldn't keep the laughter out of his voice. Not fully.

"You can't hate me. It's against the rules," Marisa admonished, pushing out her lower lip. "Especially not when I've lost count of how many people have been running by my table, and the night's just getting started. Monica's been super happy, too. She stopped by a few minutes ago to check on things, and she even gave me a thumbs-up. A thumbs-up, Alec!" There was a catch in her voice that had hooked itself somewhere within his rib cage, and damn if he didn't feel every giddy reverberation of her happiness.

"I could never hate you. God, Marisa. I'm so fucking proud of you. This is bloody amazing." The sentiment was filled with more truth than he had recent practice with, and the magnitude of it all stunned him for a moment.

Because it was true. All of it. And this woman was standing there, beaming at him like *he'd* been the one to give *her* some remarkable gift?

He had it on his mind to tell her as much, when she shifted a bit, her gaze snagging on something another partygoer was munching on. The light in her eyes dimmed a touch, and he tried to make out what it was that had caused her consternation, but he was at a total loss for how to describe what was in the guest's hand.

"Is that woman eating flowers?" he asked.

Marisa shook her head. "Not real flowers. They're gingerbread meringue poinsettia petals."

"So, not flowers? Because they look exactly like flowers."

"Whatever pastry chef Phoebe has on her team outdid themselves. The bright-red flower petals and green leaves are all made of sugar and egg whites, just brushed with Jamaican gingerbread extract and dusted with some edible glitter."

"Ah. Have you tried it?"

"Oh, I've tried it. Totally tastes like betrayal. It was also . . . Ugh, it was also really damn good. Like, really, *really* good." Then she bit her lower lip and traced a hesitant finger around a plastic-wrapped piece of Alec's face-fudge, her self-confidence visibly unraveling through the worried action. "Phoebe made good on her threat, that's for sure, though I'm surprised I haven't run into her yet so she can gloat properly. I guess I'm just worried everyone's going to compare gingerbread flavors and find mine lacking."

"Uh-uh!" Eden held up a finger in correction before handing two more treat boxes to Cal to ring up. Then she swatted her open palm lightly on Marisa's forehead. "Stop it. Just stop. No one will give a festive fuck about whose gingerbread flavor is better than whose because they'll be too busy sinking their teeth into Alec like the snack he is."

"Ha!" Cal's boisterous laugh rumbled around them, puffing out his massive chest and giving all the ladies floating nearby an eyeful of his straining shirt buttons while the men grumbled into their drinks. "I'll have to agree with Miss Eden on that one. How many times have you had a store-bought birthday cake that tasted delicious solely because you were biting into something eye-catching?"

"See!" Eden threw out her hands in Cal's direction. "The man knows what he's talking about."

"Not usually," Alec muttered, feeling ten kinds of uncomfortable being the subject of what should be spotlighting Marisa instead of him. "He just really likes cake and isn't one to discriminate against its upbringings."

He was itching to flip that flame around somehow. He didn't deserve a bit of the genius Marisa had poured into her business. And he certainly didn't deserve any credit for what she'd crafted onto the face-fudge. It was her idea to model him in such a way, her idea to put him in his kit and plop a Santa hat on his head. He'd done his fair share of photo shoots and sponsored clothing ads, so he was used to the attention his physicality afforded him and viewed it as a whole lot of nothing special. The important thing was that he and Marisa were in this together. The more eyes that connected him to the game of rugby, the more favor he'd win in the negotiation game when the season ended, and the more recognition her business would gain.

Except, well, he hadn't thought much about the negotiation bit recently, had he? Not since he'd worked out an option with Argentina that was looking like it could suit. No, it wasn't perfect. He'd still be countries away for most of the season, and he wouldn't be playing anymore, but he would still be involved in the game, in a way that seemed like the right choice, even if his heart hadn't come round to fully accepting the scope of the decision just yet.

But it would. *He* would. For her. Because she was worth it.

For fuck's sake, she wasn't just worth it. She was everything, wasn't she?

The realization tilted his lips into a smile, and he let that feeling warm him as he stepped back and watched his woman work. And by God, she was magnificent in her element. The way she schmoozed confidently with the guests, the way her bare shoulders were anchored well below her ears without a touch of tension, it was all an exercise in how long he could hold out before he whisked her away from everyone's attention and stole her for himself.

So he could tell her what his heart had come to learn after only a few short days of knowing her.

Fuck. I love this woman.

The thought hit him like an eighteen-stone flanker, rattling his good sense and causing his chest to expand with an unfamiliar warmth. And because he had no better alternative than to keep quiet and watch her work her magic, he did just that. It wasn't long before the two of them fell into an easy rhythm. Her smiling and shaking hands with guests and town council members interested in her business. Him catching glimpses of her self-confident smile and pocketing it away for tender keeping while he took a photo with people here and there.

It was all lovely.

It was all bloody perfect.

Marisa plucked three more treat boxes off the tower he'd stacked behind her and handed them to a waiting couple. "Here you go. Enjoy!"

"Oh, we will," said the thirtysomething woman whose face had turned Santa-suit red when Alec had shaken her hand in thanks for the purchase.

The night pressed on pleasantly, with the kind of merriment only found among happy couples free of children on snowy evenings in December. Even though the tent was heated and the crowds thick, it couldn't keep out all of the crisp air, which was a godsend because breaks had become few and far between for Marisa.

Once a rare lull in the action finally found them, she'd managed to chug a few gulps of water and looked out over the attendees, then back at the treat boxes she'd worked so hard to prepare, which had dwindled to an envious few.

"Wow," she said. "We really did it, didn't we?"

"*You* did it. I was just the hired help."

He hadn't meant anything by it. Really, who did? *Hired help* was a common enough phrase in colloquial speech. But it had carried a different meaning between the two of them, one that had started what seemed like a mutually beneficial business arrangement but had turned into something so much more.

Marisa must have realized his gaffe as well, because she replaced the cap on her bottle of water, tucked it beneath the table, and sidled closer to him. Not making eye contact, staring out at the crowd, she said, "I have a crazy idea."

Alec stilled, curious at the question at first, but then recalled another time not long ago when she'd confessed another crazy idea. One that had led to a kiss and a promise. "Oh?"

She bit her lip, still focusing on the crowd before them. "What if I asked you to put your arm around me?"

Alec couldn't keep the adoration from his voice if he tried. He smiled down at her and said, "I'd remind you that I have two arms."

He stood behind her and pulled her to his chest, holding her as close to his heart as possible.

"Oh, I'm sorry. I didn't mean to interrupt anything." A tall older gentleman had approached their table, but he stopped short when he saw Alec and Marisa embracing.

They peeled off each other, and Marisa stepped forward. "No, you weren't interrupting anything. Welcome. I'm glad you stopped by. Would you like to try a specialty treat box from Sweetest Heart's Desire? We're a local gourmet confectionery, and we've put together an exclusive assortment for all the guests in attendance tonight."

"Actually, my wife has already sampled the offerings. Quite good, I'll say, including the, uh . . . uh . . ."

"Gingerbread fudge?"

The crimson in the man's cheeks flushed all the way north to his receding hairline. "Yes, that's the one. Actually, that's what I came over to talk about."

"Oh?" A deep V formed between Marisa's brows as she jockeyed her gaze between Alec and the man. The latter had pulled out a business card and was offering it to Alec. But before Marisa could inquire further, a contingent of council members approached Eden and Cal looking for her. "Please excuse me."

Then she was off, leaving Alec alone with the bloke and his business card.

"I'm Martin Penhaus. Good friends with Arthur Doley. I was just speaking to him. I know he and Monica are so happy with the turnout you all have been able to garner for the event. Biggest numbers they've seen in years."

"Ah, yes. Alec Elms," he said, shaking the man's hand. "Nice to meet you. Glad to hear it."

"Oh, believe me, the pleasure is mine. Smart bit of advertising for Great Britain, as well." Martin gestured toward the squares of face-fudge Cal was handing out at the far end of the booth.

"I can't take credit for it. That was all Marisa's doing. The owner of Sweetest Heart's Desire. And my girlfriend," he tacked on, loving the way the words felt on his lips.

"Well, whoever's idea it was, they should be congratulated, and I also wanted to make your acquaintance personally. I'm an executive producer for the Global Sports Matrix in New York."

Well, *that* made Alec's antennae stand at attention. Global Sports Matrix was *the* premier international sports broadcasting network.

"I have to say, this turnout has led to more people talking my ear off about rugby sevens than anything."

"That's a good thing, I wager. More exposure for the sport is always appreciated."

"Absolutely. Which is why I wanted to speak with you. I've been trying to bring more awareness to international sports Americans may not have learned to love yet and see whether there are opportunities for primetime coverage. I'm sort of on the hunt for the right candidates and whatnot. I'm thinking the sevens circuit might be a good option."

Alec's lips thinned, and whatever curious enthusiasm he had when Martin had introduced himself grew annoyingly threadbare.

Great. Another one of these blokes.

He'd had these conversations before, always to a room full of suits who still thought an eight-to-ten-o'clock evening airing window was the zenith of appeal for audiences and advertising dollars.

And just like before, he had his speech at the ready, though he made sure to round off some of the more aggressive corners lest his comments get back to Arthur and Monica and negatively impact Marisa in some way.

"Mr. Penhaus, I think I know where this is going, and I'd like to offer a different perspective, if you'd permit me."

"Please. You don't get to be my age without appreciating the value of a captive audience, whether on the giving or receiving end."

Good. That was . . . good. A better start he'd received than most, at least.

Alec cleared his throat. "Rugby, and rugby sevens specifically, doesn't play in what is commonly thought of as primetime in the domestic viewership markets, because it is an international game, played monthly for a weekend at a time in different countries all across the globe. Primetime markets, as you call them, are for an aging generation, not the sort that appeals to the streaming audience, who tune in on their terms. If you want people and advertisers to see rugby as appointment viewing, you'd be better served to meet the streamers where they are. Give them a reason to have the sport play in the background during the middle of a workday, or find broadcast opportunities that get to know the players more so that people will actually develop a fondness for the athletes representing their country and want to follow them. Doing so will make them actually *want* to watch a game that airs at five in the morning and even make it something they prioritize. It's not a coveted timeslot advertisers are after, in my experience, but who they can advertise *to* that is more important. Give people a reason to show up on their screens, and they will. Once you accomplish that, I suspect the money will follow."

Martin scratched beneath his chin. "Interesting take, I will say. It's a hard sell in our markets, though, you're right."

Alec lifted a shoulder. "Always is. That's why it's just my opinion."

"A valued one, nonetheless. You've given me something to chew over, even if it is a bit tougher than what I'm used to gnawing on." Then Martin smiled and refunded Alec's shoulder shrug before looking down at the sparse array of leftover face-fudge, which hadn't been enough to fill any more treat boxes with. "And is this what you'd have in mind for developing player attention?"

"Maybe? Though you'd have to talk to the boss about that." Alec gestured toward Marisa, who was still excitedly talking, if her hand gestures were anything to go by, with the council members.

"Perhaps I might." Martin plucked a pack of fudge from the table and nodded down at the business card in Alec's hand. "Great meeting you, Mr. Elms. Keep in touch."

"Aye. It was a pleasure."

As the older man got in line to make his purchase, Alec fidgeted with the corners of the card, one with information he'd ultimately pass off to Brennan when he spoke to the man next.

Which would be soon. He'd promised to sign and send over the Argentina contract once Christmas had passed.

"My boyfriend's face is a huge hit." Marisa's voice had almost a euphoric tinkle to it as she drifted closer to him and hooked an arm through his, her chiffon gown whispering against his legs. She beamed up at him.

And that damn gorgeous smile of hers was enough to send his heart vaulting into his throat.

Bloody hell, the way she looked at him . . . it was a precious gift he didn't deserve, one that had come to mean everything.

"You're the hit. I'm just the packaging."

"Pretty packaging, though."

He chuckled. "If you say so."

"Oh, I say so. So many so's."

Marisa rose on tiptoe to kiss him but skittered away when his phone began vibrating in his breast pocket, tickling her chest. "Hey, careful with the lace," she admonished teasingly. "I just got this."

"Noted. I'll be sure to have the nimblest of touches when I peel it off you later."

He winked as he took out his phone, then quirked a brow as Marisa chased another electronic vibration, this one from her phone that she had tucked beneath the table.

Odd.

It wasn't until the color had drained from Marisa's face as she stared down at her screen that a worried pressure began forming in his chest.

He unlocked his phone and gazed in horror at the social media post and its headline.

RUGBY STAR ALEC ELMS FAKES RELATIONSHIP TO SAVE DYING CAREER

For a while, Marisa just stared at the screen, trying to make sense of what she was seeing. The video was a dark, blurry concoction accented with neon lights that looked like they came from glowing beer signs.

Which made sense. The arms next to each other in the shot, only visible from the elbows down and filmed from above, were resting on a bar. She could practically feel the sticky furniture rings and sliminess of the paper coasters resting beneath the dirty martini glass gripped in the impressively manicured hand on the right.

A hand that was precariously close to the thickly knuckled one that had been holding hers all night.

Alec.

But that was where the fuzzy feelings ended, at least the ones that had been gliding her around through the best night of her life.

There were no faces shown, just the conversation's audio transcription scrolling along the top as two unmistakable voices spoke.

"Since when do you notice anything that isn't rugby related?"

Phoebe. Marisa would know that voice anywhere, especially the grating trill on the upward inflection whenever the woman's indignation would fire up. Lord knows Marisa had been on the receiving end of that experience more than she'd wished.

The word *notice* ground on her quickly unraveling nerves, given the shocking headline of the video.

ALEC ELMS FAKES RELATIONSHIP...

With her. As in, Why did he bother to notice *her?*

The subtext was all over the sentiment, and the implications were quickly becoming a raging sea she had no hope of swimming through.

And just when she thought she'd calmed her limbs enough to keep her floating and stationary, Alec's voice in the video sent her reeling against the rocks all over again.

"I was damn foolish."

"I ... know ... the difference between right and wrong."

"It was a mistake ... but this has all gone too far."

Those were all his words, spoken in his brogue, but Marisa recognized none of them. No sweet inflections. No tender humor.

Just phrase after phrase of painful ... Oh, God, she couldn't hear this. If she watched any more, she was liable to vomit all over Monica's carefully crafted tablescapes.

And yet she couldn't look away, and she sure as hell couldn't look at Alec, who had remained at her side glued to his phone, his posture torturously stiff in her periphery.

"Marisa ... She's not your girlfriend."

Her stomach sank at hearing her name, a confirmation of her implication in whatever the hell she was watching, but still, she couldn't look away.

Because she knew what would come next, and like any good car wreck that stole much more than it saved, she had to witness it for herself.

"No, she's not. I'll ... be leaving her alone."

Tears rose up until the words before her were nothing more than a blurry sheen of betrayal.

Marisa tossed the phone into her bag, grabbed her coat, and ran out the back entrance of the tent. Her heels' frenzied scrapes against the shoveled walkway mimicked the frantic beat of her heart as the damn muscle gasped out whatever confidence she'd worked so hard to fill it with.

"Marisa!" Outside the tent, Alec's head was on a swivel. Once they locked eyes—hers tear-rimmed, his crazed—he wasted no time vaulting over a large garbage can to get to her. "Marisa. This . . ." He held up the phone. "I didn't say . . . Those weren't—"

"Your words? They sure as hell sounded like your words. Unless you think Phoebe was wrong and I'm actually dating a slew of other Scottish guys in North Jersey."

"Dammit, can't we just talk about this without the sarcasm?"

"Why? Why are you allowed to have your armor, but I'm not? Why are you allowed to meet with her and have a private conversation about me, and I'm not allowed to combat it with the only weapons I have?"

"Jesus Christ, will you just listen to me? *Please.*" Something akin to heartbreak twisted his features, strengthening the plea in his voice and causing her resolve to falter slightly.

"Explain," she bit out, trembling from rage rather than cold. "Now. Why were you even with her, after how she treated me?"

Alec shook his head in frustration, dragging a hand over his face. "I set up a meeting with her, aye. But I did it because I discovered her involvement in sabotaging your efforts for the Ball."

Her blood froze. "What?"

"The Jamaican ginger extract. She was the one who snuffled up all the supply after she saw how popular your gingerbread post was on social media. I confirmed it with the grocer when I was trying to see whether I could get a quantity in for you by some bloody miracle."

Marisa's throat tightened around the few breaths she could still summon. "I don't believe you."

"You should, because it's true, and I went to confront her about it."

"Why didn't you tell me?"

"Because I didn't want to drag you any further into my mess. Lord knows I've fucked up enough already."

"That's what partners do, though. They drag each other into their messes, knowing they'll each have the other to lean on through it all."

Unless she'd read the room wrong this whole time.

Unless they weren't actually partners.

His sentiments from the video rose up to strangle her over and over again, with nary a stammer or misstep to be found. Nothing but smoky, low-timbred surety delivered in the precise number of words needed to deliver his message. Nothing more. Nothing less.

"Marisa . . ." Alec entreated.

"I can manage my own life, you know," she said through a thick throat. "Despite what my family thinks, or what the whole fucking world thinks, I can manage it. I'm a person capable of making the right choices." She stomped her foot, but even that couldn't help the statement sound less hollow.

"Of course you are. You're brilliant. Marisa, you're—"

"Just not someone you could trust to help you sort through your mess, even though you had no problem swooping in and tidying up mine. Without asking me." Then she looked at him and had to hug herself tighter for the only strength she could rely on. "Why did you say those things? Why did you lie to me?"

"I didn't lie. I lo—" He called back whatever he was about to say and kicked a neatly packed mound of snow instead. "For fuck's sake, I didn't lie."

"Were those your words? Tell me the truth, Alec. Was it your voice that said those things to Phoebe? Were you the one speaking to her?"

He couldn't lift his eyes to meet hers. "Aye."

The dagger of his declaration sank deep, so deep that she had to take a step back to steady herself lest she crumple to the ground and trip over her shredded heart.

The tent's rear flap was swept aside, and Eden came running over to them. Her chest was heaving, and it was clear from her bewildered expression that she'd been trying to run damage control at the booth and was failing miserably.

Because Marisa, and by extension her business, was a failure, a fake, and now the whole Internet knew it, too.

"Monica's looking for you. What do you want me to tell her?"

A numbness had begun to take hold, packing Marisa's veins full of cement. The lights on the Christmas trees surrounding the tent couldn't even infuse her limbs with the warmth needed to combat the sluggishness.

But they were strong enough to illuminate one thing she was kicking herself for not seeing earlier.

"I'm glad you were able to get your coat back from Phoebe," Marisa said, gesturing to the familiar woolen peacoat Alec had thrown on, a coat she'd not given another thought to all the time they'd been together the past couple of days.

She'd never thought to ask how it had been returned to him or when.

The fact that he'd kept it from her seemed to hurt far worse than his public treachery.

Marisa lifted her chin and accompanied Eden back into the tent to deal with whatever shit storm had begun swirling around and mucking up everyone's Christmas Eve.

Alec didn't call after her and didn't follow her.

Because what more could he say that he hadn't already told the world?

CHAPTER 29

Alec whipped the reading glasses off his face and pressed the pads of his fingers into his eyes. It did little to help alleviate the pressure that had been festering there for the better part of three days, but at least when his eyes were forced shut, he didn't have to stare in the mirror.

Because holy fuck, what a bleak picture that had become, or so Cal had unhelpfully informed him. Alec couldn't even remember the last time he'd brushed his teeth properly, let alone run a razor across his cheeks. It was no wonder his brother shook his head in disgust every time he tossed a plate of food in front of Alec's nose, as if he were doing some great service by keeping Alec alive.

For the record, he wasn't, at least not with his cooking. Then again, Alec didn't deserve the comfort of good food, or even good company.

No, he'd torched those options spectacularly.

Truth be told, he couldn't trust himself with either. Didn't deserve to. Because trust was one of those earned things only shared with the most important people in one's life, and no matter what sort of excuses his frantic mind kept coming up with, none of them changed one crucial heart-wrenching fact.

Marisa was right. He had lied to her. Because he trusted himself more to do the right thing and fix his fuck-up with Phoebe, rather than confiding in Marisa and letting her see the flaws of his past, hoping she might accept him anyway.

And look how bloody well that turned out.

Alec picked up his phone again and scrolled through the call history, hope still high in his heart that he'd see her name returning one of his countless calls. When he didn't, he darkened the screen and tossed the damn thing in the end table drawer. Again.

"Still no word from her?" Cal asked, cracking open a beer and handing him one.

"What do you think?"

"I think three days of silence speaks volumes." The words were gentle, caring, but they sliced deeply.

"I know."

"Do you want to hit the gym again?"

Alec scoffed and mindlessly tossed Hugh his rope toy.

When Christmas morning had rolled around and he hadn't heard from Marisa, Alec had sped over to her apartment and all but sprinted out of his car to see her, to beg her to listen to him, so he could explain how much of an arse he'd been and hope she'd understand. He already knew forgiveness was likely out of the question, but he had to try regardless. Instead, Enzo had been there, standing outside the restaurant and brandishing a pizza peel like it was a semi-automatic weapon. With one silent gesture toward Alec's parked car, the man evicted him from Marisa's neighborhood and her life.

The gym had been his refuge after that, but even pushing his body to exhaustion couldn't help him escape all those bloody mirrors reflecting his raw selfish stupidity back at him.

So, no, he didn't fucking want to go to the gym.

"I'm almost done reviewing this contract. I'll sign it and send it back to Brennan. Then that'll be done, and we can all just move on."

Cal took another sip and leaned over Alec's shoulder to read the documents. "I thought you had negotiated for the remote-work clause. Did I miss it, or is it on another page?"

"This is the original contract. I asked to revert back to it."

Hugh pounced over to Alec with the rope toy in his teeth and shimmied just out of reach when he went to grab it.

That was just fine with him. He had no interest in forced revelry, let alone being dangled about by a dog.

"Why the hell did you take it out?"

"Because there wasn't a point in keeping it in any longer."

"Yes, there is. It would free up a bit of your time to—"

"Do what?" Alec seethed, hating the clog of emotion he couldn't keep from his voice. "Waste it here? She doesn't want to see me, and I've done enough damage. I won't be adding on the pain of my presence to her plate."

And that was perhaps the heaviest truth of all, the one that tipped his scales so extremely, there was no recovering from it.

He'd *hurt* her and likely ruined her business's reputation in the process.

"I get that she won't talk to you, but you'd be foolish not to give it some time. Maybe she's not interested in hearing from you now, but in a week? A month? Wouldn't it only make things worse if she finally gets to a point where she's ready to hear your groveling and you've taken your explanation halfway round the world with you? She deserves to hear the whys of it all and take as much time as she needs getting to that point, but if you rob her of that, she might just hate you more for it."

"I'm pretty sure she couldn't hate me more than I hate myself."

"I'm pretty sure that's a bet you wouldn't win, but what the hell do I know? Phoebe played a fucking awful hand. I knew she was jealous, but this was a new level of treachery."

And there was the other name Alec was trying so hard not to think of. Phoebe. Fucking Phoebe. She of the Plant Nanny narcissism who wore bloody camera glasses to meet him at a bar and spliced his words together so she could ruin all the things he cared about.

Because he'd fucked her life up, too. Strung her along with promises he knew he'd never fulfill because rugby had had more of his heart than she had at the time.

And now, he had nothing.

Despite his fingers itching to strangle the woman or threaten her with litigation, none of it would make the situation any better.

None of it would bring Marisa back or reverse the absolute crushing heartache that destroyed the damn near perfect smile he'd put on her face seconds before everything went to shit.

"I'll deal with her. Preferably from an ocean away and through a mountain of legal paperwork. She knows what she did, and she'd be a fool to assume I wouldn't bark back. But I don't entirely blame her. Oh, don't get me wrong," he amended when Cal lifted a single brow, "a vile part of me would like to take one of her precious plants and wrap it around her bloody neck, but I'm the reason she did what she did to begin with. When I last saw her, I told her to be well and that I hope she finds peace. I genuinely meant it, too. So, if this is the route she needed to take to do that, it's my own bloody fault for hurting her to the point where she felt such drastic measures were her only way out."

Cal plopped his large frame onto the couch and hooked his arms over the back. "You're a better man than I am, that's for sure."

Not even a little bit. Not by half. And that's why I have to leave.

Alec cleared his throat, already hating the response he knew was heading for him, but he couldn't avoid it any longer. "I'm leaving."

Cal's brows furrowed, and he leaned closer, his beer dangling from his fingertips. "To where?"

"England."

"But Dr. Campbell hasn't cleared you yet, has she?"

"No, but I'll not wait around for it. I need to go back, get out of the States. I can finish recovering at home, perhaps even faster once I'm away from all this chaos. Hopefully rejoin the lads for the January leg and start to make arrangements to sell my flat come the spring. Finish out the farewell tour of the season Great Britain says they want to throw me and whatnot."

It was the only course of action left. Start the transition to coaching so he wouldn't have to think about all he was leaving behind, both on the pitch and in Jersey.

"You are such a fucking coward." Cal shook his head and brought his beer to his lips, not bothering to meet Alec's eyes.

"I ruined Marisa's life, her goddamn livelihood. My face was the one plastered all over her golden ticket, and it all came crumbling down because I thought she'd be ashamed if I confided in her about Phoebe, and then my stupid words hit the Internet and torched the rest of her good reputation. I humiliated her, Cal. What right do I have to stick around? Just so I can cause her more pain? I'm doing the right thing here. The honorable thing. I'm giving her the space she requires to rebuild what I ruined. The last thing she needs is seeing the likes of me showing up to remind her of what she lost and why."

Cal took his measure with a long, hard stare, then shrugged his shoulder and took another sip of his beer. "Like I said. Coward."

A fresh coating of rage painted his vision. Was he serious with this coward shit?

Alec shot to his feet, but Cal was already there, his beefy

arms a bulwark against whatever aggression his brother saw in Alec's eyes.

"The reason I say you're a coward is because you're allergic to teamwork."

Alec's ire paused its trembling assault. He blinked. "What?"

"You heard me."

He blinked again. "I'm a bloody rugby player. A team captain!"

"And when it comes to your personal life, you're shit at relationships because you think everyone should exist in a vacuum. That each person has a job, and that job should be executed accordingly. One person kicks, while the other tackles. And that may work on the pitch, where the integrity of the win is determined by roles and responsibilities, but none of that matters when it comes to who you care about. Relationships are not transactional. You either love someone or you don't, but if you can't communicate that, how the hell do you expect them to behave? They can't read your bloody mind."

Alec was about to say . . . Well, he wasn't quite sure what, because Cal's words had wormed their way into the spaces between his simmering emotions.

He hadn't been in love with Phoebe. He'd always known that, but had he ever really communicated that to her?

No. Instead, he'd strung her on for two years because the illusion of happiness for both of them seemed a fair imitation of the real thing.

But with Marisa . . . Their entire short time together had been nothing but a transaction, a fabricated sort of teamwork based on mutual goals and methods of achieving them.

Except then he'd gone and fallen in love with her, and he'd had no earthly clue how to handle it.

Alec plopped his arse down into the armchair and scraped his hand across his scalp in frustration. "Fuck."

He'd never bothered to parse out their roles and responsibilities, because for him, he'd do anything just to see her smile again. No transaction. No stipulations. No expectations. Just . . . joy. Every kind look and gesture she gave him had turned into a precious gift, and he'd gone and showed his compensatory gratitude by assuming that he needed to keep the unpleasantness of his life away from her as much as possible.

He'd assumed she couldn't handle it or that she shouldn't need to, but that had never been Marisa. That glorious woman had shown him nothing but courage, and if he could ever hope to see her again, even for one moment, he'd need to show her the same.

"I've got to, um . . . Shit." His mind sprinted in a thousand different directions, desperately searching for the right one that would lead him back to her. Anything. He'd say anything, *do* anything, to show her what she meant to him, to show her that—

"*Ow!* Hugh! God*dammit!*"

The beast, lost in the joy of tearing something to shreds, backed his big arse right into Alec's calf, knocking his knee into the coffee table. Cal already had the right of things, as he'd had the foresight to lift his beer in the air and back out of the wrecking zone, all the while laughing at Alec's misfortune, the bastard.

Alec rubbed his aching knee and leaned down to Hugh, who had an assortment of not-rope-toys in his muzzle. "Give it here. Whatever you're destroying deserves a proper burial."

But what Alec plucked from Hugh's jowls instead were several sheets of his contract that had fallen on the floor, along with a small bit of paper that was thicker than the rest and still hanging on for dear life on the dog's fang.

Alec extricated the discovery from the canine tooth it was hooked on and stared at the punctured paper.

It was a business card. The one Martin Penhaus had slipped him at the Crystal Christmas Ball. The one he'd planned to pass to Brennan as a simple courtesy, but hadn't thought anything more of.

But as he fingered the jagged edges of the unassuming scrap, the ripples of an idea began to take shape.

One that would only work if he got his arse in gear right the fuck now.

Alec tossed Cal his phone. "Pull up flights to England for me, will you? Whatever the soonest feasible one is."

"You're still going?"

"Aye. I need to settle some things first, but I don't have much time. I've got a lot of people to talk to, and I need to catch them all before they go on New Year's holiday."

If the crazy road he hoped his future might lead him down was to be paved, it needed the proper foundation first.

He just hoped that, after what everyone on social media had witnessed, the people he needed to speak to would still be interested in hearing him out.

CHAPTER 30

If an empty pizzeria could give hugs, Sal and Enzo's place was doing its best. Unfortunately, it was the *A for effort* best and the kind of reluctant yet obligatory side-hug siblings had to do when mothers screamed at them to hug it out after a major fight.

Always taken for granted but also always there. In the morning hours before the pizzeria was open to the public, Marisa had no problems breathing in the reliable yeast or shuffling her boot around until she found a patch of floor that wasn't sticky.

Sal had just taken out the latest batch of pizza dough to finish proofing on the counter and had done the much-needed good work of wordlessly restocking her Dr. Brown's supply in the fridge.On the top shelf this time. An angel, that man.

After several days of staring at the walls of her apartment, she'd finally had to admit defeat to her sad-sack emotions and venture outside. Besides, she'd used up her last pack of ramen and had vowed to stay as far away from sugar as possible.

Or any of the other sweet memories that seemed to strike out at her with every room she went into.

It was funny. Marisa had never been one for the dramatic and had always prided herself on hobbling through whatever horrors life threw her way, but this time, things felt different.

It felt almost permanent and unshakable in its reminders of just how much of a sucker she really was.

The chair in her living room where Alec had let her care for him after a misunderstanding with the boys, her sad menorah that still sat untouched, all drippy and frozen from the last time Alec had put candles in it, the doorframe of her bedroom where Alec had stood in nothing but his boxer briefs and that delicious smirk that made her insides go all a-flutter . . .

Dammit.

Marisa's eyes began to mist over again as the shame of her foolishness rose hot and heavy, even after she'd done her best to put it all from her mind, put *him* from her mind.

She couldn't speak to him. Didn't want to hear any excuses regarding his regrets or guilt.

She had quite a bit of her own to deal with, not the least of which was what the hell she was going to do with her life now that Sweetest Heart's Desire had been embroiled in the confectionery world equivalent of a holiday sex scandal.

Marisa hadn't bothered to reopen her online shop after she'd shut things down for Christmas. Any orders that would come in were likely only out of pity anyway.

And she was doing damn fine hosting her own pity party, thank you very much, in a pizza parlor no less.

But God, it all hurt. *Hurt.* Like a chunk of her had been ripped out and lit on fire as part of a public spectacle level of hurt. She'd always thought she could handle loss a bit better than most people, but that had been before Alec had rolled the stuff around in an extra-thick layer of rejection and betrayal.

No one alive could have swallowed that and come out topside.

A thousand questions still plagued her, not the least of which was *why oh why*, but she told herself she'd just need to be content with not knowing. Answers wouldn't change what had happened.

They wouldn't change the way her heart had been torn into a million fragile pieces with each one crushed beneath some absurd designer planter.

None of it seemed to make any sense on the surface, and perhaps that was what stung worst of all. The words, those hateful, *awful* words, had been his, but for the life of her, she couldn't reconcile the truth of them with the man she'd come to know, the man she'd come to care so deeply about that this whole nightmare felt like a part of her had turned the knife on herself.

It was another reminder that she hadn't known Alec at all. How could she after only a few short days of mutually agreed-upon falsehoods?

The whole thing made the betrayal that much thicker, until it turned into a vile sludge behind her breastbone.

The sharp *tsss* of the cream soda was the first jolt she needed to send her morose thoughts packing for a bit. What did she care that it was still solidly in the a.m.? Poor life choices and poor dietary choices often went hand in hand, making both a bit more palatable.

And she desperately required palatable.

The second jolt she needed came in the form of a sharp knock on the glass window next to the flipped-over *Closed* sign. Eden stood there, eagerly shaking her leg in greeting because her arms were full with three distinct colors of takeout bags.

Sal grunted his approval at the off-hours intruder, and Marisa went to let her in. Yup. Total freaking angel.

Before Marisa even had the thing fully open, Eden burst through the door and immediately plopped one of the bags, a brown one, on Sal's counter. "Payment for early entry."

The suspicious pizzaiolo arced a large bushy brow before

wiping his floury hands on his apron, reaching into the bag, and pulling out a glistening, crusty elephant ear pastry easily the size of a calzone.

"Is that from De Luca's?" Marisa asked, her mouth already watering.

"Yup. The first of many stops on this morning's *Eat Our Feelings But Not Our Pride* parade route."

Before Marisa could question her friend further, her hands flew out to keep her soda from toppling as she was greeted by a flurry of bags being dropped on her table. From the corner of her eye, a flash of white curled itself around the brown paper bag. When she looked back, Sal was gone, along with the elephant ear, a thin cloud of flour dancing in his wake.

"Damn, that man moves fast. What else was in that bag?"

Eden winked as she finished setting up her spread. "I got the last of the Christmas struffoli before they started switching out cases with the New Year's desserts."

"Oh, you are a queen."

"I know." She grinned. "Now, here. I got the good coffee from Alice's Coffee and Kitchen, hazelnut with almond cream, of course. Then I got the good bagels from Beta Bagels and Bites over on Claremont. The French toast ones were right out of the oven, but they also had those whole wheat sesame ones you like. Grabbed some scallion cream cheese, too, along with the walnut raisin. They didn't mix it with as much cinnamon this time, I'm guessing. The color's a bit light, but I already taste tested it and can confirm it's equally delicious, as always. They might have some new employees making the cream cheese. Not sure, but still so good. Yum."

Marisa marveled at the spread before her and breathed in each distinct scent that had already gotten to work on loosening the pressure behind her ribs. "I love you."

"I love you, too, and never forget," Eden said, lifting a heavily schmeared French toast bagel to her lips, "carbs and caffeine will always love you back."

"Amen."

After they saluted their cream-cheese-smothered bagels and proverbially clinked paper coffee cups, the euphoria of Marisa's creature comforts had begun to settle in enough that she was finally able to have an adult conversation with her childhood best friend.

Except this time, boys were sure as hell off the table.

"So, what are your plans for the New Year?" Eden asked.

"My parents need help putting their Hanukkah stuff away. They said they'd pay me in hot dogs and sparkling rosé, so I don't think I'm in a position to turn that down at the moment, given the state of my fridge."

"Of course. What fool in her right mind would say no to a couple of Hebrew Nationals and a three-dollar bottle of not-Champagne? And on New Year's Eve, no less."

"You joke," Marisa said, feeling the need to defend her gloomsday meal, "but it's not like I have anything better to do. You chose to betray me as well."

"It's not betrayal. It's a job. A holiday-pay-rate job. I'm a bartender. It's literally my tax season."

"Still feels like betrayal," Marisa muttered, "even if it is understandable."

"I'm just saying, there are better places to be than château de Silver right now."

"I know, but this is likely the one time where my parents' total lack of enthusiasm for my career might be beneficial. They probably won't know what happened. I can't imagine they follow me on social media, so I won't have to rehash anything. I can just clean off all the candle wax like a good little robot and check the box for visiting them when they asked me to."

"What if they ask about Alec?"

"They won't." And oh boy, did she spit those words out almost as fast as she thought them. "They already knew he was going to be rejoining his team after Christmas. If they keep prodding me with anything else, well, that's what the three and a half bathrooms are for. After such a long GI-straining holiday, no one would question why I would need to excuse myself so often. Besides, they invited me to their block's small fireworks show, so, you know, there'll be an eventual time when conversation about me would have to stop so my mother and Aunt Gail could resume their favorite topic of community noise complaints."

"Your family members are the literal last people on the planet who I would think would want to be anywhere near fireworks."

Marisa took a sip of her coffee. Mmm. So good. "My mother calls anything spicier than a campfire *fireworks*, but it's literally just a cul-de-sac of sparklers. At any rate, even though it breaks my *bed by eleven* rule, avoiding my family altogether would only put more attention on myself eventually."

And that was something she definitely did not want. After her time as Alec's fake girlfriend, she'd had all the attention she could take for a couple of lifetimes.

When Eden didn't immediately fill the silence like Marisa expected, she lowered her coffee cup and sized up her friend. Sure enough, the woman was staring way too intently at a bottle of ketchup on the table and had started using her finger to scrape nonexistent cream cheese off her plate.

Marisa thinned her lips and kicked Eden's leg.

"Ow!"

She would *not* be the person people walked on eggshells around, no matter how fragile she felt. "Just say it. I know you want to."

Eden rubbed her calf, but the sadness in her friend's eyes was laced with the kind of regret veterinarians must feel whenever the phrase *euthanasia* came up on their patient schedule. "Any word from Monica?"

Monica. Now there was another Christmas wreath-wrapped boulder Marisa had been crushed beneath.

"Not since I spoke to her at the Ball."

After the news broke about the video, Monica had expressed concerns about what had happened and how it may have impacted the event and the recreation board's (re: *her*) reputation. With no suitable words of explanation or even understanding, all Marisa could do at the time was hide behind the standard millennial response given to all boomers when it came to clarifying such Internet scandals. Handling West Meadow's premier boomer benefactress was no different.

"Technology is weird, and no one ever really understands it."

"Social media is finicky. Don't believe everything you read on the Internet."

"Short-form video is so fleeting. No one will even remember this in a week."

Yeah, well, it had been a week, and Marisa still hadn't heard whether Monica had made a decision about including Sweetest Heart's Desire on her vendor list.

The silence was speaking volumes, though.

"I'm so sorry." Eden reached across the table and grabbed her hand, squeezing it to impart the comfort Marisa needed.

And, God, she hated that she needed it, but she did. Because, as delicious and warming as the bagels and her best friend were, they still couldn't touch the frigid chill that had iced over her heart.

Marisa sat back in her seat, removed the to-go lid from her cup, and took the biggest scorcher of a sip her mouth could take, hoping to get any infusion of heat that might stop her lips from shivering in sadness.

Instead, the only thing that seemed to worm its way through was more bitterness.

CHAPTER 31

The email that came through early the next morning had been the last thing Marisa would have pictured herself receiving, let alone responding to.

Let alone agreeing to.

But curiosity had a funny way of yanking a person out of whatever equilibrium they'd managed to work up. Even if that equilibrium was still just barely balancing sanity with survival.

Marisa trudged along the street, with her chunky scarf and tasseled wool hat serving as the only armor she had left against the situation she was about to walk into.

Pretty pathetic, but all things considered, she couldn't imagine anything hurting her more than what she'd already endured.

The coffee shop she entered wasn't one she normally frequented. Not only was it on the complete opposite side of town from her usual haunts, but it featured drinks that never sounded like coffee. Marisa was more than happy to get on board with fun foams, flavored roasts, and alternative milk choices—hello, sensitive tummy—but she tended to say *no thanks* to any drinks that were crayon-box colored with prices that rivaled her car payment.

But she wasn't there for a drink. She was there for one reason and one reason only.

Marisa's steps slowed once she laid eyes on who she was meeting with. Not just slowed but came to a complete stop. She was half inclined to run outside and double-check the signage to make sure she hadn't gotten the location wrong.

Nope, she hadn't, but that didn't make her any more comfortable.

Red hair she had only ever seen perfectly frizz-free and infuriatingly defiant of the elements sat arranged in an artfully messy bun. A few wisps had broken free here and there, framing a face that looked far more gaunt than glowing. Gone were the carefully lined lips and smug expression, along with whatever haute couture had usually been called in to pinch hit for perfection.

A pair of mauve sweatpants and an oversized gray sweatshirt swallowed the woman who had her unpainted fingers curled around a steaming cup of something.

"Phoebe?" Marisa waited for confirmation that the scene before her was real and not a mirage.

Sure enough, the Plant Nanny herself lifted her head and immediately got to her feet. "Hi. Thank you for meeting with me."

Marisa didn't say anything, and even though she had driven all the way over there before she had to make the schlep to her parents' house, she still couldn't make her feet go farther. "Your email caught me off guard."

"I can imagine. Would you like to sit? Um, with me?" Phoebe stepped to the side and gestured to the chair opposite her.

It was clear that neither of them was in their element, and the only thing Marisa could deduce from that situation was that they were finally on a level playing field.

Marisa pulled out the chair and sat down, but she kept the seat turned out and her left leg positioned toward the door in case more shots were fired and Phoebe intended to start Marisa's year the way the woman had ended it.

"I didn't have a way of reaching you, so I figured the contact form on your website was the next best thing."

"You didn't want to rifle through Monica's vendor applications when she wasn't looking and snatch my phone number instead? Seems like more your speed."

Phoebe tensed. "I deserve that."

"Yes, you do."

The Plant Nanny's deep breath was unexpected and only served to set Marisa's nerves on edge even further. "I invited you out today hoping you would agree to speak with me because I want to apologize. For everything."

Marisa narrowed her eyes in suspicion. "What?"

"The night Alec and I met at the bar . . ."

Oh, she did not want to hear this. No way in hell did she want to hear this. Hadn't she heard enough about that night? Hadn't the entire Internet heard enough?

"I remember exactly what you two talked about. You don't need to reiterate."

"No, you don't. You don't know anything about that night, because what was leaked online was a fabrication." Phoebe pressed a sternness into her words that Marisa hadn't heard before.

Between the woman's shrieking and blaming and threatening, each with their own vocal registers, she thought she knew all the flavors of Phoebe. But this one was new and smacked with an earnestness Marisa hadn't thought the woman capable of.

"You two faked that entire conversation?"

"No. Alec's words were his own, but they were taken out of context and mashed together in a different order." Then she pinched the bridge of her nose, and for the first time, Marisa noticed the bags beneath her eyes and the frayed edges of her sweatshirt collar, along with some discoloration around the wrist cuffs and . . . Was that an old stain on one of the sleeves?

The Phoebe Marisa knew would rather die buried beneath her potting soil than be caught out in public, let alone in such a disheveled state at a bougie coffee shop.

The shock to her system was almost enough to make her miss the gigantic truth bomb foisted on top of her.

"I'm sorry. What?"

Phoebe's shoulders rose and fell with a sad, shaky breath that seemed to humanize a woman Marisa had always thought of as untouchable. "Alec and I were together a long time, but we weren't really *together*, you know?"

No, she didn't know, but she would soon find out.

"Regardless, I still resented him for how it ended. I realize now that I wasn't resentful of him so much as his ability to move on so easily, while I had been trapped inside the sunk-cost fallacy of what we had. I used to think that, if you put a certain amount of time into something, that thing then owed you in reciprocal dividends, which is foolish. Even a brand-new car decreases in value the second you drive it off the lot."

She took a sip of her coffee and played with the little plastic tab over the mouth opening. "And then he started dating you. Or not dating you. I don't know what you two ever were, to be honest, but seemingly overnight, there he was again, basking in his rugby glory once more, but this time, with a different woman to smile along with."

Then Phoebe sat back, straightened her posture as only one trained to do so would, and smiled sadly at her. "I'm not the first entrepreneur in my family. My mother founded her own wealth management company in her mid-twenties and already had several high-rolling clients before she was even legally allowed to rent a vehicle in most states. My father was a licensed therapist in the trauma therapy space, but he made his living by opening up several practices that employed other trauma specialists to do the counseling instead, while he ran the operations and handled the insurance. My younger brother Anton has already started up and sold two different tech companies, and he's working on his third. And me? I babysit plants.

"I'm sure you can imagine what our Thanksgiving dinners are like, but in case you're curious, no, my family doesn't ask me about my business, because they don't view it as one. Despite my company's healthy profit margins, and despite me literally showing them the fucking receipts of my success, my interests still aren't exactly legacy worthy in their eyes. But they liked Alec, or his status, I assume, even if, deep down, I wasn't entirely happy all the time I was with him. So, when I saw Alec and you together, I was envious and . . . hurt. And that led me to do some awful, stupid, desperate things."

Marisa's body slouched forward as she shucked off her *never let them see you cry* battle armor and flattened her palms on the table to brace herself against the shock.

She was jealous? Of me?

Phoebe went back to fiddling with her coffee cup lid. "Alec reached out to me. Wanted to clear the air, he said, and I couldn't very well refuse since I still had his coat and I didn't want to look at the thing any more than I had to. So, I met with him under the guise of returning his belongings. My *former* social media manager was aware of the meeting and suggested I record the conversation. I wasn't a fan of the idea, but I had already gone down an avenue that was so unlike my usual planning, I couldn't risk going back, convinced that even awful plans might have some merit in them." Then she gave Marisa another sad smile. "For example, I was the one who stocked up on all the Jamaican ginger extract, knowing you were on the hunt for it. Not one of my finer moments, and I apologize for that, too. Hell, I don't even like ginger." She sniffed. "The pressure to be perfect really does suck, doesn't it?"

And that right there was the painful distillation of what Marisa's candy making had tried so hard to battle against for so long. Already, the heated tension that had ridden her hard on the way in had begun to ease slightly as it sought companionable relief in, of all people, the Plant Nanny. An unlikely fellow member of People Pleasers Anonymous.

"Yeah," Marisa breathed. "Totally does."

Maybe matching headbands were in order or something.

They sat there in silence for a few moments, and Marisa tried to parse out what she thought she once knew with what she'd come to learn. Like any form of enlightenment, however, a ton of crap first had to be moved out of the way before one could get to the good stuff.

"You still recorded him," Marisa reminded her. "Without his consent."

The glimmer of camaraderie that had seemed to spark between them quickly extinguished. "I did. I had already hit record by the time he sat down, and I didn't want to draw attention to the fact that I was wearing the glasses by turning them off. But almost immediately into our conversation, I knew I would never do anything with the recording." She twisted her lips. "He made me realize that it was doing neither of us any good to hold on to my anger. That by doing so, I was only dragging out our bitter ending, instead of cherishing the times early on when I was truly happy. He told me"—she cleared her throat and Marisa felt the urge to look away but didn't—"he told me to be well, to be happy, and for the first time in so long, I finally wanted to. But my social media manager got to the footage before I had a chance to tell her I'd changed my mind. The rest is . . . regrettable."

Then she lifted remorse-filled eyes to Marisa, and she was struck by the genuine truth of her words. "I'm so sorry. I know sorry doesn't fix anything, but I need to tell you regardless. This is not who I am. This is not who the Plant Nanny is. Not anymore, at least. That's exactly what I told Alec when I spoke to him yesterday."

"You talked to him?"

She nodded. "Told him everything. Apologized. I needed to clear the air as much as I could, even if it meant pushing all the foul smog of my own making back my way."

"I, uh, haven't spoken to him since the Ball." But the excuse that had once felt powerful and strong, like a true statement piece, now rang hollow in the light of his true involvement.

"You should. He cares about you. I can tell you're important to him."

Marisa wanted to believe that, she really did, but she couldn't ignore the impetus for the secret meeting between him and Phoebe, the one he'd chosen not to include her in, despite her being a central figure in it all. The thought pricked her eyelids, but she was helpless to blink away the memories.

I'm still not important enough to be trusted fully, though.

Marisa tried to bury her thoughts back down, but Phoebe was still talking, pulling her away from the mental dig site.

" . . . focusing on my New York clientele will be better for me anyway. Jersey's great, but I have more room to grow in the city. Denser populations and whatnot. Besides, so many of those high rises have restrictions on pets, so people there tend to load up on plants instead."

"New York? What about Monica's vendor list? Her referrals are legendary."

Phoebe wrinkled her nose. "Didn't get added."

"No shit," Marisa breathed, absolutely stunned. "I haven't heard from Monica. I just assumed she went with you instead. That I had lost."

"Turns out, we both lost. But hey, this whole situation could be worse," Phoebe said, a new idea giving a bit of life back to her dull eyes. "We might be people pleasers, but at least we can enjoy good Jersey pizza in the process. Alec's stuck with whatever passes for Chinese takeout over in England."

Marisa's almost-smile faltered, and her heart tripped over itself. "England?"

"Yeah. He flew back a few days ago."

CHAPTER 32

The entire drive to her parents' house, Marisa could barely keep her mind focused on the road. It was only due to pure survival instincts and her car's muscle memory that she managed to avoid the regularly scheduled potholes riddling the Parkway exit ramp.

Never in a million years could she have expected her encounter with Phoebe to have gone the way it had. It was a jarring thing to have one's certainties questioned, especially when precedent had done its damnedest to ensure a consistent experience, good or bad.

Nothing about her time with Phoebe had been consistent. Instead, it had been eye-opening on more levels than Marisa was ready to explore. It took a big person to admit when the rival they thought they knew was perhaps more like them than they could have imagined. And sure, did she spend her highway miles replaying all their interactions together and start picking out moments where, had Marisa been paying closer attention, she might have seen how the hurt and fanfare were all just a cover-up for deeply rooted insecurities?

Yes, yes she did. But that wasn't the only thing playing on repeat as she pulled into her parents' driveway.

Alec was gone. Not just gone, but across-the-ocean gone. Different-country gone. The reality of it rankled her and sat heavily on her chest with an unease that made it hard to breathe.

He hadn't truly said those things, those awful, hurtful things that had publicly humiliated her and her business. And she'd not given him the chance to explain himself, to tell her the truth from his mouth directly.

Phoebe, of all people, had been the one to clear the air in that regard instead, and, God, Marisa wished the woman hadn't busted out the original recording of her and Alec's bar conversation in front of the coffee shop audience the way she had. After days of not hearing his voice, the brogue came back to claim Marisa's heart all over again.

"She's not your girlfriend."

"No, she's not. I mean, she is, now, I think, but wasn't before, though even that doesn't sound at all fair."

"What is she, Alec? It's a simple question."

"She's . . . she's mine."

Already, her tears were doing their level best to force her sadness to the surface, and there was no way she'd let her broken heart ruin everyone else's New Year.

It was doing a bang-up job of ruining hers.

"Dry this for me, honey bun, will you?" Marisa's dad handed her another sterling silver something or other. What had she been polishing again? Oh, right. A dreidel-shaped serving tray.

As if summoned by the stately piece's appearance, her mother swept into the kitchen with a slew of to-be-assembled boxes under one arm, with a caddy full of bottles, sprays, and cloths dangling from the other, each one still wearing their yellowed price tags from decades ago. It was a testament to just how often the stuff got called into service.

Marisa had to smile at that. Perhaps seasonal neglect was more of a family trait than she realized.

"I've put the rest of the Hanukkah items on the living room table so we can tackle them like an assembly line. Now, the porcelain platters will be the hardest ones to wrap, but I got the tiny bubble wrap this year, which does a better job around the contours, so I'm hoping that won't be a problem. For the menorahs, especially the ones from the party, I already picked off as much of the wax as my arthritis would allow. The rest is up to you two. Remember," she said, setting down the caddy and pulling out each bottle with care, "first, you use this spray to remove the wax. Let it sit for five minutes so it gets nice and loose, then you use one of these cloths to wipe it all away." She held up a jar with an angry-looking dispensing spout. "Once that's done, grab a glob of this silver polish—a *good* glob—and schmear it all over the metal. That one should stay on for *ten* minutes, not five. Make sure it's all ten minutes. Very important. After that, wipe it off with the cloths in *this* canister, which are different from the other ones. These have a cream on them or something." She picked up the container and narrowed her eyes as she tried to confirm her directions with the label's fine print.

Yikes.

"Okay, Ma."

"Yes, dear."

While her mother kept going on about proper polishing techniques—with hand‑gestures Marisa could have really freaking done without—her father had quietly already returned from the living room, one of several wax-stained menorahs in hand. Out of the corner of her eye, he turned the sink faucet to scalding and, standing behind the protection of Marisa's back, stuck the first menorah beneath the hot water. In seconds, all the wax disintegrated. A quick swipe of a soapy sponge later and the thing was gleaming with glossy pride. The whole endeavor took ten seconds tops.

Marisa blinked, then whipped her head back at her mother, who was caught up in balancing all the bottles upside down so the products would come out faster that she hadn't noticed a damn thing.

Her father grinned and whispered out the side of his mouth, "Don't tell your mother. Making a fuss makes her happy."

"But this could all be done in, like, five minutes."

"And if she couldn't worry over this stuff, what do you think she'd spend the time worrying about next?"

Marisa thought about it for all of two seconds before she reached for more of what he'd brought over from the living room—a cluster of serving utensils this time. She gave him a playful shove. "Make some room at the sink, will you?"

They fell into a comfortable routine. Her father dousing the metal in hot water, Marisa wiping it all down, and her mother flitting around like a fly trapped inside, desperate to find a window—or something else to clean.

God, the woman was just not happy if she wasn't moving. Which made sense. When Marisa thought back to all the Hanukkah glitz and glamour that had dripped down these halls only a week ago, it was kind of sad to say goodbye to it all. For eight days, her family fussed and ate and sang songs and ate some more and, yeah, poked her about parts of her personal and professional life she'd rather not offer up for scrutiny, but somehow, packing all of it up didn't make her feel any better the way she thought it would.

"Oh," her mother said, pointing a finger in the air. "The fireworks are starting at nine thirty, but the Jamesons are firing up the grill at six. I said we'd bring over all the hamburgers and hot dogs and such. Hank, can you get everything out of the fridge? It's all bundled in the plastic bag in the door."

"Sparklers," Marisa mumbled, wiping down a carving knife and setting it aside. "They're just sparklers."

"They're exploding sticks of gunpowder."

"Pretty sure they haven't used gunpowder in sparklers for, like, the last century or so. Aunt Gail would know. I can't imagine there's a History Channel documentary she hasn't seen. Speaking of which, where is Aunt Gail? Doesn't she usually like to supervise when we put everything away? I remember her having very specific opinions on how to properly wrap and store the Star of David serving dishes."

By the time Marisa finished drying down all the silver and neither her mother nor her father had spoken, she knew something was wrong.

And, yup, she'd sure as hell nailed that one when she saw the two of them exchanging worried glances. Again, that stupid knot began forming in her stomach.

"Honey, there's something we should probably tell you."

"Okay . . ."

Her mother twisted her fingers in the hem of her sweater. "Aunt Gail and Uncle Max are getting a divorce."

"*What?*"

Her father went into the fridge and pulled out the plastic bag of *meats and treats*, as he liked to call them. "That's right. My stepbrother's finally cutting her loose."

"About time, if you ask me," her mother added.

"I think Max thinks so, too. I know he hasn't been happy for years, but at their age, change doesn't come easy. I did talk to him this morning, though, and he already sounds so much better now that he's finally settled into the decision. He even has an eye on this property in Puerto Rico he's been dying to get his hands on. Once the paperwork goes through, I suspect we'll see an invitation or two."

"Hold on. Just hold the fuck on for a second." Marisa put her fingers to her temples but stopped rubbing when she saw what was in her dad's hands. "Are those brats?"

"Sure are, honey bun."

"*Pork* brats?"

A confused crease crossed her mother's brow before a dawning look of awareness smoothed everything out. "Oh, sweetheart," she said, patting Marisa's shoulder in a *my sweet Southern child* rhythm that Marisa did not appreciate. "We haven't kept kosher for years."

"*Years?*" Aaand the tension headache was back. Yup, just sitting there right between the eyes. "I'm not hearing this. I am *so* not hearing this."

"Hear it or not, it's the truth. Gosh, I can't even remember the last time we had any kosher meat in the house that wasn't catered by your aunt."

A niggling feeling crept its way into Marisa's mind in the form of a strange hunch she'd never given legs to before. "You did all of this for Aunt Gail?"

Her father put the brats and other assorted meats on the kitchen table. "We didn't really have a choice. Think what you want of her, but she's helped us out a lot over the years financially, and your mother and I weren't always in a position to turn her down. Let's see," he added, holding up his fingers to tick things off. "There was the roof leak thirteen years ago that started out as a patch job but turned into a total replacement."

"Then the neighbor's tree came down in that summer storm, and a huge bough broke off and landed on our shed. What a nightmare that was. Did you know that if a single branch hangs over your fence, you're responsible for it, even if the tree itself is planted on another person's property?" Her mother shook her head. "We had to replace the entire structure *and* the lawn mower *and* the snow blower."

"There sure were a few years where we got dealt some crummy cards, honey bun. Your Aunt Gail was always the first in line, ready to cut a check." Then he slipped his hand to the side of his mouth. "Though she made sure everyone knew about her *generous goodwill.*"

"Made me sick." Her mother huffed. "But we had no choice,

so we thought it best to appease her and some of the other less savory members of the family by hosting the holidays. We had the space, after all, and it was just easier to make her happy. You see, dear . . ." Her mother drew Marisa close and cupped her shoulders. "Your aunt was, well, a bit of a bitch."

What came out of Marisa's mouth next could only be described as a guffaw.

"I get the shock," her father said through a warm chuckle, "especially because you only ever visit on the holidays when she's around. I can understand why you stayed away, though." He found a spot of water on the counter that urgently needed drying off. "Never liked the way she was so disapproving of your candy business. It wasn't right. Your mother and I should have spoken up, but we could never find the courage, given all the gifts we accepted from her over the years. But we know now that all the flashy funds in the world don't entitle anyone to speak about our daughter that way, family or not. I'd give every cent back if I could, and I'm not going to fall in line anymore out of fear for family reactions. Your mother and I are just so damn proud of you, honey bun. You're making a life for yourself on your terms in a way the two of us were never able to."

"And with that handsome Alec no less. Oh, by the way," her mother said, slinking closer. "Jules showed me a picture of the gingerbread fudge. You remember him, don't you? We like to play pickleball together now," she said, smiling. "But would, uh, you happen to have any extra? It looked mighty delicious."

"Um, Ma? Ew."

Her father wrinkled his nose. "Gingerbread's not my style, but I ordered three boxes of your buttermints a few weeks ago, and I'm almost out. I hadn't realized you closed down your online shop, though. What do you say to hooking your old man up?"

"Wait." Marisa panted through the double hug of parental love she'd been unexpectedly sandwiched between. "Dad, *you're* my buttermint buyer? The one who buys three boxes every two weeks like clockwork? That was *you*? But your name wasn't on it, and the shipping address was different."

Her father shrugged. "Had them sent to my golfing buddy Arnold's house. I didn't want to embarrass you by seeing your good old dad's name show up on orders twice a month."

"Holy shit. Embarrass me? You thought you would *embarrass* me?" Marisa couldn't keep the snort-laugh in anymore. She let it flow wild and free, not caring a whit about the wads of tissues her mother kept bunching into Marisa's hand or how her dad kept doing the *it's okay, kiddo* back pat that just made her laugh even harder. "Those orders were literally the things that kept me going."

All this time, she'd thought the worst of her family. Well, not the worst, but certainly not the best.

The failure, the stigma, the disappointed looks and hurtful comments. How many of them had been from her parents? She searched her mind for examples, but all she came away with were images of the silent worry scrawled on their faces while Aunt Gail spoke her thoughts freely, and the other cousins and such fell in line for fear of being cut off.

But Aunt Gail would no longer be a part of the family soon, and while Marisa wasn't exactly happy to hear someone's marriage was ending, she also wasn't *not* happy.

"Just know that you'll always have two very happy customers of Sweetest Heart's Desire, and I imagine Alec as well." The hope in her mother's voice was the drop-tower plunge that shot Marisa back to reality.

Alec.

He was gone, and she had to disappoint her parents all over again, though this time for a different reason entirely.

"He, uh, had to go back to England."

Her parents gave her a sad look and nodded their understanding. Then her dad added, "To finish his season?"

"Yeah, to finish his season."

It was as good an answer as any, and who knew? It might have been true. That had been the plan originally, but then again, she couldn't help but remember how capable he was of going rogue.

He didn't need to run anything by her or include her in his plans. Never had.

Marisa felt the wave of emotion rising in her stomach, so she forced a smile and gestured toward the food on the counter. "Hey, uh, why don't you guys take the hot dogs and stuff over to the neighbors' place? I'll join you after I use the bathroom."

"Sounds good, honey bun."

She hugged her parents, dearly this time, and meant every bit of the squeeze she gave, but she had held back a bit, too, so they wouldn't see the sad little part of her that wished for a slightly different miracle than the one this Hanukkah had given her.

After splashing some cold water on her face, Marisa bundled up and stepped out into the crisp evening air, determined to enjoy the non-firework fireworks and a few brats, when a broad figure stepped out of the car in front of her parents' house.

Marisa started at first, not sure whether she should run, scream, or heave the bag of ketchup and mustard at the person's head. But when the man moved up her driveway, farther into the spray pattern of the porch light, the shaggy blond hair and reserved gap-toothed smile that greeted her stole the tension from her limbs.

And replaced it with a different sort of terror.

"Cal? What are you doing here? Is everything all right?"

"Oh, aye, I suppose. Now, before you go thinking me a creep, know that Eden gave me this address and told me where you'd be. If you have any issues with that, take it up with her. I'm not interested in getting arrested tonight."

"Um, okay?" Then she noticed the folded piece of paper in his hand.

Cal lifted the thing in the air between his index and middle fingers. "I'm just an errand boy. I've been told to deliver this. That's all."

Her heart was in her feet again, weighing her to the spot. And Cal seemed to get the sense that movement was beyond her, so he graciously walked toward her and handed it off.

She recognized Alec's handwriting instantly.

"Have a read. Then have a drink. It'll be a new year soon. No one should be left with a cold belly. And if you choose not to forgive him, I'll respect that and still pummel him properly in recompense." He winked at her with a charming smile she was certain was a family trait. "Good night, Marisa. Happy New Year."

Then he was gone, and she was left holding a note that felt far heavier than the flimsy paper ever could.

Slowly, with trembling hands, she opened the flap and read.

Marisa,

In case I don't get to you in time, there are some things I need to tell you.

First, as I write this, I'm sitting here with a box of blueberry candy canes. They taste like the worst parts of a Jolly Rancher and those hard sucking candies my Nan used to have in a dish at her front entrance. Reminds me of cough medicine and that concentrated syrup that goes on shaved ice. They're truly vile fucking things . . . and I love them. I love them because I know you love them.

I'm not smart enough to find the words to fix what I've done. And, no, that's not a cop out. I say this because I have a gnawing fear that I've broken your trust by trying to take care of things in the only way I knew how. I fear I've done irreparable damage, and trying to say <u>I'm sorry</u> just sounds so paltry and pointless.

I left New Jersey, which I'm sure you've learned by now. I went back to England, but not for the reason you might think. You see, I've been thinking about stories and how the story I'd always written for myself no longer seemed to fit the way it had. And I realized why.

That version didn't have you in it, and I needed to see what I could do to change that. I'll not waste space here on details, as there are far too many and you deserve to hear them first and in person.

I know this is all vague and you have no reason to trust me or even agree to see me again, but all I can say is that, when you were with me, nothing about it was fake on my end. You are my everything, Marisa.

So, what kind of a man would I be if, by some bloody miracle, I get you back, but I haven't done the work to earn you?

I'll be traveling for a bit and don't know how reachable I'll be, but know that I'm working my way back to you, so you can rail at me in person and batter me with all the blame I deserve.

I'll take it all, because I'm working on giving you all of me—my heart, my body, my soul, and whatever else I can do to round out the package.

Wherever your heart is at, I'll accept it. But it'll

never stop me from loving you or finding my way back to the best choice I ever made.

The right choice. The only choice.

-Alec

Marisa swiped at her leaky eyes and yanked her phone out of her pocket. She barely had her glove off before she tried his number.

And tried again. And again.

After five times of being sent to voicemail, she finally gave up and let the tears flow.

CHAPTER 33

It was one in the morning by the time Marisa finally parked her car in the parking garage near her apartment. The only spots left had been the rooftop ones, as everyone else in the neighborhood had wisely left their cars at home on New Year's Eve.

She'd never claimed to be wise. If she had been, perhaps she could have connected the dots of her dismay a bit sooner and spared her heart the misery.

Marisa's limbs were achingly sluggish as she hit the walkway that led to her apartment. Her fingers and ear were numb from the constant tries at getting a hold of Alec, and she'd finally had to stop when her drained phone battery barked at her. Apparently, the thing didn't like the cold either and gave up the ghost a minute after midnight.

The air was always a few degrees colder in West Meadow than where her parents lived, and tonight was no different, though her town's higher elevation came with the lovely added benefit of more snow. Made for a miserable time trying to pull her keys out of her purse, but she managed, though not without dropping the things into a gray slush pile feet from her front door.

Happy frickin' New Year to me.

She took a deep breath and squeezed her eyes shut. God, she couldn't handle this. And she certainly wasn't looking forward to walking into her tiny, empty apartment again, except this time with Alec's letter. His words alone would take up all the remaining space she'd constructed for herself, space she'd carefully crafted to keep the bad parts out and the good parts protected.

And he'd gone and muddled all that up, throwing her nice, safe pillows on the floor and rattling her previously sturdy shelves until all her emotions fell free.

Emotions that had no place to land and were as churned up and restless as the snow drifting around her.

Cursing seemed like too much effort, so she picked up her keys in begrudging silence. When she got to her feet, however, a set of long legs stretched out on the sole strip of dry pavement beneath her awning.

Legs that were connected to a brawny body that sat slumped against her front door.

Her heart skipped several beats.

Alec lifted his head at her approach and quickly got to his feet, brushing off the bits of snow that hadn't been kept away by the overhang. A duffel bag sat on her doormat. "You're home."

She couldn't breathe. Had it only been a week since she'd seen him? His winter wear did nothing to hide the creases and exhaustion wrinkling every part of him. Even from where she stood, she could see the bags under his eyes and the every-other-day shave his face hadn't seen in a week. Patches of his beard had already begun to fill in his hollow cheeks like mossy overgrowth finally given free rein.

He looked positively travel-rumpled and miserable.

"What are you doing here?"

"I just landed at Newark."

"In this? It's snowing, and it's New Year's Eve. Well, technically not anymore, I guess, but how are planes even flying now?"

"Not easily, but they're managing. We touched down at eleven, and I came straight over."

"You . . . what? You've just been waiting here? Until I got home?"

"My phone was shut off on the flight, and I wasn't sure whether Cal gave you my letter . . . or if you were even interested in reading it." A haunted graveness painted a new desperation on his features.

"He did, and I did," she admitted, though she wasn't sure what she was admitting. That she'd read his apology and it squeezed her heart with more questions and trepidation? Or that she still hurt every time she wondered whether she could trust him?

Because she wanted to. Desperately. But there was so much standing in the way of that decision, and sometimes, to keep oneself safe from the bad stuff, some of the good stuff had to be locked outside with it.

Alec nodded and threw his fists into his coat pockets, eyeing the sky as if he were expecting the snow to give him a cue for what to say next.

"You left," she reminded him.

"I did. I had to. I needed to find a way to inject some of the worth you once saw in me back into the man I'd become."

"And did you? Find a way to do that?"

He smiled sweetly at her, the corner of his mouth lifting that scar higher. "I bloody well hope so. I met with Brennan, and together, we called a last-minute meeting with the higher-ups on my team. We managed to successfully negotiate the termination of my contract with Great Britain. Provided Dr. Campbell clears me in a couple of weeks, the team agreed to let me resume play for the rest of the season, in addition to giving me a nice retirement sendoff as I round out the remaining months."

"That's good. That's what you wanted. It'll free you up to go to Argentina. I'm sure the fans will be happy they get to celebrate you properly. You deserve it."

He was silent for a moment. "I'm not going to Argentina, Marisa."

She pushed her hat up higher on her head so she could make sure his lips said what she thought they said. "What?"

"It's true, my career as a player will be ending, but not because I'm not getting out on my terms." He took a hesitant step forward and freed one hand from his pocket, but he seemed to think better of reaching for her. "Seeing you so excited going after your dreams and telling stories through your confections, despite the box others put you in for it, got me thinking about what excited me about rugby to begin with and the damn box I wound up in myself."

The snow wasn't letting up, nor was it a whipping chilly mess. The sky felt heavy but patient, as if it were holding off the worst of the weather just so Alec could finally say what Marisa had refused to hear for days following the fallout.

"Growing up, I had a neighbor. Robbie. He was the biggest Scotland Rugby Sevens fan. Literally. The man was the size of a small car, and back when Scotland had a team of its own, he was always following the lads. His enthusiasm for the sport was infectious, and I got swept up in it and never looked back. I even traveled to games with him when the team was playing locally, and Cal and I went over to his house to watch what international matches we could. Those were the best games, the ones we all enjoyed from the couch with crisps and Coke. Robbie was just so animated, he would jump up in front of the TV and act out the plays. Had my brother and me laughing our arses off. The bloke did a fair better job at keeping us engaged than any broadcast announcer, that was for certain. So, when I was old enough, I joined the local youth league and never looked back. Rugby has been my life and love, but I see now it was only ever meant to be a *part* of my story. The rest of it I've yet to write, because you've made me realize that my true enthusiasm for the game doesn't just lie on the pitch but in the telling of it as well."

His exhausted gaze claimed hers, but this time, a spark of hope seemed to smooth out and brighten the haggard lines around his eyes. "I've still got so much more to say about the sport I love. So, I needed to make sure things were right with Great Britain before I hopefully move into the New York broadcasting booth at the start of the new season in October."

Marisa sniffed and shook her head, not sure what she was hearing. "Broadcasting? How?" she squeaked out, emotion choking off her vocal cords and making her words go all whiney.

"The bloke I met at the Ball. Martin Penhaus. You remember him?"

She nodded and dragged her arm beneath her nose. Totally gross, but she was past the point of caring.

"Apparently, he liked what I had to say about gaining viewers through investment in the streaming platforms and meeting fans where they are. I gave him a call, and we had a nice, long chat. Started telling him a few of my favorite rugby stories, both ones I featured in and ones I grew up hearing. He said he'd like to talk to the board at Global Sports Matrix and entertain some ideas about positioning the network to become the premier Rugby Sevens broadcaster for the American market, of course with a few key investments, sponsoring the next tournament, and whatnot. The first of those key investments, he said, would be acquiring eager and noteworthy names to set the network up for success with its initial broadcasts. If his proposal to the board passes in the New Year and he gets approval to move forward, he'd like to sign me on as a lead broadcaster doing analysis and interviews live from the pitch and, more importantly, from the booth in New York. That last bit was a requirement for me, as I'm now in the market for property in the tri-state area. That was one of the reasons I had to fly home, to make arrangements to get my flat in order so it can be listed on the market come the spring."

Alec took both hands out of his pockets and grabbed Marisa's, tucking them inside the warmth of his open coat against his chest. To her surprise, she'd fisted them so tightly while holding on through Alec's speech, her knuckles had begun turning white. He started slowly unfurling her frozen fingers and, like old times, massaged the stiff joints, releasing every knot of tension into the snowy night air.

As she huddled closer to him, relaxing under the memory of his comforting heat, all of Marisa's anger seemed to lessen and entangle with the torrent of happiness that she felt so damn guilty for leaning into.

In short, she was a goddamn mess, so the only thing she could manage to say was also the least contextually sensible thing. "I know those words weren't really yours." Alec stiffened, and realizing how he took her statement, Marisa rushed to clarify things. "The ones in the video, I mean."

Marisa had to wait the entirety of five Mississippis before his shoulders fell and he spoke again.

"I am so sorry, Marisa. I was such a bloody fool thinking I had any right to step in and fix what you were more than capable of handling. I should have trusted you. Fuck, I *do* trust you. With all my goddamn heart, I trust you." He pulled her closer against him, and this time, she was more than happy to slide her hands farther underneath his coat and wrap them around his broad chest.

"Phoebe told me everything. Surprise: neither of us got on Monica's approved vendor list," Marisa murmured, hating how the admission of her business's failure was some of the first words spoken in the New Year already. "She's not as bad as I thought, though, honestly. I think Phoebe's more misunderstood than anything."

"Most people are, which is why there was one other thing I needed to do before I could allow myself to come back to you."

Marisa looked up at him, confused.

"I wasn't kidding about what I wrote in that letter. I could stay like this, with you in my arms and be selfishly content for as long as you'll have me, but if I don't truly earn your forgiveness and give back what my callousness took from you, then what's the bloody point?" He pressed his warm lips to her nose and stepped back quickly, as if that small kiss was all he'd permit himself. "Check your email."

"Why? It's one in the morning on a holiday. Anything that's in there can wait."

"It's technically one fifteen, and I need you to check it. *Please*, Marisa."

It was the *please* that gave her pause. Never had she heard that type of desperation in his voice, as if the very ground would swallow them both up if she didn't pull out her phone.

So she satisfied him and looked.

The latest email at the top was one he'd been copied on, but she didn't recognize the sender's name. "Who's Veronica Baker?"

"Martin Penhaus's wife. She was at the Ball with him. Keep reading."

A burst of butterflies took flight behind her sternum, fluttering so fast she would likely be airborne in another few seconds unless she did something about it. Nervously, she clicked on the email.

Dear Ms. Silver,

I hope this email finds you well and that you are enjoying a wonderful holiday season. I am Veronica Baker, and my family owns the Baker Arena and Sports Complex, home to the Bergen County Blue Devils Minor League Baseball Team. Our facility also includes the largest indoor ice-skating rink in the county, as well as a field house for regional track and field and gymnastics competitions.

Additionally, I am the wife of Martin Penhaus, and the two of us are quite thrilled to be the newest admirers of Sweetest Heart's Desire. While in attendance at the Crystal Christmas Ball, I had the good fortune to sample your gingerbread fudge featuring a wonderful picture of the famed rugby player Alec Elms, who was gracious enough to share your contact information with me and who I have also copied on this email.

To be quite frank, I was completely enamored with your confections, specifically the sports-themed fudge, and would love the opportunity to speak with you about bringing your products into the concessions offerings at our facilities. For some time, my family and I have been looking for a way to expand Baker Arena into other markets beyond facility rental space. Whether you intended this or not, your idea of putting Mr. Elms as the face of your business was brilliant. I should like to entertain more of this genius, perhaps in the form of exclusive team-branded candies for licensing and distribution in the arena. Such items could feature seasonal offerings of your designs throughout the year or even designs for regional and high school teams, etc.

Please don't hesitate to contact me at your earliest convenience. I very much hope such a partnership might interest you in the future.

I look forward to speaking with you and trying more of your offerings.

Sincerely,

Veronica Baker

Co-owner of Baker Arena and Sports Complex

Vice President of Operations and Licensing

Fat teardrops blurred out the rest of the email signature,

along with the vague cartoony animal holding a baseball bat that appeared at the bottom. Before Alec would let her waterlog her electronics any further, he carefully took the device from her hand and slipped it into her coat pocket.

Ugh, she was a total mess and couldn't seem to get a word out without sniffing through it. A licensing opportunity for her business, one where she could test her creativity in the concessions realm? Marisa knew next to nothing about the number of people who would normally come through an arena of that size, but crowds were crowds. And *steady* crowds could be profitable. That much she knew.

Already, her mind was spinning with what this meant for the future of her business and the varieties of treats she could offer that would fit a sports-themed clientele.

"I can see the gears turning, and it makes me glad." Alec rested his hands on her shoulders and rubbed them with a quick nod of subdued satisfaction, as though he'd checked the final box on a wish list before resigning himself to what awaited him on the other side.

And that would not do.

Marisa grabbed him by the lapels and kissed him. She didn't care that her face was a snowy streaky mess or that whatever wetness she was painting on his cheeks might have been of undesirable origins, given her sniffles. All she cared about was having Alec in her arms and clinging to him like a spider monkey so he wouldn't turn around and walk out of her life again.

"I've missed this," he said against her lips, grabbing her tighter and hauling her up against his chest so her boots dangled. "I was afraid."

"Of what?"

"That I'd destroyed any hope of getting you to trust me again. That I hadn't done a good enough job of making you believe that I'd never *ever* say such awful things about you. That

I had given you even the smallest reason to doubt how much I love you."

She'd seen the word on paper, scrawled in his hasty hand before he deposited the note with Cal and ran off to the airport. But on paper, it seemed different, not entirely like any other word. After all, once written down, there were so many things a person could love.

She herself had drawn several *Marisa loves so-and-so* doodles on countless notebooks all through junior high. And then there were the Sweethearts—heart-shaped candies with the word *love* printed all over them. She was a candy maker. Hearts and love were her jam. Seeing the word caused no more shock than an EMT encountering blood at a car accident. Par for the course.

But hearing it from his mouth, whispers away from her own? For some reason, his accent thickened the word, strengthening the emotion into the sincerest, most unbreakable declaration. When Alec said he'd loved her, there was no room for incredulity.

It was a pledge. A promise. A vow.

And not a damn hint of anything fake.

While Marisa took the time to sit with the realization, Alec kept going, listing off so many faults and worries that she was convinced he must have kept a spare supply of his shame in his duffel bag.

"Alec," she said, touching her finger to his lips and putting an end to his self-deprecation. "I forgive you."

His eyes widened as much as they could given the bags weighing them down. "Truly?"

"Truly. Because when you love someone, it's easy to forgive them."

Misty-eyed, she gave him a squeeze around his middle, and the largest, brightest smile broke out across his face. The twirling came next, along with more kissing and her laughing against his scruffy cheek as snowflakes gathered on their eyelashes and landed on her teeth.

It wasn't until her elbows knocked against something hard that she asked him to put her down. "What's in your pocket?"

He didn't answer. Just moved his arms out to the sides and let her root around for the offending object that had stopped her fun. When her fingers brushed against something smooth and narrow, she pulled out her hand to reveal . . .

"Blueberry candy canes?"

Alec shrugged an *Eh, what are you going to do?* and plucked a choice one from the small bundle. "They've grown on me."

"Okay, I take it back," she said as she handed him her keys and forced him to open her front door while she began unwrapping her purloined treat. "You're not so easy to forgive. These ones were mine, from my private stash. I can't get these again until next year."

"I suppose you'll just have to make some of your own. Still love me?"

"I guess."

He barked out a laugh and kissed her cheek. "My kind of miracle."

EPILOGUE

October

Sal and Enzo's pizza kitchen had been built to handle speed and efficiency, but even those seasoned pros were having a tricky time keeping up with the staggering number of orders flying at them from the packed restaurant. Not that Marisa doubted their prowess—she didn't have a death wish or a desire to find a new apartment—but she'd also never seen the place so stuffed to the gills.

And though celebrating the start of the Rugby Sevens season at the pizzeria was her idea, she wasn't exactly thrilled she had to get in line for her standard white cheese and broccoli slice.

At least she'd had the foresight to go back to hiding her full-sugar Dr. Browns from the customers. Marisa shuddered. She didn't know what she'd do if she had to settle for the diet stuff.

Above the drink fridges, a large television was positioned at the optimal viewing angle, and everything was set for show time . . . Well, except for Eden angling her phone beneath the

TV, trying to capture the QR code on the screen so they could log into Global Sports Matrix's streaming app.

"Multifactor authentication can suck it. That's all I'm going to say." Eden finally lined up the code within the shaky colored lines on her screen and plugged in the info it asked for.

"You know what sucks worse than multifactor authentication? Identity theft." Marisa swiped a garlic knot from her previously secured stash and offered it up to her friend in dutiful commiseration.

With Eden's thumbs engaged in careful tapping, she kept her eyes on the screen as she leaned her mouth over to the proffered knot to take a bite. "Joke's on them. I've got about a buck fifty in my checking account, a good twenty grand left in student loans, and an old Payless Shoes charge card I opened freshman year of college. Pretty sure I'm not worth the effort, but who am I to judge someone's career choices? Yes, got it! Finally." Eden took the rest of her knot as payment for her accomplishment, grabbed a few sodas from the fridge, and plunked them down on the table where Sid, Captain, and Manic were deeply engaged in the tiny screen before them.

Manic scratched the buzzed side of his head, careful not to mess up his mohawk, and squinted at the video footage of Alec's final match with Great Britain he'd played back in May. "So, they're not called touchdowns or goals. They're called tries."

"Correct," Marisa said.

Sid bit into his Sicilian slice. "And when they kick a field goal—"

"Conversion."

"Right, when they go for a conversion, it's how many points?"

"Five for the initial try, and two points for the conversion. Each chance at scoring gives them the opportunity to earn seven points total."

Captain shook his head, his long braid swinging dangerously

close to the toddler's eager grasp in the high chair next to him. "They do all of this without passing the ball forward? Like, at all?"

"Yup. They can only throw it to a teammate who's behind them."

"With no gear," Sid reminded all of them.

"They're wearing mouth guards, but otherwise, nope."

"Man," Captain grumbled, "and I thought prison was tough."

Their admiration was easy to love, especially when their eyes filled with wonder as they watched a replay of Alec flying through the air with the ball out in front of him and landing on his stomach to score the final try of the game and the final try of his on-pitch career. The conversion, however, and the glory of earning the two points that would secure Great Britain the win, he left to another teammate.

That had been her favorite part. Up until now, at least. In a few minutes, they'd be able to see Alec's first on-air interview as the Chief Rugby Sevens Analyst for Global Sports Matrix. The match wasn't happening for another hour, and that was just fine. That meant she got to watch Alec, decked out in an under-wear-scorching suit, lean into the role he'd been working so hard to prepare for over the past few months. With a slate of player interviews and coaching questions, some of them prere-corded, he'd quickly found his stride in storytelling.

It made her heart squeeze all over again at how much she loved that man.

"Mom, can I go up and get more gummies?" Next to the toddler, who was again thwarted from nabbing Captain's braid, the older brother was popping a final fistful of candies into his mouth and looking forlorn down at his empty napkin.

"Sure thing, honey. Here, buy another bag for all of us, will you?" The mother handed the kid some cash and gasped when her daughter's chubby fingers found their mark on Captain's braid. "Oh, I'm so sorry! Ellie, no!"

"It's fine," he said, making silly eyes at the young one, which made her kick her feet in hysterics. "I've got sisters. I'm used to hair pulling."

Marisa took a pull on her soda and leaned into the exuberant joy expanding her rib cage as she took in the sight at the counter, one she still hadn't entirely gotten used to. The boy handed Sal the money and excitedly grabbed another bag of Sweetest Heart's Desire's Rugby Try Treats out of the tabletop display. It had taken her a solid three months to get the shaping right, but once she had it, the method had been easy enough to adapt to some of the other offerings she was putting together for the arena.

Her cheeks pinched the tighter her smile got as the boy rooted around in the bag of fruit-and-cream-swirled rugby-ball-shaped gummies. When his fingers came free with the watermelon ones, she quietly gave her nod of approval.

Watermelon was a sleeper flavor and a personal favorite of hers and Veronica's as well.

Alec had been the odd one out in the flavor favorites department. Apparently, whatever seasonal-treat damage Marisa had done had stuck around for the rest of the year. The man still preferred blueberry.

And she loved him for it.

"Oh, it's starting!" Eden bumped up the volume as high as it would go, and the entire restaurant's customer base set their heads on swivels toward the screen.

Except for Marisa. She'd chosen to stand near the counter, with her shoulders supported by plexiglass and her line of sight unobstructed and pinned perfectly to the man who had filled out the frame with no shortage of Scottish charisma or, as the women around her pointed out with tittering appreciation, his resonant brogue.

She successfully managed to make it through the first two ten-minute interviews before she had to grab some gummies and shove them in her mouth lest she start finger-whistling her approval for how amazing he was doing.

Hold it together, Marisa. Hold it together . . .

"Here." Eden handed her a basket of freshly fried zucchini sticks and warm marinara sauce. "They count as a veggie. I checked."

"Thanks." Marisa began to nibble on her molten-hot sustenance, grateful to her friend for recognizing the imminent waterworks and stopping the flow before she made a complete — "Where did you get that hat?"

"It's a sample I was working on for your new logo, and I wanted to see what it would look like on some merch. Do you like it?" Eden modeled the baby-shit-green trucker hat that made the business's swirling heart logo look like something the CDC should issue warnings for.

"It's hideous."

"Okay, but what do you think of it in mustard yellow?" Like some tricky magician, she quickly swapped out hats, her excited smile anticipating a reaction that not even Marisa, with all her previously earned experience on the lying circuit, could pull off in good faith. That was when, to Marisa's horror, an entire box of colored cap monstrosities poked out from beneath the table next to Eden.

"I think . . ." Then her heart softened as Alec's voice pulled her attention back to the TV screen. "I think we've got some fun choices to make."

And that thought alone? Man, it was a keeper.

With her business not only having its legs solidly under it but running the equivalent of at least several respectable 5Ks, and having Alec by her side forging a foundation for his new career, her life had become nothing short of a firehose of happiness.

So, yeah, she'd gladly take shitty hat options any day of the week and couldn't wait for more weird and wonderful fun.

Alec smiled at the camera, his eyes twinkling beneath the studio's lights as he answered his co-host's question about match strategy. "I hope the lads on the pitch today all go out and make the right choices one after another. That's all it takes for the game to flow and for each team to find their footing early. If they can do that, they'll only have the best of choices in front of them from then on out. Should make for a good match-up. I'm excited to see what they can all pull off. Some real top talent out there, for sure."

Alec held his confidence and smiled a beat longer so the camera could soak it all in, but the way the scarred side of his mouth rose almost imperceptibly higher than the other side was all for Marisa.

Their secret signal. A quiet nod that spoke of exciting futures and thrilling promises.

All sweet choices they would make together.

NOT QUITE READY TO say goodbye to Marisa and Alec just yet? Good, because Alec just got invited to his first big New Jersey Thanksgiving celebration with Marisa's family (oy!), and the craziness is far too much to be contained within these pages. Claim this exclusive BONUS EPILOGUE to *The Hanukkah Hoax* when you sign up to my newsletter (https://BookHip. com/FDQCRKL) to see what Marisa's parents have in store for the holiday, and whether Alec's decades-honed athleticism will be enough to tackle what's waiting for him when he walks through that front door.

THANK you so much for reading *The Hanukkah Hoax!* If you loved seeing Marisa and Alec's relationship grow, let your friends know. Help other readers fall in love with this couple by leaving a review.

ACKNOWLEDGMENTS

There's a certain amount of weirdness that comes with being a writer and, despite the plethora of words available to me, I find myself at a loss for how to explain it all.

How do you explain, for example, that you want to write a Hanukkah romance, but it's mostly centered around Christmas, but it's sure as hell not a religious story, and it's also funny, but not the kind of funny that's usually okay for holiday romances, and, oh yeah, the male main character plays a sport that's entirely unpopular in the States compared to other sports, and how many people even care about the importance of good bagels? Also, mastiffs drool a lot. Ew. And they're not labs.

But then you tell all this to your insanely supportive husband who uprooted himself years ago to start a life and family with you in Jersey and all he says is: "Sounds good. Let's do it."

To Ben, who has officially lived in Jersey long enough—and paid enough tolls—to earn his "New Jerseyan" gold card status, I love you. Thank you. We should get pizza some time. Or Korean food. I'll bring the soju.

ABOUT THE AUTHOR

Aimee Robinson used to drive ambulances and write for medical publications, but, instead, thought it better to lie for a living. Years later, she's entrenched herself in that choice and couldn't dig herself out if she tried, even if those dangling modifiers continue to get her every. single. time.

After publishing many romance novels, two things remain true: she'll never miss an opportunity to give voice to the characters in her head, and she still has very specific preferences when it comes to a good dirty martini.

Aimee lives in New Jersey with her family and an Anatolian Shepherd rescue who doesn't know what personal space is.

www.ingramcontent.com/pod-product-compliance
Lightning Source LLC
Chambersburg PA
CBHW021136310726
48971CB00002B/344